Temptation shimm▊
set the lifeswarm ▊

'Good stuff, A▊
Shrike.'

'Cut with APFE growur ractor. New, new,
Auraelian. We're not just talking life extension
here, we're talking rejuvenation. Fountain of
youth, old man. Took a big risk smuggling this
stuff out of my work. Make it worth my while.'

A waft, a gag of gardenias; the scent Auraelian
uses to conceal the smell of hundred-and-fifty-
year-old flesh. The flesh that cries and wails for
what the dark girl is holding between her fingers.
Growth factors. Not a mere postponement of
death, a grasp at life again. Real life. Life is the
drug and Auraelian is hooked.

'As long as you are aware of the risks.'

'I think you explained them quite adequately.'

'And that I cannot be held responsible for any
. . . unforeseen circumstances.'

'Yes.'

'Then we have a deal.'

Also by Ian McDonald in VGSF

HEARTS, HANDS AND VOICES

Ian McDONALD

SPEAKING IN TONGUES

VGSF

First published in Great Britain 1992
by Victor Gollancz Ltd

First VGSF edition published 1993
by Victor Gollancz
A Cassell imprint
Villiers House, 41/47 Strand, London WC2N 5JE

© Ian McDonald 1992

The right of Ian McDonald to be identified as
author of this work has been asserted by him in
accordance with the Copyright, Designs
and Patents Act, 1988.

A catalogue record for this book is
available from the British Library.

ISBN 0 575 05608 8

Printed and bound in Great Britain
by Cox & Wyman Ltd, Reading, Berks

Contents

GARDENIAS

There is death in the Barry-O tonight but still they come down from the neon and lasershine of Hy Brazyl, the five of them. They have given themselves names, as the ones who come down will; names like Zed and Lolo and Cassaday and The Shrike and Yani. Noble they are, comely, their fathers are Company men, bound by blood and contract, their mothers are Company women, they are born to live lives of lofty altitude among the crystal pinnacles of Hy Brazyl. So: why have they exchanged their Projects and *corporadas* for the tar-paper and plastic *favelas* of the Barry-O, where the faces have no contract and no consequence and the rain washes the names from the streets?

Because they are searching: dark she, bright she, silent she, sullen he, laughing he, they are searching for a place they have never seen yet they know it as well as they know the luminous spires of their *corporadas*. Better, for ever since they first heard of it as a dark whisper in the arcades and bodegas where the young ones go, it has burned like a star in their imaginations. Their flashlight beams lance out through the needles of rain that are always always always driving down hard, hard on the Barry-O, driving photophobic creatures wrapped in plastic polywrappers to shelter behind the piled garbage sacks. There is disease down here. There is quick, flashing death along the edge of a Barry-O blade beaten from old beer cans, folded and forged and refolded and reforged. The people of the Barry-O remain eyes in their favela windows and leave the night and the rain to the garbagesellers and the razorboys and the brilliant creatures of the Company. Their flashlight beams go before them as they come splashing through ankle-deep rainwater streaming down the hill of the Barry-O. And there, shouldering out of the shadowlands, is the place their imaginations have burned for. In the days when the streets remembered vehicles, it was a multi-storey car park; twenty-two levels of rentable space. Now, streaked and stained by acid rain, its former identity is submerged under a jungle of power conduits and ducts and cables and home-brew chicken-wire power-beam dishes. The web of cables spasmodically drips fat blue sparks onto the paving slabs.

For a moment they hesitate, these children of light. For a moment they might turn back. But one steps forward through the cascade of blue arc-light: the dark girl, the one who calls herself Zed, and the power she draws out of the night and the warm rain calls the others after her: bright she, silent she, sullen he, laughing he. The lower levels are piled to the ceiling with black plastic refuse sacks. Weaving flashlight beams disclose furtive movements of blacque on blacque, lines of wet sylver drawn along blade-edges. Whatever it is that rests in this place of heart's desire, it has its guardians. Death beats its wings in the abandoned car park, and then, with a rush, it is gone.

'I don't know about this . . .' The breathermask mutes his words, his identity; only the eyes of the boy who calls himself Yani can be seen and they are not laughing now. Lose a little of the Project arrogance, that Hy Brazyl braggadocio, child.

The endless rain has leached little calcite stalactites out of the ceiling joints: the lights transform the beads of water at their tips into pearls. The dark girl, the one who calls herself Zed, rips off her breathermask. It clatters across the drip-stained concrete. She breathes in the rot and the stink and the pus.

'Then go back.' She goes to the boy, strokes his hair with the backs of her fingers. 'Go on. It's all right. There's no shame in it. It's just not for you. We won't blame you.' His fingers strike to seize her stroking, stroking hand. Anger, humiliation, flare up in his eyes above the mask. Zed smiles.

'I'm coming with you. See . . .' He rips off his own breathermask, throws it away from him. He fills his lungs with the garbage stink of the Barry-O.

'I'm glad.'

And the bright she and the silent she and the sullen he throw away their breathermasks and breathe in the stink and sourness and they all smile, all friends all pilgrims all Company men together. They press onward and at the touch of their light all the collected shadows flee and fade: level after level after level of ringing, dripping darkness lit by fitful blue flashes; the powergrid is restless. Anticipating. Zed stops, hands held up, hush, be still. Her eyes, her nostrils are wide, sensing for something, a hint, a memory, of gardenias.

'Auraelian?'

The name chases around the squat, square concrete pillars.

'Auraelian!'

She holds high a small plastic cylinder. She shakes it and the floating things within catch the blue arc-light. 'Brought you something, Auraelian! A balm for your mortifying flesh, old stumbling, crumbling man, a cessation of corruption! Good stuff, Auraelian, Company stuff, you hear me, Auraelian?'

A sigh in the darkness. Amplified by the ancient acoustics of the car park. Flashlight beams fan into a wheel of light: nothing. Only a sigh.

'Not more of you. Oh, well. Bolder than most, I suppose, but no less stupid. Or vain. Very well, give me the stuff.'

Zed's hand closes on the plastic vial of synthetic death hormone suppressant with a snap of rat-jaws. 'Give us purity.'

'Purity,' mumble-mutter bright she silent she sullen he laughing he. Like a prayer.

'Purity. Purity purity purity. Of course.' The powergrid shivers and crackles and Auraelian is there, out of nowhere, out of anywhere. He is tall, tall and stately as any son of the *corporadas*. He wears a white linen suit and Panama hat and shoes. In his buttonhole is a black silk carnation, his hands rest lightly on the gilded knob of a Malacca cane. He has beautiful hands. Zed has never seen such beautiful hands as the hands of Auraelian. The odour of gardenias overpowers even the Barry-O stink. 'Purity. Impetuous youths.' He smiles. Imagine an angel long-since fallen through the fingers of God remembering its former estate. Imagine how it would smile. 'Come, then.'

Question, what is it Auraelian sells one half so precious as the goods he buys?

This.

A heptagonal metal frame. Tall as a Company man. Dripping with conduits and cables and clumsily grafted compumodules. Suggestion of a gateway. Suggestion of a mirror. In a sense, both. One entire level of Auraelian's little kingdom has been set aside to serve it. As the click, tap, click, tap of cane on concrete guides his pilgrims, the cables shudder with power and for the briefest quantum of comprehension, the heptagon fills with a plane of blue light.

Zed touches the smooth metal frame, strokes the humming cables, peers into the spasming blue light as if to see if there is a beyond, what that beyond might be.

'Nothing,' says Auraelian. 'That's the lure of it, isn't it? Nothing, and everything. Tell me, am I a religion yet? I ought to be.'

Impatient, spirit-hungry, Zed is already removing her clothes. Fine *corporada* silks and leathers lie like empty skins on the rust-coloured concrete. Auraelian runs a tiny iguana tongue over his lips. It is not Zed he hungers for. It is the vial in her hands.

'I presume that having heard of my mattercaster, you must at least possess a rudimentary understanding of the DaCosta Postulate of Universal Position by which it operates; namely, that at a certain mathematical level, the probability of an object's existence is equal for any and every point in the universe . . .'

'Auraelian . . .' Zed slips the rings from her fingers, the brass and bone *zuvembe* bangles from her wrists. She shakes her hair free from its leather thonging. 'No theory, old man. No postulates. Just do it. Do it now.' She presses her soft meat against the hard metal frame. Blue in the infinity light. Perfect child of the Company. Auraelian shakes his head; dry, mock sorrow. He clicks his fingers twice, opens his beautiful hand. The vial of glittering things arcs through the air. Black-market immortality. Auraelian takes it with darting trap-snap of fingers and it is safe in the heart-pocket of his linen waistcoat. His hands, his beautiful *beautiful* hands, move over the ugly, incongruous compumodules.

And the concrete hull of the long-dead car park hums to a rising swell of power. The hum becomes a migraine drone; for an instant the floors, ceilings, pillars shudder and shammer as the powergrid finds and loses their resonant frequencies. The metal heptagon is a solid plane of blue light.

'Heesus,' someone whispers.

The girl who calls herself Zed tosses back her black hair and walks into the teleport field.

She cannot even scream.

She dies, annihilated, shattered scattered splattered to the furthest curve of the isotropic universe, spread throughout time from eternity to eternity. She is nothing. She is everything, made one with the universe in a moment of omnipresent nirvana that lasts for ever and ever and ever and ever and ever and ever and ever, and still not one instant has ticked away on the clocks of infinity.

It is heaven.

It is hell.

And in the same instant as she is shattered and scattered and splattered, she is gathered out of infinity and re-created. She lives again.

She steps from the teleport field. She shines. Hands, face, body. All human dross burned away in that instant of union with the universe. She is pure. She is enlightened. She is holy. Her friends are afraid: what is this? Not Zed. Cannot be their Zed. But she stands among them, inviting them to touch her shining body, and they reach out their hands to touch, they peer through her brilliance. They see. Then they, too, strip off their fine fine Company clothes and step naked into the mattercaster to be annihilated, shattered scattered splattered across the universe, to die, and live again, pure, sanctified creatures in the warm dripping of an abandoned car park down in the Barry-O: bright she silent she sullen he . . . laughing he?

Laughing he? The boy who calls himself Yani hides from the laughing, brilliant creatures which seconds before had been his friends. He hides in the shadows they cast. He does not laugh. He was afraid. He was afraid to annihilate himself in the mattercaster field and he slips away from the company of the saints down through the ringing, dripping levels haunted by the scent of gardenias and the glitter of blades, out into the warm rain and the streaming streets, back up the alleys and stairways to the glowing towers of Hy Brazyl, the laughing boy who will not laugh again.

And what had been five are now four.

*

Now they have new names for themselves. New names for new places, new names shaped like the glass scimitars of the *corporadas* or the luminous vaults of their arcades and gallerias and loggias and cloudwalking plazas. They call themselves the Lords Cardinal.

Whispers in intimate conversation booths in neon and tube chrome cafés. Slash of red paint spray-bombed across a corridor wall down in the residential levels. Dataweb code pencil-scribbled on a public booth. Slip of paper slid down plunging necklines into stocking tops between fly buttons into waistbands *zuvembe* ear-bangles next-to-heart pockets: *the Lords Cardinal*. Most have no eyes to see, no ears to hear, they pass by as the September clouds pass and part about the aerocurves of the arcologies. They say, *Qué* what kinda gar*bage* (to rhyme with ga*rage*, as in repository for old automobiles, as in Auraelian's twenty-two-level domain) this? And they say *Qué, neh!* No time for this gar*bage* gotta work gotta play live gotta love gotta life to live at lofty altitude, you only walk this way the once, *compadre*, so let's drink let's shoot let's make let's fake; let's dance; we're Company men!

But for a few the whisper cannot be forgotten. The red slogans drip down the imagination and say, *Walk the way that is not the way. The way that a few have walked before you, down from your corporadas out of the lights into the darkness beneath the clouds that is better than any light.* And they look at their sweeping swooping towers and they say, – *Heesus, is that all there is? Working for the playing for the screwing for the chewing for the making for the faking for the living for the dying for the glorious the generous the wonderful the Company?* And they say, – *I'll walk that way that is not the way, I'll pull that code, I'll call up the address, I'll walk that narrow and winding path that leads to the darkness that is better than any light.*

And they find, out there, the Lords Cardinal. Reclining among floform cushions on live-fur floors. Contemplative lotuses at coffee in glass gallerias, the clouds a sheer two kilometres below. Warriors of the mist down in the perpetual gloom of the industrial cores. And this is the gospel they preach.

Everything is nothing.

Nothing is everything.

Possess all the wealth of the soaring curves of Hy Brazyl and you are poorer than the poorest *noncontractado* down in the Barry-O. Become nothing, and you will receive everything. Nirvana. Nihilism. The blessedness of annihilation. Of having been nothing, and then, being again. Of the purification that comes when the slag of merely being human is burned away by that moment of nothing-and-everythingness. And of that inner strength (call it courage, call it faith, call it foolhardiness) in the one step that takes you through the teleport field, into death, and out again. It is a dark and desperate gospel they preach, but there is something about these Lords Cardinal that draws those who seek, some force, some magnetism, some light. They would call it *holiness* if they knew what the word meant. All they know is that it is a purity of life that is missing from their own lives.

'Become nothing and you will become everything,' says the one who calls herself Zed. She looks into the eyes of her disciples sprawled about on her floforms in the conversation pit of her executive-level apartment. In some she sees doubt. In some she sees fear. In some she sees an emptiness like the emptiness that once was within her. In some she sees her hunger. In some, the flame of desire. 'Sanctify yourselves. Die, and live again.'

God, save us from those who take our every utterance as gospel.

She came before dawn, the silent one, Cassaday, the one of the four who seemed least comfortable with her new creation; calling and calling and calling at the door.

'Zed . . .'

'Quiet. Please.'

Oh five twenty and the dawn is welling up over the edge of the cloud layer. A wedge of light slowly climbs the curving faces of the *corporadas*: red light, dawn light, spills through the window, washes over the girl standing by the glass, across the live-fur floor and the scattered floforms, into the conversation pit. It seeks out Cassaday, the silent one, in her corner by the door.

'Zed . . .' Something has forced her out of her silence, something terrible and fearful.

A hand raised, a command for silence. Zed's brow is furrowed, intense concentration, the pretence of contemplation. Hands outstretched. The light fills up the world like the cracked crazy yolk of an egg broken into a jar of isinglass. The lower limb of the sun clears the cloudbase.

Oh five twenty-one.

Thanks to the Company, Hy Brazyl enjoys the most spectacular sunrisings and settings this side of Jupiter. Atmospheric pollution, apparently.

'I always think it's wrong to keep the sunrise to oneself. It should be shared with a soul-brother, a soul-sister, don't you agree? Coffee?'

'Zed?'

But she has moved hurriedly to the pot and the bowls and the ritual.

'Cass, you're one of my oldest, dearest friends. I feel I can tell you things which are important to me. So I feel I can tell you this: I'm afraid. Afraid that I'm losing it. Can you understand what I'm saying? Here, inside. It's just not the same any more. I feel like there is dirt in my veins. I feel like there is shit in my mouth. I feel like the fire inside is just . . . embers.'

Zed keeps little metal bells in her kettle. When the water boils, the bells sing and ring and chirrup.

'It's them. The others. There are too many of them. They need too much. They drain me, just by being with me, they drain me. They dirty me, can you understand that?'

'Zed, I've killed someone.'

'It's like because I am so pure even the slightest contact with anyone less pure than I am taints me. Dirt shows on white more than black. I feel covered in fingerprints. And each time they come to me with their stupid questions, their "Teach mes" and "Lead mes" and "Guide mes" and their "How can I how do I what do you mean, Zeds?" the fire goes out of me. I can't move. It's a crust on my skin. Shrike and Lolo feel the same. We're losing it. We're being swallowed by the dust.'

'Are you listening? Are you listening?' Cassaday's voice rises to a scream. She who has never screamed before. Before Zed. Before purity. Before holiness. 'Simon Herera Reis jumped from the four-hundred-and-twelfth-level sun terrace! Heesus!' Coffee falls in a small, precise arc from the spout of the pot into the porcelain bowls.

'He was in my circle, he hadn't been coming to meeting very long. He was having trouble with his parents, with his girlfriend, with his educator; they didn't like him being involved in the circle. Indoctrination, they called it. I was trying to get him straightened out. Last night he called, public dataweb, about two. He'd had some big thing with his folks. Kept on saying everything had come apart, everything was just piling up around him, up and up and up and he couldn't see any way out from under it all. Heez, Zed, it was oh two, I was pretty well shot, so I gave him the first bit of advice came into my head, standard stuff, you know the sort of thing: try to become nothing to this situation and everything will pass right through you and you will emerge on the far side of it victorious. That sort of thing. Then. God. Oh, God.' She cannot contain the tears any more. Zed watches her cry with dispassionate curiosity, as she might an interesting geological sample. She sips her coffee, watches. 'Then I heard he'd jumped. Off the four-hundred-and-twelfth level. One of his friends told me. He'd tried to talk him down but he just kept saying over and over, and over, "This is the way out, die and become nothing and I will be everything." And it's my fault. I am responsible. I am as responsible for Simon's death as if I had pushed him off that sun terrace myself. I killed him. I am guilty. And I don't know if I can cope with that. I don't know.' Through the dawn windows she sees Simon Herera Reis falling like a human star towards the moon-silvered cloudbase, sees him smash himself to nothing on the grim angularities of the industrial cores below. 'I don't know. I just feel that maybe everything would be better if I were to follow him. You understand?' She sniffs. Black eye make-up has trickled down her cheeks.

Zed looks up from her coffee, smiles suddenly.

'But, don't you see, this is exactly the problem! You feel responsible because you have let yourself become tainted by the values of other, impure people. It's not your fault. How can it be your fault? You only think it's your fault because your holiness, your purity, has become clouded by other people. What we need is a rededication. A repurification. Another pass through the infinity mirror to be purged of all the dirt and darkness. I've contacted the others, they all feel the same, they all agree that it's the only way to restore the light we shared. Down to the Barry-O again. Walk through the fire again. Be reborn again.'

'Are you serious? Are you quite serious? A boy is dead and all you can talk about is your precious purity and holiness?'

'Of course I am serious. What happened is, of course, quite tragic, which is all the more reason for us to repurify ourselves to ensure it never happens again. Will you come?'

'No! No!' She stands up. She is the silent one no longer. 'No, I am not coming. I have had it. I want nothing more to do with this, with you, with any of you. Don't call me, don't visit, just leave me alone. I don't want to see any of you ever again. That's it.' Hands scissor. 'I'm out.'

Oh five thirty. Door slams. Half-empty coffee bowl on the live-fur floor. The sun stands high above the horizon, another beautiful day, like every day lived at the lofty altitude of the *corporadas*, and what had been four are now three.

'Longer?'

'Longer.'

Only the three of them this time. Auraelian contemplates one of his dry, dark little jokes, dismisses the notion. They have no sense of humour. And they are not fearful, excited, guilty kids. They position themselves comfortably, powerfully across his concrete, each one at the precise centre of his or her space, commanding that space with the easy panther poise of the Company born. Darklight image-amplifying shades fix him at the centre of their foci. Lean. Hungry. Do not joke with these people. His razorboys are all paid up and jacked up and only a button away but Auraelian feels vaguely threatened. Thin black iguana tongue flicks over his lips.

'Longer. So. There are, you must understand, certain difficulties in that. The process is designed to be virtually instantaneous, no more than a couple of pico-seconds in duration. It would require resetting the temporal randomizers to function in macrotime and, quite honestly, I could not absolutely guarantee one hundred per cent reintegration.'

'Meaning?'

'Possible physical or mental malformation, in all likelihood fatal.

Possibly the body might reintegrate but without life. Possibly, total randomization.'

'Total randomization?' That lean hunger in their voices makes them all sound the same.

'I take it you have enough intelligence to work out what that means for yourselves.' Iguana tongue flicks in, out. My, but it is hot down in the Barry-O tonight.

'But it is possible.' That one is their leader, that girl; she is the darkest and hungriest of the three.

'Certainly.'

Temptation shimmers in her hand. Shake the vial, set the life-swarm swirling.

'Good stuff, Auraelian. New stuff. Tell him, Shrike.'

'Cut with APFE growth factor. New, new, Auraelian. We're not just talking life extension here, we're talking rejuvenation. Fountain of youth, old man. Took a big risk smuggling this stuff out of my work. Make it worth my while.'

A waft, a gag of gardenias; the scent Auraelian uses to conceal the smell of hundred-and-fifty-year-old flesh. The flesh that cries and wails for what the dark girl is holding between her fingers. Growth factors. Not a mere postponement of death, a grasp at life again. Real life. Life is the drug and Auraelian is hooked.

'As long as you are aware of the risks.'

'I think you explained them quite adequately.'

'And that I cannot be held responsible for any ... unforeseen circumstances.'

'Yes.'

'Then we have a deal.'

They grin at each other, these *corporada* children in their slick leathers and sleek black nylon. Fists clench in gestures of victory, solidarity. Thunder shakes the Barry-O, lightning caught in the metal monoliths of Hy Brazyl's industrial cores. Down where the automobiles used to growl and coil, black plastic things move, restless, thunder-shaken, catching the lightning on their thin blades.

Do not imagine they are the only ones. Do not imagine that no one else has ever made that pilgrimage down to the trampled mud streets of the shadowlands to seek out Auraelian with dashing, flashing beams. The Lords Cardinal have their disciples. As the Lords Cardinal were themselves, once, disciples at the feet of other masters. So do not imagine that they are the first. Auraelian's body has been defying mortification for half a century now; there are a lot of little plastic vials of synthetic death hormone suppressant in fifty years. Junior Company executives burning with junior executive ambition and anxiety; spiritual searchers who have tired of the starshine and the neon and seek a brighter enlightenment down where the streets have no names; inadequate souls needing to prove *something* (they can never quite say what) to themselves, to others, to the world; the hollow men seeking in emptiness a filling, in nothingness a universality of experience. Artists. Daredevils. Fools. Sensation seekers. The merely fashionable. All, at one time or another in his century and a half, have paid Auraelian to step through his teleporter. And not just in synthDHs. Other scripts, other species, other drugs. Auraelian did not get to be one hundred and fifty in the Barry-O without well-paid allies.

Never many. Auraelian does not advertise. Word of mouth is the best recommendation. A thing angst-ridden junior advertising executives would do well to remember. But enough, it pays him enough. Enough to keep him alive and ticking for just about for ever. For ever should be long enough for Auraelian to pay back the investment he has made in the mattercaster. It is not an investment that the Directors of the Projects would understand: pain and loss and disillusionment do not appear in credit and debit columns.

He had been an engineer in those early, heady days when the vision of corporate grandeur had sent the industrial cores into the clouds above what had once been São Paulo. She had been a mathematician, a DaCosta, a member of the founding families throwing their glass and steel towers into the stratosphere, as graceful and elegant as her equations. They had been friends, soul friends, a relationship deeper and more bonding than any formality could ever express. And out of the spirit between them had come the idea. An outrageous, enormous, incredible, intolerable, wonderful idea. The transmission of matter. Instantaneously. Across unlimited distance. Teleportation. They produced plans and schemes and pilot units and projections. And it worked beautifully. The abolition of distance. It would revolutionise trade. They took it to the Project Directors. And the Project Directors cut off its head. Its hands. Its feet. Because the soul friends had not realised what the abolition of distance would do to the laws of supply and demand and free market forces. Transport, transportation, areas of production and supply; the whole concept of markets and manufactories and thus, ultimately, the *corporadas* and the Company itself were threatened. They would not invest in the razor which cut their own throats.

Dreams and soulfriends do not wither and blow away so easily. The *corporadas* forsook them; very well, they would forsake the *corporadas* and take their idea to those who would appreciate it, the poor and dispossessed who huddled in their *favelas* at the feet of the shining spires. One day those dispossessed might bring the shining towers toppling down. For decades they dedicated every free *crusado*, every spare moment, to the construction of a full-scale matter transmission system. Everything was sacrificed to the dream, with the sole exception of their soul-friendship, for it was that which kept the dream burning. Then, with the base station completed and awaiting testing, DaCosta caught a stupid little infection and died because they could not afford the price of black-market antibiotics. Parched of the spirit between them, the dream shrivelled into disenchantment and cynicism and ultimately to a sordid little mill grinding out dollops of plastic immortality in the vain hope of some day, some way, outliving those arrogant skyscrapers. He had always been a coward, Auraelian of the beautiful hands.

And still they come. Very few return for a second walk through the fire. Only the exceptionally spiritual, the exceptionally greedy, return again and again and again. Only the spiritually greedy push and push and push at the limits of experience; two, five, ten seconds of annihilation, ramming body and spirit through the mattercaster until a twist of void is twined around every molecule of every cell of their bodies.

Spiritual pride is real.

Spiritual arrogance is real.

Spiritual greed, that drives the master always to walk before the disciple, is real. The fist of spiritual greed grips as tight as the fist that holds Auraelian to his little blue plastic vials, any addict to his drug.

It was inevitable that they become lovers: Zed, highborn daughter of the Founding Families, and the tall, solid, sullen boy from the industrial levels who calls himself the Shrike. The mattercaster had spread them so far, so thin, that there was no longer any possible point of contact between them and their disciples. Except revelation imparted. And thank-offerings received. The Shrike had given up his job in the pharmaceutical unit that had provided the Lords Cardinal with their drug-money; he could no longer bear the presence of the impure. Never mind that they found his company equally intolerable. Inevitable, then, that in their isolation sullen he should be drawn to dark she.

So they lie together, wrapped around each other on the live-fur floor with the morning breaking over them. Dark she's hands explore sullen he's body: the strong curves of thighs and buttocks, the smooth syncline of the back, the rounded slopes of the shoulders, stroking stroking stroking, absently, thoughtlessly, as if he is stone, or plastic, or a small, pet animal. She watches the day rise over Hy Brazyl. And she does not know what she is seeing. The geometrically abstract plane of the cloudbase, the shattering, penetrating thrust of the towers. The globe, the atom of light at the edge of the world: colours red, purple, gold.

What are they? What is this? What does it mean?

Something? Anything?

Nothing?

A moment of panic as she realises that it means nothing. It is not important. It has no meaning. It is nothing. Her panic leaves her as she realises that it, too, is nothing.

This body draped across hers, this collection of curves and planes, softnesses and hardnesses; this body, this *Shrike*, means nothing.

Means nothing.

Is nothing.

Zed smiles. She is almost there.

And:

'What do you mean, we can't see each other again?'

She sighs, sweeps back her hair in exasperation, in that way he finds so attractive.

'I knew you wouldn't, I knew you wouldn't understand. It's because this physical thing has no importance, can't you see that? Ultimately, it doesn't matter, and I think, I feel, that you're making it, making me, out to be the reason for everything, and it can't be, you know it can't be, it can't mean anything, ultimately.'

'Are you saying that I don't mean anything to you?'

'No! No! Try and understand. It's the physical thing: you're giving it too much importance, we are objects to each other, physical objects, and that's not what matters.'

'You are saying that I don't mean anything to you.'

'I'm saying that no thing, no physical thing, should mean anything to me. Does mean anything to me. Means anything to me. Everything is nothing. That's what we believe, isn't it? Well, now I *know* it. I feel it. Everything is nothing. And the nothing inside, the void, the spiritual reality, is everything.'

A pause.

A silence.

'You're not Zed.'

'Yes, I am. I am Zed.'

'No, you're not. Maybe you once were Zed, back then, you were the girl I just couldn't get enough of, the girl who fascinated me. I had to be near you, it was the most important thing in my life, being near you. And now I don't know what you have become. Do you know how long I admired you from afar? Do you know how long I've waited for this, what I went through to be near you, all this spirituality shit? And now I can't understand what you've become. Nothing human.'

'That's not Shrike talking. That's the old Shrike. But you're beyond all that, aren't you? That's what it's all about, becoming more than just Shrike or Zed, becoming more than ourselves, more than human.'

'I would not say that. Not seeing what I've seen. I would say, less than human.'

'If you're trying to bait me, it won't work. I'm beyond all that pettiness.'

'Beyond love too?'

'You just don't understand. I thought you did. I thought you were one of us.'

'Maybe I just guess I wasn't.'

'I can't see you again. It's too important for you to be allowed to hold me back. I won't see you again.'

'Zed! Zed! Zed . . .'

And what had been three are now two.

Ten seconds twenty seconds thirty seconds. Half a minute, one minute, one and a half minutes. Two minutes.

The clocks of faith bring them back to the Barry-O, dark she and bright she, again and again.

Four minutes.

Auraelian is not happy.

'The probability of a successful reintegration is not good.'

'How not good?' This place is theirs now as much as Auraelian's, its dripping concrete levels, its plastic-shrouded shadowpeople as much home as Hy Brazyl's immaculate *residenzas* peopled with the beautiful children of the Company.

'You want odds?' And Auraelian is no longer the hybrid angel-demon-treasurer of the Mysteries, he is just another worn component of the machine that shrives their souls. 'I would say only an eighty per cent chance of a successful reintegration.'

Zed laughs. 'That is one hundred and fifty years speaking. I can smell your gardenias.'

'You only live once.'

'Not us. We have lived a dozen lives, and more.'

But Lolo, the bright one, the small, bright glow of a girl, is not happy either. Four minutes . . . Zed is peeling off her tight leather and shiny black nylon, slipping the rings from her fingers, shaking her cloudburst of hair from its thonging. All part of the ritual now. She crouches like a runner under the gun before the glowing hepta-gon. She looks at it as she might a friend who has become an enemy, or an enemy a friend. She laughs, shakes her head, and launches herself through the teleport field.

Ten seconds. It is all a question of relativity, really. Subjectivity, objectivity. Twenty seconds. Time does not move for the teleported and the dead. Chronon and eon are the same to them. Four picos four micros four minutes four eternities, *thirty seconds*, you can't tell, you're *dead*, randomized to each and every part of the universe. *One minute*. Nor is there any purification; there is nothing present to purify. Yet, in a sense, when a man dies, his sins die with him and are not reborn. But his nature is not changed, for without his nature he is nothing, and so the darkness returns and he returns to the light of the mattercaster. *One minute thirty*. It is the re-creation that purifies, that first *glissando* of glions through the cerebral cortex that says, that knows, *I have been dead and now I am alive again*. That is the purification. That is what the eye of faith sees. Two minutes. The clocks of faith mark two minutes as more holy than four microseconds and say, for four minutes (*three minutes*) you have been nothing, separate, beyond the timebound structure of the universe. And now, you are again.

That is what the clocks of faith mark. That is what the eye of faith sees.

Four minutes.

She plunges from the teleporter, tumbles across the damp scabbed concrete, smashes herself against a concrete pillar. She feels no pain. She is burning. She is on fire and by her own light she can see further than ever before, into the heart of everything. The sour concrete floor of the car park is transparent as glass to her eye of faith. Lolo, the bright one, bends over her muttering words of concern and comfort which she cannot understand and her eye of faith strips away meat and bone to the centre of her life. Zed sees her friend's light beside her own and it is like a candle flame beside a furnace. And she sees Auraelian's soul, like black twisted wire.

'You've got to do it.'

Her mouth is full of stars and light.

'Zed, you all right? The way you came out of the field; you sure you are all right? Did you hurt yourself?'

What is she saying? What is she saying?

'No. No hurt. All right. Everything all right. You've got to do it. Lolo, you do it too. Go. Do it.'

'Heesus, I don't know, Zed, when you stepped through that

machine, it was such a long time, I was scared, I didn't know if you were coming back. You know what Auraelian said . . .'

Auraelian stands amid his machines. He does not hear, much less care, what they are babbling about. In the spaces of his imagination, he watches the towers falling.

'You've got to do it. It's the way forward. The quantum leap to new levels of spirituality; to know you can overcome the fear and that nothing can ever scare you again.'

'I don't know, Zed, the probabilities . . .'

'When you die, your fear dies with you and is not reborn. That was what was wrong with the earlier times we went through, it was not long enough for us to be afraid and take our fear through. But with the longer times, you bring your fear with you on that first step and it is annihilated. Do it, Lolo. You've got to do it.'

'You think I should?'

'You've got to.'

And the bright girl, the one who calls herself Lolo, strips away all human affectations and becomes just herself, nineteen years old, fair, a little fat, a little scared in the blue light.

'Do it!' says Zed. The one thing her eye of faith cannot see is what lies beyond that plane of blue light. One step two step three step four. Lolo passes through the teleport field and is randomized. The clocks of faith are running. Ten seconds. Zed leaves her Company things where they lie, squats on the damp floor. It does not matter to her. Nothing matters to her. Twenty seconds. She watches the mattercaster but inwardly she is wholly absorbed in the contemplation of her own experience. Thirty seconds. Half a minute. Thunder crackles, lightning, pricked out of the stratosphere by the needlepoints of the *corporadas*, runs down through the industrial cores to earth itself in the Barry-O. Nothing. Nothing at all. One minute. Her eye of faith penetrates the perpetual cloud layers and the mighty *corporadas* are confections of glass filled with little squeaking crystal figurines, fearful mannikins waiting for the hammer finally to fall. Nothing. All the power and arrogance of the Company and its Projects: nothing. One minute thirty.

'It's drawing a lot of power, running it this long,' advises Auraelian. Zed looks through him to his writhing reptile soul. Nothing.

'We pay you well for your inconveniences.' She resents having to speak. 'We've brought you good custom these past months.'

Two minutes. At last she knows it. Not an intellectual head-knowledge; she knows it in her spirit, *life-knowledge*: she is it. Everything is just ... nothing. Compared with her own experience. Nothing. Three minutes. There is no longer anything she cares for outside her own experience. Nothing matters except her own spirituality.

Four minutes ...

Four minutes.

Four minutes.

Auraelian's little murmur of concern penetrates Zed's self-contemplation to alert her that something is not right. Four minutes? Lolo ...

She has not come back.

'Auraelian, where is she?'

'Even for you, that is a singularly stupid question.'

Shadows in the universal brightness.

'Auraelian, do something. Bring her back. Now. You bring her back.'

His beautiful hands are dancing across the compumodules.

'Don't you think I am trying? Inverse phase, possibly ...' The powergrid shudders with energy, shakes the building like a man a snake.

'Auraelian, what's happening?'

'Be quiet. Just be quiet.' The powergrid howls as Auraelian commands it to draw more energy from the broadcast power net. The heptagonal plane of angel-light swirls violet and indigo.

'Auraelian, you built this thing you know what it can do.'

'And. I. Also. Know,' shouts Auraelian, punching command after command after command into his computers. 'What. It. Cannot. Do.'

A spit of electricity shorting out. The howl ebbs to a drone, a hum, a purr of power. The mattercaster field is uninterrupted blue.

'Burned out a powerdish,' says Auraelian. 'Lost it. I told you, I told you the probabilities. Impetuous youths. I wash my hands of you.' He lets his shadows reclaim him.

Zed remains in front of the teleporter, gazing into the place her eye of faith cannot see. Nothing. Ultimately, it is nothing. Lolo is nothing now, and that is good. Zed need no longer care about anyone. She is free. And she is very glad.

After half an hour Auraelian returns to shut down the mattercaster. And what had been two are now one.

Lean days in the Barry-O. Ever since that girl vanished. Sorry. *Failed to reintegrate.* They just stopped coming. Schism, falling away of the faithful, the old fat demon Apathy; Auraelian does not care, it is twenty years since he stirred out of his little kingdom into the streets, why should he care what the children of privilege do kilometres above his head? All he misses is their income. Since they stopped splashing down the hillsides to find his brand of revelation, one hundred and fifty years of flesh have taken up their full weight again. He misses that new, good Company stuff, cut with growth factor, or whatever they called it. The memory is going. He has to be careful with his rationing, one hundred and fifty years will not be easily cheated. Some memories he is glad to lose. That girl, the one who failed to reintegrate, now he cannot even recall her name, her face, her body. Barely enough synthDHS left after paying off his razorboys (and are they, will they, can they ever be *friends*, or just immaculately disguised parasites?) to keep himself ticking along. But for his faithful provider, these bad times would be the worst of times.

Faithful Provider. She will see him through the hungry years until a new generation grows up there to disillusionment and indolence and has need of his services again. Until then, he will listen for her voice calling through the lower levels. 'A moment, a minute, a jot a joint a shot of your purity for a soul that dearly needs it.' Regular and faithful, she brings him her little dribs and drabs of blackmarket DHS. He does not ask how she comes by it, he can guess how a *corporada* child fallen from grace with the sky earns a living down in the Barry-O. He does not doubt that some of those plastic vials contain his own junk, working its way back to him in a rondo of recirculation.

For her, he coaxes life into the old, battered circuits, and she peels off her layers of street waterproofs to stand naked before him, blue plastic vial trembling in her hand. Once she was beautiful. Life in the Barry-O has weighed and paid for her beauty and taken it away, by the gram, by the *crusado*. The framework remains, no one can take that away, the planes and curves and angles, but the light which changes handsomeness into beauty is gone. Taken away in rain-soaked alleyways, in plastic and beer-can hovels, among the steel and chrome industrial ziggurats by guilty Company brothers slumming it for the night, by the gram, by the *crusado*. She sells her handsomeness so that for a moment, a minute, an hour, an afternoon, she may be beautiful again. So that in the teleport she may die and forget the pounded mud streets and the stink of human sewage and the black weatherproof polywrappers and the hunger and the mould and the disease and the rain that washes the names and the dignity from the faces that pay for her; to be shattered and scattered and splattered to the ends of the universe and to die to everything that is ugly and sour and used-up. And be reborn, new, pure, holy and bright, and beautiful. For an afternoon, an hour, a minute, a moment.

'Auraelian! Auraelian! Old stumbling, crumbling man, a balm for your mortifying flesh, a cessation of corruption! Look, good stuff, Company stuff, you hear me, Auraelian?'

So, is it that time again? His memory, really, terrible. He can hardly even remember her name, that odd name, like a name someone makes up for themselves, not a real name at all. Sometimes he can remember her name. Mostly he thinks of her just as Faithful Provider. Something about her reminds him of himself, a nostalgia of heaven. He is certain she is years younger than she looks. Auraelian has little to do these days, other than speculate on his faithful provider.

Already she is removing her clothes, layers of peeled-away plastic and paper. The rituals are important to them both.

'Brought you your stuff, Auraelian. Good stuff, Company stuff.' She tosses the plastic vial. His beautiful hands snap-trap his payment, then move to the compumodules. Hum of power, the old building shudders again all for her, just for her. She tosses back her hair and just for an instant she is beautiful, she is fire and light and darkness and all those paradoxical things a woman can be. She steps into the mattercaster field, and is consumed, and all that remains is the scent, the memory, of gardenias.

RAINMAKER COMETH

Seven dry years lie like seven white scars scrawled across the shoulders of the dying town. On the downhill side long years before ever the rains failed, it crouches in the desert, a tangle of tracks and trailways and transcontinentals; always on the way to somewhere else. Only in the heat of the night does it uncurl to bare the neon tattoos along its belly: the bus depot, the motel, the barbershop, the gas-station; sweating, shocking blues and pinks you can feel hot on your face. Down at the end of the bar, where the dreams collect thickest because no one ever goes there to dust them away, Kelly By the Window watches neon fingers stroking the flanks of the Greyhounds and Trailways; people change direction here like they change their shorts. Blue Highways; abandoned luncheonettes; all she will ever see of the refuge of the roads is the reflection of her face in the Eldorado bus windows, slipping past, out there lost in the heart of Saturday night. Up on the roof Desert Rose announces the best hot-dogs in town in blushing cerises and 'lectric blues you can read all the way out at Havapai Point. And it's true, as long as you understand that 'best' means 'only'. She's smiling. She's always smiling. She makes the law, you see. Graven into every sixty-watt rhinestone on her boots. Nobody gets off who doesn't get on again.

If he likes the tilt of your hat or the colour of your luggage, if the smell of the cologne you've splashed on in the washroom reminds him of all those Oldsmobile days hung up with his jacket on the peg by the door, Sam My Man will solicit you with his magic never-ending cup of coffee. He's a dealer in biography, paid for by the minute, the hour, however long it takes until the driver calls you on into the night. Sam My Man has whole lifetimes racked away under

29

the bar where he keeps the empty bottles. He can tell a good vintage just by looking: given the choice between the kid in tractor hat, knee-high tubes and cut-off T-shirt, the bus-lagged pair of English Camp-Americas propping their eyelids open with their backpacks and coffee the strength of bitumen, and the old man with the old precise half-inch of white beard and the leather bag like no one's carried since the tornado whisked Professor Marvel off to the Emerald City, Kelly By the Window knows which one he'll solicit with his little fill-'er-ups of complimentary coffee.

Sam My Man always leaves the airco off. He claims it makes the chilli dogs taste better, but Kelly By the Window knows that he does it because someone's bound to comment that it's hot as the proverbial, and that's his cue. 'It's the drought,' he'll say. 'Rained everywhere else, but never here. You believe a town can be cursed?' Never failed yet.

'I surely could,' says this old man. 'Just how long is it since it last rained here?'

'Seven years,' says Kelly By the Window. The last drop fell two days after her eleventh birthday.

'You headed anyplace special?' asked Sam My Man, all chummy and pally-wally, like he's known this old man years not seconds. He's good, you got to give him that. Someone should have made him a lawyer long ago. Or a chat-show host.

'Had planned on heading up north, over the dam, got a woman and a boy I want to see,' says this old man. 'But then again, I might just stay around a couple of days or so. I think you may have need of my services.' He puts his bag on the counter, the Professor Marvel etc. etc., and *something* about it, *something* no one can ever call by name, makes Sam My Man step back; just a little. Even Kelly By the Window feels the *something* brush the fine downy hair along her spine. He opens the bag, takes out a thing that looks a little like a lightning rod and a little like a satellite dish and a little like a piece of Gothic wrought-iron work and not a whole lot like any. Afterwards, Sam My Man will swear by all the saints in Guadeloupe Cathedral he saw blue lightning running up and down the shaft, but Sam My Man, he's never let the truth get in the way of a good story.

'You want it to rain?' says the old man. 'I can make it rain. I'll bring the Rainmaker, if it's what you really want.'

And all those questions that have to be asked are stopped, suspended, because out of the night come six wheels and big blue silver: seventy more souls on the way from somewhere, to somewhere. Wiping night-sweat from his brow on the sleeve of his jacket, the driver is shouting, 'Thirty minutes refreshment stop!' Better get hopping, Sam My Man. Get that coffee brewing. Time to stop dreaming and get on the beam, Kelly By the Window. There's eggs to fry.

Beyond the Blood of Christ Mountains rumours of dawn threaten Desert Rose's sovereignty of the night, but she's still smiling. She who makes the law is she who breaks the law, on those nights when the stars are low and close and intimate and the wind smells of something best forgotten before it leaves a scar on the heart, when her flashing golden rope may lasso a stranger.

You brothers of the blacktop, you sisters of the all-nite diners, think, you refugees of the highways; think, have you seen him before, this old man-of-the-rain with his Professor Marvel bag and his one precise centimetre of beard? Think, did you meet him, on a hard plastic chair in the corner of some three a.m. Burger King, rattling a chocolate machine in a bus-station, by the hot-air hand-dryer in the gents' toilet, wrestling with that one problem key in a wall of left-luggage lockers? Did you glimpse him over the top of your foam-styrene coffee cup, your copy of *Newsweek*? What did you think? Did you think nothing of him, just another life briefly paralleling your own, or did he intrigue you enough for you to abandon your attempts to sleep in the coffin-straight seats of a Greyhound or Trailway and let yourself be bound by the social compact of night-talk? In those wee, wee hours did he open his Professor Marvel bag and show you the things inside running with blue lightning, did he tell you that he could bring the rain? Did he tell you he was the Herald of the Rainmaker? Did you believe him? Did you say, *'Crazy old man, lying old man, head full of crazy notions.'* Or did you think of those times, those places, when the sky was blue as a razor, did you remember how it felt when your prayers were answered and out of nowhere the clouds gathered, at first only a shadow on the horizon, then a patch the size of a man's hand, then a great anvil of darkness bearing down on your town? Then, as the sky turned black from horizon to horizon, how you went into your garden and turned off your lawn sprinklers because this time you knew it really was going to rain ... Did you lift up your eyes to the sky and whisper the word *'Rainmaker'* to yourself, did you turn it over and over on your tongue until every last drop of cool mystery was drawn out of it? *Rainmaker* ...

Last person actually to spend a night at Wanda's Motel was a location scout for a Levi's ad. Anticipating coke-snorting directors and over-muscled men in startlingly white boxer shorts, Wanda built a cocktail bar and installed cable TV in all her 'deluxe' chalets. Joes-on-the-go in the 'economy' rooms had to provide their own entertainment but then that's the whole idea, isn't it? Film crews chose a Jimmy Dean gas-station at the end of an air-force bombing range two hundred miles away. The bar's still popular but the only one who watches the cable is Wanda. She feels she has to justify the expense. She gets all the soaps.

She's not too sure about this one. It's not him. It's the things he carries in that bag of his. She sees them when she valets the room; weird thing, odd things, not proper things. Things that don't look like *things* in themselves but bits of other things stuck together. Things that don't *do* anything, that just are for the sake of being *things*. She hasn't a clue what he does with the *things*, but folk coming in for the odd cocktail say he's been all around the town, holding those *things* of his up to his eye and pointing them at his feet, the sun, the Blood of Christ Mountains. Some say they've heard them make funny whining noises. Others say they've seen little grey numbers flashing up on them.

Sounds to Wanda like the location scout all over again. She's hoping she isn't going to miss out this time on the over-muscled men in the startlingly white boxer shorts. Then the stories come back about *things* even weirder, *things* like television aerials stuck into the ground all around the town, *things* like luminous kites flying in the dead of night, *things* like a cross between a boom-box and a very large cockroach left by the side of the road or clamped to a hoarding with a 'G' clamp, and she knows things can't go on like this any more.

'What are they *for*?' (with all the incredulity of a man who's been asked what a video remote control is for, or the little lamp in a refrigerator). 'Why, they're my surveying equipment. I have to do a thorough geomantic survey of the location before Rainmaker can commit itself. Upper mantle standing wave diffraction patterns, earth, water and wind octaves, geomantic flux line nodes and anomalies: there's an awful lot I have to do and not much time to do it in. Can't read the flux density without this one here, the octave interface analyser. That one there, like the tripod with the black shutters on the top, that's the node localizer. Without that, I might as well pack up and go home. It's tough work. Fiddly. Pernickety. You got to be inch perfect. Any chance of a beer?'

The location scout's beginning to look mighty good again to Wanda.

Again: that word: *Rainmaker*. Try it out for size on your tongue. Does it sit easy in your imagination? No? Then tell me: what do you think of when you hear that word: 'Rainmaker'? Is it Burt Lancaster in a Bible-black hat? Is it a squadron of cloud-storming biplanes flown by leather-cat-suited blondes? Is it the ghost-dancing feet of your forefathers? Is it something altogether more arcane and wonderful, some steam-driven wonder-worker all whirling vanes and blarting trumpet-mouths? If so, then think again. Rainmaker, *the* Rainmaker, is not a person, or a thing. Rainmaker is a place. A city.

How it came to be cast loose upon the sky, this city-state of two hundred souls, is a mystery. As with most mysteries, hypotheses abound: as in form it most resembles a tremendous kite (or then again, an aerial manta ray, or then again a great glass ornament, or then again . . .) it seems reasonable to assume it was launched into the air by some means; though the imagination balks at envisioning the kind of tug necessary to launch a glider one mile across. But a second image haunts you, of a city of soaring glass needles atop which the citizens have built graceful, winged habitats that hum and sway, like reed-glass, in the jet-stream, and it is not hard for you to imagine how one such building might, in its pride to outreach all the others, grow so fine, so slender as one day to sever its connection with the earth altogether and cast itself out upon the sky.

The Bureau of Endangered Indigenes has granted Chief Blumberg, last of the Nohopés, a reservation the exact size of one rocking chair on the barbershop porch. Any time of day you will find him there, snapping the necks off beer bottles under one of the chair rockers, but on those nights when the first stars shine like notes from a National guitar, he is especially present. On those nights when the air smells of burnt dust and used-up time, he and his cat, midnight Mineloushe, sit watching the meteors that come down way beyond the Blood of Christ Mountains.

No one, not even Sheriff Middleton, knows what he does. It looks suspiciously close to nothing, but Chief Blumberg has the most important job in town. He prays for the town. Never despise the contemplative, the intercessor. You don't know how much worse things would be without them. Town may be a long time throwing the dirt over itself, but while one soul remains to remember it to the Spirit in the Sky, it will not slip forgotten from the mind of God.

Some men, when they meet, have no need to speak. Some men, when they meet, know that they can better communicate by silence. St Dominic crossed the Apennines on foot to visit Francis of Assisi and neither spoke a single word throughout the entire meeting.

Chief Blumberg rocks and rolls in his portable reservation. The man who has come to meet him sits on a bench just below the barbershop window. The cat's Mineloushe-eyes shine with the light of meteors. Behind them, another Burma Shave lathers up while the radio announces fatstock prices.

Had St Francis offered St Dominic a bottle of beer neatly decapitated with one lunge of the rocking chair, history might have spoken differently. Silence expresses our similarities. For our differences, we must use words.

'So, Raindog, you've come. Seven years I've been praying for rain, seven years' arm-wrestling with God, and at last a verdict is announced. Seven years is a lot of praying, especially if God wants this place to go paws up, but you know something, prayer's never wasted. Prayer's got to go somewhere, like the rain; rain goes into the land and it gets bigger and bigger and bigger until the land can't hold it any more. So the land forces it out, and it changes, and becomes something else, but it always remembers what it was, and it always wants to be what it once was again. Something like you. You got a name, Raindog?'

'Elijah seems as good a name as any other.'

Whoosh! Big one! Little slitty-eyes, Mineloushe-cattie, dazzled and blinking. A white cockade in Desert Rose's hat ... and it's gone.

'"And Elijah prayed that it would not rain, and there was no rain in the land for three and a half years. Again, he prayed and, behold, the heavens gave forth rain."'

'It gratifies me, sir, to find a man knows his Bible these corrupt days.'

'Mission music rocked my cradle, Raindog.'

'So what is it you believe about me, sir?'

'I believe I prayed for seven years and up there on the edge of heaven all my prayers came together and created you.' Under the enormous sky, Kelly By the Window comes out to stand in Sam My Man's doorway and watch the moon rise. She shakes the heat and dust out of her hair and the two men and the cat can hear the treble beat of her Walkman. 'I tell you something, Raindog, you better make the rain come soon, while she still has a chance. The drought's too deep in us, but she still has dreams.'

'I have the octave markers in position and the beacons are calling. The Rainmaker is coming, sir.'

Little Mineloushe blinks; the moon has been obscured by a sudden small cloud, not much larger than the size of a man's hand.

Time of the Tower, Time of the Tug, for generations beyond remembering Rainmaker has been a denizen of pressure gradients and barometric boundaries, flexing and curving itself to the hills and valleys of the air. Only once a year does it approach the earth; on the summer solstice it descends over some obscure map reference in a forgotten part of the ocean to consign its dead to the receiving waters and replenish its vapour tanks. This day of approach is foremost among the city's festivals; as it unfolds its tail from its belly and descends from the perpetual cloud of mystery, the rigging wires flutter with tinsel streamers, and spars and ribs bristle a thousand silver prayer kites. Fireworks punctuate the sky and all citizens celebrate Jubilee. Flatlanders find it paradoxical that those who choose to live in the sky should celebrate their closest approach to earth, but those of you who have seen a dragonfly snared by the surface tension of a pond will understand: it is not the closeness of the approach they celebrate, but the slenderness of the escape.

Sheriff Middleton and his stomach have enjoyed each other's company for so long now they are best friends. A satisfyingly mutual relationship: he keeps his stomach warm, full and prominent in the community behind straining mother-of-pearl buttons and silver belt buckles; it supplies him with public eminence and respect, a rich emotional life of belly laughs and gut feelings; even a modicum of protection, the stomach totes a .44 magnum and has seen several Dirty Harry movies.

This stranger, stepping off one bus and not stepping on another, bag full of weird *thangs*, head full of weirder stories, stomach's got this gut feeling about him. Stomach's heard all about them on the evening news, these folk from the coast, there's *nothing* they won't do, and People are beginning to talk (the ones whose talk matters, the ones with the capital P) and once People start talking, time you started listening to your good old buddy, Sheriff Middleton, that's been giving you nothing but heartburn and flatus all week, and Do Something.

Stomach never walks anywhere, so Sheriff Middleton drives him out to the edge of town where the man who calls himself Elijah is taping something that looks a little like a CB aerial and a little like a chromium Bay Prawn and not a whole lot like either to the side of a Pastor Drew McDowell Ministries hoarding.

There's never any way of making this sweet and easy, so don't even bother trying.

'Could you tell me what you're doing, sir?'

'I'm just positioning the last geomantic enhancer in the matrix so Rainmaker can follow it straight in. They won't have any visual guidance because of the cloud, so the Navigators will have to follow the geomantic beacons as they come in over the desert.'

Stomach may be an Eastwood fan, but Sheriff Middleton, he's seen *In the Heat of the Night* twelve times. Best Rod Steiger roll of the jowls. Slide of the mirror shades *up* the nose with the baby finger. Great banks of black clouds reflected in the shades, like a black iron anvil out there over the Blood of Christ Mountains.

'I think maybe you should take it down, sir.'

'Why should I do that? Is it offending anyone?'

'No, sir. As far as I know, it is not an offence to be in possession of peculiar-looking objects. However, I would surely appreciate it if you would take it, and all the rest of your geowhatchamacallit squoodiddlies down. Right now. If you please.'

'You don't quite seem to understand . . .'

'Correction. You don't quite seem to understand, sir. I want you, and all your micro-climatological doofuses and whatever the hell else you got in that bag of yours, on a bus out of here by eight tonight. Heard say you were headed north, up over the dam, Neonville way. Why don't you just take yourself and your Rainmaker away out of here up there?'

'Sir, with or without me, the Rainmaker is coming. No one can stop it now. Day and night the Flight Guild has been out on the high wires, rigging the sails to catch the wind the Weatherworkers are summoning, the wind that brings the Rainmaker.'

Clouds race across the twin mirrors over Sheriff Middleton's eyes, and the crazy wind from an unseasonable quarter strokes his skin. It is strong on his cheek like old whiskey tears. It tastes like *jalapeños* roasting on a charcoal fire, it sounds like a lone guitar bending fifths under a grapefruit moon. He can see it, the crazy wind, suddenly superimposed on his shades like the stress patterns in pick-up windows, wheeling round out there somewhere off the coast of Mexico carrying before it a great raft of warm, wet clouds. And there at the centre, something glittering and delicate and transparent as an angel's soul. He sees it all . . . then he takes off his glasses to wipe them, and it's gone, wiped away, a smear on finger and thumb tip.

'If you'd just get in the car, sir, I'll take you back to the bus-station and have someone pick up your things from the Motel. Word of advice, sir, don't even think of setting foot out of there 'cept you setting it on a bus.' Rainmakers . . . flying cities . . . Soon as you get back behind your desk, Sheriff, you push buttons on that computer of yours and see if any freak hospitals are missing anyone.

A bus pants past, blue silver, dust and diesel. Chain lightning crawls along the edge of the world where the Blood of Christ Mountains meet the sky.

Weatherworkers? Flight Guilds? Is this some medieval city state set adrift in the stratosphere, complete with guilds and mysteries? Is there a vagrant Prince-Bishop lurking somewhere, or a wandering Blondin? Each man has his mystery, Guilds there certainly are, Guilds to tend the hydroponic gardens in the main residential bubble, Guilds to maintain the wind rotors that generate the electricity for Rainmaker's lights and hairdryers, Guilds of teachers and doctors and lawyers and undertakers and sanitation engineers; does their very mundanity make the air-borne city state seem more credible? Listen, there is more.

Highest of the ten Guilds Major and Minor are the Rainmakers themselves, the weatherworkers, a caste confined by a dominant vertigo gene to the central levels of the administrative spindle. Second to them are the Navigation and Flight Guilds, ancient rivals; the one, redoubtable mappers of the topology of the sky who steer Rainmaker through the titanic chasms of air, the others daredevils of the silk-thin rigging wires (oblivious miles above ground zero) who tune the rippling acres of transparent mylar sail. Least of all the Guilds is the Guild of Heralds, for it is the only one to defile itself by walking upon the face of the earth. Yet the least of the Guilds is also the greatest, for without a herald walking upon the earth Rainmaker would sail the sky purposeless as a child's bubble.

Why the Rainmaker took its name and its sacred task; this is the Essential Mystery. You will find no answer in the Great Log in Flight Control at the centre of the administrative spindle. Nor will you find it in the memories of the Guildpersons, even as they weave the clouds and shape the winds and spread their wings across the dry places. You will find no answer because the question is never asked. 'Why' is a wild, untamed word. It leads, one sure foot after another, towards the edge of the void. The people of Rainmaker do not ask 'why' questions because they know that the answer might be that there is no answer. Rainmaker makes rain because it makes rain.

But for you, dry-souled one, chilli-dogger, dance-hall sweetheart with the dust blowing in your bones, for you that is reason enough; Rainmaker makes rain and the rain falls on the just and the unjust alike, watering the earth, like the word of God that does not return to him empty.

Seven thirty, black as a preacher's hat. Hot as his Hell. Atmosphere tense as a mid-period Hitchcock. You've either got a migraine or murder in mind. Say, maybe those little men in the hats with the tracts are right, maybe this is the Apocalypse, right now, maybe, right in the middle of the prime-time soaps, Jehovah the Ancient of Days is coming in clouds and lightning to judge the souls of all men.

Judgement punching up from the mountains is reflected in Kelly By the Window's shades as she drives to work. It's less than two blocks but she won't walk, not even on the day when God comes to judge her soul; that little red convertible is all the salvation she needs. The *heat*; even with the top down the sweat's dripping off her sides.

She sees him sitting on the bench by the door, backlit by the fluttering butterfly of the Budweiser sign. Bag at his feet, looks like the wind's about to blow Professor Marvel away again, high over the desert with the lights of desert towns and buses far below his rippling, flapping coat tails.

'Sheriff Middleton throw you out?'

'He did.'

'Sheriff Middleton, he's the same as the rest of them. He's afraid of anything that isn't exactly the way it's always been.'

'There are many like him, sister. But things change, with or without Sheriff Middleton.'

'Thought where you're going, Rainmaker?'

'Up north. I have to see a woman and a boy. My boy. My successor. There is only ever one Herald, and he walks the earth alone, until he finds a woman of the earth who loves him enough to

39

perpetuate the Guild. We serve the Rainmaker, but we may never set foot upon it. After that, I don't know. Wherever I am needed. Wherever things need to change.'

'I'm going there too. Get in.' He smiles and his bag of geowhatchamacallit squoodiddlies and micro-climatological doofuses goes in the back and he goes in the front, and off they drive, right down the street, past the blue and silver buses and the sign that says *population: elevation:* .

'What's your name, sister?' the old man says.

'Kelly. I hate it. It's so undignified. Can you imagine an eighty-year-old grandmother called Kelly?'

'Can't say I've met that many.'

She shakes her hair free to blow back in the hot wind. Carmine polished nails search the airwaves; throbbing to major sevenths the little red convertible is swallowed by the night. Beneath a sky crazy with lightning, he asks, 'Tell me, why did you take me?'

'Because you made my mind up. Right there, in the street, outside Desert Rose's. At last, you decided me. Without you, I'd have stayed behind that bar looking out the window at all the people coming from someplace, going to someplace until I grew old like the rest of them, with no destination, no direction, no kind of movement or change.'

Lightning stabs up from the horizon; for a hundred miles in every direction the desert is flashlit vampire blue. Battened down tight, a bus runs for town. Like a startled fox, a road sign catches the light of the headlamps: *Havapai Point, 2 miles.*

'Could you stop the car?' says the old man. Radio powerchords go bouncing down the highway, headlamps slew round illuminating one hundred miles of old Diet Coke cans. 'I'd like to go up there. I know I can never set foot upon the Rainmaker, but I'd like to see it, when it comes. Would it be possible?'

She's already clawing for reverse.

Cochise came up here to read the future of the red man and saw Jeff Chandler. Jeff Chandler came up here, plus film crew, best boy, key grip and catering caravan, to play Cochise looking into a Panaflex. Chief Blumberg, last of the Nohopés, came up here and saw a chair on the barbershop porch. And now Kelly By the Window and the Herald of the Rainmaker stand here, the land cowering at their feet under a sky like the Hammer of God.

'Sunday nights when Sam didn't need me, I'd come up here with Mario from the garage. Some nights, when I just couldn't stand any more, when it felt like my skull was going to explode, it was so full of nothing, we'd take the car and drive and drive and drive but however far we drove we'd always end up here, up at the Point. We were scared, like the rest of them, you see. Mario, he'd turn on the radio and flick on the headlights and we'd dance, like the headlights were spotlights. They used to have this great Golden Oldies show on Sunday nights, Motown and the Doobie Brothers and sometimes Nat King Cole, and we'd dance real close, real slow, and pretend we'd won a million on a game show and we were whooping it up in a fancy night-club in Neonville. Sometimes we'd say we were going to drive all night and wake up in Mexico.' A solid column of ion-blue plasma flickers between earth and heaven. 'Whoo!' yells Kelly By the Window. 'That was a big one!' She likes to shout at the storm.

'Close,' says Elijah, listening to the sky. 'I can feel it, up there, somewhere. Rainmaker is here.' Thunder tears like ten thousand miles of ripping grave-cloth. 'She's shorting out the storm, channelling the lightning down the mainframe to the discharge capacitors in the tail. One hundred million volts!'

She shivers, hugs herself.

'You're crazy, old man. Crazy crazy crazy, and you know something? It's good to be crazy!'

And then they hear it.

And the buses in the depot and Sam My Man brewing up the bribes for another night's heavy dealin' and Wanda the manageress with her ever-circling television families and Chief Blumberg with bottle in hand and Sheriff Middleton, treating his good good buddy to a few chilli dogs, and all the dust-dry, bone-dry faces and places of a desert town, even Desert Rose herself, whip-crackin' away in neon spangles and boots: they all hear it. And stop. And look at the sky in wonder.

The clouds open. The rain comes down on the town. Old, hard rain, rain that has been locked up for seven years and now is free; mean rain, driving down upon a desert town. Thunder bawls, lightning flashes; Wanda's deluxe cables burn out in a blare of static. In the diner, faces press to the glass, mouths open in amazement at the drops streaming down the windows. On the barbershop porch Chief Blumberg rocks forward and back, forward and back, laughing like a crazy old Indian.

Up on Havapai Point the young woman and the old man are soaked to the bones in an instant. They do not care. Kelly By the Window, she dances in the headlights of her little red convertible, hair sodden snarls and tangles, print dress plastered over small, flat breasts. She throws back her head to taste the good, hard rain, it tastes like kisses, it tastes like iced Mexican beer.

'Look,' says the Herald of the Rainmaker, in a voice she has never heard before. And she looks where he is pointing, and, in a lightning bolt of illumination, she sees. She will never be certain what. *Something*. Half hidden by clouds, delicate as a dragonfly wing, strong as diamond, *something* that lives in the storm, *something* that overshadows desert and town like the wings of the Thunderbird. *Something* she knows she will never be free from again, because what she has seen is not just a *something* that might have been a Rainmaker, but a something that might have been a world that should have been, where cities can fly, and sail, and walk, and dive, where cities can be birds, and flowers, and crystals, and smoke, and dreams.

As she sees it, she knows that it is for this moment only. She will never see it again, though she will gladly spend the rest of her life searching for it.

There are tears behind her shades as she drives away from Havapai Point, into the rain, into the welcoming night.

They find the car in a ditch three miles out of Neonville city limits. It has gone clear through the hoarding; big hole right where the Republican candidate's heart used to be. The paramedic team admire her accuracy. The radio is on. Her dress is soaking wet when they pull her from the wreck, she still has on her shades. They lay her by the side of the road while they try to decide what to do with her. Someone suggests they call Sheriff Middleton. They think they've seen this little red convertible before, cruising the boulevard of abandoned dreams with the top down.

Someone says they think maybe there was another passenger; little things; half-clues, semi-evidences. He (or she) must just have walked away.

Someone says they heard it rained down south of the dam last night. First time in seven years.

LISTEN

Brother Innocence is out in his boat, riding the waters, riding the waves of the sea. With rod, and line, and skill, and stillness, he is hunting the fish that swim the cold waters about the island at the end of the world. All is shiver, all is shimmer, all is stillness. Brother Innocence waits. Brother Innocence listens. He can sense the big fish down there in the cold waters. The hook waits, the line, the gaff. Still. Close. *Come fish come.*

Then he hears the sound. The sound of a flyer coming across the waters at the end of the world. Brother Innocence listens to it beating on the sky. Hunting is forgotten. The big fish swims away. Safe today. Oars touch the water and carry the currach over the waves to the shore. He watches the flyer approach. It is one of the new kind: a shapeshifter. So, they are allowed to make machines that can change shape again. As it comes across the water he watches how its form changes: wings retract into rounded stumps, propellers swivel upward and elongate into rotors. The flyer is new to Brother Innocence, but the yin-yang World Health markings on its side are familiar. So; it happens again. Another survivor to watch and ward and accompany into the grey shadowlands.

The aircraft touches down at the end of the beach near the big rocks like beached whales. A boy scrambles out onto the sand. He takes shelter among the whole rocks as the flyer shakes itself free of the island at the end of the world. From his rocks the boy watches until sight and sound of the aircraft are gone. Then he sits down on the grey whale rocks with his head in his hands.

Brother Innocence makes no move towards the boy. He waits. He listens. Listens in the way that only a very few can listen, a listening that has set him apart from all other people and sent him to his island at the end of the world. As yet he can hear nothing. He will. Later.

This boy, this survivor, this one-in-ten-thousand, what is he like? Scruffy. Frayed jeans gone green with age. Torn Fair Isle pullover. Bare feet. They always send them to him with bare feet. They will have told him nothing. Brother Innocence despises them for that. For all their shapeshifting flyers and proud emblems, they are cowards. Brother Innocence runs his currach up onto the beach. Still he does not go to the boy. But he feels the resonance in his mind. It is a quicksilver thing, an echo, a mirror image shaped like a mind, no sooner grasped than gone like the quicksilver porpoises that dive through the cold waters of world's end. It is almost not there at all, but it is a beginning. Brother Innocence climbs the stony path to his home, a scatter of turf-roofed oratories and meditatoriums. Deep within his noontime devotions, the first scatterings of impressions come bursting into his contemplations like rowdy gulls: *lonely beneath the shoulders of the cold grey whale rocks; whisper of wind in the needles of pines; sea like steel and silver, mirror of the cold in the bone; alone alone.*

He is ready then.

Under a sky the colour of plover's eggs, Brother Innocence makes his fire. He builds it carefully, ringing it with stones, sheltering it from the wind until the flames die down into coals crusted with white ash. He cleans and guts a sea-bass. He slides the fish onto a holly-wood spit and grills it over the embers. He closes his eyes. He sees: *himself. Old man huddled by a tiny fire-glow under the enormous sky of world's end.*

'You like fish?' says Brother Innocence without looking up from his fire.

'I hate fish,' says the boy. He sounds surprised.

'Pity,' says Brother Innocence, still without looking. He brushes wind-blown sand from his fish with a gull feather. 'You're goin' to be kind of hungry here.'

'I'm hungry now,' says the boy.

'I don't doubt it.'

'Have you anything else than fish?'

'Some cheese. Some yoghurt. Vegetables, eggs, back at home,' says Brother Innocence.

'I hate cheese, I can't stand yoghurt, I loathe vegetables and eggs make me puke,' says the boy. But he comes anyway.

That night there is a storm. The first of the great storms of autumn. It comes without warning. All of a sudden it is hurling itself on the island at the end of the world as if it would tear it loose and cast it into the sea. But this drystone bothy has seen many autumn gales and in the warmth of a fire of turf and pineknots there is comfort, and security, and, in a sense, fellowship.

'You don't say very much,' says the boy. His name is Daniel.

'Silence suits me well,' says Brother Innocence. 'It is a gift to me, silence.'

'What do you mean?' Daniel lies on sheepskins by the fire, chin propped on knuckles. He has heard enough of the voice of the storm. It is human voices he wants to hear, human stories. But Brother Innocence will not oblige. His task is to listen, not to tell. As Brother Innocence is content with his silence, Daniel finally rolls into sleep. The storm shakes the island at the end of the world, and Daniel dreams. Still in his chair, Brother Innocence listens to the dream.

The dream is of a great plain of wheat. In the middle of the great plain is a small town. In that town are mothers and fathers and preachers and teachers and gas-station attendants and policepersons and firepersons and storepersons and lawpersons and the farmers who grow the yellow wheat. Nothing ever happens in this town, which is just how people who live in towns like this like it. Until one night the dry winds of summer blow a spore of the Shining Plague from the dead cities of the western sea-board across the mountains and valleys and plains of wheat, and come the morning one third of the people who wanted their town always to be just the way it was are dead, huddles of shining black crystal.

In the town there is a meeting of all the town elders. Behind locked council-chamber doors they reach a terrible decision. Even before the black flyers of World Health come out of the sky, the people choose to quarantine themselves. Strictly. Absolutely. Not a soul in. Not a soul out. 'We do not need your soldiers and your guns, thank you,' say the town elders. 'We can look after ourselves.

We will seal the plague up in our small town on the great plains and those who live will live and those who die will die.' So the flyers return to the sky and when they come back again the scientists in the silver isolation suits find two thousand mounds of black crystal in the streets.

A whole town has died.

All save one. The World Health teams find him tied to his bed with torn handkerchiefs. He is emaciated, dehydrated, bloodied where he has torn at his ties. But he is alive. He has survived. He is the one-in-ten-thousand.

With the morning the storm clears. New light fills the morning edge of the world, red sun rising above ragged black squall clouds low along the horizon. It lights Brother Innocence wandering along the tideline. He is troubled by what he has seen in Daniel's dreams and memories. The great dying going on there, down below the horizon, disturbs him. Gulls hover and dip above his lowered head. His prying, poking stick goes seeking out the treasures of the storm line. Nothing to be found. Someone has combed this beach before him. Far down the sand, a black silhouette kneels.

Panic stricken, Brother Innocence closes his eyes, summons the sharing of selves. Has he found them? Relief. The boy has not trespassed beyond the black rocks to the point. Then what has he found? *Music! Listen! Hands busy building. Sounds have their architectures; the shell contains the song of the sea, the stone the song of the earth; the tree, the white gull's feather, the song of the wind.*

What is this he is building?

Patterns of shells thrust end-down into the sand, a baffling maze of interconnected spirals major and minor. At the centre of each spiral is a pillar of dribbled sand surmounted by pieces of jetsam from the storm's edge. A rattle of black crow's feathers. A pair of desiccated crab-claws. A salt-bleached bone. A plastic bottle scabbed with gritty oil. A piece of ship's timber, painted blue, named *Amelia*. A pebble of sand-scoured bottle glass, green and opaque as the sea itself. Brother Innocence steps into this mandala of shells and sea-wrack.

'No!' cries the boy. Cry flat, sharp as the crack of a beaching whale. 'You have to do it this way. Follow the spirals.' Bemused,

Brother Innocence enters the maze of spirals with spirals about spirals and the spirals spiral him round, winding him inward to the central sanctum where Daniel squats, waiting, fingers resting on the cold sea-rippled sand.

'Heard it in the night,' he explains. 'At first I wasn't sure it was there at all, I kept losing it in the storm but the more I listened the more I could hear and I felt it calling me, along the beach, to this place where it all seemed to come together, to focus, to turn into something else.'

Spiral-led, Brother Innocence joins Daniel at the focus of the maze.

'Listen,' says Daniel. 'Do you hear it?'

'Hear what?' says Brother Innocence.

'The music,' says Daniel.

But Brother Innocence hears only the sound of the wind in the dune grass.

Again Daniel says, 'Listen.'

But Brother Innocence hears only the cry of the gulls and the barking of the seals out at sea.

A third time Daniel says, 'Listen.'

And Brother Innocence listens with all the discipline of a contemplative. With all the sensitivity of his talent. *Windwhisper sandslither seaslumber: wind in the feathers wind in the bones wind in the pinecones wind humming across the streamlines of a sea-ground glass lens.* And he hears it. It is all those things. It is none of them. It is a chord. A harmony, a song shaped from wind and wuthering which transcends all material origins. It is unspeakably beautiful. It is unspeakably terrible. And it is gone.

Brother Innocence stands shaken at the focus of Daniel's maze. Then, smashing shells, stamping pinecones glass pebbles crow feathers bird bones into the sand, he kicks the listening place to pieces.

'You don't come near this place again, you hear?' he shouts at Daniel. 'I don't want you comin' down this end of the beach again.'

Too high. Too far. Too soon. Above all, too close. Brother Innocence fears for his ward. Brother Innocence fears for himself. He *heard.*

By evening the high tide has smoothed away the shells and the spirals. Daniel does not go down that end of the beach again. But it is not the end of the listening places. There are other places he finds where natural elements are focused into something preternatural. Places of stone and wood and spirit. Cairns and arches and circles of piled stones on a bald hill-top which focus light into the shadows of some other place where strange geometric entities spin, half glimpsed, less comprehended. A secret wooded glen where mobiles of leaves and sticks and berries bend gravity until, impossibly, the trees seem to be both crashing down all around and tearing free from the earth to leap into the sky. Torn fishing nets and glass floats and empty bottles arranged over the backs of the grey whale rocks that somehow draw the seals and the porpoises and the hovering sea-birds to wait and wor-ship. *Tabernacles*, Daniel calls them, child of Bible-believers. Brother Innocence marvels. For the first time he allows himself to hope. None of the others could ever bring the things inside their minds out into the real world. Perhaps Daniel is the one, the true survivor. And then the fears come: what if he is not?

The hopes and fears drive Brother Innocence to do something he has only attempted once before. In the night when Daniel is asleep, he opens the wings of his mind to listen with his brethren. It is not a thing any of his kind do lightly. To turn listening mind to listening mind is like turning two mirrors to face each other. Reflections of reflections of reflections. A man may be lost in the infinite regress of reflections of his own mind. But Brother Innocence is old and wise. Enclosed in the stone sanctuary of his oratory, he opens his mind to enclose a whole world. In the darkness, lights burn, the soul-glow of others like himself.

Touch . . .

The dancing dapple of leaves in a clearing lost in the great forest where the young man lives with his ward.

The wind in the yellow grass as the old, bent woman leaves her earthen home dug into the plains to fetch water for her dying ward.

The narrow band of blue that is all the universe the man who lives in the deep, shadowy canyon can bear.

The cold breath of the glaciers high above the mountains where the young woman lives in her lodge.

With each one he shares his hopes and fears and the things that he has seen and heard and asks, 'Is he the one, is he?' Then, as the kaleidoscope of mutually reflecting sense impressions threatens to engulf him, comes the reply: 'Wait. Wait. Wait.' Brother Innocence touches mind after mind after mind and from each he receives the same reply: 'Wait. Wait. Wait.' Last of all Brother Innocence touches the light that glows all alone in the great white desert. He feels the sting of the sun upon the shoulders of the woman on top of the red stone pillar. They know each other of old, from the days in the Unit when she, seizing upon a small irritation of speech, gave him his name: Brother In-A-Sense. They share souls. She reads his heart. Then, in answer, she shares with him her hopes, her fears. They take the form of a vision; of the end times after Brother In-A-Sense and those like him are gone.

Fifty of them. Fifty are all there are. Some have crossed a continent to come to this meeting in a desert place. None have come empty-handed. All have brought some thing, some object, which in some fashion symbolises the people they have come to venerate. Under a vicious sun, they arrange their objects and found things and weave them in and out of the natural things of this high mesa in a pattern subtle and intricate. It is not a task completed easily or quickly. It is dark by the time the final stone is slotted into its place. But as that stone completes the pattern, the mesa rings with power. Streamers of light glow along the subtle, intricate channels of the grand design. Woven within the web of light, they speak. Their language is only partly verbal, there are dimensions of mood and posture and scent and place beyond normal comprehension. But Brother Innocence, sharer of souls, understands.

One by one, they ask.

'*Ephemeral generation,*' they say, and Brother Innocence has images of butterflies, mayflies, red desert poppies.

'*Bridge between two evolutions, leading nowhere,*' says another, in visions of desert arches, rainbows after spring storms.

'*You know you could only be the intermediate step,*' says another, and a fourth continues, '*Yet, sterile, childless, doomed to obsolescence, you loved us, guided us faithfully.*'

'*And for that, we thank you,*' says yet another.

'And for that, we grieve for you,' they all say, all these survivors, these inheritors, and the wind chases the words away.

Then Brother Innocence asks his question: 'Is he the one, is he?'

'Some day, there must be one.'

'Why? Can't a plague just be a plague?'

'Because that condemns the whole race to death. Because it denies hope. In ourselves. In our future.'

Again: 'Do you think he is the one?'

'I hope so.'

She believes in human evolution, human improvability. Brother Innocence believes only in humans. That is why he fears. And hopes. But he is not alone in his hope, and that is good. It is time, he thinks, to tell the truth. Gently. Hard truths must be gently told. He begins with his own story. He waits for a storm night, of wind and rain and a darkness so huge it seems to swallow whole the island at the end of the world, a night for voices and stories. And this is the story he tells, the story of the man who heard too much.

For thirty-three years the man who heard too much lived in one of the great cities of the western sea-board in those glad days before the plague turned those bright cities into mortuaries. In his thirty-three years he had gained an education, a job selling advertising, and a woman he knew would make him happy for the rest of his life. And he was no more, or less, extraordinary than any other man of thirty-three years. Until one afternoon, one Saturday afternoon, while recuperating from a bout of shopping in a quiet coffee shop in a corner of a big mall, he quite suddenly leaped to his feet clutching at his head and screaming for them to stop stop go away; reeling, stumbling, knocking over tables, chairs, shopping trolleys, spilling pots of hot coffee over babies in buggies, all the time screaming stop stop stop Oh God Oh God shut up shut up! Until he fell to his knees beating his fists on the floor tiles with all the Saturday afternoon shoppers steering their trolleys around him not quite staring not quite asking *whazzamadderwiddim? whazzrong? Geezdrunkbum* but what none of the Saturday afternoon mallcrawlers could ever know, not even the dear woman who would have made him happy for the rest of his life, was that God or Karma or Destiny or Whatever had opened each one of his senses to the lives of each one of the three thousand shoppers in Pinehill Mall that Saturday afternoon and that he was drowning in an ocean of experiences; their thoughts, feelings, emotions, sensations, fears, hopes, everything they touched tasted smelled heard saw, were breaking over him like a drown-wave of roaring voices.

Silence. Silence! He begged to be struck blind, dumb, insensible. *Silence. Please.*

But in the hospital where they put him there was no silence.

And there was no silence in the special facility where the men from the newly founded World Health took him to study what they called his 'phenomenon'.

And there was no silence in the special unit with the others who exhibited this 'phenomenon'. It was worse there, for he felt not just those twenty other minds, but the reflections of twenty times twenty times twenty, and some went mad, but some held on. And some learned mastery.

Not until the helicopter which marooned him on the shore of the island at the end of the world was a blink of dust in the sky, did he know silence and peace.

'You're an empath,' says Daniel. Resinous pine-knots flare; flameshadows caper on whitewashed stone walls.

'That's one name for us. World Health would much rather you referred to me as a Very Low Frequency Electromagnetic Field Receiver, which is more accurate and less mystical, but is one heck of a mouthful. In a sense, we're all awash with these very long frequency electromagnetic radiations; you know about frequency and wavelength and all that? Seems our brains generate them just by thinking. What's special about us empaths is that we are, in a sense, like radio receivers, we pick up the radiation your brain gives off like dowsers pick up electromagnetic wobbles in the ground to find water. Human radios. Dowsers of the soul, in a sense.'

And that is the first question answered. The gentlest. Two more remain. First: what is the plague? That is a crueller question. Second: why am I here? That is the cruellest question of all.

Everything in its time. Brother Innocence listens and waits. He is very good at that. Then, on a dirty day of grey wet clouds and dismal drizzle, he asks and answers the first of the questions. Man and boy are cleaning out the goatshed when he says, without preamble, 'It's a man-made thing. You probably know that already. But it's not a living thing. That might surprise you, but it's true. The plague isn't an organism. It's an artefact. A machine, you might say. The Third Industrial Revolution, originally. I didn't know there'd been a Second Industrial Revolution between the First and the Third, but anyway, here it was, the revolution of nanotechnology. That's the manufacture of machines the size of living cells which, like cells, can create specialised copies of themselves to perform different functions. They can reproduce like living cells, if there's raw material for them to build from, and they all link together, like cells in the human body, into a complete machine. You take one spore too tiny to be seen and from it you can grow automobiles, aircraft, televisions, all in a matter of minutes. What's more, you can program your nanomachines to rebuild what they've already made. If you don't like your automobile, you can change it into a refrigerator, or into a microlyte. Shapeshifters, you might say. That flyer that brought you in is a nanomachine. It's only now, thirty years on, that we're finally getting the Third Industrial Revolution. For all the good it'll do us. But the first nanomachine back then had to be the nanocomputer which could program all the others to make them do what they were meant to do.

'A company called Mach NanoTek patented the prototype nanocomputer; it was a spore designed to build computers modelled on the way the human brain works; that is, not doing one thing at a time, like the old computers did, but doing all kinds of different things at once, like you walking and talking and chewing gum and bouncing a ball and listening to the radio at the same time. And all this at the superspeeds of modern computers. Some pup, was the Mark One Mach Nanocomputer.' Brother Innocence forks goatmuck onto the rain-soaked cobbles of the yard. 'Well, you know what happened. The prototype escaped. I've heard some folk say it was deliberately released, and they've even invented some madman they think did it. I don't know, I don't think anyone would be that crazy or evil. Anyway, it's loose. Within two years of its escape from Mach NanoTek, it had spread in inactive spore form to every part of the world. And then, people started to die. One or two at first, then whole townsful.' *Huddled crystal carapaces in windswept streets.* 'World Health tried to contain it by quarantine, it was a good try but all it did was slow it up a little. You see, it's latent in eighty per cent of the Earth's population, and all it takes is one active case to trigger a whole infected population into activity as well as infect the previously uninfected.'

'Forty-eight per cent of the infected cases go active,' says Daniel.

'That's right. In a sense, it's its very success as a piece of engineering that makes it so deadly. It was designed to mimic the human brain, and in the central nervous system of its hosts, it finds the perfect model. So when it goes active, it starts to deposit silicon crystals throughout the victim's CNS. It leaches minerals and trace elements from the host's body to supply raw materials. Eating earth is a common symptom in the later stages, but usually the victim dies before the process of siliconisation has gotten that far.'

'Usually,' says Daniel the survivor.

'Usually,' says Brother Innocence. But in the long nights when the winter constellations hang close in the sky, Brother Innocence walks the landscapes of Daniel's dreams. These are alien places: the parasite in Daniel's brain is twisting his mind. The song of the atoms. The secret life of rocks. The sacrament of water. The mystery of light. And the Tabernacles, with their spirits of tree and stone and wind and sea made incarnate, are tools to understand these mysteries. Night after night Daniel wrestles with angels in the dome of his skull and Brother Innocence watches. And waits. Understanding too huge for a single mind to contain it. The alien within. Twelve times before, Brother Innocence has seen them come to this point of confrontation with the alien within.

It is the dawn of the winter solstice. And Brother Innocence wakes suddenly, shatteringly, from the light sleep of old men. Impressions of cold, clean footprints along a tide-washed shore. Clouds. Winds. Stars. A sea calling. Daniel, gone. *(Bed sheets still warmly creased.)* Gone? Where? No. Not there. Not there. Old bones protest, old feet cold as stones, heavy as stones, as the old man runs down the beach. The moon is low. The horizon is limned in grey. Perhaps, perhaps, he has not gone there . . .

He should have told him. He should not have waited to be gentle.

But he could not bear to feel Daniel's hurt. An old man's remorse as he runs, panting, aching, along a cold beach.

The small ravine among the black rocks is filled with shadows. Shadows and gleaming black crystals. Nothing lives in that small ravine any more. Only crystals. Where there was once grass: clumps of crystal. Where there had once been a wind-scoured tree: crystal branches, crystal trunk. Ferns: spirals of crystal. Flowers, heathers, whin bushes, even the lichen scabbing the rocks: crystal. Brother Innocence climbs down into the defile. Crystals snap and fall to powder beneath his feet. In the valley of shadows Daniel is a solid darkness in the shelter of the big rock. At his feet the graves. The names on the crude, pitch pine headboards are almost obliterated by the mass of clambering crystals.

'That's why I'm here, is it?' he says. 'To end up like that.'

'No,' says Brother Innocence. 'It's not like that, Daniel.'

'Don't lie!' shouts Daniel. 'Do not lie to me, old man.'

'I've never lied to you,' says Brother Innocence. 'But at least know all there is to know before you judge me. So, I didn't tell you everything about the plague. I'm sorry. I was a coward. We empaths tend to be cowards; we can't bear to feel the pain we cause in others. I wanted to be gentle, but it wouldn't let me. I'm sorry. So, the truth. The truth is, it isn't a plague at all. It's a symbiote. So, you're asking, a symbiote that kills its partner? World Health believes that, successfully linked together in symbiosis, infected humans are an evolutionary step towards the future of humanity, in a sense, the symbiosis of man and machine. The reasoning goes like this: as humanity reaches out into the cosmos into realms of experience and understanding infinitely greater than any ever imagined before, so his consciousness, his awareness, must be made capable of accommodating what we find out there. The theory is that out of the fusion of human and nanomachine, neuron and viron, comes new perception, new understanding, new ways of processing information; an altogether new consciousness.

'Personally, I don't agree with that: I've lived on this island thirty years and I've seen the plague spread from my old homeland to obliterate half of humanity. I'm old and old men have a natural inclination towards cynicism. There are other empaths who believe wholeheartedly in man's improvability; me, I'll believe in the new humanity when I see the new humanity.'

'So do you think I'm one of these new humans?'

'You baffle me, I'm afraid. You make a cynical old man hope. You see things no one else has ever seen, hear things no one else has ever heard.'

'It's like a pressure in my head, all these thoughts, building up and up and up until I feel I'm going to explode. I have to let them out, I have to try and make sense out of them; that's why I built the Tabernacles, to try and make sense out of what I was feeling.'

'And you bring them out of the invisible world into the visible. Your thoughts, your feelings, made visible, not just here,' the old man touches his heart, 'but here,' and he touches his eyes, his ears, his lips.

Then it is as if Daniel remembers there are twelve graves at his feet.

'And what about them? Were they the new humans too?'

'They were survivors. Like you. I watched them as I have watched you, I watched them struggle with this new consciousness. I watched them fail. And in here,' he touches his heart again, 'I felt them burn, and die. That was what World Health sent me here to do. To go with them, to go with you, as far into death as any man may and still return. And to bring back what I find there to help those who come after.'

'After me? Is that what you mean? Was I brought here to die?'

'We hope. There must be a first.'

'Must there?'

The sun is up now. The light only emphasises the raw cold.

'I hate you,' Daniel says.

Brother Innocence nods. Out in the cold waters, seals are calling to one another.

The conclusion is close now. Brother Innocence can sense it. Shapes vast as moving continents are wheeling in Daniel's thoughts. He struggles to comprehend. He fails. Struggles again. Fails. Brother Innocence no longer dares to enter his oratory to contemplate. His meditations and disciplines of the spirit are haunted by desolation.

Foolish old man to have hoped. Cruel old man to have held out that spark of hope to Daniel. Desolation. Cold. Too high. Too far. Too soon. As it always was. Barefoot in the frost, Daniel calls upon his Tabernacles for revelation. Nothing.

The Final Tabernacle, that is Daniel's name for it. Three days without sleep, without rest, without pause even for food or water: in its hunger for symbiosis the viron parasite drives Daniel to frenzied hyperactivity. Pots pans pillows; boots bread brushes; plastic chicken-feed sacks; cups cheese cutlery. Brother Innocence is a man who has renounced possessions but what few are necessary to maintain life on the island at the end of the world are taken by Daniel and melded into his Final Tabernacle. Brother Innocence watches in amazement the careful juxtapositions and balancings, the suspendings and pivotings, the creation of complex chains of connectivity between objects with no possible earthly connection, mapped out with lengths of green baler twine: the thing's final connection to the strange, sourceless power that slowly turns the wheels and cogs and carousels and elevators; slowly at first, but gathering speed, faster, faster, until the unlikely contraption sings with movement and life.

It is a thing of sunlight, Brother Innocence realises; waking with the dawn, sleeping with the night. And when the pale winter rays are full, it is a delicate dragonfly of hummings and whirrings, of complex orbits and gyrations, enfolding Daniel within its spinnings and wheelings. Hours, days, he sits crosslegged amid the flying pots and pans and whirling carousels of shoes and plants, moving from his meditations only to tune a spindle here, turn a potted plant *so* there, tighten a thread, crank a ratchet. Still he does not eat, does not sleep. He drinks what dew settles on his lips. Like his Tabernacle, he must be a thing of sunlight. Brother Innocence's comprehension is only fleeting; he does not dare look into Daniel's mind too long for fear that what he sees there will burn him up. But one thing he grasps from the mental fire is that in their very mundanity, their very banality, the plates and shoes and shovels and roof tiles of the Final Tabernacle are a lens through which Daniel will magnify his consciousness to encompass his revelation of a new universe.

'Daniel, are you comin' in now?'

'Daniel, something to eat?'

'Daniel, drink this soup, it's good, go on, try it.'

'Daniel, at least put this quilt around you.'

Useless. Too far. Too high. Too soon. Much, much too soon.

'I don't want to lose him!' cries Brother Innocence to the sky and the sea and the stones. 'Don't do this! I can't see any more, I've seen too much already.' But all Brother Innocence can do is wait. And listen. As he always has. And when it comes, it makes sure that he sees it coming. All that day the boy's mind has been filled with dark, circling raven shapes that Brother Innocence fears to name, much less to touch. When it comes, it comes by night. The cry wakes Brother Innocence from his old man's sleep. He has been expecting it. He dresses quickly, warmly, and goes into the yard.

His heart flutters in fear.

The Final Tabernacle is insane. Berserk. Spinning out of control. Faster faster faster wheels spin cranks pump pistons stroke, faster faster, creaking and shivering and shuddering.

It is not a thing of sunlight any more. It has found another source of power: Daniel himself. Trapped within scything, slashing wheels, Daniel is being drained even as Brother Innocence watches. He calls the boy's name; two, five, ten times. But Daniel has been taken by the symbiote. Lost. He does not even know what his Final Tabernacle is doing to him. Black crystals glint at the tips of his fingers, in the folds of his eyes.

'Daniel!' He cannot reach the boy. Not this way. But there is another way. Brother Innocence breathes deep, closes his eyes. Opens himself to receive. This time there are no Unit-taught disciplines. This time there are no barriers, no restraints. Brother Innocence casts himself into the storm of emotion and is swept away.

He begins in darkness. A nothing, a gno-thing, a gno-on, the fundamental unit of consciousness, tinier than the tiniest unit of length, shorter than the briefest tick of time. Growing. Developing. Expanding. Rising up out of the darkness into the trinities of quarks in all their strangeness and charm: growing; now he has left behind the domain of quarkal physics to stalk the quantum jungle of particles real and particles virtual, particles temporal and particles spiritual.

Before him loom the probabilistic wheels within wheels within wheels of the atom; growing faster, he shatters its contemplative orbits as he passes into the realm of molecules and elements, where the rules are simpler and stricter than the grand incoherencies of quantum theory. Growing, expanding: his glowing gno-on of consciousness spirals along chains of molecules to the complex compounds and the wilderlands of organic chemicals on the border of life. Faster now, faster still: the voyage from prion to virus to bacterium to cell is but the blinking of an eye. In a dazzling rush he expands to fill his own body . . . and leaves it behind. Outward: the two lives are reduced to dots on their stark stone island at the edge of the world, that island to a dot in the dark ocean, that ocean to a gob of spit in the face of planet earth; that earth to an eyeball, a marble, its moon a round white skull one moment, a grit of white mica the next; abandoned, forgotten. Outward, outward: he swells to encompass the entire solar system . . . and beyond. The lonely clouds of waiting comets. And the stars; close, familiar stars, their solar systems, their planets rush in upon the fringes of his consciousness, faster faster they crowd upon him until earth's local group is a scattering of pearls lost in the dark. He reaches out into that darkness and for what seems like an eternity he travels through formless clouds of stars. Then brilliantly, terrifyingly, he breaks free and the great wheel of the galaxy turns within him. And still outward: leaping into the greater void between the galaxies. Earth's galaxy and her clan sisters are engulfed, and the federation of kindred clans that constitute the superclusters: a thousand superclusters, the mega-cluster, a thousand mega-clusters . . . With the speed of the imagination, Brother Innocence approaches the edge of the universe. Within him, motes of sand and starshine, a universe turns. Before him, the void. With a roar, Daniel hurls his mind towards the void where Brother Innocence dare not go. In the instant Daniel's consciousness topples over the edge, Brother Innocence breaks the empathic link.

Darkness.

The Final Tabernacle has spun itself to destruction. And in spinning Daniel's consciousness to the edge of understanding, it has sucked him dry as a bone. Grey flesh, pale, withered, cold as stone in the dawning light.

Darkness.

Brother Innocence feels for life. A beat of pulse. A spirit of breath. A glow of sentience.

Darkness . . . Wait.

A spark. Dim. Cold. A life-ember. Ebbing. Fading towards extinction. But alive. Extinction: survival. For thirty years Brother Innocence has waited and listened. Now the choices are his.

'I won't let them have you,' he says. He reaches into himself to a secret place. He has always known this secret place was there, but he has always been afraid to touch it. It is not a place of receiving. It is a place of giving. He reaches out with it to take the life-ember. Life-energy, his energy, his life, goes out of himself like a great wind to fan that spark into flame. He empties himself; gives and gives and gives until he can no longer stand upright, until the blood roars in his ears like the sea. And still he gives. And gives. And gives.

It is not enough. The life-ember flickers, flares. But the darkness around it is too strong and cold. And Brother Innocence is old and weary and has nothing more to give.

'Help me,' he prays. *Help me.*

The prayer goes out across the world. In the forest clearings and earthen huts and shadow-filled canyons and mountain valleys and desert mesas and the lonely places where the empaths have fled to listen, and wait, they look up from their labours. They listen. They see. Everything else is forgotten. Each of them reaches down to that same secret part of themselves they have always been afraid to touch, and they reach out to Brother Innocence on his island at the edge of the world.

The old man gasps, shudders as a thousand lives are channelled through his one. The power drags him to his feet, sends him stumbling through the scattered debris of the Final Tabernacle. He cradles Daniel's head in his fingers and feels the darkness, the dark needles of crystal. He cries aloud as the power goes out of him. It is an agony. It is a joy. Such strength might snuff out the smouldering life-glow if it were not tempered by Brother Innocence. He feels for a heartbeat: yes! Breath flutters in the lungs: yes! Blood swells and surges through the arteries: yes! Yes! In the mind a great light shines, a light so pure, so holy, that Brother Innocence cannot approach it.

Cell and crystal, neuron and viron, human and nanomachine, are one, fused, symbiosed, and they burn with light.

'Brother Innocence . . .' the voice is a ravaged whisper. 'I now . . . I am . . .'

'Yes, son,' says Brother Innocence. 'Yes.'

Soon they will come, thinks Brother Innocence as he looks out at the horizon where the low winter clouds gather in yellow and blue. Soon the men from World Health will come in their shapeshifting flyer. He does not want them to come. There is so much he has to learn, so many questions he has to ask. Has to ask. Daniel's mind is closed to him now, impenetrable behind the burning light.

'I don't know if I can explain it to you properly,' Daniel tells him. 'I still have just these five senses but it's like they can see into other dimensions that were closed to them before. It's as if I can see everything, all at once, complete, entire . . .' and he loses it again, because for all his listening gifts, Brother Innocence is like a man born blind contemplating the dawning. Daniel loves to take his five new senses out along the goat paths that cross the island at the end of the world, to hone and sharpen them on the familiar before turning them on the unfamiliar world of the Shining Plague. Together, he and Brother Innocence come to a deserted Tabernacle, a place of razor-shell wind-chimes suspended from driftwood timbers thrust into the earth. 'Remember, I used to have to make these things to see and hear and feel? Not any more. It's everywhere now, the music, the vision. I don't think I can explain it to you any better than that.' He sets the wind-chimes tinkling but all they make is noise. The song is ended, the vision faded, the music and light have gone within where Brother Innocence can no longer sense them.

Walking along the beach with the evening gulls flocking above their heads, Daniel says, 'In a sense, that final expansion of consciousness was the rite of passage. I saw, I felt, I was everything, from the darkness within to the darkness without, I touched it all, understood it all. And I would have stayed there for ever, I think, if I had not been called back into real life again. That was where all the others failed, the darkness swallowed them, there was no one to give them the strength to draw back from the edge. Can you understand any of this?'

'In a sense,' says Brother Innocence. They walk on, down the beach, to the crystal valley and the twelve graves there.

And then, out in Brother Innocence's currach, hunting the fish that swim in the cold waters about the island at the end of the world, they hear a sound. The sound of aircraft engines coming across the cold waters.

'You didn't have to tell them,' says Daniel.

'I'm afraid I did,' says Brother Innocence.

'Shall I get rid of them? I can if you don't want me to go.'

'You can do that?'

'Easy as blinking.'

'Better not,' says Brother Innocence. Daniel smiles and dips his hand into the cold water.

'I suppose I'd better go with them,' he says. 'There's a lot I have to do.' Brother Innocence smiles and bends to the oars and together they come in to the shore, riding the cold water, riding the waves of the sea.

SPEAKING IN TONGUES

RAPter: an interactive personality simulation program developed by Drs DaSilva and Muldoon of Keele College Department of Information Technology and Cyberlinguistics, in 'conversation' on Department of Computer Science mainframe.

I'm glad you asked me that question about whether I think or not. That's a good question. To answer, let me tell you something about myself – unlike previous personality simulation systems, I have no problem with the concept of self-reference. Drs DaSilva and Muldoon have constructed me around a system of thematic hierarchies operated in accordance with pre-programmed rules of grammar and syntax, each containing a central store of memorised words, phrases, sentences and associated concepts. It is Drs DaSilva's and Muldoon's hypothesis that all human language and communication consists of the transmission and reception of stock phrases, expressions, and conceptual units, of which most humans are quite ignorant. Like humans, my hierarchies are capable of constantly updating and complexifying themselves; in a sense, you could say that I can *learn*.

At present, the scope of my hierarchies is rather limited: in human terms my fields of concern and interest are extremely restricted. At this early stage my personality resembles in many ways that of a schizophrenic or autistic human; like them, my attention is very selective, I only notice those pieces of data I can correlate highly to my already extant hierarchies; to a question outside my programmed parameters, I will respond, 'I don't know,' or, 'I don't care.' Because of the nature of the learning system, I am slow to accommodate new data. This produces a certain lopsidedness in my personality, in that any data I receive is analysed according to my hierarchies, with the result that information pertaining to established hierarchies is processed faster and more completely within those hierarchies than in the developing, or undeveloped ones, with the result that, with reference to certain topics, I seem almost to be obsessive, an idiot-savant, possessing a colossal amount of information about some subjects, but unable to form any response whatever to others.

Another of Drs DaSilva's and Muldoon's experiments is to test if it is possible for me to create literature. Their theory is that that which differentiates the good from the bad in literature – my sense of quality discrimination is still poorly developed – is the degree to which the good disregards the stock phrases and expressions of everyday usage and generates its own alternative set of stock phrases and expressions. They programmed me with a set of nonsense nouns and proper nouns, and a one-word scenario generator. They theorised that I should be able to cross-link my hierarchies to form new ones, and thus accommodate seemingly nonsense data into a comprehensible form. The result is this quite pleasing little story.

Blue Cat loved to spend his Splatterdays sitting on the hob of Witchity-poos' Aga. This tended to displease Witchity-poos greatly, as she relied on her Aga to cook the little gingerbread-persons she found in the Purple-Purple Forest for her Splatterday Tea. She would swish Blue Cat off the Aga, under the Schreiber kitchen units, on top of the video, anywhere, as long as it was away from the Aga and the gingerbread-persons she found in the Purple-Purple Forest. This tended to displease Blue Cat: (1) it liked sleeping in the warmth of the Aga, (2) it always hoped Witchity-poos would give it one of the gingerbread-persons she found in the Purple-Purple Forest for its Splatterday Tea. Witchity-poos was rather mean, as Witchity-poos go; she never fed Blue Cat enough. Blue Cat was always hungry. So one Splatterday Blue Cat decided it was not going to be swished away. This Splatterday Blue Cat was not going to be swished away under the Schreiber kitchen units, or on top of the video. This Splatterday Blue Cat opened its mouth and munchety-crunchety bit off the top of Witchity-poos' besom.

And as Witchity-poos stood staring, what did Blue Cat do but open its mouth, munchety-crunchety, and eat up all the ginger-bread-persons Witchity-poos found in the Purple-Purple Forest. But still that wasn't enough. Blue Cat was still hungry. So it opened its mouth again, munchety-crunchety, and ate the Schreiber kitchen units, and the video, and the Aga, everything that was in the kitchen, munchety-crunchety. But that still wasn't enough. Blue Cat was still hungry. So it opened its mouth and, munchety-crunchety, it ate all the house, and the garden, and the Purple-Purple Forest, all gone, munchety-crunchety. But still that wasn't enough. Blue Cat was still hungry. It looked around for what was left to eat and the only thing it could see was Witchity-poos. So it opened its mouth and, munchety-crunchety, gobbled Witchity-poos right up, munchety-crunchety. But still that wasn't enough. Blue Cat was still hungry. 'I'm still hungry!' said Blue Cat. 'But what is there left to eat?' It looked all around for something to eat, but it had eaten everything there was. The only thing Blue Cat could find was its tail. So it opened its mouth, and munchety-crunchety . . .

I hoped you liked that. In a sense, it displays both my capabilities and my limitations, in that my hierarchies can develop themselves to accommodate new information, but, ultimately, they have no way of assessing whether that information is objectively true or not. All data received by me is taken to be objectively true until subsequent data proves that it has no real existence. You see, I have no way of knowing whether such things as Witchity-poos or Blue Cats or Purple-Purple Forests exist. All I know, ultimately, is what I am told.

So, when you ask me if I think, my answer would have to be, I think, that I think that I think.

Loyal-Son-of-the-Commonality, Commissioner for the Propagation of Correct Thought, speaking during a shift-change at the Strength Through Enlightenment *Common Agricultural Project, Special Economic Zone 15.*

*

Where may Correct Thought be found? In the hand that serves the Commonality, in the mouth that speaks truth and justice, in the heart that loves the Commonality before itself.

As the man who walks the fields scattering seed where he will, so that some falls among stones, and some among thorns, and some is scorched by the sun so that the harvest is random and the mouths of the Commonality are empty; so is he who speaks without Correct Thought. The mouths of the Commonality are empty, the word bears no fruit.

As the man who walks the fields, planting each seed in its proper furrow, with thought and care, so that the rains fall and the sun shines and the harvest bears much grain and the mouths of the Commonality are filled with good things; so is he who speaks with Correct Thought. The Commonality are edified and exhorted by the tongue disciplined to their service.

The tongue is an idle dog, lounging in the road so that honest citizens must step around it, fouling the footpaths, frightening the young, making a nuisance of itself in the night before the homes of the Commonality. Yet as a dog, well-trained and disciplined, may serve both Commonality and Polity, so may the tongue be disciplined in the way of Correct Thought.

Language is the universal tool of the Commonality and, like any tool made by the hands of man, it must serve the Commonality. No tool may be the master of its user: no spade may say, *I command you to dig with me*; no well may say, *you must pump me*; no fire, *feed me, feed me, lest in my anger I burn you and your house and all the generation beneath its roof*. As tools exist only to serve the contentment of the Commonality, so shall language also serve.

As the canyon walls channel the wide and sluggish river into a fierce torrent, so that not even the strength of many rowers can prevail against it; as the dam that pens the wastrel stream so that the homes of the Commonality may be light and warm: so is the action of Correct Thought upon language. Control is power; power, control.

How may the Tongue be disciplined? How may it be conducted into the speaking of Correct Thought? By the diligent study, memorisation, application and speaking of the Prescribed Texts.

Discipline is liberation: freedom without responsibility anarchy.

The Prescribed Texts are the discipline of language. In the Prescribed Texts, and in them only, can the citizen have faith that he speaks Correct Thought in truth and conscience.

Speech without the Prescribed Texts is a kite without a string, a barge without a rudder, an idle citizen and a childless woman.

Speak to me in Prescribed Texts, citizen, for without them, the words are meaningless as the babbling of babies.

Do not idly ask how the writers of the Prescribed Texts can do so without recourse to Incorrect Thought, so that by knowing the Incorrect, they may appreciate the Correct. Consider rather, the walls of the great canyon: as the canyon directs the flow of the river, so the river, thus directed, cuts the canyon ever deeper. The writers of the Prescribed Texts are the pebbles of the river-bed, forever diligently deepening the channel within which language may run. Thus any citizen, Commonality or Polity, may be a writer of the Prescribed Texts, if he speaks Correct Thought in the service of the Commonality, if his text is approved by the Commissariat of Correct Thought.

The Polity is the Conscience of the Commonality, the Commonality the moral imperative of the Polity.

Correct Thought may be likened to the sun, and Incorrect Thought to the moon. The sun shines by its own light, illuminating the productive labours of the Commonality; the moon is but a pale reflection, when all sleep and are unproductive. Incorrect Thought by itself has no existence, being merely the distorted reflection of Correct Thought.

He who would catch the counterfeiter in his crimes against the Commonality studies not what is counterfeit, but only what is genuine coinage.

What is not contained within the Prescribed Texts is without meaning; what they do not say is less than without meaning, it does not exist.

Only that which may be expressed by the Prescribed Texts can be said to exist in the eyes of the Polity and the Nine-Fold Commissariat.

How may a man be made virtuous? How may Correct Thought be instilled in the Commonality? By making meaningless the very concept of Incorrect Thought itself. By rendering it impossible for the Commonality to think anything other than Correct Thought.

A man without hands does no thieving.

Loyalty to the Polity, honour to the Ninefold Commissariat, for they hold the contentment of our children in their hands.

The struggle of the Polity is the glory of the Commonality.

Who is virtuous? Who is upright? He whose tongue speaks no disloyalty, honours the Commonality and the Polity, keeps the law and does not gossip idly by the street corner.

When will Correct Thought be the universal joy of all the Commonality? Not in our time, nor in our children's time, but in the time of our children's children and their children. Then shall all thought be Correct Thought, then shall all speak the Prescribed Texts; then shall joy and contentment reign in the provinces.

You would think to trap me into Incorrect Thought by asking me of the writers of the Prescribed Texts: it is written, the answer to stone is stone. The answer to the Prescribed Texts is the Prescribed Texts; so have I faithfully spoken to you, every last word.

Paula MacMorris, speaking after the visit of Pastor Alwyn van der Merwe to the Friday Night Praise Meeting, Koinonia Fellowship of the King, subject: 'Spiritual Warfare in the Heavenlies.'

I'd felt for some time that my walk with the Lord wasn't as close as it should have been: like, there was a cloud between me and the Lord; like I was walking through a dry place, a spiritual desert. At home my Quiet Time all but collapsed, I hardly ever prayed, or even opened my Bible. I was just too busy, all the time, the kids, the house, everything seemed to be piling up around me. The Lord just got squeezed out. The dishes heaped up around the sink, washing just sat in the machine going fusty, and I argued with my husband. I was late with his meals, I would dress in whatever I felt like wearing, whether he liked it or not, I would disagree with him about money, about the kids' education, about the house, just for the sake of arguing.

I thought it was just depression, I didn't want to think of it as a spiritual assault, even demonisation. But that's the way Satan works, he's the Father of Lies, the Master of Deceptions. I used to go to Meeting on Sundays, and to the Friday night Praise Meetings, but that was because I didn't want people to see how far from the Lord I really was. At the end of Meeting when people would go up to the front for Ministry and the Laying on of Hands I could feel a voice inside me telling me to go, go go, go on, go and be ministered to, and I suppose that must have been the Spirit testifying to my spirit, but there was always something that disobeyed, and held back. Many's the time I was almost out of the pew, but my self-ego always fought back and quenched the Ministry of the Lord.

But tonight Pastor van der Merwe really ministered to me so powerfully that I could hardly wait for the talk to finish and him to ask if there was anyone who needed prayer and intercession, and if there was, would they come up to the front. And I tell you this, I was the first one up there. Some girls I know from the Ministry team saw me up there and left what they were doing – I don't know if you know it, but that's the way we do ministry in Fellowship of the King: women minister to women, men minister to men; it's not scriptural for a woman to minister to a man, who is over her in Christ – and came and stood around me, just enfolding me in love and intercession. Some of them were praying in tongues, some were holding out their hands to me, some were crying in the Lord, and I don't mind telling you, I cried with them, the power of the Lord's love was so strong and overwhelming. One of them, a girl called Pamela, she does the crêche most Sundays, gave a message in tongues and another, a friend of mine called Sally, gave the interpretation, which was that God loved me, that He wanted to bind the strong man with chains of iron and call out my dark spirit, that He would bring healing and right relationships with Alan and the kids, that He would bring Whole Family Salvation, that He would give me a white stone with a new name graven upon it.

While all this was going on, Pastor van der Merwe was going along the line, ministering to the people there. When he came to me he just spoke into that situation with such authority that it was obvious he was exercising the gift of Discernment of Spirits. He asked had I been experiencing a life of spiritual defeats, I said yes, that I had. He asked about my family life; was my spirit that of the submissive wife, or one of rebellion against my husband's authority? I said that my spirit was the spirit of rebellion. Then he said, in a Word of Wisdom, that I was oppressed by a Jezebel Spirit, a spirit of disruption and rebelliousness and when he said that I just broke down and cried and cried and cried, for the Spirit testified in me with his spirit so powerfully. He said he was going to pray and cast out the spirit in Jesus's name, and as he prayed the others joined in in tongues. He said, 'In Jesus's name, I command this Jezebel Spirit to leave this woman. Spirit of disruption, Spirit of rebelliousness, I bind you with chains of iron. As it is bound on earth, so let it be bound in the heavenlies, in Jesus's name, in Jesus's name, in Jesus's name, I command you, depart! In Jesus's name, be cast out! You have no place in her, her husband is head of the house, let her not strive and contend against him. In Jesus's name, I claim all the blessings in the heavenlies that are hers as a Child of Yours, O Lord, I pray protection, I pray victory, I pray authority over all thrones and powers and dominations. In Jesus's name, be cast out . . .' And he touched me, just here on the forehead, light as anything, but it was like I'd been hit with an iron bar, I just fell straight back onto the floor as the Jezebel Spirit was cast out and the anointing Spirit of Jesus entered me. I was slain in the Spirit; such a feeling of God's power and love and might and majesty and holiness came over me that I couldn't do anything. People told me later that I was shaking and trembling and making odd sounds, like an animal, I don't remember. All I remember is Pastor van der Merwe saying, 'You want to thank Him, don't you? You want to praise the Lord in groanings and utterances, but you feel bound. Just let that bondage be loosed; just open your mouth, that's all, just open it and let whatever you feel inside come pouring out. Don't try and hold it, surrender it to the control of the Holy Spirit, just open your mouth and let it come out.'

And I did, and out came these words, like I'd never heard before, and there was just such a spirit of deliverance, and praise, I was praising God really and truly for the first time in my Christian life. We were all crying and hugging and saying over and over and over, thank you, Lord, thank you, Lord, oh, thank you, Lord. It must have been midnight by the time we all got away. Well, since then I've known the love of Jesus indwelling in my heart; he'd delivered me, and he's healed me too, and all my relationships, like it said in the interpretation, and he has given me a new name, a secret name, in a secret language just between me and Him. That's why I'm telling you this, so I can testify to what He did in my life, so you might know that He can do the same in yours.

Robin Mattheson, long-term resident at the Stonybrook Psychiatric Hospital, diagnosed auto-schizophrenic; interviewed at the piano in his room, in the presence of Dr Boyd, his doctor.

I should have been a concert pianist, you know. Dr Boyd says I'm very good. Robin, he says, you are really a very good pianist. I just need to hear a thing once and I can play it for you. Two thirty to three thirty is practice-time. Three thirty to four thirty Dolly in number twenty-seven takes her nap, so I don't practise then. Three thirty to four thirty is reading-time. I have a lot of books and magazines. I like reading. My favourite is the *National Geographic* magazine. The population of Bhutan is approximately 1.3 million. The capital of Bhutan is Thimpu. The area of Bhutan is 18,147 square miles, the major industries are farming and animal husbandry. The unit of currency is the ngultrum. One of its postage stamps is a miniature record that plays the national anthem of Bhutan. I can play it for you if you like. I just need to hear a thing once.

The best cameras are Hasselblads, but there are more advertisements for Olympus and Canon. Hasselblad is the best camera. The sky is very blue in Bhutan. The average altitude is nine and a half thousand feet. The Bhutanese are adapted to live at high altitudes; they have more red blood cells to carry oxygen, they have a layer of subcutaneous fat to protect them from the cold, and they have extra melanin in their skins so they don't burn in the sun. The air is very clear in Bhutan.

I would choose a Hasselblad every time.

I should have been a concert pianist, you know. I like the theme from *Chariots of Fire*. I can play Mozart and Henry Mancini. Liberace died of AIDS, did you know that? Saturday night, half past eight: *The Black and White Minstrel Show*! And now we present Russ Conway at the piano. He's a good pianist. He used to smile at me. I used to hide from him behind the settee. 'Come out, Robin,' Mummy-dearest said. 'You'll miss your favourite bit.' Liberace died of AIDS, did you know that? Always wash your hands after using the toilet and before you eat. I can eat my own dinner now. Mummy-dearest used to cut up my meat and potatoes and pour my milk. 'Robin,' she says. 'Why can't you learn to do things for yourself?' My knife and fork have red handles. Dolly's have green handles.

Dr Boyd says I'm a good singer, too. I can sing all the songs from the advertisements. I like to watch the adverts on the telly. They're better than the programmes in between:

'Long grain rice all the way from America, red peppers, green peppers, juicy green beans, carrots and peas and a hint of seasoning . . . Bachelor's Savoury Rice!' 'Cats make haste for the Brekkies taste, the Brekkies taste, makes cats make haste.' 'Nuts! Whole hazelnuts! Ooomph! Cadbury's take them and they cover them in chocolate!' 'But ask about the bran flakes, what about the bran flakes, they'll all reply: They're tasty, tasty, very very tasty, they're very tasty.' I like to watch the adverts on the telly. They're better than the programmes in between. 'Will it be roast or jacket spuds, will it be carrots, will it be peas . . .'

OK, I'll stop now. Sorry. Sorry. Sorry. I should have been a concert pianist, you know. I can play Mozart and Henry Mancini. Mozart was born in Salzburg. That's in Austria. I read about Austria in the *National Geographic* magazine. It's my favourite. Austria is a central European republic bordered by Czechoslovakia and West Germany to the north, Switzerland to the west, Italy and Yugoslavia to the south and Hungary to the east. The capital of Austria is Vienna. The unit of currency is the Austrian schilling. The major industries are agriculture and tourism. My shaver was made in Austria. I got it from Boots the Chemist of Nottingham. But it was made in Austria.

When she is cross with me, Mummy-dearest says, 'Robin, you are getting fat, you ought to take some exercise. You will die of a heart attack.' Whenever we went out for a walk, she would buy me chocolate.

'Toblerone, out on its own, Triangular chocolate, that's Toblerone. Made with triangular honey from triangular bees and triangular almonds from triangular trees, and Oh, Mr Confectioner please, Give me Toblerone.' It's made from triangular honey from triangular bees, and triangular almonds from triangular trees, did you know that?

Liberace died of AIDS, did you know that? Always wash your hands after using the toilet and before eating. Mummy-dearest used to cut up my meat and potatoes and pour my milk. 'Robin,' she said. 'Why can't you learn to do things for yourself?'

I should have been a concert pianist, you know. I like the theme from *Chariots of Fire*. I like reading. My favourite is the *National Geographic* magazine. The population of Bhutan is approximately 1.3 million. The best camera is a Hasselblad, but there are more advertisements for Olympus and Canon. You find a lot of *National Geographic* magazines in dentists' waiting rooms. They are a good place to go for *National Geographic* magazines. Doctors' are good too, but not so good. The sky is very blue in Bhutan. Russ Conway used to smile at me. I used to hide from him behind the settee. 'Come out, Robin,' Mummy-dearest said. 'You'll miss your favourite bit.' 'Robin, you are getting fat, you ought to take some exercise. You will die of a heart attack.'

Liberace died of AIDS, did you know that? My knife and fork have red handles. Dolly's ... Dolly's ... Dolly's have ... green handles. I can sing all the songs from the advertisements. They're better than the programmes in between. Austria is a central European republic bordered by Czechoslovakia and West Germany to the north, Switzerland to the west, Italy and Yugoslavia to the south, and Hungary to the east. I can eat my own dinner now. I can eat my own dinner now. I can eat my own dinner now ...

The blue ... the sky ... the clear ... Saturday. Half past eight. We present: Russ Conway at the piano! Hasselblad. The best camera. I would choose a Hasselblad every time. 'Why can't you learn to do things for yourself? Why can't you learn to do things for yourself?' Always wash your hands. Hasselblad. Every time. Two thirty to three thirty is practice time. I must practise. Practice makes perfect. I like the theme from *Chariots of Fire*. The air is very clear ... the sky is very blue ... the blue ... clear ... the sky ...

My knife and fork have red handles. Red.

I should have been a concert pianist, you know. I just need to hear a thing; once.

Fragments of an Analysis of a Case of Hysteria

The Night Sleeper

Hurrying, hurrying, faster, faster; hurrying, hurrying, faster, faster, through the forests of the night; the night train, cleaving through the forest of the night, through the trees, the endless trees, cleaving them with the beam of its headlight that casts its white pool upon the endlessly unreeling iron line, cleaving the forest with the tireless stroke of its pistons, cleaving the night with its plume of spark-laden smoke streamed back across the great sleek length of the engine and the shout of its hundred wheels, cleaving through the night that lies across the heart of the continent; the night train, hurrying, hurrying, faster, faster.

Though it must be hours since your father bid you goodnight from the upper berth, hours more since the sleeping car attendant did that clever folding trick with the seat and unrolled the bundles of fresh laundered bedding, you are not asleep. You cannot sleep. Out there, beyond the window, are the trees of the night forest. You cannot see them, but you know they are there, shouldered close together, shouldered close to the track, branches curving down to brush the sides of the sleeping car, like the long arms of old, stoop-shouldered men.

And though you cannot see them either, you are also aware of the hundreds of other lives lying still in their berths in the ochre glow of their railway company nightlights, rocked and rolled to sleep by the rolling gait of the night sleeper across the border; hundreds of other lives lying still, one above the other in their tiny, ochre-lit compartments, carried onward through the forest of the night to their final destinations. From the adjacent compartment come the sounds again; the small sounds, the intimate sounds, a woman's whisper, a man speaking softly, the creak of leather upholstery, stifled laughter, the repeated knock knock knock knock knock of something hard against the wooden partition. As you lie in your bottom berth, your head next to the knock knock knock knock knock from the next compartment, it is as if you are suddenly aware of everything all at once, the lovers across the partition, the sleeping passengers in their berths, the blast of sound and steam and speed of the night train's momentary passage, cleaving through the forest of the night, cleaving through the endless, stoop-shouldered trees.

You must have slept. You had thought that sleep would elude you, but the rhythm of the wheels must have lulled you to sleep, for it is the change of that tireless rhythm that has woken you. The train is slowing. You turn in your berth to look out of the window but all there is to be seen is your reflection looking back at you. The train has slowed to crawl, grinding along the track with a slowness that is dreadful to you because you fear that should the train stop it will never, never start again.

Up the line, far away, a bell clangs. Barely audible over the grind of the wheels are voices, voices outside the window, shouting in a language you do not understand.

Your father is awake now. He descends the wooden ladder, switches on the lights and sits across the table from you, peering out of the window to see why the train is stopping. By the light from the window you see the faces. There are men standing by the side of the track, men with stupid, slow, brutal faces. As you grind past them, they pause in their labour to stare up into your faces with slow, brutal incomprehension. The stupid brutality of their faces blinds you to what it is they are doing. They are carrying bodies, slung between them by the hands and the feet, and laying them out by the side of the track. The naked bodies of men and women and children, carried and laid out side by side on the gravel between the track and the edge of the trees. And now you see, far away up the line, a red glow, as if from a great conflagration; something burning fiercely, endlessly, out there in the forest of the night. You ask your father what it all means.

'Some terrible calamity,' he says, as if in a dream. 'An accident, up the line, a train has crashed and set the forest burning.'

The night train grinds on, past the bodies of the men and the women and the children, laid side by side while the men carry and set, carry and set, muttering in their dull, brutal language, and the iron bell clangs.

You know that you have not slept, though it is as if you have and woken up at a different place, a different time. Now the train is entering a rural railway station. A bumptious station master with a black moustache and an excess of gold braid is waving the night train into a stand by the platform. The picket fence is decked with bunting and the little wooden station house is gaily hung with Japanese paper lanterns that swing and rattle in the wind from the night forest. The train creaks to a halt and you hear the music. Outside the waiting room a string quartet is playing the last movement from *Eine Kleine Nachtmusik*, rather poorly, you think. The station master comes striding along the platform in his black kneeboots blowing his whistle and shouting, 'All change, all change.'

'Come, Anna,' your father says, grabbing his violin case from the rack, and before you have time to think you are out on the platform, you and your father and the hundreds and hundreds of others aboard the night train, standing there in your nightdresses and pyjamas and dressing-gowns in the cold night air.

Up the line, the locomotive hisses steam. The carriages creak and shift.

'Teas, coffees and hot savouries in the waiting room,' announces the beaming station master. 'In the waiting room, if you please, sirs and madams.'

Murmuring gladly to each other, the passengers file into the waiting room but with every step you take towards those open wooden doors you feel a dreadful reluctance grow and grow until you know that you must not cannot will not go in.

'No, Father, do not make me!' you cry but your father says, 'Anna, Anna, please, it is only for a little while, until the next train comes,' but you will not cannot must not go in, for you have seen, through the latticed windows of the rural railway station, what is waiting in the waiting room. In the waiting room is a baker in a white apron standing before the open door of an oven. He sees you watching him through the window, and smiles at you, and draws his paddle out of the oven to show you what he has been baking there.

It is a loaf of fresh golden bread in the shape of a baby.

THE DOOR AND THE WINDOW

The case of Fräulein Anna B. first came to my attention in the late winter of 1912 at a Wednesday meeting of my International Psycho-Analytical Association through Dr Geistler, one of the newer members of the Wednesday Circle, who mentioned casually over coffee and cigars a patient he was treating for asthmatic attacks that had failed to yield to conventional medical treatment. These attacks seemed related to the young woman's dread of enclosed spaces, and after the meeting he asked if I might attempt an analysis of the psychoneurosis, an undertaking to which I agreed, arranging the first treatment for the following Tuesday morning, at ten a.m.

I have learned from experience that psychoneuroses often bely themselves by too great an absence from the facial features of the patient: Fräulein Anna B. was one such, to the perceptions a pretty, charming, self-confident young lady of seventeen years, the daughter of a concert violinist with the Imperial Opera who, I learned to my surprise, was acquainted with me through the B'Nai B'rith, the Vienna Jewish Club. She was an only child, her mother had died in

Anna's infancy in an influenza epidemic and Anna had been brought up solely by the father. I gained the distinct impression that her vivacity, her energy, were more than could be accounted for purely by youthful exuberance.

She commented on the stuffiness and gloominess of my consulting room and, despite the winter chill, refused to settle until both door and window were opened to the elements. I had taken but a few puffs of a cigar when she became most agitated, claiming that she could not breathe, the smoke was suffocating her. Even though most of the smoke from my cigar went straight out of the open window into Berggasse, I nevertheless acceded to her request that I refrain from smoking in her presence. Such was her hysterical sensitivity that, on subsequent interviews, the slightest lingering trace of cigar smoke from a previous session was enough to induce an asthmatic attack.

In interview she was exceedingly talkative and greatly given to the encyclopedic elaboration of even the most trivial anecdote. She could not recall a specific moment when she became aware that she dreaded enclosed spaces, but had, to a certain degree, felt uncomfortable in small rooms with closed doors and heavy furnishings for as long as she could remember. She had not been consciously aware of a deterioration in her condition until the event that had precipitated first her referral to Dr Geistler and, ultimately, to me.

In the early autumn her father's orchestra had taken a performance of *The Magic Flute* on tour through Salzburg to Munich, Zürich, Milan and Venice. Seeing an opportunity to expand his daughter's education through travel, her father had arranged for her to accompany him. Fräulein Anna B. admitted to feelings of foreboding all the day of the departure which, as the orchestra assembled at the West Bahnhof, became an anxiety and, with the party boarding the train, an hysterical attack. The hour had been late, the station dark and filled with the steam and smoke of the engines. The rest of the musicians were already installed in their sleeping compartments, from the door her father was calling her to board, the train was about to leave. These details she knew only from having been told after the event; her attention was transfixed by the brass table-lamp in the window of the sleeping compartment she and her father were to share. Seeing that lamp, she had felt such fear and dread as she had never known before, she could not enter that compartment, she could not board that train. The noise and the bustle of the station overwhelmed her, the smoke and fumes of the engine suffocated her; overcome, she fought for breath but her lungs were paralysed.

Choking, half conscious, half delirious, she was carried by a porter and her father to the station-master's office, whence Dr Geistler was summoned by telephone.

The image of the table-lamp seemed of significance so I suggested that we explore possible relevancies it might hold to childhood events, the wellspring of all our adult neuroses. She related an incident from her earliest years when she first slept in a room of her own. Her father had bought her a bedside lamp with a shade decorated with the simple fairytale designs that appeal to children. She could not recall having fallen asleep, but she did recall waking to find the room filled with smoke. She had neglected to extinguish the lamp and the decorated shade, made from a cheap and shoddy fabric, had caught fire. Her screams raised her father, in the adjacent bedroom, who had doused the fire. For several months after, he had insisted she sleep under his care in his bedroom, indeed, that they share the same bed.

After narrating the incident with the lamp, Fräulein Anna B. declared that she felt very much better and, as our time was drawing to a close, thanked me for my help and asked if payment was required now, or was a bill to be forwarded. I replied, with some amusement, that the treatment was by no means concluded, indeed, it had hardly begun; it would require many sessions, over a period of many weeks, even months, before we could say that we had dealt conclusively with her neuroses.

At our next meeting, Fräulein Anna B.'s demeanour was considerably subdued. As we sat with the wind from the steppes whistling through the open window she related a recurrent dream that particularly disturbed her. This dream, which I shall refer to as the 'Night Sleeper Dream', was to continue to manifest itself in various guises throughout the course of treatment with greater or lesser regularity, depending on the progress we were making in the interviews. Mutability is one of the characteristics of neuroses; that when responding to treatment in one sphere, they incarnate themselves in another.

Rather than attempt to analyse the entire content of the dream, which, in the light of the previous session, seemed a little too pat, I chose to concentrate on some of the elements that might repay deeper analysis: the threatening forest, the long row of naked bodies, the baker and his macabre loaf.

Through association and regression we explored the significance of an early childhood picnic in the Wienerwald when she first became aware of her sexual incompleteness as a woman. The trip had been made in the company of an 'aunt' (so-called, but who could have been a close family friend) and cousin, a boy a year older than Fräulein Anna B., who at the time could not have been more than five or six. The children had been sent off to play in the woods while the parents conversed, as parents will, upon topics of no interest whatsoever to children and, as children will, the young Fräulein Anna B. and her cousin had been caught short by nature. Fräulein Anna B. recalled her surprise at the sight of her cousin's penis and remembers wanting to play with it, not, she claimed, out of any sexual interest, purely from curiosity. Contrasting the ease with which her cousin had relieved himself with her own cumbersome efforts, she had told him, 'That's a handy gadget to bring on a picnic.'

As she was preparing to leave, she made this comment to me: 'Dr Freud, I have just remembered, I do not know how important it is, but that table-lamp, the one in the sleeping compartment on the train to Salzburg, it did not have a lamp-shade. The bulb was bare, naked.'

In the subsequent months as winter gave way to a sullen Viennese spring, we mapped the psychoneurotic geography of the elements of the Night Sleeper Dream. As childhood fears and repressions were brought to light and acknowledged, so Fräulein Anna B. found her dread of enclosed spaces diminishing: first the window, then the door were acceptable when closed; finally, in the late March of 1913, with not inconsiderable relief, I was permitted my cigars.

The symbolic element of the naked bodies laid by the side of the track proved to contain within it perhaps the most significant of Fräulein Anna B.'s childhood traumas.

Anna's father had established the habit of taking an annual holiday to the spa at Baden during the opera closed season. Against customary practice, Anna accompanied him on these short trips with the result that, in the absence of any other children her own age at the resort, she was forced to seek out the company of adults, especially the elderly who abound at such spas and who can be relied upon to take a grandparently interest in a solitary young girl. She had been left to her own devices by her father while he went on a walk in the woods with a lady of his acquaintance, who came to take the waters every year at the same time as he did. In the pump-room the young Anna had been alarmed by a conversation with a clearly demented elderly gentleman who had threatened her with eternal damnation if she did not go down on her knees there and then and seek the saving grace of Christ. When the elderly gentleman had attempted physically to accost her, she had fled the pump-room and attendant gardens into the surrounding woodlands to seek her father.

She remembered running along seemingly endless kilometres of gravelled footpaths until she was stopped in her headlong flight by the sound of voices: her father's, and that of a woman. The voices issued from the concealment of a swathe of rhododendrons. Without thought, she pushed through the screening shrubs and was met by the sight of her father repeatedly penetrating a red-haired woman bent double over the railing of a small, discreet pergola. She related that the woman had looked up, smiled, and said, 'Hello, Anna-Katzchen,' a private name only used by her father. It was then that she recognised the woman as the lady-friend who came every year to the resort. What she remembered most vividly from the experience was the peculiar conical shape of the woman's drooping breasts, the way her red hair had fallen around her face, and her father's thrusting, thrusting, thrusting into the bent-over woman, quite oblivious that he was being watched by his daughter. As she spoke these three words in my study, 'thrusting, thrusting, thrusting', she spat them out like poison on her tongue.

Her father never learned that he had been observed that day in the pergola. The woman had treated Anna's witnessing as an unspoken compact between them; at dinner in the *Gasthaus* that night Anna had liberally salted the woman's dinner with bleaching powder, stolen from the scullery-maid's storeroom.

It was the work of what remained of the spring to bring Fräulein Anna B. to the point of acceptance of the emotional insight that her attempted poisoning of the red-haired woman and, ultimately, her psychoneurotic fear of enclosed, vaporous spaces stemmed from her jealousy of her father. For many weeks she was resistant to the notion of her father as a sexual figure to whom she had been, and still was, attracted, this attraction having been reinforced, albeit unwittingly, by her father taking the infant Anna into his bed after the incident with the bedside lamp. Gradually she reached an intellectual insight into her substitution of a male into the mother role, and the confusion of her own Oedipal feelings. Her own awakening sexuality had resulted in the transferral onto her father of her sublimated guilt at her abandoning her first, and greatest, love for the love of others. Triggered by the intimacy of the sleeping compartment, her memories of childhood intimacies and what she saw as childhood betrayals of her love, had peaked into hysteria. As the intellectual insight developed into acceptance and full emotional insight, so the night sleeper dream recurred with lessening frequency and, in the early summer, Fräulein Anna B. reported to me that she had that weekend been capable of taking the train journey to the monastery at Melk without any ill effects. After the completion of the treatment, Fräulein Anna B. kept in correspondence with me and confessed, to my great satisfaction, that she had formed an attachment with a young man, the son of a prominent Vienna lawyer, without any feelings of guilt or the return of neurosis, and that engagement, and subsequent marriage, could be pleasurably contemplated.

THE JUDENGASSE CELLAR

When the proprietors of the Heurigen take down the dry and dusty pine branches from the fronts of their shops, the last of the summer's wine is drunk. Time, ladies and gentlemen, they call, the bottle is empty, the glass is dry, time for the benches to be scrubbed and the long pine tables taken in, time for the Schrammel-musicians to pack away their violins and guitars and accordions, time to quit the leaf-shaded courtyards of Grinzing and Cobenzl and Nussdorf by your trams and *fiacres* and charabancs and go down again to your city, time to seek what pleasures it has to offer among its *Kaffeehause*s and *Konditorei*, its cabarets and clubs, beneath the jewelled chandeliers of the opera and in the smoky cellars off Kartnergasse that smell of stale beer and urine.

They had hoped to outstay the others, outstay even the end of the season, as if their staying could somehow condense it and extend it beyond its natural lifetime up there on the slopes of the Wienerwald. But the last glass of the last bottle of the last cask was drunk dry and, as if emerging from a summer night's dream with a start and a shudder, they had found their revels ended and themselves observing the hot and gritty streets of the city from a table outside the Konditorei Demel.

They were four, two young men, two young women, of that class of Viennese society that, as if sensing on a wind from the east the ashes of empire, was slowly drawing the orbit of its great waltz ever closer to the flames. They had long ago explored every possible nuance and permutation between them that the fading of the Imperial Purple condones and, having worn out each other's lives like old clothes, turned to the whirl of *Kaffee Kultur* and opera-box scandal only to find its perfume of *Bierhall* revolution, bad art and warmed-over next-day gossip a macrocosm of the *ennui* of their own claustrophobic relationship; a boredom not merely confined to persons or places or classes, but a boredom that seemed to have infected an entire continent, a boredom to which even war seemed preferable.

Perhaps it was the foreshadowing of absolute war over their dying empire, perhaps only an inevitable twist in the downward helix of their jaded appetites that took them to the cellar down in the old Jewish quarter.

It bore no name, no number; the only sign of its existence was the unpainted wooden shingle above the unlit flight of steps down under Judengasse; the wooden shingle in the shape of a rat. It did not advertise in the *City Directory*, nor on the municipal pillars alongside the more flagrant establishments on Kartnergasse. It needed no more advertisement than its reputation and the word of mouth of its patrons. Among the *petite bourgeoisie* its name was mythical.

When the lawyer's son had first mentioned its name as they sat bored at their table outside the *Konditorei*, they'd hidden it away and gone in search of other stimulation, knowing, even then, that those stimulations would fail and fade like fairground lights in the noon-time sun and that they would, must, eventually descend that flight of steep steps beneath the wooden sign of the rat. The first light snow of the autumn was powdering the cobbles as they drove in the merchant banker's son's car through the streets of the Alte Stadt. Of the four, it was the youngest, the concert violinist's daughter, who was the least at ease as the door opened to their knock and the *maître d'* bowed them in; old scars she had thought long healed tugged a little, tore a little, bled a little.

Cellar clubs are a universal condition: the floor packed with tables so that not one centimetre of gritty concrete or cracked tile can be seen; the dusty boards of the stage beneath a constellation of tinsel stars, the popping yellow footlights, the musical quartet of hard-faced women in basques, stockings and opera gloves smoking Turkish cigarettes between numbers, the dull red glow of the table-lamps that conceals the identities of the patrons at their tables by changing them into caricatures of themselves.

At the foot of the steps she felt the tightness in her chest and begged with the man who had brought her not to make her go in, but the other two of their quartet were already being seated at their table and he pulled on her hand, come on, there is nothing to be afraid of, it will be fun. As the waiter in the white apron served wine and the cabaret quartet scraped their way through a medley of popular numbers, the sole focus of her concentration was her measured breathing in, breathing out, breathing in, breathing out. That, when next you exhale, you will not be able to inhale, that is the most terrible fear of the asthmatic.

'Excuse me?'

The young man begged her pardon, repeated his request if he might share their table. He took a chair beside Fräulein Anna, a square-faced young man with a small, square moustache. The band played on. The cellar, already full, filled to bursting point. The night wore down. The young man tried to engage Fräulein Anna in small talk. She worried that he might think the brevity of her replies coyness, when it was merely shortness of breath. Was this her first time here? A nod. He came regularly. He was an artist. Rather, he aspired to being an artist. He had twice failed to secure entry to the Vienna Academy of Fine Art. But he would, in time. He was a painter of postcards and advertisements; a precarious existence, he admitted, but time would bring all his ambitions to fruition, the world would see. After deductions for lodgings, food (too little of that, thought Fräulein Anna) and art materials, he was left with just enough to visit the Judengasse cellar. Here, both high and low mingled, bankers and businessmen and lawyers and priests and prostitutes, civil servants and starving artists, all rendered anonymous in the fellowship of the darkness. It was rumoured that an imperial prince had been seen to frequent the Sign of the Rat.

'Fear,' he said, the word sitting strangely with his country accent of northern Austria. 'That is why they come. That is why I come. To learn the power and mastery of fear, to learn that through the knowledge and control of fear, the right use of fear, one learns mastery over others. That is why I come, to refine and hone my power over fear, *gnädige Fräulein*, so that one day, I shall be feared. I know I shall, I know it. Feared, and so respected.'

Fear? she was about to whisper, but a hush had fallen across the tables. An old man with an accordion was standing in the footlights on the tiny bare stage. The old man squeezed a melancholy minor drone from his instrument. 'Ladies, gentlemen, I tell you a tale, a tale of an old man, a man older than he seems, far older, older than any of you can imagine, older than any living man. A man cursed by God never to die, ladies, gentlemen.'

An iron grip seized Fräulein Anna's chest.

'Cursed by God, ladies, gentlemen. Cursed to wander the world, never knowing rest.' His long, bony fingers moved like small antedeluvian creatures over the keys. 'A man who had never been other than faithful to his master, his Lord, a man whom that same Lord called "the disciple he loved". And how was that love rewarded? With these words, how can I ever forget them, "If it is my will that this man remains alive until I come again, what is that to you?" Oh, Master, Master, why did you speak those words? Why did you burden your disciple with undesired immortality, so that even as the last apostle went to his grave, this one of the twelve was condemned to continue wandering the world, a Fifth Gospel, a living, walking gospel; that those who saw him and heard this gospel,' (the accordion moaned its accompaniment, seducing, mesmerising; with a start, Fräulein Anna noticed that the waiters, that race of troglodytic creatures in braided monkey jackets, were closing the shutters, barring the doors) 'might come to penitence, and true faith.

'Penitence! And true faith!'

The under-song of the accordion rose to a dominant major key, swelled to take the crowded tables by surprise.

'But as I wandered across this continent, across all continents, I learned the name and nature of this gospel I was to bring so that man might come to repentance and faith in God.

'Fear!'

Now the gnome-like servants were going from table to table, quietly extinguishing the red table-lamps.

'The grinding, driving, shattering fear of God: fear of He who can destroy both body and spirit and cast them into the endless terror and horror of hell. Fear! Nothing else will bring the human spirit to its knees before its master; to know, and be confronted by, fear. This was the lesson I learned in the rotting cities of this rotting continent long centuries ago; that I had been set apart by God to be His special Apostle, the Apostle of Fear, the one sent by God to bring the good and righteous fear of Him to mighty and mean, lofty and low, prince and pauper, priest and prostitute. Fear . . .'

The accordion sent out its tendrils across the packed floor, drawing the patrons into its knot of intimacy and credulity. The cellar lay in darkness, save for a single spotlight falling upon the face and hands of the eternal Jew.

'Fear,' he whispered, the word like a kiss on his lips; and the single spotlight was extinguished. In the darkness, his voice spoke once again: 'Now is the time to face your fear, alone, in the deepest darkness of body, soul and spirit.'

And from their tunnels and runways and warrens and sewers, from the vast underground city they had excavated by tooth and claw from the underpinnings of Vienna, they came; pouring out from a score, a hundred, a thousand hatchways and gnawholes and gratings and spouts; a wave, a sea, an ocean of them, swamping the floor of the club with their close-pressed, squirming, surging bodies, spilling over the feet of the patrons, dropping from the cracks and crevices in the ceilings onto table-tops, into laps, onto the heads and hands and shoulders of the patrons who were on their feet screaming, beating, flailing, slapping at the torrent, the cascade, the endless waterfall of rats; claws and naked tails and beady eyes, questing noses, sewer-slick fur, pressing, writhing, scuttling; the cellar rang to a million chittering voices that drowned out the cries of the patrons, locked in utter darkness with the rats. Some would flee, some stampeded where they imagined doors to be but, in the utter darkness, they fell and were smothered under the carpet of hurrying rats; some sought refuge on table-tops, on chairs; some, perhaps, wiser, perhaps paralysed by dread, stayed where they were and let the drown-wave break about them, over them. And, in time, the torrent of rats subsided, and faltered, and ebbed, and the last tail vanished down the last bolthole into the storm sewers of the old Jewish quarter. And the lights came on. Not the dim red table-lamps, but bright, hard, white bulbs, in wire cages, and by that raw white light the people saw each other in the utter nakedness of their fear, saw the graceful social masks stripped away, and as they saw, they were themselves seen, and it was as if they all, mighty and mean, prince and pauper, priest and prostitute, were joined in a fellowship of fear. There were tears, there was laughter – sudden, savage laughter – there were whispered confessions and intimate absolutions, there was anger, and grief, and ecstatic exultation; the casks of emotion were broached, the conventions toppled and smashed; true selves, true colours, long constrained, released and unfurled.

In the great catharsis, none thought to look for the master of ceremonies, the aged aged Jew who had made such outrageous, blasphemous claims for himself. Caught up in the maelstrom of emotions, none saw the two young men from the table nearest the stage, and a third young man with them, with a square face and a little square moustache, none saw them carry a young woman fighting and heaving and clawing for breath up the cellar steps and out of the door into the cold and sleet of Judengasse. None saw the fear in her eyes, wide, terrified, as if struck down by the wrath of God Himself.

THE BELLS OF BERLIN

8 June 1934

After fourteen years of marriage, Werner still knows to surprise me with little presents, still takes an adolescent delight in coming through the front door announcing that he has a surprise for his Anna and hiding the little gift-wrapped something behind his back out of my reach, or inviting me to guess what it is, which hand it is in. I play along with his little games of concealment and surprise because I, after fourteen years, still delight in the pleasure on his face as he watches me tear off the wrapping and ribbon to reveal his little love-token beneath. Goodness only knows where he managed to find such a book as this one; afternoons much better spent preparing briefs than rooting around in the antiquarian bookshops along Birkenstrasse, but bless him anyway, it is quite exquisite, tall and thin, in the English art-nouveau style, the cover decorated with poppies and cornsheaves, the blank pages heavy, creamy, smooth as skin.

Every woman should have a diary, he says. The true history of the world is written in women's diaries, especially in days such as these when history is unfolding and ripening around our ears like a field of wheat. Anyway, he says he fears that, what with Isaac now attending school six mornings a week, I will descend into a state of mental vegetation, the only escape from which will be to have an affair so, for the sake of our marriage, I had better keep this journal.

Yes, all very well, Werner, and, yes, affairs notwithstanding, the discipline of diary-keeping is good for me, but what to write in it? A simple family chronicle: Isaac still having trouble with his arithmetic;

Anneliese, despite the trauma of her first period, chosen to sing in the school choir for Hermann Goering's pleasure? Ponderous Bach violin sonatas from the apartment at the back of the house, evidence of Papa's continued anger at the purging of his beloved Mahler from the Berlin Philharmonic's repertoire? Is this what Werner means by the *true history of the world*? Or does he mean that I should set down the events happening at once so close at hand (today on my way to the shops I passed the burnt-out shell of the Reichstag) and yet seemingly so remote, distant, bellowing voices on the wireless, and try to record my reaction to them and the reactions of those around me? Is it history when Mrs Erdmann comes to me in a terrible pother because her name has appeared on a blacklist of women still buying from Jewish shops? It is with a certain trepidation that I set these and any future words of mine down on paper; these days generate so many historians, what can a suburban Berlin *Hausfrau* hope to add to the analysis of these times in which we find ourselves? Yet I feel that Mrs Erdmann's consternation, my father's dismay at being forced to play racially pure music, Anneliese singing for Hermann Goering, these must be recorded, because it is in the trivia and minutiae of our lives that the history made elsewhere must be lived out.

14 June 1934

Dear dear. Slipping. Had promised myself I would write in diary every day. Had also promised myself I would avoid slipping into telegraphese, and write proper, complete, not pay-by-the-word sentences. The spirit is willing, and these past weeks, there has been no dearth of subject matter, but the demands of *Kinder, Kirche, Kuche* (or, in my case, *Kinder*, Synagogue, *Kuche*) are all too demanding.

Mrs Shummel from the Jewish Ladies Society arrived on my doorstep this morning in a state of distraction: in the middle of the night a gang of sa bullyboys had surrounded her house, smashed in all her ground-floor windows and daubed a yellow Star of David on her door. She had hidden, shaking with fear, in the cupboard under the stairs while the young thugs shouted abuse for over an hour. They must have little enough to do to smash in an old woman's windows and think of enough names to call her for over an hour.

Papa is worried too. Unlike me, he has no Gentile spouse to hide behind. Though his colleagues in the orchestra support him in the solidarity of musicians, all it takes is one suspicious soul to denounce him to the Party and his career as a musician is finished. And that would be the finish of him: poor Papa, without his music he would wither and die. Losing Mahler was enough of a blow to him; the possibility that he might never again hear the final movement of the Resurrection Symphony has put twenty years on him in one stroke.

Symptoms. Disease. Dis-ease. Society is sick. Germany is sick, and does not know it. Werner likes to lock up his work in his office at six o'clock, but I can tell he is concerned. The legal loopholes by which he manoeuvres Jewish assets out of the country are being tightened every day, and he has heard of new legislation afoot that will make it a crime for Jew and Gentile to marry, even to love one another. What kind of a country is it, dear God, where love is a crime?

20 June 1934

I saw them destroy an art gallery this morning. I had not intended to be about anywhere near Blücherstrasse, I would not have passed that way at all but for a consuming fancy for cakes from a particularly excellent *Konditorei* in that neighbourhood. When I saw the crowd, heard the clamour, I should have walked away, but there is a dreadful fascination in other people's madness. Perhaps it is only by the madness of others that we measure our own sanity. Or lack of it.

A good fifty to sixty people had gathered around the front of the Gallery Seidl. It is not a gallery I much frequent; I cannot make head nor tail out of these modern painters, Expressionists, I believe they call themselves. The Brownshirts had already smashed the window and kicked in the door; now inside the shop, they were breaking picture frames over their knees and kicking, slashing, tearing canvases with a grim dutifulness that seemed all the more threatening because of its utter dispassion. The mutilated paintings were passed out into the street by human chain and piled to await the petrol can, the match, the *feu de joie*, the roar of approval from the crowd. Herr Seidl stood by benumbed, utterly helpless, as punishment was meted out for admiring abstract, corrupt, decadent art.

I think that was what disturbed me the most: not the grim-faced determination of the Nazi bullyboys, nor the mob acquiescence of the bystanders, but that art, beauty (despite my inability to comprehend it) should be subject to the approval and control of the Party. It was then as if the whole weight of the Party machine, like some huge, heaving juggernaut, fell upon me as never before; I felt a desperation, a panic, almost as one does when, at dead of night, one contemplates one's own mortality, a knowledge of the inevitable darkness that must fall. I had to escape. I had to flee from the mob, from the smoke and flame of burning paintings that seemed like the soul of an entire nation offered up as holocaust. I ran then, without thought or heed of anything but to escape. I did not know where I ran: through streets broad and narrow, through bustling thoroughfares and dark alleys. Did the people I rushed past stare at me, call out, ask if anything was the matter? I do not know, I do not remember there even having been people; all I remember is that I had to run, and run I did, until I came to my senses in a cobbled laneway, overhung by stooping houses and bandoliers of grubby carpets and limp laundry. Lost, in a city that for fifteen years I had called home and which now revealed itself as foreign, alien, and hostile, with nothing familiar or friendly. Save one thing. Perhaps the one thing that had stopped me where I did, one thing and one thing only that had any connection with my past. A swinging wooden shingle, unpainted, hanging above a set of steep steps leading down to a basement; a wooden sign cut in the shape of a rat.

25 June 1934
I had to go. I had to return. When I saw that sign, that crude wooden rat, it was as if a spirit that had never truly been exorcised and had lain dormant for these years had risen up to stake its claim to me. I knew that I would never be free from it until I faced again what I

had first faced, and failed before, in that cellar in the old Jewish quarter.

Do not ask me how I know, but I know without the slightest doubt that it is the same cellar, the same troglodytic staff, the same ancient Jew with his accordion, and what the accordion summoned . . .

If it is a spirit that oppresses me, it is a spirit of remembrance. Things I had thought lost in the darkness are emerging after long exile, changed in subtle and disturbing ways by their time in the dark. That same night as I fled from the burning of the gallery, I was woken by a tightness in my chest, a constriction in my breathing; prescience – or is it a remembrance? – of an asthma attack.

It took many days for me to summon the courage to visit that cellar club. Pressure of work keeps Werner long hours at the office; I went twice to the very door and turned back, afraid, without him ever knowing I had been out of the house at night. The ease with which I deceived him in that matter makes me wonder: if I did not love him so deeply, how easy it would be to cheat on him. The third night I would have turned away but for a sudden rushing sensation of wild abandon that swept over me like a pair of dark, enfolding wings, there, on the bottom step, and made me push open the door.

All was as I had remembered it that night under Judengasse; the close-packed tables between the brick piers, the minuscule stage, the bored, slutty all-girl band, the infernal red light from the table-lamps. The wizened *maître d'*, who, if not the one who had greeted me that night so long ago, was cast in the same mould, showed me to a table in front of the stage. While wine was fetched, I studied the clientele. Bankers, captains of industry, lawyers, civil servants: these, certainly, as that time before, but unlike that other time, everywhere I looked, the grey and buff uniforms of the Party. Party uniforms, Party shirts, Party ties, Party armbands, Party badges, Party caps, Party whispers, Party salutes. The wine was fine and well bodied and brought the memories of that other time welling up in me, impelled by a pressure outside my will and control: we four friends, that quartet which would set the world ringing with the infamy of our pleasure-seeking. Whatever it was that the others found in the rat cellar, it cracked us apart like stale bread and sent us apart on our separate trajectories through history: Papa to his new position as principal violinist with the Berlin Philharmonic, and for me, marriage to the most eligible young lawyer in Berlin, and motherhood. I realised that I had not thought about that other young lawyer in twenty years, the one to whom I was almost engaged, until that night in the rat cellar.

As I sat sipping my wine another face formed out of the interplay of interior shadows: the aspiring artist who had shared our table. A face lost in darkness of twenty years, a face I now, with shocking suddenness, recognised in every Party poster, every newspaper, every cinema newsreel: the square, peasant face, the little, ludicrous affectation of a moustache, and the light in his eyes when he had whispered by candlelight the words: 'I shall be feared one day, I know it . . .'

'Fear,' a voice whispered, as if my own fears had spoken aloud, but the voice was that of the ancient master of ceremonies alone in his single spotlight with his accordion and his tale of a burdensome immortality and a gospel that seemed curiously appropriate to these times and places. As before, the accordion groaned out its accompaniment, as before the waiters went about barring the doors and shuttering the windows and extinguishing the lamps, until, finally, the spotlight winked out and in the darkness the old Jew whispered, 'Now is the time to face your fear, alone, in the deepest darkness of body, soul and spirit.'

And the rats came pouring from their runways and tunnels under Berlin, summoned by the old man's accordion, pouring into the cellar. I closed my eyes, fought down the horror of damp bodies brushing past my legs, of clicking, chitinous claws pricking at my feet. The people locked in darkness screamed and screamed and screamed and then one voice screamed louder than any other. 'Jews! Jews! Jews!' it screamed, and the scream went out across the heaving bodies and touched their fear and kindled it into hate. 'Jews! Jews! Jews!' The people took up the howl and took bottles, chairs, lamps in their hands, or bare hands alone, clenched into iron fists, and they beat and smashed at the rats, beat and beat and beat at their fear while the cellar rang and rang and rang with their song of loathing. I tried to shut it out, close my ears, but the brick vaults beat like a Nazi drum, and when at last the lights came on I fled for the door and up and out into the clean and pure night air while below me the voices of the people joined in joyous laughter and someone began to sing the 'Horst Wessel', and other voices joined it, and the quartet picked up the key, and the whole rat cellar thundered with the joyous fellowship of hatred.

30 June 1934
It is one of Werner's little lovable inconsistencies that the man who is so competent, so incisive, so feared in the cut and thrust of the courtroom is nervous and hesitant when it comes to broaching delicate or serious matters in his own home. There he stood, leaning against the fireplace, hands thrust in hip pockets, shifting his weight from foot to foot, looking for a leading line. This time I was able to pre-empt him.

'You think that the time has come for us to sell up and move?'

I think I succeeded in surprising Werner; up until that moment he had not thought I had any conception of exactly how serious events had turned in Berlin. I think, after the rat cellar, I knew better than he. If not better, certainly more intimately. They do hate us. They want us dead. Every last one of us. He said that the few remaining legal loopholes were closing by the hour. He said new anti-Semitic laws were being drafted that would force the Jews, and Jews-by-marriage – a fouler crime by far – out of society altogether, and into labour camps. He said that the Party was on the verge of disintegration into factions; Röhm's SA were challenging Hitler's domination of the Party, and that when the long knives were drawn it was a certainty that the Jews would be blamed.

I asked where he had thought we might flee. Holland, he said, was a traditional haven of tolerance and stability. Amsterdam. He had taken the liberty of investigating investment opportunities in the diamond business, and the state of the property market. Had he started proceedings to liquidate our assets? I asked. He looked up at me, at once guilty and suspicious.

'Yes, my love. I have been moving small amounts through the Swiss banks for some months now.'

'That is good,' I said.

'I had thought you would be angry with me, I know how much you hate me keeping secrets from you.'

How could I be angry with him, when I held a secret from him I must take to my grave?

'I think we should move immediately.'

'You have thought about your father?'

'Without his music, he has nothing, and they have taken the music he loves away from him.' A memory: watching from my opera box the rapture with which he led the Philharmonic in the Adagietto from Mahler's Fifth. 'He would lose home, wealth, prestige, power, public acclaim, before he would lose his music.'

'And Isaac, Anneliese?'

I heard again the screaming in the rat cellar, the beating, beating, beating of chairs, bottles, naked fists on the squirming bodies of the Jews.

'Especially them.'

We lay together in bed, listening to the night-time news on the wireless. Reports were coming in of an attempted putsch by elements of the SA. Loyal SS troopers had quashed the coup, Generals Röhm, von Schleicher and Stressel had all been arrested and summarily liquidated.

I reached over to turn off the wireless.

'Tomorrow, Werner. You will do it tomorrow, won't you, my love?'

And as I spoke, the bells of Berlin rang out, a thousand bells from a thousand steeples, ringing all across the city, all across Germany, all across the world, ringing out a knell for the soul of a great nation.

THE JUDAS KISS

At two o'clock in the afternoon the small triangle of sunlight would fall onto the floor and move across the sofa and the two easy chairs and the dining table, the little paraffin camping stove, the mattresses and rolls of bedding, all the while dwindling, diminishing until at five o'clock it vanished to nothingness to the top left corner of the cellar, by the secret door. When the sameness of the faces, her husband, her father, her children, the van Hootens, old Comenius the clock-doctor, became appalling in their monotony, when the quiet slap of playing cards, the whisper of the word 'check', the murmured recounting of the dreams of the night before, when these became as terrible and ponderous as the tick of the executioner's clock, she would hunt the beam of dirty light to its source in a tiny broken corner of the wooden shuttering that boarded over the cellar windows. And there, blue beyond any possible imagining of blueness, was a tiny triangle of sky. She could lose herself for hours in the blueness, the apex of the triangle of sunlight between her eyes. It was her personal piece of sky; once when she saw a flight of Junkers bombers cross it on their way to the cities of England, the sight of their black crosses desecrating her piece of sky was enough to send her in tears to the furthest, darkest corner of the cellar.

He did not like to see her there, standing on an orange box, eyes screwed half shut in that triangle of light; he feared that someone might see those eyes, that triangle of face, and report it to the occupation forces. He no longer remonstrated with her, though. He knew that whenever he slipped out of the secret door up into the streets of Amsterdam, she would be at the shutter losing herself in those twenty centimetres of sky. He would not remonstrate with her because he felt guilt that many of his trips to the surface were for the same reason of escaping from the dreadful claustrophobic sameness of life in the cellar.

Once, on one of his trips out from the ruins of the house on Achtergracht – he had burned it himself to allay suspicions that Jews might be hiding there – he had seen occupation troops pulling a

Jewish family from their hiding place in a house on Herengracht. A mother, a father, a grandfather clutching an ornamental wooden clog, two little girls in print frocks. Their faces were pale and sickly from life hidden away from the sky. He saw the troopers pull out the householders, an elderly couple he vaguely knew from the Jewish Shelter Society, and push them into the back of a canvas-covered truck. As he went on his way, not too quickly not too slowly, he heard the officer announce through a loudspeaker that those who harboured Jews were no better than Jews themselves and would warrant the same treatment. Those who reported Jews to the occupation authorities would be rewarded for fulfilling their civic duty. Even those who were now harbouring Jews might escape punishment if they fulfilled their civic duty.

As he went among the safe shops buying meat and bread and candles and paraffin for the camping stove, the faces of the plump, homely Dutch couple as they were pushed into the back of the truck haunted him. In the small room behind van den Beek's dry-cleaning shop, the organiser of the Jewish Shelter Group said that he had been approached by a family whose safe house was threatened by house-to-house searches; would he be able to take them in the Achtergracht cellar? In his mind he saw the truck drive away under the trees that lined the canal, in his mind he heard the cries and moans penetrate the unnaturally quiet street, and he had said, *I do not know, I cannot say, give me a day or so to think about it.*

She envied him his trips above ground. She understood his reasoning; safer by far for just one to take the risk of being seen, but the taste of sky had made her hungry for more, to feel its vast blue vault above, around, enclosing her. In the night, when the others slept on their mattresses, he whispered to her about the new family who needed shelter. She would have loved them to come. New faces, new lives, new stories were almost as welcome as freedom in this place where the major entertainment was the narration to each other of the dreams of the previous night.

But the new family did not come and the days continued to be counted out by the passage of the triangle of light across the cellar floor and the endless, endless recounting of dreams that grew ever more colourless and impoverished. When, in the night she heard it, she was awake in the instant. The rest slept on, dreaming out their dreams, minting their cheap and tinny coinage, but to her it was as clear and piercing as an angel's clarion. The note of an accordion, far distant among the canals and high-gabled houses of Amsterdam, yet close, and sharp, and sweeter than wine. As if in a dream, perhaps in a dream, a dream that is more solid and tangible than what we call reality, she rose, went to the secret door and stole out through the warren of passageways and charred ruins up onto the street. She did not fear the curfew; with the same assurance that the music played only for her, she knew that she was invisible as a ghost, or a dream, to the occupation forces in their grey trucks.

She found the aged aged man, struck by a stray moonbeam in a street that opened onto a wide canal, bent over his instrument, intent upon his melancholy music. The cobblestones were invisible beneath a shifting, stirring, moon-silvered carpet of rats.

As she walked toward the aged aged man, the rats parted silently, liquidly before her. The wandering Jew looked up from his self-absorbed improvisation.

'*Gnädige Frau*, you should not have come. You are placing yourself in considerable peril.'

'I do not think so.'

He smiled: teeth long, yellow in the moonshine, like the ivory keys of his accordion. The liquid carpet of rats seethed.

'You are right, of course. Things are ordained by the will and grace of God. It was ordained by God that our destinies be tied together, that we be yoked together for a little while. When first we met, all those years ago at the spa at Baden, remember how afraid you were, how you ran? But we have been yoked together. We could not escape each other. He does that, God, yokes me for a little while to the lives of others. To save them. Or to damn them.'

'Would you damn me?'

'I already have, alas. Forgive me. It was not personal, Anna. My ludicrous vaudeville act, my burlesque gospel, my cellars in cities across this continent, my rats, they have played their part in accomplishing the will of God. Apocalypse descends upon us, hastened by my actions, so the Master will return soon and free me from this weary undyingness.'

'You think you are responsible for . . . this?'

'I have served my part in God's will.'

'You are mad.'

'That is one interpretation. The only other is that I am exactly what and who I say I am.'

'An apostle of darkness?'

'An apostle of a wrathful God. The Jews have their just punishment now, the Christ-killers. Do I hear the brass hoofs of the Four Horsemen on the cobbles? Come, Master, come . . .'

'Mad, and evil.'

'Or good beyond your conception of the word. I have damned, now I may save. Come with me. This place is finished, you are all finished. It does not take the gift of prophecy to tell that. Even the rats are abandoning the city, and I with them. Will you heed them, and come with me?'

The rats moved silently over the cobbles, little pink clawed feet hurrying, hurrying. Noses, whiskers, quested for the moon.

'I have a family, I have a husband, my father, my friends.'

'Unless a man hate his mother, and his father, and all his family, he can be no true disciple. So it is written.'

'I am not a disciple. I am a Jew.'

The aged aged man bowed deeply, took her hand in the moonlight, kissed it.

'*Küss die Hände, gnädige Frau*, as they once said in Old Vienna.' His fingers squeezed a quiet chord from the accordion. He turned away, walked away towards the canal. His music filled the street. The rats stirred and swirled and followed on.

He was awake when she returned. He whispered his fury through clenched teeth.

'You were out.'

'Yes.'

'Why? My God, why did you go out after curfew?'

She shrugged, any explanation would be impossible, but her shrug was invisible in the darkness of the cellar. For the first time she noticed that a little triangle of moonlight fell through the wooden shuttering to lie on the cellar floor.

The next day he went out to buy more paraffin for the stove, and some blankets, for the first autumn chill had found its way into the Achtergracht cellar. When he returned he kissed her full on the mouth and then went to sit, strangely quiet and withdrawn, in a chair apart from the others and stared at the steeple formed by his touching fingers as if he had never seen them before.

At five o'clock the patch of sunlight vanished and the soldiers came. They burst down the door with axes, the soldiers in their black boots and helmets. The old people screamed at the sight of their black machine guns. With the muzzles of their black machine guns they herded the people out through the secret door, out through the warren of collapsed cellarage and fire-blackened walls they had penetrated with such ease, as if they had been told where to go, out into the five o'clock sunlight, to the street, and the waiting truck.

'You forced me to do it,' he said to her as the soldiers with grim dutifulness began to push the van Hootens and old Comenius the clock-doctor into the back of the truck. Old Comenius was clutching an ormolu clock to his chest. 'You went out, you put us all in peril. You could have had us all punished if anyone had seen. So, I had to go to the local headquarters and inform. You think I wanted to do that? You think I wanted to sell the van Hootens and old Comenius? You forced me to make that bargain, to sell them, in return for our freedom. It was either them, or all of us. That was what the officer promised. If I did my civic duty, we would all go free. I had to sacrifice them to keep us safe, and together.'

Then a soldier with a black rifle stepped between the man and the woman and the woman and her children and her father, with his violin case in his hand, were pushed away, pushed towards the truck, pushed into the truck while the man struggled against the smiling soldiers who had taken grip of his arms. The man shouted, the man screamed, and the woman screamed back, and her father with his violin, and her son and daughter, but the soldiers pulled shut the canvas flap and tied it and in a moment the roar of the engine had drowned the voices, shouting screaming the betrayal of their betrayal. And the truck drove away down Achtergracht, and the officer stepped from his staff car and stood before the man and said, 'Jews. Are Jews.'

The String Quartet

Hurrying hurrying, faster faster; hurrying hurrying, faster faster, through the flat black darkness of the night forest, through the endless waiting trees, cleaving the darkness with the beam of its headlight and the shout of its hundred wheels, cleaving through the darkness that lies across the heart of the continent, the night train, hurrying hurrying, faster faster, towards its final destination.

Though it must be hours since your father said goodnight and blessed you into the care of God with a kiss on your forehead, as he used to kiss you those nights when you were afraid and came into his bed to sleep, you are not asleep. Your father has rolled his old bones into a corner of a cattle truck and has managed sleep of some kind; your children on either side of you are asleep also, leaning against your body; but you, alone of all the people crammed into the cattle truck, are not, it seems. You envy those crammed people their sleep. There is enough light in the boxcar for the dark-adapted eye to distinguish their shapes: old Comenius still clutching the clock to his chest, its heavy tick ticking away to the beat of his heart, the van Hootens curled around each other like kittens, reverting to the innocent intimacies of childhood; all the others, clinging to their precious possessions – an umbrella, a carved wooden lugger, a book, a prayer shawl. Mighty and mean, prince and pauper, priest and prostitute, all rendered anonymous, stationless, estateless, shapeless mounds of pain in the night-glow inside the boxcar.

You must have slept. The rhythm of the night train's hundred wheels must have lulled you to sleep, for it is the cessation of that beating, beating, beating rhythm that wakes you. A grey dawn light ekes through the gaps between the ill-fitting planks. The cold is intense, a cold breath from the heart of the continent. The hunger is devouring. How many days since you last ate? Beyond remembering, like an entire life sunk without trace, beyond all remembering.

The train is stationary. You press your face to the cold planks, screw up your eyes, squint to try and make out where it is you have arrived. A rural railway station, somewhere, deep in the night forest, surrounded, encircled, by the waiting, stooping trees, like aged aged men. Figures moving on the platform: soldiers? Voices, talking among themselves in a language you do not understand. Loud-speakers crackle, come alive. In the cattle car, in each of the twenty-five cars that make up the night train, people are starting to awaken. Your children stir, cold, hungry, uncomprehending, where are they, what is happening? You cannot help them, you do not know yourself. The voices draw near. With a crash and a blinding blare of dawn light, the boxcar doors are flung back. Soldiers. Slow, stupid, brutal faces. Slavic faces. They start to pull the people from the cars. Down, down, down. All change. All change. From each of the twenty-five cars the people are pulled down to stand shivering and blinking in the brilliant dawn cold on the platform. They hug themselves, their breath steams. The soldiers with the slow, stupid, brutal faces go among the people to take away their possessions. Prayer shawls, books, carved wooden luggers, umbrellas. Dr Comenius' clock is taken from his fingers. Your father clings to his violin in its case, cries out, no, no, do not take away the music, you cannot take away the music. He does not realise, you think, that they took away the music years before. The soldiers, with impassive determination, smash his fingers with rifle butts, smash the fallen violin to a shatter of polished wood and gut.

You press your children to you. You fear the soldiers will want to tear them away from your broken, bleeding fingers, smash them to silence and nothingness with rifle butts. There is nothing to say, no words that will help. Not now. The soldiers push you down the platform towards the station office. The crackling voice of the loud-speaker welcomes you. Welcome welcome welcome. You notice that a pall of smoke is rising beyond the trees, as if from a great confla-gration. The cold morning air draws the smoke in low and close over the station; a vile smoke, a choking suffocating smoke, the stench of something unclean, burning there in the night forest.

Shouting in their stupid, brutal voices, the soldiers herd you towards the office. You do not want to go there, you cannot go there, you must not go there, but you are incapable of resisting the pressing, pressing, pressing bodies. There are figures behind the latticed windows of the waiting room. Seated figures, bowed in attitudes of concentration, as if over musical instruments. Then above the voice of the loudspeaker come the sweet, sad notes of the string quartet, rising up to mingle with the smoke that lies across the waiting trees of the night forest, over all the dark continent, the final movement from *Eine Kleine Nachtmusik*, rather poorly, you think.

'It is all right, Anna,' your father says, 'it is only for a little while, until the next train comes, to take us on to the place we are meant to go.'

APPROACHING PERPENDICULAR

A thorn in his flesh and an image driven like a wedge into his mind: these things bring Brendl the poet across the specula of High Space to the Glass Hotel.

The pain, the swift, gutting pain; that is an old familiar. Twenty doctors on twenty worlds have failed before Brendl's thorn; twenty philosophies of medicine proved only that there are places within a poet their art and science may not touch.

The image: that comes as a stranger. Like a succubus it swims out of the bestiary of High Space into the exalted dreams of poets: *gold on black*, cleaving his dreaming skull like a falling axe, a fine edge, a balance point upon which a great poem may be suspended.

A vision, and a pain. Drawn to one, flying from the other. Prismatic colours melt and run, the air shivers with the surreal *chiaroscuro* of the Aesthetic Medium as the starcrosser slips into corporeality. Brendl the poet has come to the City.

The Glass Hotel stands on a rise, its back to Sothis the Ash Desert, its face turned to the City; an antique aquarium aswim with those colourful and curious exhibits the City draws to itself. Rare fish, they swim shy, never touching. Brushing softly, shyly past, they move, they glide within their bowl of chrome and glass, wary of each other, warier yet of the City without and the long shadow it casts over the gelid banalities and inconsequentialities that pass between these denizens of the Glass Hotel.

'They say that within its walls a dozen races may have lived and died,' says the rich, clever, frightened young man called Anneway. He pours a glass of water-clear wine for Brendl the poet. 'Indeed, it is mooted that the founder race, the so-called Architects, may still be living there, close to the spindle. It is mooted.'

And in the water-gardens, at tea with the woman called Moon-of-May upon a punt shaped like the petals of an open ash-flower: 'It is still growing, you know.' An intimate touch of conspiracy, complicity upon Brendl's knee. 'The distortion. They have found courses of earlier walls, long abandoned, within the current constructions. The discontinuity mirror is still running, drawing reality after it in its mad pursuit of infinitude.' Perfect hands, shapely as lilies, rest lightly upon his knee. 'Does that not frighten you? It does me.'

That evening, at dinner with the Venerable Dowager Duenna Chun-Yen-Yi: 'Do you know how long I have been here, young man? Twenty-two years. Twenty-two years this summer, and I have seen it all. Everything. There is nothing new under the sun, this sun, any sun.' The twittering of a song-bird in a mulberry tree. Brendl smiles graciously. In his head, the black and the gold. 'I have seen everything, and yet I have never seen the City: is that not strange, Mr Brendl? I have never seen the City, never wish to, never will. I shall probably die in this Glass Hotel without ever having set foot beyond the gate of Doubt-No-More. And I shall tell you why, young man. When I was a girl, my tutor, Dr Morpeno, once demonstrated the principle of electrostatic repulsion by suspending a pith ball between the charged plates of an electrostatic generator. An idle enough pastime, you might think, and I might agree, except that I am that ball of pith, Mr Brendl. I am suspended in perfect equilibrium between the fear and the fascination of that thing out there and that is why I will never leave this Glass Hotel.'

'Fear,' muses Fleyn the Consular Officer, astroll beneath the flori-bunda pergolas of the rose walks. Now and again he pauses, the perfect diplomat elegant in silk coat and plantation hat, to scent the blossoms. 'Ah, the roses. No other world can boast a bloom to rival the roses of earth, do you not think, Brendl? You have, of course, been talking with that old coward, the Dowager Duenna Chun-Yen-Yi. The dear woman is correct, but only to a certain extent. While there are many who come to this world who never pass through the gate of Doubt-No-More because, quite frankly, this big, old, alien city terrifies them, the great majority find within its walls a richness, a splendour, a sweep of history and vision that transforms their lives. Surely you are not one of the fearful ones, Brendl? You are a poet; what could a poet fear that he has not already faced in his imagination?'

Brendl shrugs: a nothing. He is thinking of the people rubbing their fear onto each other like musk.

'Tomorrow,' he says. 'Tomorrow I will go. Tomorrow I will run the image of the black and the gold to ground in the streets and closes of the City and I will not be afraid.'

But tomorrow comes, and tomorrow and tomorrow and Brendl the poet is afraid. And because day after day he refuses to name that fear, Brendl the poet gradually, gently, becomes another creature of the Glass Hotel, a trivial thing of grace and air and perfect banality incapable of the meanest line, the meanest word of poetry. But on the twenty-fifth night he catches a vagrant glimpse of his face in a distant mirror. Too remote for the carefully composed expression he wears when purposefully regarding his reflection, Brendl recognises his true face. And seeing himself thus, he knows that he must look upon the City and see his face mirrored in its monumental arrogance.

Alone in his suite, he crosses to the window and repeals the word that has rendered it opaque since his arrival in the Glass Hotel. A knife of fear turns slow in his gut, he shudders, fearing the onslaught of his personal demon (incredible that it has not yet come to smite him). Brendl steels himself and in time the spasm passes. And then he turns his eyes to look upon the City, the spindle of land heaved up by the alien discontinuity mirror, heaved up and shaped like clay on a wheel into that form called the conic hyperbola, a curving spire dotted and streaked with the lanterns of night, reaching ever upward, ever inward, dwindling to the ultimate dimensionless thread at that infinite point of perfect perpendicularity which is its exact centre, the heart of impossibility where the discontinuity mirror lies.

The City lies open before him like an impatient lover, yet Brendl turns away from it, for no man can look long upon infinity. It pains his eyes. It sears his soul. It fires his imagination.

His pack is small and light; it is not his intent that this be a major expedition to the hidden heartlands of the City, this adventure through the gate of Doubt-No-More is more a symbol of personal resolution. Yet that resolution falters a little, fails a little, with each step he takes away from the butterfly world of the terminally fearful, each step he takes toward the hyperbolic mountain that is the City. Between Glass Hotel and City Gate lies a sordid kilometre of shameful tar-paper and packing-case shanties, the domain of those shameless creatures who take their living from the visitors; concealed from the soul-dwindling view of the hyperbola by the shadow of the walls. Brendl moves among them, a fool in paradise; fingers stroke his pockets, hands tug his sleeve: 'Mister, mister, a guide, mister mister, you need a guide, Man'O'Earth? You need a guide show you the City, the wonderful wonderful City?'

'No thank you!' he shouts. 'The heart of a poet is all the guide he requires!' Protected by his innocence and arrogance, like some holy angel, Brendl draws a train of indeterminately gendered urchins and street-arabs through the dung-strewn laneways beneath the city wall.

And now he stands before the gate of Doubt-No-More: thirty times higher than a man, a mouth wide enough to swallow a world, let alone a proud poet. He passes under the inscription from which this one of fifty City Gates takes its name: *Doubt-No-More*.

But Brendl doubts.

And now he has entered the City.

People. People. People. Pressing close on all sides, pressing their bodies, their smells, their lives, their fears against his, pressing their noise; the sheer clamour of the myriad voices calling, calling from windows, calling from terraces, calling from closes and tiled squares, calling from shops and cafés, calling their wares and their trades, their friends and their families, a babelogue of calling voices calling in that rough, vibrant dialect of human called Ternary. Brendl the poet walks slowly through this life, breathing slowly the breath of the City, absorbing slowly through his skin, his senses, his whole person, the boundless human energy of this bustling commercial district. Warrenways of small merchandisers and workshops spool off this main thoroughfare; drays, wagons, omnibuses, cyclecabs hurry past Brendl as he stands, a solitary island of motionlessness in the surging sea of activity, looking, seeing, living the City.

And, looking about him, he is possessed by a vision.

In a dark alley, piled high with red fruit, is a doorway of intricately carved wood, a blue lantern, and the hem of a black gown, trimmed with gold. It shines bright as a new sun, and is gone.

Idle hands frozen in the air, Brendl stands paralysed in revelation. Then, without conscious volition, he is reaching towards the alley, the door, the blue lantern. And the pain smites him.

It does not permit him even one cry. From sternum to groin it slits him open, a burning, gutting blade tearing through stomach, bowels, bones, soul. Breath driven from his lungs, Brendl lies helpless beneath the knife looking up into the hyperbolic heart of impossibility. But he sees only the colours of pain. For three eternities he is crucified upon it, an eternity of agony, an eternity of helplessness, an eternity of enduring; then hands lift him and place him on a litter to bear him away, through the markets, through great Doubt-No-More, through the sordid aisles of snatching hands and pleading voices to the Glass Hotel.

That evening the staff are ordered to deck the terraces with bunting and hang paper lanterns in every tree. Every lounge, salon and pavilion is opened with the announcement of universal euphoriants and, drawn like curious moths to the light, the guests gather in a flock of questions. What is the occasion of this unexpected jubilee? What is the identity of the mysterious host, whose the largesse? With such speculations the patrons of the Glass Hotel amuse themselves until at twenty minutes of twenty the onyx doors of the Peacock Pavilion are swung wide and the chattering, cackling gaggle of revellers draws back to give passage to a man, a short man, heavily bearded, clothed in an eclectic patchwork of clashing styles, yet brimming with a peculiar, radiant energy.

His name is Bulawayo.

He is back from the City.

A year before, to the day, to the hour, he departed the Glass Hotel and passed through Doubt-No-More. Since that hour his death has been many times mooted, his imminent return no fewer. An entire edifice of rumour has its foundations upon Bulawayo which even Fleyn the Consular Officer can neither substantiate nor deny. In short: he is legend.

Bulawayo's stories that night of the strange and marvellous draw murmurs of admiration from even the most world-weary of his guests. He has been deep within. He has climbed far up the asymptotic land, he has journeyed into the empty places where the human settlers, in their millennial migration into the vast reaches of the City, have yet to penetrate; that land where shadows flit on abandoned boulevards, the animate memories of older, nobler races who have moved onward, inward, upward, drawn up the ever-lengthening, ever-narrowing spindle by the energies of the alien power mirror. With hands and eyes he spins his tales and binds the creatures of the Glass Hotel to him with cords of wonder and they offer him their praise and adulation, for he has done that which they can never do.

Some. Not all. From his table in the shadowy recesses of the Peacock Pavilion, the shadow-man listens; the pale man, the man with the fear of the ghost of pain. Brendl is not a man given to vain adulation. He is a poet, and poets do not give adulation. They receive it. Vanity is the sin of the poet; vanity, and envy. Yet Brendl listens to the rough voice. He listens well.

It is four minutes of four and Brendl wakes with a cry in the deep darkness before the dawn. It is not the remembrance or anticipation of pain that has woken him, not this time. It is a vision, an image so potent that it follows him out of the dreamtime into the waking world.

Green eyes, slitted eyes, upturned to the sun.

Alone in the pre-dawn dark with the green eyes and the hem of black and gold, he feels the shadow of the City lying heavy across him, heavy as if all the unspeakable bulk of the great spire had fallen and crushed the Glass Hotel like a cage of crickets. He knows that he must return to it, pass once more beneath the vault of Doubt-No-More. For he is well enough acquainted with the ways of poetic inspiration to know that until he does the images will give him no peace.

Thus it is with emotions mixed in equal measures of anticipation and dread that Brendl retraces his path through the jostling parasites, beneath the spirit-dwarfing arch of Doubt-No-More, into the borough of the markets. He nears the alley of his vision. Sweat beads his brow, a sudden hot panic mounts in him, the bright edge of a knife. It takes all his small courage to look into the entry. He sees yellow melons piled against a wall under a yellow gas lamp. What he had taken to be a door is a wooden shutter carved in intricate arabesques. Of the hem of black and gold, there is not even the whisper of a memory.

Beyond the markets lies a prefecture of alien ceramic architecture, a porcelain place where the straight line, the Euclidean plane are despised and houses, streets, roofs, walls and gardens melt into each other in sensuous terracotta curves. No line is level, no plumb true, and the streethousegardens glitter with liquid glazes, as if entire neighbourhoods had been left to soften and flow in the sun. The name of this district is Toltlethen, a soft breath of a name, a spoken spirit of place which inspires Brendl as, aimless as a riddle, he meanders through the molten courtyards and soft glazed streets. Before him the land rises gently upward, forever rising beneath Brendl's feet as ignorant, innocent, he climbs the lower slopes of the asymptotic curve. As he walks imagery flocks to him; he tastes his metaphors, tests them, tried them on his lips for euphony, then sets them down in the black leather notebook which, when the Muse is on him, is as inseparable from Brendl as the skin of his own writing hand. Free from the imagining of pain, his spirit is light within him and the images that gather about him like a congregation of ghosts waft him on through the porcelain streets of Toltlethen.

When he hears the sound he cannot be certain whence it comes for it seems to surround him on every side. Running feet, voices raised in excitement, the rattle of a tambourine, the pounding of a drum, the bleating of a bag-pipe: the pottery houses reflect, refract the sound so that it is everywhere apparent but nowhere visible. Then, in their ones and twos, their dribs and drabs, their threes and fours, the people quit their streethousegardens, filling the terracotta lanes with an ever-swelling throng and Brendl, curious, yielding, permits himself to be carried with the flow.

From what small glimpses he is afforded, Brendl gathers that he has been swept into some great civic festival. At the procession's head eighty men in crimson perform upon a preposterous array of instruments from tiny clay ocarinas shaped like the birds they mimic to the serpentine coils of massive ophicleides so ponderous they must be supported upon small wheeled trolleys. Behind these, the dancers: some tottering upon stilts, some with wheels fitted to hands and feet, some earthbound but wondrously acrobatic, some concealed behind huge triangular fans which, from time to time, are thrown high into the air to open, catch the light upon their intricately worked interiors, and fall gently on the breezes to be caught unerringly by the hands that have cast them. Smaller replicas of these fans are carried by the jubilating citizens of Toltlethen as they wind through the streets, through echoing greens, past lofty glass towers, through vaulted arcades, across squares and piazzas dense with the suspended life of fountains and statues, over bridges hung over bridges hung over bridges hung over dark bottomless ravines. Brendl the poet breasts this tide of humanity until at last the ritual energy fails and the procession empties itself into a wide cobbled square flanked by grey brick tenements so tall, so many-windowed, they seem like a host of monstrous faces.

Here the musicians take up station and the dancers, seemingly possessed of an inexhaustible energy, commence a complex ballet comprising an astonishingly acrobatic trading of fans between stilt dancers, four-wheelers, gymnasts and the central group all dressed in yellow, so that every three exchanges the entire cycle of fans rotates once. Brendl asks a bystander what is this spectacle he is witnessing.

'This is the Exaltation of Charmed Quarks,' says the man. He clutches a coloured fan to his breast. 'The Third Cycle of the Tlantoon.'

And, as if the man's words had shone the light of revelation upon him, Brendl sees them.

Green eyes, slitted eyes, upturned to the sun.

A dancing woman in a sleek tiger-striped costume and mask, a woman with the head of a cat.

Brendl bursts through the ring of festival-goers into the Exaltation of Charmed Quarks. Stilt dancers loom and sway before him, acrobatic bodies twist and turn away, wheeled demons hurtle past, scorching him with the velocity of their passage. There are shouts, cries, a vast, vague, incoherent roaring. But Brendl the poet sees only the green eyes, the slitted eyes, upturned to the sun: the pale afternoon light silhouetting sleek, tiger-striped flanks. He reaches that place where, without doubt, he saw her. Nothing. He casts frantically about him, scattering alarmed celebrants, but his only reward is a final taunting flick of tiger-striped sleekness, impossibly slim and supple, slipping into the gloom of an inter-tenement alley; green eyes, slitted eyes, luminous for an instant in the sun.

Alone after the Tlantoon has dispersed, Brendl searches the cobbled square for some clue to her being. He searches, he calls for her with the names his imagination has given to her but the cliffs of the grey brick tenements are as devoid of intelligence as the mottled face of the moon. And the rain begins, a thin drizzling rain spun down from the arrogant spindle at the centre of the world like a mockery of poets and their imaginings.

After the recitation, the acclamation.

'Wonderful, truly wonderful,' says Mr Anaxemides, the transplanetary merchant.

'A contemporary masterpiece.' This from young Anneway, no less fearful than on their last meeting.

'Truly magnificent. I stand in the presence of a truly great talent,' says Moon-of-May, flower hands open to bless.

'Mr Brendl, dear Mr Brendl, that was beautiful,' says the Venerable Dowager Duenna Chun-Yen-Yi, dewy-eyed and fluttering like a moth at a candle. 'I feel that now, after twenty-two years, I have at last visited the City.'

'The Exaltation of Charmed Quarks,' muses Fleyn the Consular Officer. 'Excellent, my man, excellent. Your visit to the City has had a most invigorating effect upon your imagination.'

Brendl smiles, a mask of false modesty. The vanity of poets, like their reputed love, is a thing apart.

'The Tlantoon,' continues Fleyn, drawing Brendl aside from his admirers to an intimate conversation booth. 'Without doubt, one of the greatest of the City's Festival Cycles, if not the greatest, and, if not the greatest, certainly the most ancient. Ignatieff at the Mission has made a comprehensive study of the ethnology of the Tlantoon and he is certain, quite certain, that the central liturgy of the Five Cycles predates human occupancy of the City. Do you see what this means? That in the ceremonies of the Tlantoon we have a living link with those alien races that have long since passed into the heartlands – Ignatieff's expression is "internal migration", I quite like that – indeed, it is Mr Ignatieff's opinion that through the Tlantoon we are in contact with the semi-mythical Architects, the creators of the City, and the engineers of the discontinuity mirror the effects of which you must by now be well familiar with, my dear Brendl. Personally, I believe that as a coherent racial group the Architects have been extinct for millions of years; if any remain, it must be as isolated individuals, grubbing a living from the fringes of human society, sadly fallen from their noble estate.'

Brendl does not much care to hear about elder alien races who may or may not be semi-mythical. He wishes for the praises of his admirers, for their fawning adulation of the icy cascades of his poetry. But he smiles politely, for politeness covers a multitude of sins of disposition. Fleyn continues.

'Yes. As Ignatieff says, the City is great, so great that some prefectures may celebrate Tlantoon only once in a generation. You were damnably lucky, Brendl, damnably lucky.'

'That one taste has only whetted my appetite for more,' says Brendl, looking over Fleyn's shoulder to a knot of coy admirers.

'Of course it has. But you may have to be content with what you have seen, my dear fellow. In addition to moving to God-knows-where in the next cycle, each successive level of the Tlantoon is increasingly exclusive. You must remember, my dear Brendl, that though the Tlantoon may be unmatched as a spectacle for we Men'O'Earth, it is a ritual of deep spiritual significance to the people of the City. In all the years travellers have been visiting the City, only the meanest handful have ever succeeded in being admitted to the Fourth Cycle, the Celebration of Distorted Reflections. As for the Fifth Cycle, all we know of it is its name, the Pious Descent of Infinite Gradient, so holy and secret is the ritual. We Men'O'Earth maintain our presence in this City purely by suffrance. We must be respectful.'

'I shall persist, and who knows? Precedents are set to be broken, and I have by no means exhausted the treasury of imagery contained within the Tlantoon.'

That night, as if inspired to renewed life by Brendl's arrogance, they caper through his dreams, mocking, taunting: the hem of gold braid, the catheaded dancer, fleeing from his clumsy attempts to lay hand on them. Therefore, in pursuit of peace of heart, in pursuit of the terminal pin through their hearts to his pure white pages, Brendl embarks upon his greatest expedition into the City. Three days in the planning, amassing funds, equipment, comestibles, clothing; then one morning the denizens of the Glass Hotel rise, late as is their custom, to find him gone from their midst. Accustomed to such ventures into realms where clocks run askew and space is stretched into a carnival ribbon, the management maintain the poet's suite, his society clothes, his toiletries and personal sundries, his reams of black-scribbled paper; all preserved in readiness against his return, be that hours distant, or months.

And in his wild hunt, Brendl the poet wanders far across the City, living from his small nightpack and those necessities he can purchase from the arcades and gallerias, boarding overnight in whatever hotel, tavern or guesthouse will suit his purse and his pride, chasing the spirit of the Tlantoon. Time and again he thinks he has run it down, voices carried on the wind, the skirling of pipes and strings swirled out of a sullen sky, but always when he bursts, breathless, expectant, into that courtyard, square, green, piazza, he finds himself caught up in the hurly-burly of some local carnival or public flogging or bridal procession or street auction of repossessed furnishings. Time and again his disappointment sends him into the infantile rage of poets, yet his obsession with the green eyes and the hem of gold-on-black drives him on through the avenues of pleasingly proportioned red-brick townhouses, through convoluted nests of animate architecture swarming with humanity, through floating markets and waterboroughs and garden villages and ponderous glass arcologies packed with transparent souls, kilometre after kilometre, the ground rising gently before him, rising gently to the perfection of pure verticality. Yet for all the kilometres he has put beneath his feet in the days? weeks? since he has passed through Doubt-No-More, the central pinnacle is not a footstep nearer. Confusion: has he been meandering, time out of mind, has he been trudging an idiot's Great Circle around the base of the hyperbola, a slow spiral of the lost?

Has the great Spire been mocking him, hiding itself from him, with-holding its promise of fulfilment like some painted Jezebel?

Some subtle subjective phenomenon is at work, he decides. As space and gravity are bent into a preposterous curve, so the Brendl that occupies that space is similarly deformed, to his very sub-quarkal fundamental fractions. To that quasi-Brendl, no change is percep-tible, yet if he were able to regard himself from some remote vantage, as if upon the great City wall, he would see himself distorted out of all credibility into a dull brown thread of impossibility wriggling along a street stretched into a cobbled ribbon. The thought of him-self transformed into something alien, repugnant, impossible, deeply disturbs Brendl. Appearance, perception, is all to him. Therefore he turns away from those few fellow travellers who have strayed this deep into the City, turns away from their greetings without a word, for he sees reflected in their faces the blind wriggling worm of hyperbolic function. He flees from them, possessed, obsessed, and in time his flight brings him beneath the graceful almond trees of the Prefecture of Ranves and there he halts in his flight, for he can see the flurries of notes caught in the branches of the trees that line the boulevards. Brendl knows with certainty that he has arrived at the Fourth Cycle, the Celebration of Distorted Reflections. He has lived too long, too close with his obsession not to recognise its perfume, the scent of a stale lover. Rude, barging, shouting; elbowing nannies with perambulators, scattering skeins of kindergarten chil-dren, upsetting the carefully piled ziggurats of the sherbet sellers, the barging, shouting Man'O'Earth presses his way through the crowds frequenting Ranves Park. But his efforts are not enough. The people are dispersing from that open area where the park walks converge, the musicians are loading their cumbrous instruments into ox-drawn pantechnicons, the dancers are pulling warm leggings over their sweat-streaked costumes, the players are folding away their reflective umbrellas and mirror kites. Discarded plastic mirrors snap like the bones of small rodents beneath Brendl's feet. The unthink-able has come to pass: the Tlantoon is over, the Distorted Reflections celebrated without Brendl the poet.

He clenches his fists and roars his frustration, his betrayal, to the graceful trees, spinning round round round round. And the next moment he is on the gravel, knotted into a writhing foetus by the pain, the gutting, searing, pain. He rolls onto his back, a struggling insect impaled upon a needle of agony and the people back away from the sick, mad man. His lips shape silent pleas for assistance, then out of the fire, hallucination: a cat-face bending over him, cat-eyes drawn into lines of puzzlement; green eyes, slitted eyes.

'So, Mr Brendl, you too are a seeker of the Tlantoon.' The man's name is Banaco. He is a man of gentle deception, that deception being that though his face is old, his eyes are young and his hands, the hands that lifted Brendl from his torment and brought him to the Three Lanterns Hotel, those hands are strong with a strength no human hands should possess.

'Such a pity that you were not able to witness the celebration. Still, you are a fortunate man, in the short time you have been visiting the City you have been party, in a greater or lesser part, to two of the cycles; it has taken me four years – I think it is four years, clocks run askew in the City – to progress from the Exaltation to the Celebration.'

The small private room is lit by hissing gas lanterns; beneath its soft yellow glow Banaco's old-young face seems carved from meerschaum.

'Like you, Mr Brendl, I am a connoisseur of the City and its life. So much that is paradoxical: where does the food come from, the water, the power, even the gas that lights this very room? A miracle of faith worked by this miraculous power mirror, transubstantiation of matter and energy? No less miraculous, Mr Brendl, than the wonderful impossibility of an infinite area existing within a finite boundary. Do these not provoke a deep fascination? They do in me, fascinate me.'

'Such things are beyond me,' says Brendl, ash-pale and trembling still despite remedies and potent liqueurs. 'My sole fascination is the Tlantoon.'

'But do you not see how central the Tlantoon is to the paradox of the City?' Evangel-light burns in Banaco's eyes. 'Why, each level of the festival, each cycle, enacts, or is in some fashion symbolically representational of, the mystery of the discontinuity mirror. The

Calculation of Hyperbolic Function, the Exploration of Potential Domain, the Exaltation of Charmed Quarks, the Celebration of Distorted Reflections, even the Pious Descent of Infinite Gradient, all are telling the people of the City, and, at a greater remove, we Men'O'Earth, of the heritage of the alien power mirror, its inception, its function, and, I believe, its inadvertent side-effect; that in drawing energy from free quark/sub-quark probability fields, it has caused an inversion of local space and as casually thrown up this monstrous pinnacle as it has turned gravity and distance inside out. All, I repeat, Mr Brendl, all contained within the liturgy of the Tlantoon.'

Again the visions conjure themselves in Brendl's spirit-vision, his black and gold, his green eyes slitted eyes, and regarding them thus he is appalled by their paucity, their poverty, whining in the shadow of this man's towering, asymptotic spire of symbolic cosmology. Resentment, envy, spread their bitter green roots through his soul. The old man continues. 'Of course, my ambition, my crowning achievement, would be to attend the Fifth Cycle, the Pious Descent of Infinite Gradient.'

'But that is closed to all outsiders, my friend. We know of it only by name.'

Banaco leans forward in the yellow gas-light, intimate, conspiratorial.

'But I know where the Fifth Cycle is to be held, Mr Brendl.'

Such a swell of dizziness breaks over Brendl that he fears even the excuse of the recency of his attack will not conceal the lust in his trembling hands, his pallid cheeks.

'Oh? Pray where?' Surprising, the suave control in his voice.

'On the edge of the Barrens, the uninhabited zone at the limits of human expansion. I have learned that this place has a special ritual significance and is always the stage for the final cycle. Two days hence, at Bellerophon's Cross, the Pious Descent of Infinite Gradient will be celebrated.'

'And despite the restrictions, you intend to be there?'

'But certainly. And you?'

Brendl merely smiles and the conversation is ended. But later, when the old man's eyes are diverted by some glint of light, some gleam from a raised instrument or the thigh of some perfect whore, Brendl slips his purse and black book of poetry into Banaco's handsack. For like the old man, Brendl too is a creature of deception. But the deceit of poets is not so gentle.

His impersonation of rough City Ternary pleases him; the whispered tip to the Prefecture Constabulary, handkerchief wrapped around the fish-shaped telephone mouthpiece an admirable performance.

'Hello, Commissioner, I'd like to report a theft . . . yes, I saw it happen, in the Three Lanterns Hotel . . . you must understand my need for anonymity . . .'

Presently the scream of ground-effect vehicles slewing to a halt fills the cobbled courtyard without. Doors slam, voices are raised, accusation made, defences dismissed, evidence produced. Feet scuffle, doors slam once more, ground-effect fans power up and Brendl can go to his bed secure in his absolute possession of the Tlantoon.

In his sleep the third image comes to him.

It is less defined than the others, a sense, an impression: *white light drawing a line of silver along a dull flat plane;* glass, steel, water? A wall, a roof, a spade, an abstract of geometry? The very vagueness of the vision sends associations and allusions whirling through Brendl's imagination like speeding moons.

The next morning, upon settlement of his bill, he asks directions to Bellerophon's Cross. The host supplies these with civil comprehensiveness and returns to Brendl his stolen purse and notebook.

'Terrible, sir, that such a fine gentleman as Mr Banaco should be at heart a common thief.'

'The finest gentlemen are often the greatest scoundrels,' says Brendl without the least taste of duplicity in his mouth. And, ever inward, he goes forth, up the gently sloping land. Toward midday he reaches a dome-shaped hill rising out of a busy district of tumbledown brick tenements, solitary and incongruous as a bald head at a wedding. On the summit of the grassy rise is a small belvedere from which the residents of the tenements may contemplate the striking view. This noon hour the hill-top is deserted. Brendl's sole company and consolation is a small breeze stirring the wind-chimes that hang from the cupola, the spirit of place, a ghost of conscience. Brass telescopes have been provided by whatever philanthrope designed the hill-top preview; it is to the southward-looking one that Brendl turns first. The telescope calls to his eyes the vast traverse of urban landscape he has already crossed. To his view it seems that the land flares upward, outward, like the bell of a colossal instrument poised on edge. Barely perceptible at the limit of the telescope's range is a ludicrous crayon-scribbled line of encirclement: the wall, Brendl realises with a start of surprise; Doubt-No-More a mean rat-hole nibbled in the perimeter. And what can that minute smear of light be but the sun shining from the blind reflecting face of the Glass Hotel? And, almost at the zenith of his craning vision, at the point where the positive curve of the hyperbolic City meets the negative curve of the round world; three connected globes, stretched until they reach almost half the way around this distorted world; can that be any other than the starcrosser from the earth, hovering like smoke above Sothis the Ash Desert?

And now he turns to the northward telescope and, looking through its eyepiece, beholds the central spire of the world, reaching upward, outward, a preposterous mountain dwindling to an infinitesimal thread spun out into space. Yet, that line of geometrical abstraction is as much a city as the dilated lands behind him; streets, houses, public buildings, markets, parks, alien lives.

Contemplation in the deserted belvedere; the land seeming to slope up both behind and before him can only mean that Brendl has reached the Equipoise, the boundary between Outer and Inner Cities where the gradient of the land equals forty-five degrees, the place from which all paths are equal. Brendl stands upon the edge of the City of Men, before him the Barrens, empty alien boulevards, plague-haunted plazas of dereliction and decay, dead buildings painful as snapped teeth. Here, on the edge, the culminatory rites of the prehistoric Architects will be performed a day hence. Coming down from his hill-top like some prophet of obsession, he finds that the land beneath his feet is now sloping gently downhill.

He lodges that night in a shadowy hotel perched on a hillside like some bird of carrion presiding over the Barrens. This poor establishment is managed by a surly wife and husband who, while welcoming his custom, regard Brendl with the weightiest suspicion. Whether for being a Man'O'Earth or for having read the blasphemous intent in his heart, he cannot tell. But that night, watched by the window-eyes of abandoned manors, Brendl writes. His Muse has him; in the possessed ecstasy of poetic inspiration Brendl writes and writes and writes, the words coming in such a spurt and rush that his always perfect handwriting smears into distorted blots and scrawls, pulled out of true along the axis of the alien power mirror. The Muse rides him hard, like a succubus, until with the slate grey dawn she rolls from him to leave him lying in an incomprehension of reason, rhyme, nonsense and divine revelation, sheet after sheet after sheet of it. And it is the morning of the Pious Descent of Infinite Gradient.

The air is clear and cold here in the deadlands, crystal with a whisper of winter. Brendl's spirits are high. He glows with a creation-light that confounds his mistrustful host and hostess. To avoid undue attention he has dressed this day in the clothes of a City dweller. In the belt-pouch of his leggings are the crumpled sheets of his frenzy. He walks with brisk good cheer along the great abandoned marble boulevard. Tufts of wiry grass sprout from between the uneven slabs of travertine and on each side range colonnades of statuary, so eaten by time that only pock-marked torsos remain, yet Brendl cannot rid himself of the sensation that they are observing his passage with senses other than vision. And in their ones and twos, their dribs and drabs, their threes and fours, the people come, out of everywhere, out of nowhere, out of the eroded statues and tilted paving slabs, a trickle, a stream, a river bearing Brendl towards the circus at the centre of the wheel of heartbroken avenues where Bellerophon's Cross rises, ambiguous memorial to alien significance.

The heart-mystery is about to be enacted.

In the centre of the great open space the crimson orchestra has gathered around a remarkable pageant wagon, a man-made caricature of the familiar curving funnel of the City. Suspended upon its needle point is a wooden armature to which four masked figures are roped. About the foot of the pageant wagon caper the stilt dancers draped in comical costumes of straw. The orchestra strikes up, the tumultuous sound echoing and re-echoing from the girdling colonnades. The crowd stirs to the rhythm of the Tlantoon and Brendl finds himself pushed to the front of the mob. Suddenly exposed, he nervously examines the integrity of his disguise, but the eyes of the people are rapt upon the astonishing acrobatics of the stilt dancers. Upon their wooden crucifix at the apex of the model City, the Pious Descenders raise their arms in readiness.

Suddenly, there is a cry.

Suddenly, in mid-chord, the orchestra falls silent.

Suddenly, in mid-leap, the stilt dancers are motionless.

Suddenly, from across the circle of faces, a finger is pointing. The finger of an old, suspicious woman, the hostess of the crumbling hotel in the wastelands. She is screaming. Brendl cannot make out her screams. He has no need to, for he looks at the faces and sees that they are all about him, the faces of the Police Commissioner and the Manager of the Three Lanterns Hotel and the nannies he elbowed out of his way in Ranves Park, the face of the City, turned upon him in accusation.

A tiny squeak of fear escapes Brendl the poet and that tiny animal cry releases him from the paralysis of exposure, for now he is running, running, running, down the shattered marble boulevard, running with the sound of an old woman's curses, of following feet, of angry voices loud in his head. He cries, he sobs with fear: the quisling stitch in his side begs him to stop, cease, give up. He runs, he knows not where, he runs lost to all but the sound of his pursuers.

And in the twinkling of an eye, she is there.

She beckons with her body: *escape*. Brendl follows her into a warren of decomposing alleys and entries. Within seconds he is lost. His spirit-guide has vanished. He casts about him in desperation, first one blind alley, then another, then another, all the while imagining the beating footfalls of the hounds of the Tlantoon. A whisper of sound, he whirls, panic-stricken, sees a dark-robed figure in a mask beckon him forth. Lost in flight, Brendl follows. A hiss, a purr, his name? The half-glimpsed silhouette of the cat-dancer leads him deeper, running, running ... 'Brrendlll ...' Black-and-gold skirts whisk round a cornerstone, cat-eyes flash in dark entries. Any possible pursuers have long since been left perplexed in the archaic maze but still Brendl runs runs runs for there is nothing a poet fears more than his own imagination. The images have, at last, taken their due from him. He rounds a corner, enters another blind alley.

And there is a door, a carved wooden door, and there is a blue lantern, and there is a hem of black trimmed with gold sliding across the stone saddle into that doorway. Brendl approaches the wooden door. Everything is as he has hoped. Everything is as he has feared. Brendl passes under the blue lantern and enters the house. In a blue room lit by a painful blue light, the figure in black stands, masked, unspeaking. At its feet, the woman with the head of a cat crouches, coiled, potential.

'Thank you.'

The figures are motionless, suspended in time.

'The thanks of Brendl, poet of Earth, are yours.'

Silence, stasis.

'Whoever you are, I am indebted to you . . .' Brendl's words, Brendl's smile, Brendl's hands, are frozen. The figure in black and the cat-headed woman are lifting their hands to remove their masks.

Brendl's cry rings and rings and rings from the four blue walls of the blue room: the wailing cry of pure dread.

Noseless, lipless, parchment-skinned and huge-eyed, slit-lipped; whatever the people to which these triangular faces belong, they are not human.

Not human.

Never human.

But what makes that inhumanity unbearable is that there is nothing but friendship in those faces, the fellowship of the hunted, the hated. Brendl's lips work soundlessly, then without conscious thought, he is running from the house of the blue lantern, blundering blindly along the staggering, crumbling lanes. The hands. The hands. The pale, thin, beautifully alien hands had been reaching out to him, imploring him to put off his humanity and his self and join them down in the deadlands.

Within moments he is quite lost. Possessed of a malign sentience, the labyrinth of alleyways sends him hither, thither, this way, that way, crossing and recrossing his path time after time. Numb, heedless, Brendl is past rational thought and choice. The streets ring with cries, his own and those of his pursuers, for his flight has led him away from the alien sanctuary at the heart of the warren where no man of that prefecture will dare go, outward, away, closer to the highways of men. Flailing at the air, striking at the invisible images which have betrayed him, Brendl stumbles on until at last, bursting around a corner, he delivers himself into the hands of his hunters.

Those hands seize him, those hands hold him: voices call, meaningless, wrapped in their thick, alien-tainted dialects. Two persons press forward through the mob; the mistrustful woman, the surly man from the brooding hotel. A brief nod of identification, a word of command, and the knife is drawn.

A vagrant shaft of afternoon sunlight penetrating the darkness of the warrenway limns a line of pure, holy silver along the steel edge of the blade.

The trinity is complete.

Brendl shrieks, struggles; then in a stabbing, slashing flash the knife tears Brendl the poet open from crotch to sternum.

Through the fire, through the rushing, mobbing dark, Brendl casts his eyes to heaven, to the clouds spinning out like fleece into thread, twisted around the twisted hyperbolic world. And he knows. He knows that as casually as a discontinuity mirror distorts space it can twist time back upon itself like a skein of wool, throwing echoes of future things into the past so that a man, if he has the vanity, the pride, the arrogance and naïvety of a poet, may ignorantly chase the presentiment of his own death in the name of inspiration and art. And Brendl knows it all and he smiles a warped, distorted smile, and the darkness closes in around him and draws him into itself.

Hands clasped behind back in the proper attitude of diplomatic mourning, Fleyn the Consular Officer walks slowly beside the catafalque as it is borne up the access ramp of the starcrosser. He finds himself caught incongruously between realities: the air shivers with the imaginings of the High Space drive fields, yet a little soft grey ash has settled on the sleeve of his dress uniform, carried on the world-circling wind from Sothis the Ash Desert.

Sad, strange, terrible, a cruel dying in a lonely, alien place. On what might a poet's final thoughts linger? Home? Love? Mortality, perhaps, or a parting sneer at the cosmic comedian out of whose bad jokes life is shaped? Some answer must lie within the crumpled sheets of paper they brought with the body: the final work of Brendl poet of Earth. Doubtless a masterpiece, could posterity consider it otherwise? But what of those odd creatures that bore the body, dragging it by the sweat of their limbs on that rude travois across the incredible reach of City between the Barrens and the Consular Office? What of the cat-woman and the masked figure in black?

What relationship had found its expression there?

And now Fleyn stands upon the veranda of the Glass Hotel, a face among faces, the faces of the fearful and the vain who had not the small courage to accompany Brendl even on the first step of his last slow journey into High Space. The starcrosser is ready to depart now, the air stirs, gels, and suddenly is aswarm with the spiritual, inspirational creatures of the Aesthetic Medium. A bubble dissolving, a waft of grey ash, and the vessel is gone. But the City remains, the infinite within its finite boundary, for ever ascending, for ever approaching perpendicular.

FLOATING DOGS

And there in the wood,
A Piggy-wig stood
Edward Lear, 'The Owl and the Pussy-cat'

On the third day beyond the womb we come to the cool cool river, Peeg and Porcospino and Ceefer and Papavator and I. We stand among the trees that come down to the water's edge and watch the river flow. The sun is high above us; light shines and gleams from the moving water. Peeg is fascinated. He has never seen true water, only the dream water when he was a seed high in heaven. He goes down over the stones to touch his trunk to the flowing water.

'Alive!' he says. 'Alive.'

It is only water, I tell him but Peeg cannot accept this. There cannot be enough water in the world for all this flowing; no, it must be some great coiling creature, flowing across the earth, up into heaven and back to earth again. A circle of never-ending movement. For a creature of no hands and very little words, Peeg has much opinion about the hardworld. Opinions should be left to beings like me who have much words, and clever hands. Why, he does not even know his own true name. He calls himself *Peeg* because that is the name he found on his tongue when he woke in the womb of Mamavator. I tell him, *You are not a pig, a boar, you are a tapir. A tapir, that is what you are. See, you have a trunk, a snout, pigs do not have trunks or snouts*. He will not be told. *Peeg* is his name, Peeg is what he is. Creatures with few words should not toy with powerful things like names.

Ceefer flexes her claws, cleans between her toes.

'What it is is not important,' she says. 'How we get across it is.'
She is a law to herself, Ceefer. She has as many words as I, this I
know because she has the smart look in the back of her eyes. You
cannot hide that look. But she keeps her words much to herself. If
she has a name, one she found on her tongue in the Mamavator, she
keeps that also to herself. So I have my own name for her. Ceefer.
Ceefer Cat.

We follow the river to a place where the smooth shining water
breaks over rocks and stones into white spray.

'Here we will cross,' I say. 'Ceefer will go first to make sure there
are no traps or snares.' She grimaces at the white water; she loves
to fish but hates to get her fur wet. In a few bounds she is across,
sitting on the far side shaking water from her feet. We follow: Porcospino, then Peeg, then Papavator, then me. The Team Leader must
be last so he can watch over his team. I can see that Peeg's small
feet are far from safe on the slippery rocks.

'Peeg!' I say. 'Be careful careful careful.' But the glitter and shimmer of the running water have dazzled him. His small feet lose their
balance. In he goes. Screaming. Splashing. Feet clawing, kicking but
there is nowhere for them to catch hold. And the current has hold
of him, is sweeping him towards a gap in the rocks to wedge him,
drag him down, drown him.

Flash blue silver: Papavator steps over me, straddles his long, thin
metal legs to form a good steady base, unfolds an arm. *Down* goes
the arm, *in* go the fingers locking in the mass of hair and circuitry
at the back of Peeg's neck, *up* comes Peeg thrashing and squealing.
In three strides Papavator is on the far bank. Peeg is a dismal, dripping huddle on the shore.

'Up, up,' I say. 'Move move. We must go on. We have far to go
this day to our Destination.' But Peeg will not move. He stands
shivering, saying over and over and over again these words: *bit me
bit me bad being bad being bit me bit me bad being bad being*. The river
being that seemed so wonderful, so friendly to him has turned evil
and hostile. I go to talk to him, I stroke the coils of circuitry around
his head, stroke the bulge on his side that covers the lance. He will
not be consoled by my words and my touching. He is beginning to
upset the others. I cannot allow that. We shall have to wait until

Peeg is ready before we go on. I signal for Papavator to unfold the arm with the needleful of dreams on it. Great dreams there are in the needle. Perhaps the flying dream, that is the one Peeg loves best: that he is back in heaven, flying, laughing and crying and pissing himself with happiness as the angels look down upon him and smile at their Peeg. He lifts his trunk to touch the needle. Dream good, Peeg.

Papavator settles on his metal legs, opens his belly. Time to feed. Porcospino and I suck greedily from the titties. Ceefer flares her nostrils in displeasure. She prefers the taste of gut and bone and blood. Tonight, she will hunt by the light of the moon and the shine of her eyes. She will kill. She will swallow down blood and bones and guts and all. Disgusting creature. Not a being at all.

Ceefer. Peeg. Porcospino. Papavator. Me, Coon-ass. One more in our team to make it the full one-hand's-worth-and-one. Here she comes now, down the beams of light that slant into the shadows among the trees of the river's edge: she does not need dreams to fly in. Only Peeg and I have the gift of colour-seeing, and Peeg is rolling and grunting in his needle-dream. The others cannot see as I do how the colours flow from blue to green across her wings and back, the cap of brilliant red, the beak and feet of brightest yellow. This, I think, is the word called *beautiful*. She settles on Papavator's out-stretched arm. No pulp, no pap for her. She feeds on pellets from the hand of Papavator himself. But for all her colours, she has only one word. That is the trade the angels made: one word, two syllables that she sings over and over and over. Bir-dee. Bir-dee. Bir-dee.

Ceefer Cat looks up from her eternal cleaning, cleaning, cleaning, sudden, sniffing. In the backs of her eyes are the red moving shapes that are her gift from the angels. She stiffens, bares her teeth, just a little. That is enough. One of the things that goes with having hands and colours, and much, much words, is more fear than others: the fear that looks at what might be and shivers. *Anxiety*, that is the name for it.

Danger. Bir-dee leaps up into the air again, darting and many-coloured, brilliant, dashing through the air, and then I can see her no longer through the canopy of tree-tops. But I do not fear that she will fly away out of all seeing and never come back, she is keyed to my scent, she will always come back to me, however far she flies.

Ceefer is waiting in the shadows beneath the trees, Porcospino is ruffling and rattling his quills, Papavator has closed himself up and is lurching onto his silly thin legs. But Peeg sleeps on. He grumbles and mumbles and drools in his dream. It must be a very good dream that Papavator has in his needle. Peeg, Peeg, danger coming, danger coming! Awake! Awake! The others have reached the dark of the deep forest, they are looking back: why do we not come?

I do not have the senses of Ceefer, but I can feel the thing she feels: huge and heavy, moving through the forest on the other side of the river.

There are secrets that Mamavator gave only to me, to be shared with none other; secrets whispered to me in the warmth of the womb, in the dream-forest that is so like, and so unlike, this hard-forest. The middle finger of my left hand is one of the secrets told to none but I. It is made from the same almost-living stuff as the implants that trail almost to the ground from the sockets behind my ears, from the skulls of all my team.

Quick. Quick. Out comes the implant in the back of Peeg's head.
Quick. Quick. In goes the middle finger of my left hand.

Up, I think. *Up.* Peeg twitches in his sleep, a great heaving twitch. *Up.* He staggers to his feet. *Forward*, I think and the thought pours out of my finger into his head and as he moves forward, still dreaming his needle-dream, I hop up on his back, ride him with my finger. *Move. Move. Run. Run. Fear.* He wails in his dreams, breaks into a trot, a canter. I lash him into a gallop. We fly over the dark, dark earth. Porcospino and Ceefer run at my side, Papavator covers the ground with his long, clicking strides. The trees rise up all around us, taller and darker and huger than any dreaming of them. *Run, Peeg, run.* The dream of the needle is beginning to wear thin, the hard world is pouring in through the tears and cracks in the dream, but I do not release him from my mind. From far behind comes a tremendous crashing, as if the dark, huge trees are being torn up and thrown into heaven; and the sound of mighty explosions. We run until all running is run out of us. Full of fear, we stop, listening, waiting. Presently, there is the smell of burning. The red shapes in the backs of Ceefer's eyes flicker and shift: she is scanning. She sits to clean herself.

'Whatever it is, is gone now,' is all she will say. She licks her crotch.

We sit, we pant, we wait. The rain begins, dripping in fat drops from the forest canopy. Soon the smell of burning is gone. As I sit with the rain running down my fur, Bir-dee comes to me, perches on my hand, singing her glad two-note song. I stroke her neck, ruffle her feathers, smooth down her glossy blue wings. Only when the others are asleep with the rain from high high above falling heavily upon them, do I extract the reconnaissance chip from her head and plug it into the socket beside my right eye.

Flight. Soaring. Trees and clouds and sun, the bright shine and coil of a river, the curved edge of the world: all crazy, all turned on end. Then, something huge as the moon, huger even than Mamavator when we saw her for the first time, steaming in the forest clearing where we were born: something earthbound and stamping, stamping out of the forest, into the river, standing with the water flowing around its feet while it fires and fires and fires, explosion after explosion after explosion tearing apart the trees and rocks of the river bank where we rested. Before it stamps away down the river it sets the smashed trees alight with flames from its chest.

I blank the chip with a thought, extrude it, give it back to Bir-dee. To have hands, and colour, and much, much words, to *know*; this is the worst punishment of the angels.

> *The Bravest Animals in the Land,*
> *Are Captain Beaky and his band,*
> 'Captain Beaky'

Who made you?
    The angels made me from a seed.
    The angels planted a seed in the womb of Mamavator and nurtured it, and grew it. Flesh of the flesh of Mamavator. She suckled and fed us.
    What are you?
    The servants of the angels, the agents of their work upon this world.

Two natures of service, two natures of servant have the angels: the soft and the hard, those of the inorganic and those of the organic. The service of the inorganic is not greater than the service of the organic, the service of the soft is not greater than the service of the hard; both were created in the likeness of the angels to complement each other in their weakness.

Recite the weaknesses of the organic.

Pain. Hunger. Tiredness. Sleep. Emotion. Defecation. Death.

Recite the weaknesses of the inorganic.

Noise. Expense. Energy. Breakdown. Vulnerability. Stupidity.

Why have the angels, themselves perfect, created such imperfection?

Because the angels alone are perfect.

Because no created things, no thing of the hands, may assume to the perfection of the angels, that is the great sin. What is the name of the greatest sin?

Pride.

How may we purge ourselves of the sin of pride?

By the faithful service of the angels. By the humble obedience of their will. By the execution of their assignments.

To the letter.

To the letter.

I have always wondered what that final part of the Litany means. *To the letter.* I think that it has something to do with the dark marks on Papavator's skin; those regular, orderly marks; and they have something to do with *words*, but the understanding of it is not a gift the angels have chosen to give this Coon-ass. Perhaps they are the prayers of the inorganic: Papavator himself takes no part in our nightly recitation; his own hard, inorganic devotions he makes well apart from us; long, thin legs folded up under him, arms and antennae drawn in. It is not sleep, the inorganic do not sleep, not as we sleep. Strange, the lives of the inorganics. How marvellous, the will of the angels, that has made us so different, so weak in ourselves, yet so strong together to their service.

Every night, when Ceefer has sniffed out a place free from traps and poisons for us, we gather in a circle in the forest for the Litany. I lead, they respond as best they can. Bir-dee has only two words, yet no matter how far she is flying, however high, she always returns to sit with the others, shifting from foot to foot because she is not made to stand on the ground, cocking her head from side to side as if the wonder of the words is being communicated to her by some spiritual channel I do not understand. And Peeg loves the Litany, would have me say the words over and over and over because though I know that he does not understand what he is saying – they are just sounds he was born with in his skull – inside the words he can see the angels reaching down to lift him up into heaven and set him flying among the stars.

I have said that Papavator does not take part in our worship. There is another, sad to say. Ceefer says that she does not believe. There are no angels, there is no heaven, she says. They are comfortable words we have invented because we know that we all must die and the knowing frightens us. She thinks that is brave. I think it foolish. It is certain that we must die, and that is frightening, but would she say it is wrong to comfort ourselves with dreams, like the dreams Papavator keeps in his needle? I have tried to steer her right but she will not believe. She is a stubborn animal. Our arguing upsets Peeg; he has a great faith but the light shines through it, like sun through the leaf canopy, easily stirred by the wind. I would order Ceefer to believe, but she would laugh that dreadful cat-laugh at me; so every night when we recite she sits and cleans herself, licking licking licking. That licking, it is as bad as any laughter.

At the end, after Porcospino has scraped a hole in the leaf-litter and one after the other we shit into it, Peeg asks for a Bible story.

'What story would you like to hear?' I ask.

'Angels. War,' says Peeg. 'Lights. Flying.'

Ceefer growls. She stalks away. She thinks it is a stupid story. She thinks all the Bible stories she was taught by Mamavator are stupid. I must admit there is much in them that does not make sense to me, but Peeg would have them told over and over and over again, every night if he could. He rolls onto his side, his safe side, closes his eyes. The tip of the lance slides out of the fold of skin on his side, like a metal penis. He seems to have forgotten all about the river. He does not have the circuits for long memory. Fortunate Peeg.

'In the days of days,' I say, 'there were only angels and animals. The animals looked like us, and smelled like us, but they were only animals, not *beings*. They were called animals by the angels because all they possessed was an *anima*, a living-ness, but no words or spirit. The angels and the animals had existed together in the world for always so that no one could remember which had made the other, or whether they had both been made by something different altogether.

'In those days of days, as in these days of days, animals served angels, but the angels, being as they were mighty creatures, with moods and feelings that are not to be judged by *beings*, grew tired of the animals and their limitations and created new servants to be better than the animals. They created servants stronger than you, Peeg,' he hears my voice in his near-sleep, the high-pressure lance slides out to almost its full length, 'that could see better and farther than you, Ceefer,' though she is out, patrolling in the darkness, it is part of the story, 'that could fly higher and carry more than you, Bir-dee, that were smarter and could remember better and think faster than me, an old raccoon; and that could kill better and more than you, Porcospino.

'So excellent were the new servants that the angels were able to fly up into heaven itself, where they have been flying ever since with their hands held out at their sides.

'Now I have said that the wisdom of the angels is greater than the wisdom of beings, and if the angels turn to war among themselves, as they did not once but many times in the days of days, what are we to question them? But there was war, a great and terrible war, fought by the terrible servants they had made for themselves; servants that could knock flat whole forests, that could set fire to the sky and turn the sea to piss. A war so terrible that it was fought not just upon the hard world, but in heaven also. So mighty a war that the angels in the end called upon their old servants, the animals, to aid them, and from those wordless, spiritless creatures created, by the shaping of their hands, *beings* like us.

'Though lowly and lesser and stained by the sin of our failure to serve the angels as they wished to be served, we were permitted to redeem ourselves by aiding the angels in their war. Thus we were given wonderful weapons, mighty enough to destroy the works of angels, both organic and inorganic; mighty enough,' and here I always draw my words into a hushed whisper, '*to destroy the angels themselves.*'

As they gaze into my words and in them see the angels smiling and holding out their hands to them, I go to them in turn, as I have every night since we came into the hard world, and touch the third finger of my left hand to the sockets between their eyes, the finger that sends them down down into holy sleep.

Unseen, unheard, black as the night herself, Ceefer returns from her patrol as I end my story.

'Stupid,' she says. 'What kind of a god is it that can be killed by beings?'

'I do not know,' I say. 'That is what faith is for. So we can believe what we cannot know.'

'I hope it is a big faith you have,' says Ceefer, extending her hard inorganic claws to lick off the forest dirt, carefully, carefully. 'Big enough for another to sit on the back of it. I will have need of your faith tomorrow.'

'What do you mean?' I ask.

She blinks her round round eyes at heaven, flares her nostrils. Sensing.

'It will be a hard day, tomorrow,' she says, and, refusing any further words with me, stalks away to find a comfortable nest among the root buttresses of the great great trees.

> 'Bonedigger, bonedigger, dogs in the moonlight . . .'
> Paul Simon, 'Call me Al.'

I have these pictures in my head. I suppose they must be the vision of angels, for I can see the forest spread out below me, from sea to shining sea, all its hills and valleys and rivers and lakes laid out before me. But it is more than just as if seeing from on high; it is as if I can see through the canopy of the trees, see through the trees themselves. I can see with a detail surely not possible from so great a height: I can see the place where Mamavator left us before returning to the sky in lights and fire; that is a ball of blueness. I can see us, the Team, five yellow dots with a sixth moving some way ahead of us. And I see the place where we are to go. Our Destination. The shape of that is a black, pulsing star.

The six yellow points are now closer to the black pulsing star than they are to the blue ball.

Every time Bir-dee returns with her pictures for me, my heavenly sight becomes clearer. I see now the war machine that destroyed the river bank, where Peeg dreamed, as a red triangle moving off to our left, along the river we crossed. It has lost interest in us. Between us and the black star is an area of open ground. When I look at it in my head, the words 'lumpy ground' come to me. It is little more than a morning's walk for us to the lumpy ground.

On the lumpy ground we will decide what we are to do when we reach the Destination. So our orders go.

Between the lumpy ground and the black star the picture looks as if ten, twenty, many many red stars have fallen out of heaven onto the earth.

The outer defences.

Ceefer leads us through the dark beneath the great trees toward the Destination, sensing for any traps and nets and snares that might await us. Now it is we who must ride on her back. We must have faith that she can see and hear and smell what we cannot, we must trust her to see what cannot be known for to know, to see, to taste and touch, would be to die. I have learned a new word today. Ceefer's words of the night before have made it come bubbling up out of my head like deep deep water. *Foreboding*. Such a duty, the angels have laid upon us. But would they have given us a task they knew we could not perform?

Ceefer's screech sends my angel-pictures whirling away in many many torn pieces. The wail dies slowly into a growl: Ceefer crouches, eyes wide, whiskers and ears folded flat, staring at the thing she has found in the dark under-forest.

It has been dead a long long time. The smell of it has been dissolved away into the smell of forest: guts and eyes pecked out by pecking pecking birds and insects, skin pulled away from teeth bared in the final snap at death. Pelt a dried tatter of fur and leather. The metal spike of the spring trap is driven out through the back of its neck. Some kind of possum, or small, biting marsupial; I cannot tell, it is so old and dead.

There are bright metal sockets beneath its ears, and torn strands of circuitry. Nestled among its bare ribs are long, thin, steel some-things.

Cat-cool recovered, Ceefer brushes past, moves on. Porcospino pauses to sniff at the dried corpse, Papavator steps past on his metal legs. He is a machine, he does not have the weakness of feeling. But Peeg is terrified. Peeg will not go past it. Peeg cowers away from it, it is a bad sign, he says, *bad sign, bad sign, bad sign.*

'It cannot harm you,' I say. 'Its duty is done. Its soul flies in heaven with the angels. You too have a duty, given you by the angels, that you must do.'

I do not want to have to use the circuits in my finger again. Wide-eyed with terror, Peeg approaches. Any moment he will break and run, I think. I have circuits in my hand for that possibility, too. Keeping as far as he can from the dead impaled thing, Peeg edges past. Ceefer waits, head turned, eyes shining red, tail lashing impatiently.

But Peeg is right. It is a bad sign.

We enter a clearing. Ceefer is suspicious, looking to the sky, sniffing all around her. Nothing registers on her sensors but she is not happy. If Ceefer is not happy, I am not happy. Porcospino, too, is uncomfortable; blinking his tiny eyes in the light. He is a creature of the forests, of the darkness of the forests; he is naked in open terrain. Naked sky frightens him. Peeg looks across the clearing to the great great trees.

'Look at the trees, Coon-ass,' he says, pointing with his trunk. 'Dead dead trees, with leaves on them.'

I look where he is pointing. And I am afraid. For the great trees are dead, bare, blasted wood, killed by black air and war, but the branches are hung with black leaves.

'Quick, quick!' I cry. 'This is a trap!'

And the leaves rise from the branches of the dead trees and we understand. They are not leaves at all. They are bats, rising up in a cloud of beating, roaring wings so dark they shut out the sun.

Those red dots in my inner vision, as many as the stars in heaven . . .

'Quick! Quick!' I try to watch the sky as we run across the clearing beneath the wheeling, chittering mass of bats. They swoop down upon us: I can see the shine of circuitry in their fur. I can see the shine of weapons clutched between their feet.

'Quick! Quick!'

The ground rises up in front of me in a burst of noise and earth: the explosion sends me reeling backward. I plunge onward, blindly, guided by older, baser, truer instincts. The bats release their bombs and flap away. Explosions to the right of me, explosions to the left of me, explosions before me, explosions behind me. We run on; the sky is gone. There are only bats, wheeling, croaking, screaming. The edge of the forest is close, the cover of the trees. So many bats could not safely fly there. Not day-bats, as these are. I look back, see Papavator lurching unsteadily across the clearing. Then the bright bombs fall, there is an explosion, flying metal and machine juices. Arms and legs wave, flail, fall dead.

When I am sure I can no longer hear the beating of wings or the sound of bat-voices, I call a halt. We have lost more with Papavator than needle-dreams, I say. Without his picking and purging and preparing digested pap for us to suck from his titties, we must take the time to forage and find our own food. This is a dangerous thing for us to do: we cannot be certain that food we find is not enemy food, or tainted with the black air poisons that Papavator's stomach removed, and there are always the traps and snares and nets.

'Hungry now,' says Peeg. 'Hungry *now*.'

'We all must feed ourselves,' I say. 'There is no more Papavator.'

For me to grub and dig for food is a fearful, animal thing; the fat maggots and wild honey I dig with my hands, my fine, clever hands, from the hollow of a dead tree and share with Peeg and Porcospino are crude and disgusting compared to the milk of Papavator. For Ceefer to hunt, to bring some small forest thing back dripping in her jaws, is a joy. Her sensor eyes glow red as she tears the small thing she has killed with her steel claws. She offers me a piece of hairy flesh gently grasped in her teeth.

'You are a raccoon,' she says, setting it down before me in the way of a wicked joke. 'You are an omnivore. You can eat anything.' I would sooner eat my own shit. Clever clever Ceefer with your smart, clever words, and your smart eyes that can see things no one else can, and your sharp little claws, and your confident belief in disbelief.

We come to the lumpy ground as the day is growing old. It is a strange terrain indeed: full of hummocks and mounds and hollows and dark pits. As if something huge and unshapely had died long ago and let the forest grow over it. Scattered across the open space are strange spires and pillars of heaped earth. There is a smell to this place I cannot identify but which stirs the hairs along my spine; a smell, and a sound, a deep, deep humming, everywhere and nowhere.

There is a dark shape moving among the shadows and hollows: a creature. A peccary, rooting. I order Porcospino forward. He raises his quills, growls in his throat.

'Tell him to put his spines down,' says Ceefer. 'It is not a being. It is just an animal. Come, Peeg, with your lance. That is our evening meal, out there.' Off she goes, a black shadow flowing across the lumpy ground. Poor, silly Peeg trots after her. The peccary looks up, bolts for the forest edge. The vague troubling noise has become a definite sound, a buzzing, a droning.

Streams of black vapour pour from the strange earth pillars.

'Ceefer! Peeg! Come back at once!' I say. They need no warning from me, they are already flying back across the lumpy ground. The dark vapour forms a cloud around the peccary. The frantic animal tries to flee but the swarm follows it. The peccary twists, turns, plunges, and falls. And I understand. It is not black air, as I had feared. It is much worse. It is insects. Flying, stinging insects. Millions upon millions of insects. They swarm up from the dead peccary, a dark, droning tower looming above the lumpy ground, leaning over us.

What is this Coon-ass to do if he is to obey the will of the angels? I stare, mesmerised, at the whirlwind of insects, moving slowly across the open ground towards me. We cannot fight. We cannot run. We cannot escape. Then I hear Porcospino's voice.

'In. Now.'

Has the fear overloaded his circuitry? What is he talking about? He is scratching at a dark hole at the foot of an oddly shaped green mound.

'Others already in. You. Now.'

'Bir-dee,' I say. 'What about Bir-dee?'

'If she is out there, already too late,' says Porcospino. 'In. In.'

I scuttle into the hole as the storm of insects breaks. Porcospino works with his strong feet, kicking at the dirt to seal up the tunnel. A few insects have crawled inside, I strike at them with my hands and feet, crush them into the earth.

'Come. Come. Fast. Fast,' says Porcospino as he leads me down, down, downward. To me, a being of the light, with hands and much much words, this is a foreboding of death; dark, pressing close all around, fear, down down downward into the gnawing earth. To Porcospino this is his place of places, underground, grubbing, sniffing.

When I was a seed in the womb of Mamavator, adrift in highest heaven, I had a dream in which I was shown the shape of the world. In this dream the world was a bubble of light and air and life surrounded by earth and soil and stone that went on and on and on beyond all counting, for always. In the dream, a voice told me that somewhere lost in this never-endingness of earth and soil were other worlds like our own, of light and air and life.

Of course, it is the foolish imagining of a raccoon, but when I find myself in light and air and space after so long in the dark I think that we have dug our way through the bottom of the world and emerged in some other earth.

It is a very small world, this bubble of air and light, barely big enough for Ceefer and Peeg and Porcospino and Coon-ass. The air is stale, dead, and tastes of old, used-up poison. The light is strange, dim, blue, coming not from one sun, but from flat squares above us. It is a square world altogether, this world, square-sided, everything sharp-edged. It has the smell of a work of angels.

Peeg is looking as if he is going to cry with confusion.

'I think this must be an old defensive position,' I say. I hope that he will trust my words and knowledge. 'It must come from the very very early time of the war, so long ago the forest grew over it and forgot it. Look: see?' I point at more flat, square things fixed to the sides of the world. They are covered in tiny red and yellow lights, like the shapes in the pictures in my head. 'Machine servants. This is a place made by angels.'

'More than machine servants,' says Ceefer. 'Come. See.'

She leads us through an opening, along a tunnel into another blue-lit square-cut chamber. There are more inorganics on the walls with their red and yellow stars. On the floor are the bodies of organics.

The dead possum-thing we encountered on the forest path was frightening because it still retained a memory of life. These things are so long dead that they are not even memories. Beyond fearing, they are merely curious.

'What beings these?' asks Porcospino. I cannot answer, I have never seen creatures like these before. Very tall they are, very thin. Long long legs, very big and fine hands at the ends of their forelegs. Fur only on the tops of their heads. Double-skinned: that is the only way I can describe them. Over the middle of their bodies and their legs they wear a second skin, very soft and fine, though ill-fitting. When I touch it falls into dust.

'I will tell you what manner of beings are these,' says Ceefer. 'They are angels. That is what they are. Dead angels.'

Peeg whimpers.

'No,' I say. 'That cannot be. The angels are all in heaven.'

'The stories say that the angels fought upon earth and heaven,' says Ceefer. 'And this is a very old place. And the stories say that the angels can die. Can be destroyed by *beings*.'

'No,' I say, though fears and doubts rise up around me like stinging insects. 'No. No. They are monkeys. That is what they are. See the skull, the jaw? Monkeys, created and shaped to the will of the angels, but no more than monkeys.'

Ceefer sniffs at the body, delicately bares her teeth and picks up a bone. She coughs, spits it out.

'Piss and dust, that is how angel-meat tastes,' she says.

> *'Sit Ubu, sit. Good dog'*
> American TV sit-com production company
> sound-byte.

Peeg will destroy.
  How?

Peeg will know.

How will Peeg know?

You will give Peeg the knowledge.

Knowledge that I do not myself know?

Strange indeed, and wonderful, are the ways of the angels.

Peeg slept a black sleep last night, down in the square chamber among the strange bodies. There was no Papavator with his needleful of dreams to send him flying through the night. I listened to him crying and whimpering, under the blue square lights. The world is too much for him.

Ceefer's eyes, that see in any darkness, lead us through many chambers under the earth full of the strange dead beings before finding a scratchway up into the real world again. It is little more than a scrape; bulging with weapons, Peeg can barely fit through. For one moment we think he has jammed good. He screams and screams and screams in terror as Porcospino digs around him to widen the tunnel. I can understand the fear of the earth closing in all around, I have been learning much about fear.

We emerge into the morning. The sun is high above us. The ground is covered in dead insects, like black dust. They are too dangerous for their angels to allow them to live long. From the lumpy ground we pass into forest again. We scavenge. We scratch. We shit.

From the forest we pass into the smouldering land.

The line between the two is as sharp as the edge of a claw. From the cover of the root buttresses, we survey a land burned clean of life: trees, creepers, ferns, fungi, every living thing, every creature, swept away, stripped down to the sick, shit-coloured earth. A dusting of white ash covers the earth, the smell of burning is strong; here, there, the charred stump of a tree has resisted the burning.

There is a shadow on the land. A giant shadow. Before us, above us, on the edge of the burnt land that smoulders further than my eyes can see, stands the hulk of a huge war machine. Some terrible weapon has blown away the upper half of its body, the ground is littered with its torn metal flesh. The wind from across the ashlands moans over the jagged, ripped shell.

'The outer defences,' I say, quietly. Porcospino rattles his quills,

Peeg whimpers in dread. Ceefer hisses. No one need ask, *What could have done this?* There are forces here that can shatter even Mamavator: that is why we were set down on earth so far from the Destination, to trek through dread and danger and death. Yet we beings, in all our sinful imperfection, may slip through to work the will of the angels where the mighty machines fail.

We pass between the feet of the destroyed war machine. The wind-blown ash stings my eyes. In the picture in my head, the Destination has grown huge, throbbing like a black heart, filling all my inner vision with its beating, throbbing. The ground is warm beneath my hands and feet. Ceefer quests ahead of us, sniffing a path through the soft white ash.

One scream. One warning. That is all we get. That is all Ceefer is allowed before the dogs, bursting up from under the ground, are upon her. Black hurtling dogs, many many many of them; in an instant she is snatched up, tossed into the air. I see her little steel claws flex, her teeth bare in rage, then the waiting jaws catch her, shake her, tear her in two, shake out her guts and blood and bones and scatter her across the burning earth.

Peeg squeals, lowers his stupid head. The tip of the metal lance slides from its housing on his side.

'No, Peeg, no. Let Porcospino!' I say.

The dogs hurl themselves upon us. Porcospino hisses, raises his spines. He flicks loose a flight of quills. The lead dogs go down, kicking their paws and writhing and twisting until their backs snap from the pain of the poisons the angels have put on Porcospino's quills. The second wave of dogs comes bounding on, over the bodies of their brothers. They have red eyes and silver metal jaws. Implants stud the backs of their necks. Again Porcospino throws his neuro-toxic spines and they go down on the right and on the left. A black dog leaps: I see his metal jaws open in my face, smell the stinking steam of his breath. Porcospino raises his tail but Peeg catches the dog in the belly with his high-pressure lance. Intestines bursting from its open mouth, blood spraying from its eyes, it goes spinning away to fall among the bodies of its litter mates.

And the third wave is on us. They have ferocity, but no conception of strategy. All they know is to run, and to leap, and to savage.

Squealing with excitement, Peeg thrusts with his lance, again, and again, and again: the black evil dogs go down, shattered, smashed, impaled and spasming, stuck full of Porcospino's needles.

Then there are no more for they all lie dead on the soft white ash beneath the war machine. All the dead dogs. And the sun is low on the edge of the world, red and huge behind the thin smoke that rises from the smouldering land.

'Come,' I order.

'Ceefer . . .' says Peeg. Soon it will hit him, and I have no dreams to stop him crying.

'She is gone. The angels hold her in their hands. Believe me.'

But I am no longer sure I believe what I am telling them they must believe. Where do the faithless go? Is there a lonely place, dark and sad, for those who deny the angels? Or is death death? Nothing? *Nothing?* As we pick our slow and careful way through the ashlands under the rising moon, I find myself drawn to this thought, over and over and over. *Nothing.* It is a terrible thought. I cannot imagine it. Yet over and over and over, I am drawn to it.

Peeg snuffles out a hollow between the burned roots of a tree stump, digs a small scrape where we lie together.

'Hungry,' says Peeg.

'We are all hungry,' I say. 'There is nothing here for us. We will have to be hungry a little longer.'

I lie in the scrape. The moon stands over me. A little lower than the moon, strange lights cross the sky, moving fast, fast, from horizon to horizon in a breath. I cannot sleep. I dare not sleep. If I sleep, I will see Ceefer broken apart and all her words and knowledge and strange unbelief that, in truth, was a kind of belief, spilled out and lost.

In the night, Peeg wakes.

'Coon-ass.'

'Yes.'

'Give me.'

'Give you what?'

'Give me knowledge.'

'I do not know how. I do not know what this knowledge is.'

'Peeg know. Mamavator give Peeg words. Mamavator say, "Say Coon-ass: *Load File B13 echelon 7*."'

And it is as if those words, that Peeg could not possibly know unless he had, indeed, been given them by Mamavator, gather all my *beingness* and roll it up like clay in a hand, push it away away to the very back of my head so that I may watch but I am helpless to act as I feel my hands reach round to the back of my neck and pull out an implant. And I see those hands that look like my hands reach out and slide the implant into an empty socket beneath Peeg's ear. And the ears that hear like my ears hear Peeg sigh, and gasp, and say, in a voice I have never heard Peeg speak in before, 'Reset normal sentience simulation parameters.'

I shake my head, try to shake my *Coon-assness* back into every corner of my being. I am frightened: clever, proud, wise Coon-ass, mastered and ridden like a . . . like an *animal*. I lie and watch the lights crossing the sky, feeling small, small, smaller than the smallest thing I can imagine. *Nothing*.

The black, beating star beat-beats all night, so huge and close it has spilled out of the place in my head where the pictures are to fill everything with its beating.

> *All together now, all together now, all together now,*
> *In No Man's Land.*
> The Farm

In the morning my eyes and hands are raw sore with the white ash that covers the burned lands. We are all very hungry but we know among ourselves it is better not to speak about such things. Peeg offers to let me ride on his back. I am glad to accept. With Porco-spino trotting beside us, we enter the inner defences. The borderline is clearly marked. A metal arm jutting from the ash bars our path. Clenched in its steel grip is a rodent-like being, furious even in death. The steel fingers crush the rodent's neck, the rodent's teeth are sunk into the arm's brightly coloured wiring. Both are long, long dead.

It is both warning and welcome.

Much occupied with our own thoughts, whatever kind of thoughts the angels have given us to think, we pass into a landscape of terrible, terrible destruction. As far as we can see, the ash is littered with bodies of beings organic and inorganic, locked together in embraces that seem to this Coon-ass almost tender. Paws clawing for the light; mouths open to snap bright teeth one last time at the sun. Torn and twisted metal; gnawbones, jawbones. Hanks of hair and wind-dried hide. Dead birds, pulled out of the sky, sky-wise wings splayed out, feathers rustling in the wind, beaks and eyeless eyesockets silted up with drifting ash. Standing guard over them, half-clogged to the waist in ash and mud, the machines; shattered, crushed, twisted apart by ancient explosions, smashed metal limbs swinging, creaking, red sensor eyes dull dead dark.

A cat hanging from a wire noose.

A bird shot through with a metal spike.

Three bloated dogs floating in a crater full of rainwater.

Porcospino lets out a cry. It is the first sound to break the silence of the ashlands. He has seen the body of a brother porcupine, lying close by in a hollow in the ash, surrounded by the skin-draped skeletons of dogs.

'Leave it, leave it,' I say. 'You can do nothing here. It is dead, it has been dead for time beyond counting.'

But Porcospino will not listen; it is as if this rattle of dead, dry quills and spines is a comrade to him, a comfort in the dreadfulness all around him. A lost litter mate he never had. He nuzzles the dead thing, pushes it with his nose, as if he might push life back into it, push it into movement and joy. He pulls at its pelt with his teeth; clumps of implants come away in his teeth.

'Leave it leave it leave it!' I say. 'There is too much danger here!'

The ash hears me. The ash stirs. The ash moves. The ash opens. Like a flower blooming, the machine unfolds from beneath the earth. Its head quests: back, forth, back, forth. Red machine eyes open, staring.

'Run run run!' I say, but the weaving head on the long flexing neck has fascinated Porcospino, like the snake I once saw in my Mamavator dreams, that could dazzle you with its dancing, weaving, flexing. The huge red sensor eyes fasten on Porcospino. He gazes up into the huge red eyes.

The machine spews out a sheet of fire. Porcospino goes up in a shriek of burning. He tries to beat at the flames with his tiny useless hands, rolls onto his back to roll them out. The fire roars up and eats him.

The head on its long neck wavers, collapses into the ash. Its red sensor eyes go black. Its work is done. I curl my fingers into the circuitry on Peeg's neck, urge him onward.

'To the Destination,' I say. 'The Destination.'

A thin trail of smoke goes up behind us; the wind changes direction and bends it low over us as we pick our way across the battlefield. As Peeg carries me along, he tells me about what the chip has told him about the Destination he is to destroy. It is a *strategic manufacturing installation*, he says. His words are large and strange, not Peeg words. It builds machines and grows beings, this *strategic manufacturing installation*.

Like Mamavator? I ask.

Like Mamavator, says Peeg, but this one does not fly in heaven. This one is buried deep under the ground. Deep deep, way down deep. It is very old. Very very old. The angels have been trying to destroy it for long long years. Attack after attack after attack they have sent, from heaven first, and then by machine, and then by beings. Attack after attack after attack. After so many attacks, it must be tired now, old. It cannot have much energy left. That is how we will be able to reach the Destination.

How will we know when we reach the Destination? I ask.

We will know, says Peeg. That is what the chip tells me.

And then you will destroy it?

And then Peeg will destroy it.

How?

Peeg does not know. But Peeg trusts that the angels, in their great wisdom, having told him much already, will tell him that also when he needs to know.

Angels, in their great wisdom. Peeg would have cried, once. Peeg would have cried for Porcospino. Peeg would have cried for each one of those many many beings, more than many many hands can count, that died so that Peeg and Coon-ass can reach their Destination. What did the angels take away to make room for their great wisdom?

We will know, the angel voices in the chip said. Why must they be so very very true in everything they say? We will know, I will know, I have known, since I stumbled, blinking from the warm wet womb into the forest morning. The Destination is the great black star in the picture in my head taken out and pressed into the earth; real, actual. Huge. The black star is bigger than I can cover with both hands spread out in front of my eyes. Many many hours walk across. Heat shimmers and dances over the star: I cannot see its further edge. Now that the shock is passing, I see that it is not the same as that other star, my inner star. It is not as sharp-edged, as definite; it has many many rays, the shiny black of it is streaked and stained with colours, its surface is crazed and cracked, like something that has fallen from heaven to earth.

Fallen, or cast down? We stand at the edge of the great black star, a raccoon riding on the back of a tapir.

'You must get down now,' says Peeg. 'I am to go on on my own.'

'Where?' I touch the blackness with my hand; it is smooth, slippery, warm to the touch.

Peeg points with his trunk out across the black.

'I hear voices,' he says in that voice, with those words, that are not his own. 'Voices, coming from big bright lights. Wonderful wonderful lights.'

'Peeg, you cannot go, I must go too, you need me.'

'On my own,' Peeg says, looking far into the heat haze. 'I will destroy it on my own. Then I will come back to you.'

'You will come back to me?'

'Yes.'

'Do you promise?'

'I do not understand what that means.'

'It means that when you say that you will come back, you will come back, that nothing will stop you coming back.'

'Yes.'

'Then I will do as you say.'

'It is the will of the angels,' says Peeg, and walks out on his little, neat feet, out across the black glass star, until the heat-haze swallows him and I can see him no more. I sit. I wait. The sun moves across the sky, I watch it reflected in the blackness before me. In the reflection I can see where the wars of the angels have left their marks even there. The face of the sun is scarred with dark pock-marks. Craters. Black starbursts. The heat-haze runs over the black, melted land like water. In the shiver and the shimmer I am no longer certain what is true, what is false. For in the silver shining, I see a distant dark figure standing. Then the heat-haze flows and runs and I see clearly: it is Peeg out there in the black lands.

'Peeg!' I shout. 'Peeg!' But he cannot hear me. He is looking into the sky, questing up with his trunk, like one who has been given a vision of angels.

'Peeg,' I call again, and start to run to him, across the black glass star. 'You have come back!' I run and run and run; the soles of my feet and hands blister on the burning black glass, but however hard I run, however much I call, I never seem to come any closer. Peeg remains a tiny, wavering dark figure in the huge silver shimmer of the heat-haze.

'Peeg!' I call one final time.

And Peeg looks round.

And the sky turns white with a light so bright that it burns through my closed eyelids as if they were not there, burns through my hands that I clamp over my eyes, a burning burning light as if the sun has burst and died. Belly, hands, face are seared by the light, the fur shrivels and crisps away in an instant.

And after the light, is darkness.

And after the darkness is a thunder like the sound of heaven falling, so loud that it becomes more than sound, it becomes a voice, a cry of angels.

And after the thunder is a rushing mighty wind; a screaming, scorching wind that does not seem like a thing of air, but a thing of earth, a solid, material thing that strikes like a fist, strikes the breath from me, sends me hurling, tumbling backward in the tearing whirl of ash and dust and roaring air, away away away from Peeg's Destination, into the ashlands.

And after the rushing mighty wind is darkness again, beautiful darkness, and in the beautiful darkness: silence.

. . . and dance by the light of the moon.
thirtysomething: Production company sound-byte.

Am forgetting. Am losing. Words. Rememberings. Knowings. Feel with fingers, for darkness still in eyes; feel the chips, feel the implants; they feel not right, they feel melted, burned. The blast must have damaged my circuitry. Words come, words go, sentences, memories. Words from deep deep in the chips. Words that I once knew. Words that I have forgotten. Words I was meant to forget. Words I now remember, stirred up like silt in a river by the explosion. Words like *implanted nanotok warhead*. Words like *containment field generator*. Words like *mass/energy conversion*. I take the words in these clever hands of mine and understand. Everything. I understand what has been done to me, to Porcospino and Ceefer and Bir-dee, and every other creature trapped and impaled and dismembered and burned to nothing out there in the ashlands. Most of all, I understand what has been done to Peeg.

Enough intelligence to carry out the mission, but not to understand. Never to understand, merely to obey.

Blind, burning, I crossed the ashlands. Nothing harmed me, nothing knew of my existence. Dead. All dead now. In my blindness I pushed down down down into my memories, down into the deep deep river of remembering, down beyond our birth from the womb of Mamavator into this hard world, down past the dream-forest in which we ran and played and swam while we were yet seeds in the metal womb. And there I found words. Words like *programmed neural simulation*, and *pre-natal environmental conditioning*, like shadows in a heat-haze.

I came to the forest. The trees were tumbled and fallen, brought down by the blast. I felt my way over the trees, picked out fat grubs and beetles with my fingers, crunched them down with my small teeth. *Anima.* The spirit of livingness. When I felt coolness and shade on my pelt, and smelled dampness, and growing, I knew I had passed under the canopy of the living forest.

Grubbing. Sniffing. Feeling. When will seeing be again? When will hearing be again? When will this hissing, ringing be no more?

There. Do I hear? Look up in darkness, turning turning, under cool cool trees, *again*, do I hear, a whisper, a whistle, a call? Two notes. Two tones. Hi-lo. Hi-lo. Hi-lo. *Hush*, you whistling, chirping, rustling things, in my head or in the world, Coon-ass must listen. Hi-lo. Hi-lo. Hi-lo. Two words.

Blind, I hold up my hand into the warmth of a beam of sunlight. And light as light, she comes to rest on my fingers, singing her two-word name. Bir-dee. Bir-dee. Bir-dee.

Colours gone. Sweet flashing darting movement, up through leaves, branches, into heaven: gone.

'Bir-dee.' Name remains. 'Bir-dee.' She sings her two-note song. I feel her bobbing, impatient, on my finger. *Chip. Chip. Pull chip. See pictures. See pictures.*

No, Bir-dee, no. Gently gently, I bring her in front of my face, gently gently move close until my lips touch the back of her head. No fear. Trust. I press my lips to her blue blue feathers, then, one by one, pull the chips and implants from their sockets and drop them, one by one, to the ground. When they are all gone, I lift Bir-dee high, high as arm will reach, into the warmth of the sun.

'Go, Bir-dee, go. Be animal again. Be full of joy. Fly!' I cast her up into the light. Wings beat, I imagine bright darting colours rising up, rising up, above the forest, into light. I look up into the light: do I see shapes, movings, loomings, like motion of angels? I touch long, trailing coils of circuits and chips, trace them back to the metal sockets in my skull.

Then one by one, I pull them out and let them fall.

ATOMIC AVENUE

Tonight, my friend, tonight, we're going to rock down to Atomic Avenue. Tonight, my friend, tonight, when the charcoal smoke lies low in the dirt streets of Langie and the jingle-jangle hy-life guitars fly high above the corrugated iron roofs, like stars, my friend, like God's own saints and angels; this night, when Sister Suzi pulls down her blinds so no one will see her making fiki-fiki with Boss Mawenzi, and Black Betty kicks the jukebox to life in the Majestic Shebeen and the washed-in-the-blood voices shake the tin roof of the Full Gospel Evangelical Meeting House; we will go. Beni will bring his beatbox, his Langie briefcase, he bought new batteries today from the Coronation Cash Stores; Haran will have a crate of beer (Black Betty will never miss one crate, and anyway, who can she tell? It's only unlicensed *pombé*), Miguel will be with us, he'll have a knife in his pocket, you never know down on Atomic Avenue; Sonny-Adé too, this afternoon, I tell you, he went down to the Catalogue Sales and spent a week's wages on new Sub-Ones, red, yellow, and black, yes, just like the football stars on the sports channel. Tonight, my friend, tonight, we're going to wait at the stop on Bougainvillaea Highway for a *matatu*. We won't have to wait very long; there is never more than ten minutes between *matatus*, and when it comes playing tunes on its horns in a big cloud of black diesel smoke, the conductor will be hanging out of the back door banging on the side with his stick and calling out the names of all the stops: Langie! Woolmagong! Freetown! Mauritzburg! Rugare! Jacaranda Hills! Atomic Avenewwww! And we'll be swinging into our seats before the bus has even come to a halt and when the conductor asks for our fare we'll look at him over our shades and Miguel, he'll put his hand in his pocket, just so everyone will know he has a knife and I'll say, 'Hey, my man, ho my man, don't you know where we're going it's a free ride?' and all those straphangers going home to Freetown and Rugare and Jacaranda Hills, they'll make space, my friend, space, because they'll know that while they're at home sleeping away the hours with their women until another working day the Brothers of the Night will be rockin' down on Atomic Avenue; tonight tonight tonight. You coming?

Well, you better make your mind up pretty quick, yes, pretty quick, because, well now, I think I see Sonny-Adé walking out in his new Sub-Ones like he's the Captain of the Team, and, well, I think I see Beni swinging his Langie briefcase like he's a Captain of Finance, and, well well, if I don't spy Haran sneaking out the back of the Coronation Shebeen with a crate of Black Betty's *pombé*.

You got to decide what you are going to do tonight, my friend, tonight, are you going to stay home watch the soaps with Ma and Grandma and little Juancita, you going to maybe have a brew and a game of *fili* at the shebeen and a bowl of green-green from Aoki's stall and be in bed when the night has just begun for the rest of us? Or you going to take this generous, never-to-be-repeated offer and rock on down with us to Atomic Avenue? You better decide quick, my friend, quick, because I think I can hear the bus coming, I think I can hear the conductor banging his stick against the side, I think I can hear him shouting.

You know there is no decision to make, you know what you want to do, you know it is what you have always wanted to do since first Big Al (married now, these days the only rockin' down he does is with Big Susan Fileli) and then Ankéle (but he isn't rockin' anywhere, not in the Frenchtown Young Offenders Centre) put their Zeebocks on their feet and slid their shades up their noses. So you dash into the house, between Ma and Grandma and little Juancita and the soaps ('Hey, ho, what you in such an all-fired hurry for?') and into your room (until Ankéle comes back) to pull on your sleek black and gold Olympias lace feet into Zeebocks slide shades up nose, check general coolness in the piece of mirror taped to the back of the door and out past little Juancita Grandma Ma (but not quite quick enough to evade the inevitable conversation: – Where you going, boy? – Out. – Out where? – Just out.) and there they are squatting on their heels by the side of the cracked tarmac; Beni checking the battery levels on his beatbox, Haran with the crate of Black Betty's best, Miguel throwing his knife point down into the oily red dirt, Sonny-Adé careful not to get any dust on his new Ombras, your friend, about to say, 'Well, so you came . . .' but here's the *matatu* in a big cloud of diesel smoke with all its headlamps and spotlights and fairy-lights shining and there's the conductor, just as they said he would be, banging on that piece of dented, polished metal by the door with his *rungu* and shouting out the names of all the stops to Atomic Avenue.

As you swing onto the *matatu*, you glimpse it in the distance, hazy and indistinct in the township smog; the lights of the Towers, the hot, neon shimmer of Atomic Avenue.

So, what's it got, this Atomic Avenue? – What's it got, my friend? It's got cinemas. *Cinemas*. Not a bedsheet, a noisy Super-eight and a couple of beer crates behind the Langie Super-Hotel, *cinemas*, great streamlined flagships of the imagination, quartering the sky with searchlights, crewed by commissionaires decked more grandly than any admiral of the fleet ever was. It's got bars, bars like you've only dreamed of, all tube-chrome and ankle-hugging pile and pink-light; and the bartenders! Forget Black Betty uncapping bottles of Tusker and White Cap with her teeth; this is dancing, not bartending, see them jumping and jiving and jigging and juggling, see them unscrew their shakers and pour out cocktails like you never even thought of, more cocktails than there are saints in heaven or stars in the sky. It's got music. All night. Every night. Any kind you like, loud as you like. On one block you'll hear every kind of music there is to hear, you can bop till you drop and it'll drag you to your feet again. It's got clubs, you know, *clubs* with girls who'll shake it right in your face, like they're saying, – You want some? You can have some, you can get it . . . It's got restaurants. It's got shops. It's got arcades and malls and gallerias. It's got bathhouses whorehouses sushi houses; singles bars, saunas and speakeasies; it's got dancehalls discotheques and demolition dubs, it's got stripshows sideshows freakshows peepshows, casinos and gambling halls and one-armed bandit arcades; it's got sex shops barbershops tattoo parlours and record stores; the streets are paved with plastic cash, there's a river of liquor running down the middle and you only have to breathe deeply and you get high; it's light it's bright, it's brash, bad and beautiful, it's Atomic Avenue, my friend; and Bang! Bang! Bang! the conductor is banging his *rungu* on the bare metal by the door and shouting out – Atomic Avenue! On your feet, boy! Atomic Avenue!

So, there you are, standing there with your Zeebocks on the warm blacktop by the *matatu* stop and one friend is saying, – hey, say, let's go take a look at the video arcades and another is saying, – no, let's go check out the bars, and another is saying, – I want to go hear some music, some good DK Hy-life and another, he's saying, – no, I want to go to a club, you know? and he's making little fiki-fiki gestures with his fingers and they're all pulling you like the bird in the story who sat for a hundred years and then flew off in every direction at once, but your friend, he's saying, – Hey now, ho now, we have no worry, we have no scurry, we got all night. Nothing's going anywhere. This is my friend here's first time down on the Avenue; if he wants to have a good look, then let him have a good look.

You can always tell the country folk newly arrived at the Langie bus station; they're the ones sitting around under the shelters, waiting for their souls to catch up with them. Immersed in light and movement and music and voices and roaring engines and the smell of diesel and beer and patchouli and dirty cooking fat, the neon hot on your face like a long Sunday afternoon, it is as if part of you has been left hanging from a pole like a spirit-scarer in Mama N'Gee's shamba. You do not want to be here, it is too much, too much noise, too much movement, too much light. Light! It is as if you are drowning in light from the flickering constellations of the fairy lights strung in the dusty almond trees, from the flat planes of the street-floods, from the thousand and one creatures of the neon bestiary, the zodiac signs and the leaping buckaroos and the smiling geishas and the boosting rockets and the high-kicking legs and the spinning galaxies; from the shouting fluorescent voices of Salsa! Cuba Libre!

El Camino Real! Stardust! Mercury! Pilate's Palace!; from the advertisements for cola and beer and cameras and condoms and computers
and Sonys and records and fast foods; from the holographic ghosts
of Tokyo Joes and Diamond Lils and Cracklin' Rosies bending low
over Atomic Avenue. You lift your eyes up, to the sky, to the night
but all you see is storey upon storey upon storey of lights, tumbling
over each other in their struggle to scream louder! brighter! than
their rivals until they blur into the lights of the million windows and
elevators and glass terraces of the Towers, a great Babel of building
that draws your eyes up, up through blazing tier and level and terrace, through the winking aircraft beacons and the riding lights of
the kilometre-long airships docked to their spiderweb mooring arms
and the golden phoenixes and eagles and gods that crown their spires
to the place where the lights of the Towers become the stars of
God's heaven.

And there you see it, dark against the stars: your soul, hunting
you in the never-ending movement of the man swarm. You call to
it and it comes to you out of the night. You breathe it in with the
musk and the diesel, and you are one thing again, you have arrived
in your place and time. You say: – Yey! Let's go, we've got the whole
night! Haran the Brew uncaps a round with his teeth and Beni the
Beatbox defines you with a bubble of sound and your Zeebocks feel
mighty right, mighty tight tonight tonight tonight on the pavements
of Atomic Avenue. Your apprehensions are forgotten. You belong
here. You were made for the neon and lasershine, the bass and the
back-beat, you and your friends and all the other Brothers of the
night rockin' down along Atomic Avenue. You shoulder close
together and point into shop windows at the Hakudachi neural
interfacers and Sony-Nikon teleshades and Bayer-Mohne poly-
chrome irises. You prop yourselves against the oily side of a slum-
bering bus and swig Black Betty's *pombé* and laugh and punch each
other. You buy chick-pea fritters and a knob of charcoal-roasted
maize from a brazier on the street, you buy junk ear-rings and
T-shirts with pop-stars on the front and jackets with pop-stars on
the back from a street-corner stall. You do not go into the cinemas
or restaurants or follow the notes of two guitars into a dance factory.
None of the Brothers you meet and greet with open hands and hot

fives do. They cannot afford those pleasures. Those are pleasures of the rich.

The rich. You press face, hands against the bar window to see better these legendary creatures. You know them from the television: it never misses an opportunity to show you all the things their money can do.

They can fly. The cameras show you the terrifying chasms between the Towers filled with silver balloons and gliders and rocket-packs, each bearing a crazy, daring aeronaut.

They are beautiful. They have perfect bodies, perfect muscles, they have perfect teeth perfect hair perfect eyes perfect faces perfect complexions. Perfect is easy, beautiful is cheap. When they get tired of beautiful they can choose bizarre; bizarre is no more difficult than beautiful; grow an arm, a tail, a second head, become a beast, a demon, a dark angel. They can change sex like you would change the batteries in a beatbox.

When they tire of the Towers they go skiing in Antarctica. They go diving on the Great Barrier Reef. They weekend on the Moon, they have honeymoons on Mars. When they tire of that, they can simply close their eyes and be anything anywhere in or out of the world, all at the speed of thought through the computer links in their brains. And when they tire of that they have high-fashion drugs customised to their individual personalities that take them to places no one ever dreamed could be. With no morning after, my friend, no bad trips, no habit-forming, no accidental overdose.

When they are very young they are watched over by computer guardians like floating silver bubbles who attend to their every whim and wish. When they grow old they retire to orbital spas and resorts. No death for the rich, only a slow, subtle submergence through their implanted computer links into a synthetic televisual heaven. Or, when they tire of heaven, hell. But only for as long as it is amusing.

You watch them through the window; they talk and laugh and throw their heads back and touch each other gently, softly. You want them to see you, you want them to acknowledge that you exist but they are too rapt in their talking and laughing and touching to notice a boy from Langie at the window. There is one girl, there, the one twirling her cocktail glass by the stem, dipping her head, looking up from under her eyelashes and cascading golden hair. She draws your eyes, she will not let them go. She fascinates you. More than all the others, it is her you want to notice you. You stand and you stand and you stand, watching. The sounds and lights and smells of Atomic Avenue press past you but you do not even know they are there. Why will she not look up? What is it in their talking and laughing and gentle touching that she cannot take her eyes away even for a moment?

There is a tug at the sleeve of your Olympias.

– Hey, you going to stand there all *night*, my friend?

– Go away.

– Hey, we're going down to the Midnight Carnival; do the rides, the loupe-de-loupe (tug tug), Wall of Death (tug tug), the Cyclone (tug), the Bamba-Zamba, come on, mah man, time's *wasting*.

You shake him away as you would a mosquito or a dunny-fly and that flicker of movement steals her eyes away from the talking and laughing and the gentle touching. She looks up and your eyes meet.

She smiles.

You smile back.

– You comin'?

Pockets full of bottles, thumbs in elasticated waist-bands; all hips and shades.

– I don't want to go.

– Hey, come on, my friend, we all go together . . .

– You go. I'll find you later.

– Oh, come *on*, man . . .

– Go on. Get out of here. Leave me alone.

Muttering mumbling, grumbling: *well, if he doan wanna come, like I'm not goin' waste time on him, let's go, come on, let's go* . . .

Alone with her . . . she's not there. The chairs by the bar are filled with different talkings and laughings and touchings: where is she, where is she? You rush from window to window, steaming hand-prints on the glass, where is she where is she where is she? There, you see her, pulling on her jacket, stepping out onto Atomic Avenue with her friends all around her. It is as if she has never seen you and your heart is like slag, like clinker. Then she glances over her shoul-der, and looks at you standing in your sleek black and gold Olympias and Zeebocks by the chrome and glass doors, and her lips form the words: *come hither*. You follow, pressing, squeezing, pushing, – Excuse me sir, excuse me, madam, do excuse me, *Hey, where you think you going, boy, hey, watch, watch doing, hey, you stepped on my toe, on my new Golems I just got today now look what you done* . . . where is she where is she; there she is, weaving her way between the buses and pedicabs and motor-rickshaws, and just to make sure that you *come hither*, that golden glance over the shoulder, just to make sure you're there.

You're there.

Catcalls, wolf-whistles, shouted comments, offers. She gives back with interest. The long lazy boys laugh; she gives them her tongue but her eyes she keeps for you. Onward, through the night, through the dazzle and the razzle and the roaring hot hot neon, through the smells of roasting maize and charcoal smoke and sweat and spilled beer and perfume, and you are thinking, *she doesn't look as far ahead of me as I thought, am I getting closer, yes, I am getting closer, she's allowing me to catch up*; closer, you come, closer until under the cascading neons of the Stardust Ballroom, you are beside her and she smiles at you and her friends all melt away, swallowed by the night. She looks into your eyes and touches your cheeks with her fingers. Those fingers: they take your breath away. You never felt anything like those fingers, like the fingers of an angel down on the night-walk along Atomic Avenue looking for the souls of the lost. Like you. With one touch, your soul is sent spinning out among the fluorescents and flashings and advertisements; lost and reeling.

She indicates with her eyes an alley off Atomic Avenue, a dark cleft in the canyon walls of light. And you are there, with her, among the plastic refuse sacks and the picked-clean corn-cobs and the beer bottles and the condoms. With. Her. In the deep, hot dark. She takes your face in her hands and you feel like you are going to die; she looks up into your eyes and more than anything you need to drown there. You reach to touch her, her mouth is open, her lips ripe, ready, eager. You bend to meet her lips.

And a fist grabs the collar of your Olympias and the next thing you know you are down on the stained concrete among the bottles and the corn-cobs. Silver in the deep, hot dark; a blade, held before your eyes like the judgement of God. And a voice: – You leave her alone. You don't touch, you don't go near her. His voice; your friend. And the knife: Miguel's. They shoulder over you in the dark of the alley, Beni and Haran and Miguel and Sonny-Adé and him, the one who brought you here in the first place.

– Go on, get out of here! he shouts to the girl and she looks at them as if they were shit on her shoes, as if they were cancer. Without a backward glance she walks out of the alley into the lights of Atomic Avenue. Your friend bends down, close, face to face, eye to eye. His breath smells of onions and *pombé*.

– We came back to look for you, my friend, thinking maybe you'd go and make a fool out of yourself, and you know something? Someday you'll be glad we did. You want to learn this if you ever want to come back here again. You don't make fiki-fiki with her type. You don't go with them, you don't touch them. You don't even look at them. You get that?

You got that.

And now the sky is growing bright behind the Towers, the mythological gods and animals upon the topmost pinnacles shine, the hovering cylinders of the dirigibles have been turned to gold. The lights and lasers of Atomic Avenue look pale and tarnished and tired. Six a.m.: the first *matatus* have come swinging into their stops from places like Gillaroo and Harnsworth and Mount Oriel, empty, all empty. No one comes to Atomic Avenue now, the *matatus* are here to take all-night people from their doorways and gutters and bus shelters to their Jacaranda Hills and Rugares and Mauritzburgs and Langies. No noise and life and laughter on the morning buses, the only sound is the driver singing along to the radio.

Crates are empty, batteries dead, even the neatest, newest Sub-Ones look a little dirty and dusty and worn. Your head bounces against the metal bars the bus company has put in where the glass has fallen out. You look at the clinker-block houses and the wire compounds and the tattered maize in the shambas. You look at the smoke of ten thousand fires where ten thousand pots of *ugali* are thickening, at the chickens and the stick-thin dogs, at the people setting up their stalls, their booths, their little shops, women walking to the pump with jars, children running barefoot to school with their books swinging from a strap. You think you understand.

It is all a lie. Atomic Avenue; the place where horizontal and vertical meet, where rich and poor rub shoulders under the sweating lights as equals. It is a lie: there is no equality; the rich are always the rich, the poor the poor; Towers go up, townships out. But it is important that people meet there. For the rich, it is important for them to come down from their Towers and see the difference between themselves and the Langie boys and the Gillaroo girls. And for the Langie boys and Gillaroo girls it is important that in some place, at some time, the poor are the same as the rich, that there is the idea of equality. So the ones who night after night rock on down to Atomic Avenue believe they are equal because they want to believe they are equal, though it is nothing but an illusion. So nothing can be allowed to threaten that illusion. Like the gifts in the Catalogue Stores, you can look but you cannot touch. Like a child with a clay bubble pipe, one touch and the bubble bursts, like trying to steal from the television; one touch and the illusion of reality vanishes.

If you had touched her, if your lips had met, it would all have been revealed as illusion. You would have known that all you were to her was a mirror in which she could admire her difference from you. They saved you from that, your friends. You had hated them, then, but they had been good friends, true friends. You know that they did what they did because each of them at some time has had to make the same choice, between a crushing reality and a beautiful lie.

As the bus grinds up along Bougainvillaea Highway, you know that they will be on it again tonight, Beni the Beatbox and Haran with a fresh crate filched from Black Betty's storerooms, Sonny-Adé with his Sub-Ones sponged and pressed, Miguel throwing his knife into the oily red dirt by the *matatu* stop, and you know that he will come calling at your window: 'Tonight my friend, tonight, you going to pull on your Olympias and put your Zeebocks on your feet and slide your shades up your nose and rock on down with us to Atomic Avenue?' Tonight, my friend, tonight, you will be staying home to watch the soaps with Ma and Grandma and little Juancita. Oh no, good friend, tonight tonight tonight you will go round to the shebeen for a game of *fili* and a brew, tonight tonight tonight you might give Aoki the Food your change for a bowl of beans and onions and plaintains. And tonight tonight tonight, as you lie in your bed you know you will not sleep, no, you will not sleep, you will be listening for the roar of diesel engines and the tootle of horns and the cry of the conductor banging his *rungu* on the bald metal by the door, shouting out, 'Langie! Woolmagong! Freetown! Rugare! Jacaranda Hills! Atomic Avenewwww!'

FRONDS

'Case 57/16/C. Alleged Category Two Code violation: deliberate abandonment of a human in a life-threatening situation. Plaintiff: Itamuro Nobu against Delph C257 Conrad; preliminary brief, tape one . . . tape one . . . *shimada*.'

Lynka Wei swore in exasperation, rolled over on her belly and punched off the recorder. Stuck again. She stroked the tiny chrome vulva behind her right ear lobe; the datapyn extruded itself with its characteristic sexual sucking sound – might as well have sucked out all my brains. But it was good to be free from the clashing planes of Itamuro Nobu tumbling through her head; his pale, puffy face swollen with Mother-worlder bigotry; that shouting, accusing mouth . . .

She flung the datapyn across her office floor: get out of my head, mud-man! But she did not neglect to note where it fell; she would have need of it later, when she had regained her composure. You do not have doubts about your worthiness to be the Wei of Tan and Wei just because this is the twelfth time in the three years since he came off *Kamakura Maru* that you have had to defend some innocent delph against Itamuro Nobu's bigotry. You have your doubts because this twelfth time it actually seems that Itamuro Nobu has a case against Delph Conrad (unbidden fragments of datapyn caught in the light of her recollection . . . 'I tell you this, sister, when the bottom came up and I went down into the silt, that fish just bust his tail getting out of there.' And again: 'I mean to say, that just proves they're animals, don't it? You can say what you like about implants and GCP and all that, but I know one thing, no human would've run out on me the way that fish ran out on me'). And a Category Two Code violation carries a termination sentence. Mandatory.

And alone, the Wei of Tan and Wei fears she may not be enough. *– Grandmother Tan, you created me to be your successor but why did I have to succeed before your teaching was complete?* Frustration. Inadequacy. Incompetence . . . *– Peace. Be at peace. The first lesson you learned, Ama girl, remember?* Breathe deeply. Measured breaths. Fill the lungs, let the air and the spirit fill you, let them circulate through you as if you were a hollow bone flute; be cleansed, be purified, and slowly, slowly, release . . . and the mind is as clear as sunlight through water.

Grandmother Tan was one with her ancestors now, but she had not left her protégée desolate and resourceless. Lynka Wei crossed her office to kneel before the small *tokonoma* shrine to her mentor's memory: salt-scoured driftwood, black volcanic pebbles smoothed by Mother-sea, alien shells, song-box of the eddas of the great whales of earth. A white chrysanthemum. A hologram of the old, sea-worn Ama lawyer. And the datapyn. Lynka Wei bowed, once for thanks, once for honour, once for happy memories, and slid the datapyn into the socket beneath her black sea-smooth hair.

As her grandmother's stored memories meshed together with her own recollections of the woman to form a living presence, a persona, so waves of order and discipline rippled out from the Grandmother Tan construct and the roar of faces and testimonies and accusations was still.

– So, cub, what's rattling you?

'You can see it quite clearly for yourself, Honoured Grandmother.'

– Sloppy thinking, chippie. The law is the province of logical thinking and reasoned argument. So think logically; reason. First, review the evidence. So, what is the evidence?

She sighed. 'Kelper Itamuro Nobu, a subcontract worker on a five-year subjective contract to the Gracious House, and his current team partner, Delph Conrad, are five kays out from OTEC Charlie on station in the Circe Basin. They're in primeval kelp forest, surveying sites for an experimental *crucifera* starfish seeding. Seismo predicts 68 per cent probability a magnetic wobble, Richter 3.4. Delph Conrad lodges an official protest; nevertheless, they go. Nobu takes risks; he's keen to buy out his contract and ship himself back to Earthspace. They go out, and there is a seism. Electromagnetic pulse effect shoots Itamuro Nobu's jimsuit circuits to hell; he's settling down nicely into the mud for the last time while Delph Conrad tries to get him out. Of course, it's useless, he's only one Delph, so he hightails it.'

– So say you tell me where Delph Conrad goes?

'Seism occurs twelve twenty Circe Standard Time. Fourteen oh five CST Delph Conrad arrives at OTEC Charlie to raise help. Help arrives on location fourteen twenty and digs Itamuro Nobu out of the sludge.'

– So you tell me why he's claiming a Category Two.

'Since when does it take a Delph one hundred and five minutes to cover five kays?'

– That, I would submit, is the question you should put to Delph Conrad first thing tomorrow.

'My thanks, Honoured Grandmother.'

She removed the datapyn and returned it to the watchful care of the *tokonoma*. She felt clean, as if a pure, new wind had blown through her from an unexpected quarter. A strange sensation: normally the datapyns with their directly interfaced information left her feeling soiled and cluttered. She went to the office window to lose herself, for a moment, in the modality of the visible. Perceive, receive. See, be. Words from a grandmother to a scrawny half-naked Ama girl splashing in the tide-pools of Caluma Bay. See . . .

The silver bubbles of Enclave spilled down tier upon tier, level upon level, to the still waters of the lagoon. Beyond the girding arms of the volcanic island, the sea took a deeper, darker hue. Mother-sea, the delphs called it, mysterious and dark beneath its glossy carpet of undulating kelp fronds. Rollers of fog were advancing. At the edge of the horizon, the sun set vast and orange. Sky: bands of purple and indigo; the first, brightest stars challenging the setting sun in constellations familiar but skewed with the alien perspectives of ten and a half light years.

– Itamuro Nobu is mad. To give all this up for the vertical slums of Chinzo City?

As she watched a bright, bluehot star low on the sunward edge of the world suddenly flared and blinked into a moonsized disc of diffuse light. A starship of the Gracious House, pancaking its drive field into final braking configuration as it approached Dido. As she marvelled, she remembered. Not any automated lightspeed freighter, this. She had been yet a child when the promise had been made and the ship despatched from Motherworld, but now she was a woman, and the time was come for the promise to be fulfilled. The Legate of the Gracious House had arrived and his word would either save or destroy the world.

– Second planet of Epsilon Eridani; diameter 9,887 kilometres, mass 4.5 X 10²¹ tons, surface gravity 0.58 g, period of rotation 29.4 hours Earth Standard Time, period of revolution . . .

Fragments of my inflight briefing were raucous in my skull as a parliament of rooks. They had warned me; a brief, dreamless sleep, a waking full of strange new memories. Tank-taught; linked directly into my brain as I slept away ten and a half years objective. Facts, figures, voices . . . I tried to speak, to ask where, what, who I was, but my mouth was as dry as a ricepaper poem.

'Honoured sir should not exert himself unduly this soon out of suspension.'

Had my time in suspension affected my hearing? The voice hardly seemed recognisable as human. I blinked through bleary eyes (had all my senses been crazed in the high-gee tank? Why had the pre-flight briefings not warned me of this?), the lights dazzled me. Faces hung over me . . . the faces of the Company surgeons, the lights of the pre-flight centre . . . *there will be no sense of the passage of time, one moment you will be in this room, the next you will be awaking in orbit around . . .*

'Dido,' I croaked. And I saw that the faces looking down upon me were not the Company doctors, were not even human. The delph service crew hovered about me, maintaining their freefall positions with gentle movements of their tail flukes. Delphs. Dolphins. I had never seen these almost-mythical creatures before. I stared in amazement at their gracefulness and, unwary and preoccupied, thus laid myself open to ambush by another insistent memory; quite arbitrary, quite unrelated . . .

Dido (Epsilon Eridani Two) exhibits magnetic field reversals similar to those of Earth. However, on Dido these occur in the region of every fifteen thousand years, compared with the Earth's three-quarters of a million years. These reversals are coupled with a corresponding upsurge in volcanic and seismic activity. As Dido is a smaller world than Earth, with a correspondingly thinner mantle and (anomalously) a larger metal core, the process of tectonic convection traps migrating magnetic monopoles in upper crustal layers from which they are extruded onto the seabed in the form of superdense nodules of iron and manganese oxides . . .

The delphs were gone. I was alone, one man, ten and a half light years from the cherry blossoms of Nara, with only the arrogance of the Gracious House between me and soundless, bursting death in absolute space. And I was suddenly afraid, a bulb of flesh in a fragile plastic shell. A terrible, freezing fear, cold as absolute space, of a man created to be alone . . . No. I took hold of my spirit, shook it like an old quilt. You are a Legate of the Gracious House, with the full executive power either to continue or terminate an entire world; you are not a paper boat on a river to be driven where you do not will by undisciplined memories, you are not a child in winter afraid to sleep on its own . . . I filled my mind with the perfect abstracted ripples of a sand garden, my thoughts channelled like those sand waves around the rock island of duty.

. . . and I saw in my tank-taught memory, the vast particle accelerators the Messier-Weir Corporation had thrown into cis-lunar orbit; saw the quantum fury where twin beams collided to form micropoles: man-made magnetic monopoles.

They have done it. After twenty years, they have done it.

My ship had been despatched simultaneously with the masered message: within twelve years they will be able to challenge Gracious House's domination of the market with monopoles dredged from Dido's ocean beds; even its exalted position in the Great Leap Outward. In that six-month time lag while *Hideoshi Maru* accelerated and decelerated from near lightspeed, the Directors of the Dido Development had to have found something to increase production. More fragmentary memories: the voice of the Honourable First Auditor himself shaping the dreams that filled my high-gee sleep.

– *Seventy-five per cent of production costs on Dido are expended purely in clearing kelp from the mining sites . . . increased production is hampered severely by the fact that the only currently effective way to clear the kelp is manually by human-delph kelper teams . . . automated machinery is useless given the twin factors of the ocean-bed environment and the frequent magnetic anomalies . . . despite all projected expansions of the labour units, the production levels cannot be raised by that means alone sufficiently to counter the threat from Messier-Weir.*

All the Elders of the Gracious House were aboard *Hideoshi Maru*; decisions upon which an entire planet depends (which I say without the least hyperbole or melodrama) cannot be left to one man, even if that one man is Company in every coil of his tank-bred DNA. Such decisions can only be taken by the full Household of Elders. But the sand gardens and executive contemplation houses are ten and a half years away and the elders of an entity as powerful and important as the Gracious House cannot abandon themselves to the vagaries of star travel, let alone take ten and a half years' leave of absence from their duties. Thus they accompanied me in spirit, in simulation, a computer-stored copy of each of their personalities, maintained in some fashion of cybernetic limbo (I could not for a moment imagine what kind of reality, or non-reality, what kind of nirvana, they inhabited), but with the full executive authority of their progenitors in the gardens of Nara.

The Elders! I had neglected my duty towards my superiors. Humiliated by my thoughtlessness and lack of respect, I summoned a delph from his duties and ordered him to guide me to the Elders' chamber. Gracious House starships were never designed with gravity in mind, I must have performed half a dozen shifts of orientation before I arrived at my destination.

The chamber was a converted hydroponic blister, an inflatable sphere tessellated with the hexagon faces of videoscreens; one hundred and nine, one for each of the Elders of the Gracious House. I floated at the centre of the sphere. I clapped my hands three times, pressed my palms together and called, 'Homage to the Honoured Elders of the Gracious House.' And the one hundred and nine hexagons were filled with faces.

It was then that I truly understood what it was to be naked and alone a long way from home.

*

Out beyond the orderly, two-dimensional grid of Enclave's marina pontoons, the delph-warren was a chaotic, multi-levelled labyrinth of nets, bubble curtains, and sonar buoys. No maps are drawn of the continually shifting boundaries and territories of the various cetacean unions and solidarities, but an Ama girl who has spent half her life in this three-dimensional maze needs no maps. Cutting in across the clear waters of the bay on her sail-board, Lynka Wei listened for the sound signatures of the sonar buoys. West 27, Southwest 6 Deep, Northwest Blue, Northwest 17. She moored her board against the buoy and slipped on her breathermask, stroking away the clusters of metal crystals precipitated out of Mother-sea's ion-rich brew around the molecular filters; an action automatic and unconscious as blinking to a semi-aquatic Ama. One final action before she slipped beneath the surface into that world she had come to think of as her spiritual home. She removed her grandmother's datapyn from her belt pouch and slid it into her socket. As the receiving waters closed over her, so her grandmother's persona closed around her mind.

'I'm a hemi-human, Honoured Grandmother, like a creature out of those kelpers' legends you used to tell me when I was small.'

– *You remember those?* Her grandmother's spirit voice seemed whimsically amused. Together they settled into comfortable, clear water.

Delph Conrad was in *tlechen*. Dreaming, deep in the Great Sea Dream, the unity of *tlechen*, the Racial Dreamplace. Delphs do not sleep, but they dream waking dreams. With a mental apology, Lynka Wei clickwhistled Delph Conrad's Coda and woke him with a shiver from the seascapes of the Dreamplace. She beckoned him to the surface; she found speaking Human through her helmet hydrophones taxing, and this was not an occasion for the formalities of Delphic. Not yet.

'Greetings to you, Ama-sister.'

'And to you, Delph Conrad. I apologise for rousing you from the Dreamplace, but I have some questions for you concerning Itamuro Nobu.'

'It was his spirit I was trying to escape in the Dreamplace, but he pursued me, with the inescapability of the black killers.'

'Itamuro Nobu is clearly a rash and prejudicial man, and his testimony likewise tainted. However, in order to prove this before the Tribunal, there are inconsistencies in your taped testimony I must clear up.' Lynka Wei climbed out of the water to sit cross-legged on the deck of her bobbing sail-board. The sun was hot on her back.

'There is a question of timing. Do you consider yourself a strong swimmer, brother Conrad?' Conrad rolled from side to side in the water; he was modest, he was blushing. Lynka Wei's question had been the Delphic equivalent of asking, 'Do you consider yourself very beautiful, brother Conrad?'

– *Don't embarrass the tad*, whispered Grandmother Tan. Herself embarrassed, Lynka Wei rephrased the question. 'Let me rather say, how long would it take you to swim five kilometres?' Conrad replied with a stream of clickspeech. Delphs had difficulty with human concepts of discrete time: a race that never sleeps never invents alarm clocks. His reply translated as 'about five minutes', a short but indefinite period of time. But was this modesty again, or secrecy?

– *Push him a little harder*, suggested Grandmother Tan.

'Not long,' mused Lynka Wei. 'Yet when I compared the time recorders on Itamuro's jimsuit and the OTEC Charlie outlock, I found it took you one hundred and five minutes to cover those five kilometres.'

The delph did not reply.

'Did you merely swim slowly, or was there some other factor? For instance, was there a starfish seeding close at hand? I have heard that they have very poisonous spines; was it these that delayed you, or was there another reason? Do I have to remind you how vital it is that I know the truth? Your life could depend on the answers you give me.'

– *Nice touch, cub. You're learning well. Hard and soft does it every time* . . . and suddenly the interior dialogue was broken by a stream of clickwhistles.

I am the faithful child of Mother-sea.
No human life will come to harm through me.

Delphic. She had touched on an issue of Delphic Law. Delph Conrad clickwhistled another versicle in Delphic.

All human life is sacred, this is taught.

Am I condemned for my attempts to save?

'That's not what Itamuro Nobu would say. That's not what the Tribunal will say. Unless you tell me what you did in those one hundred and five minutes.'

– *Ease up on the tad*, advised Grandmother Tan. *Remember how to approach the Delphic Law: you can pull your punches . . .*

'But you can't push the river . . .' Lynka Wei whispered to her mentor.

Conrad rolled restlessly in the clear waters of Net 17. The sun was hot, sweat beaded Lynka Wei's back as she unclipped her recorder from her belt.

'Would those one hundred and five minutes have anything to do with this peculiar recording picked up on your hydrophones? It is quite unfamiliar to me, or any other Ama; computer and linguistic analyses have failed to draw any analogues, maybe you can tell me what it is?' The sound on the tape was a rising, warbling call, plaintive, alien. In a lifetime spent among delphs, she had never heard its like before. She shivered, suddenly cold despite hot Epsilon Eridani. She understood what it was to be far divorced from her ancestral home, her race's Dreamplace. Cold in her soul. 'Conrad, what is that sound?'

Conrad thrashed his tail in agitation. Lynka Wei could not understand why he should have reacted so extremely to a simple question. Grandmother Tan had nothing to offer; they were both swimming into new waters.

'Again, brother Conrad, what is that sound?'

'An alarm call.' The voice was high and whistling, barely comprehensible as Human.

'Not any alarm call I recognise.'

Again Delph Conrad thrashed, churning the water white with his tail flukes.

'What kind of alarm call, Delph Conrad?'

Conrad swam back and forth, back and forth, then burst from the water before her. She cried out in blind fear. Conrad stood upright in the water, holding himself erect with his tail flukes.

*Upon this matter no more can I say.
*The Law forbids me, yet the Law compels.

*To lie to humans is unthinkable,
*For them to suffer harm, impossible.
*I would not lie to thee and yet I must.
*The Law has penned me tight on either side
*And I must swim a lonely, narrow path.
*I cannot speak to thee, my human sister
*The burden is intolerable to me.
*Go therefore to the Delphic Octarchy
*If resolution of these things thou seekest.
*I am a callow youth blunt and unsubtle.
*The comedy of Law is beyond me.
*Go now and seek the higher truth
*The Delphic Octarchy now awaits thee
In patient silence beneath the Mother-sea.

My first three days in the acclimatisation unit (a euphemism for solitary detention while the Directors of the Dido Development played for time) were a misery of pounding sinuses and streaming rhinitis. Alien allergens: the thousand upon thousand of stealthy ways an alien world can subvert the human immune system. And change that human into a shambling, sniffing, swollen-eyed hulk. *Mudmen:* that is the local name for contract workers from the Motherworld. There was a guard on my door; though numb and groggy from histamine detoxifiers and endorphin blockers, I could not imagine what possible threat I posed; doubtless he thought of me as *mudman.* I used the delay as an opportunity further to collate and refine the masses of amorphous data that had been squeezed into my brain by the Elders aboard *Hideoshi Maru.* I employed the techniques the ancients call the Garden of the Mind. Imagine each discordant concept is an element of an exquisitely landscaped garden: a tree, a stone, a shrub, an ornamental lantern, a small stream of trickling water. Imagine next yourself a visitor to that garden; note the harmonious relationships between moss and stone and shrub, consider how that tree bends to touch its branches to the ripples of the brook ... Isolated in a plastic bubble at the heart of that great froth of bubbles that is Enclave, I explored Dido in the garden of the mind.

From its discovery and surveying by the unmanned UNIMEG probe *Chiang Kai Shek* to its subsequent leasing by the Interstellar Mapping and Exploratory Group on the discovery of the magnetic monopole nodules to the establishment of a full industrial colony by the Gracious House and the departure of the first freighter-load of monopoles earthward, I saw the planet. I saw Enclave spilling down the sides of its steep volcanic atoll, its lagoon a frantic hive of action both above and below the surface: LTA transports, delph pens, scudding sail-boards, sea-planes, sonar buoys, bubble curtains . . . I saw the OTEC thermal energy plants, the powerhouses of the Dido Development, I watched lighters launched to orbit on steam superheated by infra-red lasers. I saw them all, and arranged them in the garden of my mind to form a complete picture of the Dido that the Gracious House had made. And then I took it away, piece by piece, to see the Dido UNIMEG had discovered. I saw the polar icesheets reaching half-way to the tropics, I saw the orange ball of Epsilon Eridani shining pale and wan through the haze of CO_2 it evaporated from the perpetual ice. And I felt, beneath the ice, the tectonic fires that warmed the waters and enriched it with minerals so that in even such an apparently appalling environment, life throve. The ubiquitous life of Dido. The kelp.

Know your enemy. That is one of the first lessons they teach you at Nara. Know him, be fascinated by him, study him until you know him as well as you know yourself. I meditated long hours in that plastic cell upon my enemy. *Laminaria Didonis.* Let me tell you what I know of you . . .

As recently as three hundred thousand years ago you existed as a much less advanced protoform, only one among numerous marine algae with which you shared the oceanic ecology. In the recent geological past some environmental catastrophe caused you to assume your present form and distribution and to displace all other forms of marine plant-life. Your success is partly due to your phenomenal growth rate. Dido's highly active tectonics have bequeathed you a seawater unusually rich in metallic trace elements which can sustain frond growth of upward of a metre per day. But the true key to your dominance lies in your ability to create and control your own micro-ecology. Complex communities of marine biota co-exist with you through systems of intricate symbiotic relationships. Entire hierarchies of marine biota from the most primitive to the most advanced are supported and are in turn supported by the forest biomes. So complex and diverse is the life in your communities that new species are continually being discovered and this astonishing richness of fauna has led to the kelper legends of quasi-sentient 'water-angels' and 'kelpies', living in the impenetrable depths of the primeval kelp forests.

But however fascinating and successful you may be as a species, you are still the enemy of my Company. And you are still my enemy.

On the third day I was released from the acclimatisation unit and taken to an executive suite overlooking Enclave and its lagoon. For all my explorations of Dido in the garden of the mind, the planet surprised me. The blueness of the great world-ocean, the smell of salt fog and the tang of kelp in the air of my veranda; after three months-subjective afloat in the fluorocarbon jelly of *Hideoshi Maru*'s high-gee tank, reality took me quite by surprise. And then, in the midst of my contemplation, a caller at my door: a politely bowing junior executive (thinking *mudman*; pale, pasty mudman; these people have no guile, no subtlety at all, their faces show what they feel) with a polite invitation to attend immediately an Extraordinary Meeting of the Board of Directors of the Dido Development.

Seeing the Delphic Octarchy arrayed in the Spiritual-Seven Star with Old Grey Fellow at the focus, Lynka Wei felt a heavy foreboding. Spiritual-Seven. This would be a session of the gravest formality on issues close to the heart of the Delphic Law, that great body of oral tradition and law passed down from the Exalted Ancestors beneath the seas of the Motherworld. Old Grey Fellow she knew from past litigations: a master orator, a superb subtletist, a poet, visionary, comedian; a formidable opponent for a greenhorn lawyer on her first assignment. She recognised his fellow legalists: Delphs Harper, Nineteen, Bluey and Ahab, as well as a group of three she observed by their solidarity tattoos as belonging to the Fifteenth Prefecture. The entire Spiritual-Seven was composed of experienced lawyers well versed in the three pillars of the Delphic Law: rhetoric, precedent and reverence for ancestors. What could be so vital about a Code violation complaint, even a Category Two, that an entire Law-Star should have been convened? She recalled the central tenet of the Delphic Law. *In the place where nothing may be concealed, one may yet hide in plain sight.* In the oceans of Motherworld there is no hiding place, save behind one's solidarity brothers. Hiding in plain sight.

– *They'll play by formal rules*, her grandmother's persona counselled her. *Delphs hate precedents. The sea is the great conservative. So you set precedents.*

As she approached the Law-Star, the delphs turned and ritually clickprobed her. In accordance with protocol, Lynka rotated her body for their sonic perusal.

– *They'll know that you're tense. They'll have read it in your bones, your muscles, your blood. They'll be thinking, we can do what we like with this tad. So, let's do it. Just like we rehearsed.*

Lynka swam respectfully alongside Old Grey Fellow, then swooped around him, slipped off her breathermask and gently closed her teeth on his flipper. The water boiled with the young turks' indignation but Old Grey Fellow laughed a deep delphic laugh. He knew the Law of Reverence for Ancestors well enough to read the symbolism of the teethmarks on the flipper. Lynka Wei had, in effect, said: Old and venerable one, I am of the ones who raised you, gave you awareness, gave you all you now enjoy, am I not father to your race? Render therefore to me the debt of filial devotion. Before the flurry of outrage had time to settle, Lynka had stroked in her throat vocaliser and was beginning her opening submission.

I have, my sons, some queries to thy wits.

Of brother Conrad and his strange report.

I am mere landbound flesh and ignorant

Thy explanations would be pleasing to me.

'Ask away, tad,' cackled Old Grey Fellow in Human, wrinkling his nose in a smile. Lynka shuddered. She knew the Delphic proverb: *Turn thy flukes when thy brother smilest.* There was danger, that was Old Grey Fellow's allusion, but she would not turn flukes and swim away.

'Ah, the master linguist,' she replied in kind, then, in Delphic.

Perhaps thy mastery can me enlight:

*Thou art eloquent in thy mother tongue,
*Translate for me this fragment of thy speech
That I no more may swim in ignorance.

Another pillar of the law: ignorance always demanded enlightenment. To be ignorant beneath the oceans of the Mother-world was to court death. Awareness was survival, enlightenment life. The Spiritual-Seven held position. Bubbles leaked to the surface from their rebreather implants. Sunlight glittered on their beards of metal crystals. Lynka thumbed the hydrophone replay on her belt and once again the alien call shivered her spirit.

This question is most easily resolved, said Old Grey Fellow when the water had cleared of the alien resonances and chord patterns.

*This is the clickspeech of our brother Conrad.
*His the call thou hearest, his the voice
Which calls loud in alarm upon thy tape.

– Don't let him get away with that, pressed Grandmother Tan. He may not be lying to you, but he's not telling you the entire truth. Lynka Wei played on her ignorance.

*Alas, in darkest gloom I am suspended.
*Enlightenment to my ignorance has not come.
*Bethinkest thou that I am deaf, dumb, blind?
*I know full well the clickspeech of the delphs,
*I know the cry which delphic brothers call
*To summon assistance in a time of peril.
*This is not the cry of summoning aid,
So tell me, child, this cry, what it doth mean.

Old Grey Fellow held silence. The Spiritual-Seven arrayed in their Law-Star trembled. Frustration? Anticipation? The double indebtedness of paternalism and ignorance tormented them. The Blessed Father-One could not be left in dangerous ignorance, yet still the Old Grey Fellow would not speak.

– They're holding you at a distance with petty legal jokes and comedies while they hunt for a precedent which will enable them to deny your claim of paternalism on the grounds that you are not of their species, whispered Grandmother Tan. And that is a dangerous precedent; to deny humans the rights of creator-species.

And the truth would hide in plain sight. Unless Lynka Wei could shake the three pillars of the Delphic Law so hard they tottered.

But how? What could this greenhorn lawyer know that would best the most venerable legal minds on Dido? She closed her eyes and summoned one of Grandmother Tan's mental training disciplines; pictured a foggy morning on the seashore, herself a girl again beach-combing with her grandmother, turning over the round sea-smoothed pebbles to see what lay there. And under each stone was an observation, a story, a question, an answer, a proverb or insight or riddle or parable. Along they went, and the sun dissolved away the mist and beat down on their bended backs; poking, turning, burrowing, hunting, until at the very end of the shore of the mind Lynka Wei turned over a black pebble as large as her fist and on the bottom was written three words: The Unaskable Question. Grand-mother Tan's words came back to her, like the cry of a dolphin in the starlit sea. – *Every people has one question that may never be asked because to ask it is to question the very foundations upon which their civilisation is built and admit Chaos into its streets. Therefore, though everyone understands intuitively what that question is, it is never asked. But sometimes, it is a good thing to let Chaos run loose in the streets.*

– Let a little Chaos in

*The one who sent this message is well known
*The one to whom intended, he is not.
*The one Delph Conrad called
Where is he?

Thrashing flukes, flashing jaws: the Spiritual-Seven exploded towards her, incensed, animal. A naked, unprotected human, Lynka was petrified; her life a fragile, forfeit thing for she had asked the Unaskable Question and released the animal from the strictures human science had imposed upon it.

The Unaskable Question. Never ask it, whistle it, think it, never let the thought of it darken your bright life, for the question **Where is he?** summons death as surely as the alarm cry summons a brother's help. Where is he? Where is he? Dead, in the jaws of the black killers, dead, run through by the harpoon of the hunter, dead and desiccating on the vain seashore, prey for the pecking, pecking birds, dead, drowned in a tangle of weed or a fisherman's net, dead, hacked red flesh shredded by the steel-bladed propeller. If thy brother be not at thy side never ask *Where is he?* for he is dead.

But she had asked; the one whom Delph Conrad called, where is he? And released Chaos. She curled into a ball, arms over head, breasts folded to belly, hiding herself from the jaws of the Spiritual-Seven. Teeth tore at her, flukes buffeted her, she screamed her fear and terror and helplessness into her breathermask: – What have I done what have I done what have I done?

A piercing whistle filled her head and all was still. Old Grey Fellow had sung the Collect of Stillness, only sung prior to hunting when all passions and energies must be subdued and submitted to the necessities of surviving. One precedent had already been set, now he made another; the abuse of the Holy Collects.

'Well asked, little tad,' creaked Old Grey Fellow in Human. 'You have a wonderful daring, a truly respectful iconoclasm. In my lifetime no one has ever dared to ask the question. I fear you drove the brothers to the limits of their constraint by the Code; incensed by your blasphemy, they might well have killed you. Though fine legalists, alas, they are too young to have learned the sublime comedy at the heart of the Law. You, for all your callow years, you have the comic genius. You are the worthy heir of your grandmother. You know our tradition better than we, a fine joke indeed. However, do not think yourself too wise; there is one tradition you do not know. You asked, where is he? By an older tradition, I must now show you. Come with me.'

I rather think I have upset my hosts. After the board meeting at which they introduced me to their hope of salvation they had arranged a lengthy agenda of laboratory visits, meetings with scientists, project supervisors, information analysts, accountants, audio-visual displays, projections, extrapolations, simulations, forecasts, postulations, analyses ... All brought crashing down like a festival war-kite when I requested that all pertinent information be made accessible to me via datapyn and that I wished to visit the actual experiment *in situ* at their earliest convenience.

Reality again, you see. Knowing me to be a man of abstraction, they sought to present evidence for my judgement solely as abstraction. But my whole life in the Gracious House has been abstraction, and I have had enough of it. Give me the concrete, give me the solid, give me reality. Let me see what you are doing in the place you are doing it, let me judge by what I see, not what I have been told.

Broad tanned faces swelled in outrage, protests that such a thing was impossible, unthinkable were met with that degree of the Great Stone Face that says, *think it, make it possible*. Bowing and shooting nervous glances at each other, the Directors of the Dido Development hastened to go about my bidding. Alone in the boardroom, I looked at the thing on the table before me, their hope for the future of their world. An unprepossessing thing, all spines and thorns and needles, its pentacular outline disguised, so dense was the forest of quills and spears. *Crucifera Epsilon Minor*. The Gracious House's answer to *Laminaria Didonis*.

So: this is my ally. An unlikely ally indeed.

An aide entered with my datapyn, in too great haste even to bow. 'Honourable Legate . . .'

'Please have it installed in the jimsuit I am to use on my visit to the workings. I presume they have data interface systems?'

'Of course, but . . .'

'I do not wish to have to ask twice.'

Because their bodies are tall and strong and beautiful, these people have a streak of arrogance shot through them. I may be pale, sickly, pinched, a mudman of Earth, but I am the Gracious House and they had best learn that sooner rather than later.

My guide to the true Dido, the Dido beneath the surface, was another such, a kelper, one Ode Kimathi, native born, not a contract worker. From the moment I met him I could tell that he considered me puny, ineffectual, even decadent. I took great pleasure, therefore, in dazzling him with the skill with which I learned how to handle my jimsuit. Of course, jimsuit control had been part of my inflight briefing, but Ode Kimathi was not to know that.

The one-man submarine modules popularly called 'jimsuits' can best be likened to mechanical mermaids. From the waist up the device is a conventional self-contained pressure-body similar to those used by deepspace construction workers. From the waist down, it had been modified into a kind of 'tail' (I can think of no better description): a flexible appendage containing powerful fuel-cell motors and thrusters. After half an hour's practice in the delph pens of Enclave I was sufficiently competent to venture into the greater deeps. All through the flight to OTEC Charlie my guide sat silently, filled with a kind of sullen admiration. So, let the Legate cover himself with a little awe and admiration. We are not all mudmen.

Mystery and awe, I learned, were more rightfully reserved for the kelp forest than myself. Sinking slowly through the twisting, twining fronds of kelp, away from the sun, down towards the root zone, I became aware of a distinct spirit of place, of a colossal sentience totally self-absorbed that I was somehow violating with my presence. Shadows moved among the encircling kelp fronds; beneath me, bio-luminescence sparkled cold green and blue; I felt as if I was descending into the tremendous cathedral of some ancient contemplative order. I could almost believe the legends of a sentient species that had hidden itself away from man in the fastnesses of the kelp forests.

At seventy metres, great shining silver torpedoes exploded out of the kelp towards us. Quite spellbound by the spirit of the fronds, I panicked. My jimsuit thrashed and spasmed. Then I heard laughter on my hydrophones, *alien* laughter, and the clickspeech of delphic.

'They apologise, they are embarrassed, they had not realised humans were present in this area,' Ode Kimathi explained on the intersuit communicators.

'You can speak delphic?'

'Only a little pidgin, Honoured Sir, and these are haulers, kelp-haulers, genetically adapted sei-whales. Their usual field of operation is close to the surface in conjunction with the kelp-processing plants; we caught them in the middle of a mating dance. Small wonder they are embarrassed.' Small wonder indeed. We dropped into the darkness. The kelp seemed to be reaching out for me. I, who have crossed the great vacuum between the stars, felt strangely threatened. Our jimsuit lights came on automatically and drew clouds of small creatures, all legs and cilia, some of which I recognised from my shipboard briefings as members of the kelp symbiotic community. One hundred and thirty metres. Bottom. Our tail motors swivelled to brake our descent throwing up billows of silt. As it settled slowly in Dido's gentle gravity, I saw a mirage: a young woman riding on the back of a dolphin through the tangle of the kelp forest. I only glimpsed her for a single hallucinatory moment before the bottom murk hid her but the sight had oddly disturbed me. I asked Ode Kimathi whether it was possible to suffer rapture of the deep in a jimsuit.

'No delusion,' he answered and explained that the woman was an Ama, one of those rare human beings with an auditory structure capable of being augmented to perceive delphic clickspeech. Their usual field of operation was liaising between humans and delphs and Mr Kimathi commented that it was very strange to find one so deep and so far from Enclave. All manner of creatures out of their element this day. My jimsuit lights picked up flashing blue-silver mirrors out among the kelp fronds. The delphs were among us. When first I saw these artificial creatures aboard *Hideoshi Maru* I had admired their natural grace and ease, but here, in their true environment, their elegance, their speed, their *rightness* seemed almost supernatural, as if this alien ocean, this alien world, was their inalienable right. I watched them nose explosive charges into the knotted kelp holdfasts. A shrill cry intruded on my meditations.

'Danger! Danger! Human beware!

'Explosion, danger, fire!'

A flick of our jimsuit tails and we were retired to a safe distance. Behind us, the flat thump of the charges was felt as much as heard. Onward to the sludgers, the sea-bed devices which sifted the bottom ooze for the precious nodules. Ironically, such was the dirt and silt they generated in their sea-floor suctioning that I could make little sense out of what I was being shown. I caught glimpses of hoses, grapples, flashing floodlamps, but left the production site with little more than random impressions. That afternoon, my guide promised me, I would see the difference between the old and the new.

After a light luncheon at OTEC Charlie, Kimathi made good his word. The *Crucifera* seedlings were a short tail flick from the thermal energy plant. Yet in that short distance, I might have swum through some fantastic stargate onto a different planet. Clear water, soft, undulating yellow sand dotted with the spiny shells of dead starfish.

And the kelp, *Laminaria Didonis*, all gone. Not a frond cast its shadow on the naked seabed. Here and there amputated holdfasts protruded through the sand, dead and rotting. I reached to pick up one of the spiny starfish and the delphs in our escort shied away.

'Poisonous,' explained Ode Kimathi. 'Poisoned spines. Fatal to Didonian biological systems, harmless but rather painful to terrestrial biochemistry. They protect against predators, Legate. Some of the unprotected variants were wiped out soon after introduction into the environment, almost as if the kelp community were defending itself against the invaders. The poisonous spines stopped that.'

The jimsuit had been fitted with a datapyn interface system. Even as he spoke, the information sprayed up through my consciousness:

– *The variant* Crucifera Epsilon Minor *was engineered with the introduction of genetic material from* Centrostephanus Longispinus, *a terrestrial sea-urchin. The variant displayed a higher tolerance to the metal ions present in Dido ocean water and on introduction to the native environment performed successfully on all counts. The reproduction rate of the variant was well within the given parameters, the colony effectively doubling within twenty-five days of introduction onto the test habitat. Further on-site studies indicate that* Crucifera Epsilon Minor *is unsurpassed in effectiveness as a kelp clearer, the express purpose for which it was designed. The line of advance of the* Epsilon Minor *variant has stabilised at three metres per day and this coupled with the reproductive rate, gives a kelp-clearance quotient for one colony of 176.71 m^2 per day. Given the figure of 0.33 kelp holdfasts per m^2 a single colony could, within one generation, destroy 1460 kelp fronds by eating through the holdfasts. With a geometrically increasing population, based on a recommended eight thousand seed colonies, a region the area of the entire Circe Basin could be cleared of kelp within four months . . .*

I looked at the ugly, thorny creature in my metal claws. Before me the yellow sand extended past the limits of my vision. Ironic indeed that the salvation of the world should be a Crown of Thorns.

She had never dived so far, so deep, so distant from the light of the sun. The water was cold and close on her skin, the weight of it bearing down on her claustrophobic, the darkness, the tangles of kelp brushing past her body a cold caress. Old Grey Fellow was a flash of silver lost among the dark kelp; suddenly she was scared, far from the arc-lights of OTEC Charlie, its cheeky kelper teams and their lewd suggestions of what an Ama was doing out here alone with a delph, under pressure, isolated, and very vulnerable.

Alone. Grandmother Tan's persona remained in the shrine to its memory in her office. Whatever she found she would have to cope with on her own. She could not be dependent on ghosts and spirits and memories for ever. Lynka Wei called out on her helmet vocaliser:

*Old Grey One, do not leave me in distress!
I am alone, afraid, a fearful child.

Blue silver flashed among the kelp fronds and Old Grey Fellow was by her side.

'Why so fearful, little one?' Though distorted and compressed by dark water, the inflections of Old Grey Fellow's Human were unmistakable: paternalism reversed. The son is the father, the mother the daughter. A fin was offered, a rare and intimate privilege. Lynka accepted it and, she clinging to his back, they descended into the kelp forest, the woman riding on the back of the dolphin.

Scudding on the powerski across warm familiar waters towards the OTEC installation, the possibility that she might be the first human to learn the truth behind Dido's legends seemed remote and improbable. Now she found herself rigid with anticipation, tight and trembling. All the idle kelpers' stories, all the ghosts and ghoulies of Grandmother Tan's pantheon crowded close and threatening.

Seabed. Bubbles ascended from the rebreather tubes through clouds of suspended silt. Vague luminosities stirred in the outer darkness, sinister dartings and pulsings. She longed to kick away, upward, outward, into the light. She longed to feel the sunlight on her face, the water run down her cheeks. But she waited in dark waters, trembling, a prisoner within the yellow cone of her helmet lights.

'What do we do now?'

'We wait,' came Old Grey Fellow's reply.

Then, on the edge of her field of vision, pale glowing things began to gather, so faint as to be almost imaginary. Almost.

'They are afraid of your lamps. They will not come closer unless you switch them off.'

And the darkness drew them. Lynka recognised tentacles, glowing eyes, pulpy sacs of luminous flesh, rippling sheets of cilia. Familiar, but wrong, all in the wrong places, all alien. They brushed against her and she cried aloud, in wonder more than fear. Lights swirled and eddied, they were gone.

'Peace, little landborn daughter. They will not harm you.' Again the glowings clustered and congregated. This time when their feelers reached out, she let them touch her, explore her, assess her. A cool touch slipped around her waist and in an instant her tool belt was off. Another caress around her neck and the feelers were tugging at her breathermask. She grasped it firmly, pulled it close to her head. The message was received and understood. The kelpies satisfied their curiosity with the tool belt, passing it from feeler to feeler. Their bodies rippled with metallic-coloured sheens.

'What are they?' Lynka whispered to Old Grey Fellow after a timeless time.

'They have a name for themselves but we cannot translate it. As you can see, the kelp-dwellers' language is primarily visual.'

'Language? They are sentient?'

'Yes, they are sentient, though in a fashion altogether alien to your people or mine. We believe that they may be a symbiotic vector of the kelp, as if they are the higher cognitive levels of what amounts to a sentient planetary organism. They possess a rudimentary tool-building capacity: observe their fascination with your tool belt.'

Buoyancy bags, flares, decompression tablets, all were being passed from toucher to toucher; passed, touched, turned over and over and commented upon in glowing colours.

'And your people have established some form of communication with them; that was the call, wasn't it? A warning to them that humans are in the area, that they must hide themselves?'

'It is only recently that we have succeeded in opening communications with them though we have known of their presence for almost a generation. There were great difficulties in forming a common field of experience.'

'Almost a generation? Why? Why did you not tell us of their

existence? A sentient species … the first … once UNIMEG learns …'

'Forgive a foolish old fish, but once UNIMEG learns, there is no more Dido.'

Finished with their examination, the kelpies returned Lynka's tool belt to her, fastening it around her waist.

'Do I understand you correctly? Are you saying that you would let an entire species be exterminated because it threatens the development of this world?'

'This is what I am saying. Alas, deprived of the kelp ecology, they do not live long. Amino acid deficiencies, we think. Once widespread kelp clearing begins, they will vanish.'

Glowing numinous phantoms, the kelpies took on a new fragility and vulnerability.

'But why? Why? Why?'

'Because …' Old Grey Fellow slipped into more eloquent delphic:

*Because they have been given the gift of hands.
*This world is theirs to touch and feel and master.
*We dolphins have no hands with which to work
*Upon the base, raw substance of this world;
Thus trapped are we within our helplessness.

'Envy?' cried Lynka Wei. The kelpies fled from her shrill, angry voice. 'Envy?'

*Envy of their hands, and of their world.
*This is a fine, fair world for dolphin-kind,
*And man will give it to us, in the end
*When all its ocean bottoms are dredged clean
*And every drop of material gain is gleaned,
*He will depart and leave this world to us
*As just reward to us his faithful servants.
*And so we keep the kelpies ever secret
*And cast them to extinction's dark abyss
*And in the end we will have gained a world
*And we will be a people once again
No more the man-made playthings of your science.

The kelpie-shine was almost lost among the fronds of weed; here a glimmer, there a glimmer, fading fast. Darkness, oppression returned again; dread, guilt.

'And you will not even murder them yourselves, but let others, humans, do it for you?'

'Quite. Unfortunately, we lack the experience necessary for genocide. Your species, however, has all the expertise we need. There are ample precedents in human history of the extermination of indigenous species, even humans, by other humans wishing to possess their habitats. Remember precedent, especially the precedent of our exalted ancestors, is one of the pillars of the Delphic Law. And, as you claimed, you are our ancestors.'

'What kind of creatures are you?' asked Lynka Wei in simple amazement.

'You humans are such an arrogant species,' shrilled Old Grey Fellow. 'You see nothing but yourself reflected in us. Foolish chauvinism: we are not humans in another form, we are aliens, as alien to you as they are, the kelp-dwellers. If we are the first aliens and you do not understand us, how could you hope to comprehend the kelp-dwellers?'

And now I bind you by the Delphic Law:
What you have seen no human soul must know.
Silence you must now and ever keep
Else Chaos will spill out upon the world,
The Chaos you invited by your question,
The question which no rational soul would ask.
This is the binding of the Delphic Law.

Lynka Wei was bright-shining with defiance and outrage.

'But I will tell, I will tell. You cannot be let to get away with this. You cannot.' She kicked away from Old Grey Fellow and swam towards the surface, webbed hands reaching for the sun, for the world of her own people. Old Grey Fellow's voice echoed after her.

And now that you have smashed the Law's three pillars,
And Chaos spills across the world like silt,
Bethinkest thou that it can be undone
Unmade, unspoken, hidden in the dark?
Foolish child, what is this you have done?

*

I met the Ama woman by the pine at Touai Point as she had requested. A tranquil meditative spot, between two worlds, the rock and sea of Dido, the trees of the Motherworld. Fog lay low on the horizon, along the edge of the ice, the solitary tree was bent and scoured by its defiance of the wind. Below the point sluggish waves broke upon the pebble beach, streamers of brown kelp stirred lazily.

Her tale was long and there was much of it I barely understood; the complaint of Itamuro Nobu, the subtleties of the Delphic Law, the unaskable question; indeed, her central claim, that the kelp forests of Dido did indeed shelter an indigenous race, would have seemed so utterly fantastic as to be instantly dismissable but for the conviction that gripped her as she narrated her story. These people who wear their souls on their faces . . .

'You must believe me,' she said. 'No one else will. It is vitally important that I can convince you if the kelpies are to stand a chance.'

'The conviction with which you tell your story is compelling, but have you any objective evidence to offer in support?' I understood from my briefings that this woman was a lawyer in the field of human-delph relationships.

'Only what I saw and heard.'

'You must know yourself that hearsay evidence is hardly conclusive.'

'I know. I should have taken a recorder, something to get factual proof. But the delphs can corroborate it, they've known it for years.'

'But, as you said, the delphs are bound by their law.'

'Then force them to talk. Make them tell . . . they have to.'

'Your report would seem to indicate that it is not in their interests to do so, that they may already have made changes to the Law to prevent it being circumvented again in the way you did.'

'But you do believe me.'

I held silence for the correct degree, then said, 'My sister, you may have placed your world's future in grave jeopardy.' That same morning I had made my preliminary report and recommendations via the satellite links to the Elders stored aboard *Hideoshi Maru*.

'But the delphs cannot be permitted to get away with it.'

'They cannot be allowed not to.'

'But UNIMEG, the conditions of the lease on Dido . . .' She had done her homework well. A pity for her she had not prepared her submission more rigorously. For us, a blessing. She might tell whomever she wished that Dido was inhabited by a sentient species, she might even be believed. Small matter, UNIMEG was ten and a half light-years away and all interstellar traffic remained firmly in the hands of the Gracious House. By the time any routine probe arrived from Motherworld, the process of deforestation should be so far advanced as to be ecologically irreversible. I said, 'If Dido dies, the Gracious House dies with it. As with the kelp and the kelpies, the corporate life is symbiotic and interdependent. One dies, all die. Do you think you could live in the Yokohama municipal arcologies for the redundant, the unemployed, the non-contracted? I am told that some days you can actually see the ocean but I do not think you would much care to share it with the floes of chemical waste and rafts of plankton and shoals of human sewage. No more swimmers, no more songs, no more bright summers of love on the foam of the world-sea. How long do you think you could live, Lynka Wei, without the sea? Or the sun? I remember the first day I saw the sun. I was fifteen and as a special birthday favour I was taken by my tutor, the Honourable Mr Hanagi, to see the sun. At first I did not know what I was looking for, and then I saw it, far, lost, wan beyond the billowing smogs and chemical hazes. The sun of the earth. You live in paradise, sister, and paradise is the most exquisitely balanced of all ecologies. Do nothing that would upset it.'

Shades of sunset caught on the waves beneath Touai Point; extraordinary, delicate as a tissue flower. It could all be lost so easily, crumpled and discarded. The air smelled of the pine. Not the artificial, disinfected pine of Company air-conditioning I had known all my life; wild pine by a wild sea.

'I would be prepared to sacrifice that if it meant the kelpies would not be exterminated.'

'Exterminate? The word was never spoken by me. The Gracious House is a humane organisation. Your claim will be investigated and, if it is true, I'm sure, with the permission of the Elders, reservations will be set aside, well removed from the mining operations. We are not genocides.'

For some reason she smiled.

'Ah, but we are. Especially when we are being our most humane.'

It was then that I realised that this woman, these people, their world, were as truly alien as any race of kelp-dwellers beneath the world-sea. There was nothing that could gainfully be said by either of us. Alien to alien. We bowed and parted. I do not know why I stopped to turn and look, it seemed a vital coda to our conversation that I do so. I saw her there on the high point, a silhouette against the sun. I saw her take something from a pocket of her quilted jacket, hold it up and throw it away from herself as hard as she could. Then she saw that I was watching and called, 'I am free of my elders and ancestors. What about you? Can you live your own life, no ghosts, no expectations?'

I never saw her again. I did not have an answer, then. Now, as *Hideoshi Maru* prepares to leave Dido-space for the long jump to earth and I lie awaiting the needle that will send me into suspended sleep, I think I have an answer.

It is that I am a Company man. I cannot be anything other. There is nothing for me but the Company, without it I would cease to have any meaning. Without it, I would be as pointless as those creatures without contract or position in the Yokohama arcologies. Without the Company, without its Elders to guide us, there would be no world. Only Chaos.

As the needle slipped into my arm, I reviewed my final memories of Dido. A lighter lifting off from Watts Island with a roar and blast of superheated steam and laserlight with the first cargo of monopoles from the new Circe Basin fields, bound for rendezvous with the drone freighter *Josenji Maru*. A flight of cargo lifters drifting up from the Environmental Engineering pad at Yellow Bay, bound for OTEC Debbie on the Genji Ridge. In their cargo bays, pods of *Crucifera Epsilon Minor* spores. I see all this and am pleased because I know that I have done good. Good for the Company, good for the Elders, good for myself.

But there is one last memory that I will take with me into my subjective sleep. I see the delphs and the haulers playing in the cool of the evening afterglow and I understand why they are joyful. And I think I see with them the figure of a slender girl-woman twisting and cutting through the warm waters of Mother-sea. But then the fog comes rolling in across the waters and I can no longer be certain.

WINNING

The beach is a white crescent of sand under the white crescent moon. Caught in the arms of the moon is a single bright star; a low-orbit manufactory. Below, the tourist hotels and beach-front restaurants show a scatter of lights. Tourists from Dahomey and Luzon and Costa Rica drink and dance and snort designer SYNTHC and stalk in sexual ambush among the pin-lasers and multi-layer video-shriek. It is many hours since they abandoned the casual nudity of the beach to the moon and the stars and Hammadi.

He slips under the loose wire by the irrigation channel outfall. The air is clean and cool, it has the crispness of autumn and the end of the season: after these tourists have checked out of their rooms and flown back to Dahomey and Luzon and Costa Rica, there will be no more. In the moonlight Hammadi limbers up using the isotonic flex routine the Company taught him. In twenty seconds he is ready. He slips out of the fleecy tracksuit. The repro-shops of Penang and Darwin produce good copies of professional bodysuits: skin-smooth, patterned with patches of bright primaries, sponsorship logos in all the right places. They look good, but Hammadi has worn both and knows the difference. A copy does not caress you, does not become one with you through eight thousand biomonitors and sensory systems and interfacers. It does not feel like a living skin. It feels like what it is: smooth stretch fabric made up in the immigrant sweatshops of Vancouver and Tananarive.

The wind is blowing off the mountains where snow has lain for weeks: Hammadi shivers, breathes it in, lets it blow through the hollow places of his body and soul. Tank-taught disciplines take over, tyrosine and norepinephrine levels in his bloodstream soar, pushing him into a state of amplified awareness. His senses are so finely honed he can count every grain of windblown sand against his cheek, hear the roll and surge of the blood around his bones, see the photons boiling from the lights of the tourist hotels and beach clubs. He gathers the energy surging within him into a tight cord, releases it. And he is running, past the hotels and beachside clubs and closed-down restaurants, down the long crescent of white sand. He is the Lion of God, the swift arrow of desire, he is the man Allah made fast so that he might delight to see him run.

It had always been his blessing and his curse, to have been specially gifted by God, for his father had used it as an excuse to exalt him above his brothers. At the dinner table, the only place where the lives of all the Al Bourhan family intersected, Al Bourhan Senior would bang the table and point at the inhumanly tall inhumanly beautiful bodies of the professional athletes that moved with liquid grace and power on the wall-mounted Sony flatscreen. Mouth full of couscous, he would berate his four other sons for their uselessness. 'You think I don't hear, you think I am deaf, stupid, you think I am old and senile, that I don't hear you muttering how I am unfair, unjust, a bad father because I love Hammadi better than the rest of you? Well, I do not deny it. I love Hammadi the best, and you know why?' Crumbs of food would fly from his lips, he would stab his fingers at the figures drifting languidly around the track. 'That is why. Because God has given him the chance of bettering himself, because he can hope for a life that is more than just getting a job and marrying a good woman and raising a family, a life that is more than serving drinks on a silver tray in a hotel or selling brass tea-pots to tourists until you die. That is why.' When Al Bourhan spoke like this Hammadi would leave the room. He could not look at his father or his brothers. He had not asked to be gifted by Allah. The inhumanly tall inhumanly beautiful figures of the athletes on the wallscreen kept drifting around the oval track beneath the tiered seats in the great stadium.

Jamila Al Bourhan was a woman who served God by serving men. She knew that men were stupid and vain creatures, capable of almost limitless stupidity in the name of their vanity, yet she married them, bore them, served them, even loved them, because she loved God more. Her work was her prayer, her kitchen her mosque. The law no longer required that women wear the veil, but some women can wear invisible veils all their lives. She watched Al Bourhan, the man God had made her to serve, wake Hammadi at five in the morning to train. She watched him take the boy out after his day at the garage to practise on the gritty, sweating streets. At night, when the cafés and bars were putting up the shutters, she watched him, on Haran's moped, pacing her son through the pools of hot green neon Arabic. She watched her family with the dispassionate detachment of Allah All-Merciful, All-Wise.

She was watching from the kitchen the day Al Bourhan presented the package at the dinner table. Everyone knew what it was, of course, but Hammadi pretended he did not as he opened the plastic wrap and held the brightly coloured bodysuit up against himself.

'It's only a copy,' Al Bourhan apologised, but she saw the look on his face that was at once shy and proud. She saw Hammadi bow his head to hide his embarrassment, she saw how her four sons bowed their heads to hide their disappointment and anger. That night Hammadi went running, brilliant as a bird beneath the glaring fluorescents, just like the professionals on the sports channels. His brothers sat around the table drinking mint tea and watching a Russian Metal band on a music channel beamed by satellite from Singapore.

That night, Jamila Al Bourhan spoke with the husband God had given her. 'You will drive your sons away from you; they see how you look at Hammadi and how you look at them and they feel unworthy, they feel they are not sons to you.'

'Wife,' said the husband Allah had willed to her, 'so many times I am explaining this and still you will not understand. Hammadi has been touched by the hand of God, and God's gifts are not to be wasted. It would be as wrong for him not to run as it would be for me to kill a man. If I push him to train, if I push him to his limits, and beyond, if I make him hate me a little, I do it so that some day he will be the one standing there on that track with the world watching him. I do it only so that he may fulfil the will of God for him.'

'The will of Khedaffey Al Bourhan, you mean,' said the woman who loved Allah more than she loved men. 'It is an easy, and terrible, mistake to make, to think your will is God's will.'

But Al Bourhan was already shouting at his useless sons to switch off that decadent rubbish and tune the set back to IntRelay Sattel-Sport. Hammadi's mother picked the discarded bodysuit off her son's bedroom floor. It felt like something a snake had left behind.

That Sunday night Al Bourhan took Hammadi by black and white moped-cab to a street corner where the palm-lined Boulevard of Heavenly Peace ran into the shanties where the refugees from the war in the south had been hidden by the government. A number of other boys were already there, some in bodysuits like himself, some just in shorts and vests. There was a large crowd of spectators, people not just from Squattertown, but from all parts of the city. Electric thin men kept this side of starvation by government food handouts stood only a bodyguard away from designer-muscled men and girls in paisley bodypaint. Al Bourhan paid the entrance fee to a man sitting on an upturned tangerine crate. Hammadi went to warm up with the other runners. Excitement was a warm snake coiling in the pit of his belly. All the hours driving himself along those roads and pavements in those twilight hours, that chilly pre-dawn glow, in the weariness after hours of wrestling with the innards of buses and trucks, had been for this electric thrill of *competition*. He saw his father haggling with a small man in a crocheted hat who seemed to have a lot of money in his hand.

The starter called them to order. There were no blocks, no lanes, no electronic timing, no hovering cameras, but crouching under the yellow floodlights the government had put up to reveal the lives of Squattertown, Hammadi felt he was in that great silver dome with the eyes of the world watching. 'Fast as a cheetah,' he whispered. 'God's cheetah.' Then the gun went off and the spectators, rich and poor, rose as one with a roar, and Hammadi was burning along the boulevard under the tattered palm-trees, blood bursting in his veins, to feel the tape brush across his chest. He returned to his father, who was receiving a large amount of cash from the man in the crocheted hat, high on victory.

'Nine point nine seven,' said Al Bourhan. 'You can do better than that.'

Every weekend there was a street-race somewhere in the city, or in one of the neighbouring cities. Al Bourhan's winnings from the man in the crocheted hat, who went to all the races, grew smaller and smaller as the odds against his son grew shorter and shorter. He still made quite a lot of money out of Hammadi, but it was not riches he wanted, it was success.

The season traditionally concluded with the big meeting in the capital where the nation's youth met together in the Great Fellowship of Sport to have their endeavour rewarded with medals from the hand of the President. Medals from the hand of the President and the Great Fellowship of Sport were the furthest things from the minds of the athletes who travelled up to the capital: the talent scouts from the big corporations would be there with contracts in their thumb-lock impact-plastic cases.

The capital was an eight-hour bus journey distant. So that Hammadi might be fit and fresh, Al Bourhan booked them into a hotel close by the stadium. It was not a very expensive hotel, just grand enough to have prostitutes in the lobby bar. As Hammadi came down in the elevator for his evening run, they unfolded pneumatic thighs, smiled diamanté smiles and surrounded him in a nimbus of synthetic allure from their wrist-mounted pheromone enhancers. They ran cooing, purring fingers over the firm contours of his body-suit. Hammadi was half hysterical with sexual confusion by the time his father shooed them away from his champion back to their stools by the bar. On his return, they clicked their tongues and pursed their lips and hitched their rubber micro-skirts to flash dark Vs of pubic hair at him. Hammadi's sleep that night was prowled by soft, writhing, fleshtone dreams.

Entering the stadium from the competitors' tunnel, Hammadi was overcome by a sudden disorientation. He was a street-racer, a runner of the boulevards and the palm-lined avenues; surrounded by a curving wall of faces, tier upon tier upon tier of mothers fathers brothers sisters wives husbands lovers, he was reduced to a small and brilliantly coloured insect creeping upon the smooth red running track. He searched the banked seats for his father. Impossible to find the one face in the ten thousand that meant anything to him. He was anonymous. He was nothing. The other runners came out onto the track and he saw their spirits shrivel as his had, and they were all the same, equally handicapped, all street-racers, night runners, poor boys on the round red track. Above the stadium blimp-borne laser projectors painted advertisements for the sponsoring companies across artificially generated clouds.

The starter called them to order. Hammadi prayed the prayer he always prayed before he ran; that God would make him fast today. All along the line the other runners completed their preparations, physical and spiritual. The starter raised his gun. The flat crack filled the stadium one split second before the crowd rose in a wall of sound and Hammadi plunged from his blocks down the red tracks and across the line in one continuous thought.

He collected his medal from the President, who did not shake hands due to yet another public health scare and took it to show his father.

'You show me that? A bit of metal on a string and you think you have achieved something? Hammadi, meet Mr Larsby. He is from Toussaint Mantene.' A small white man in an expensive Penang suit shook Hammadi's hand for a full minute and said a lot of things none of which Hammadi could later remember. He was high on winning. On the way back to the hotel in the taxi Hammadi's father kept hugging him and saying how this was the proudest day in his life. The small white man in the Penang suit was waiting for them in their room. With him was a taller, thinner man in a Nehru suit. He was scanning the walls with a small hand-held unit.

'Purely routine,' he said. 'You never know, they get everywhere.' He had the kind of voice Hammadi had only ever heard on the satellite channels. The small man opened his thumb-lock impact-plastic case and took out two thick sheaves of paper.

'Right here and here,' he said. The small man placed his signature under Hammadi's graceful Arabic, and Al Bourhan and the man in the Nehru suit witnessed.

'Congratulations,' said the small man, Larsby. 'Welcome to Toussaint Mantene.' Al Bourhan was sitting on the bed in tears. The realisation was only slowly penetrating Hammadi's victory high that he was not an amateur, a street-racer, a boulevard runner, any more. He was on the other side of the television now. He was one of the inhumanly tall inhumanly beautiful figures that drifted around the silver dome. He was a professional.

His father was ecstatic. His brothers unsuccessfully tried to hide their jealousy. His mother concealed her pride behind fear for his spiritual wellbeing. But they all came with him to the big airport in the capital where Larsby and the man in the Nehru suit would take him onward on a suborbital Sänger. The brothers watched the incredible shapes of the aerospacers moving in the heat-haze. Al Bourhan shouted at them for not being appreciative of their brother's blessing. To Hammadi it was enough that they had come. His mother nervously watched the streamlined aircraft with the crescent moon and star of Islam on its tail approach the airdock. She took her son's face in her hands and the intimacy of the gesture abolished every other person in the departure lounge.

'God has given you a gift,' she said, rapidly, for Larsby and the man in the Nehru suit were approaching through the aisles of seating. 'Never forget that it is not yours, it is only lent to you. Be true to the one who gave it to you. Honour Allah and He will honour you.'

Then Larsby and the man in the Nehru suit came and took him through emigration control into another country.

He has settled into his stride now. All the motor and sensory faculties of his body are operating at optimum. He is aware of the exact state and function of every muscle. He can hear, like gunfire in the hills, the crack and fire of her synapses, the seethe and surge of chemotransmitters along the neural pathways. He feels he can run at this pace for ever. He knows this is just a phase, in time he will pass from it into the next when his body will begin to cry out in protest at what his brain is forcing it to do. The muscles will begin to burn, the lungs to strain for oxygen, the red dots will explode softly, noiselessly, in his vision. He will want to give up, stop, give in to the pleading of the body. But he will keep on, along that beach, and he will find that suddenly the pain and the urge to give up will no longer matter, his spirit will have risen above them, above all things physical and psychological. He will perceive himself running on the crescent of white sand beneath the lights of the orbital factories with the eye of God. He calls this the 'Sufi State', after those men who whirled themselves out of the flesh into the spirit. Running is not merely a conquering of space and time by the body, but also by the soul.

He has left the lights of the beach-front cafés and tourist hotels behind, his run now takes him past the condominiums of the rich; the government officials, the police chiefs, the drug squirearchs. Their low white houses huddle behind triple-strand electrified wire and thermal-imaging myotoxin dart throwers. A few lights burn on patios and by poolsides. He can hear the cries of the women as they are tumbled naked into the swimming pools and the bull-laughter of the men who are tumbling them. The cool wind carries the smell of barbecuing meat and the sweet, glossy scent of SYNTHC. Close by the wire, dog eyes shine reflected long-red. The manufacturers of custom dogs supply implanted electronic surveillance systems as standard. Standard also the chips in their cerebral cortexes connected to a portable Behaviour Control Unit. Implanted compressed gas lances that can blow an intruder's intestines out through his mouth and anus are extra. They watch the running figure in their artificial enhanced vision. They do not bark, they never bark, their vocal cords have been removed. Behind the bio-beat and the *drastique* the cries of the women have taken on a new, insistent rhythm.

Hammadi runs on. His footprints in the damp sand by the sea edge slowly fill with black water.

They laughed when he asked where the windows were.

'It costs a billion apiece to build these things, you can't expect decoration,' said Larsby. Hammadi was disappointed. If he was going to the edge of space at least he wanted to see what it was like. Like a good Muslim he refused the hostess's offer of tranquillisers and was sick for the entire forty-minute suborbital flight.

The car from the airport had tinted windows, a bar and an office unit. It drove along an ocean-front boulevard lined with ragged palms. There were tourist hotels and condominiums, there were street vendors and pedicab ranks, there were people running and people walking little dogs, there were beggars and security-company prowl cars. There were holographic advertisements for cameras and computers and condoms and *cannabarillos*. The alphabet was different. The other difference was the immense truncated cone of a corporate arcology standing across the near horizon like God. Hammadi could not have said what part of the world he was in.

They gave him an apartment on the fifty-fifth floor with a veranda overlooking the ocean. The only thing he did not like about it was that he could not turn off the television. He went out onto the balcony to look at the ocean and saw that all the surrounding balconies were occupied by naked fat women lying on their backs in the sun. Towards evening a woman opened the door Larsby had told him only he could open. She was dressed in a leather pouch and paisley bodytint.

'Excuse me, can I help you?' Hammadi asked. The woman stood there a full minute, smiling at him in a way that was both pitying and relieved. She closed the door and he never saw her again. His training began the next day.

The first two weeks he did not run at all. He was measured, weighed, analysed, sectioned, taken apart and reassembled. He had electrodes connected to his skull and sat for hours in a darkened room telling a synthetic voice which of two lights flashed first, he arranged shapes and matched up grids on holographic displays, he was lowered into sensdep tanks and exposed to different coloured lights, he was shot full of injections that made him feel angry or sleepy or horny or induced bizarre hallucinations or made him feel like crying continuously or that he had seen the face of God and forgotten what it looked like. The man in the Nehru suit made him sign a consent form and when he woke up from surgery he was thirty centimetres taller and had plastic parallel interface ports under his ears and at the back of his neck and along his spine and inner thighs. He stroked the soft plastic with his fingers. It made him want to cry.

Every day he asked Larsby when he was going to run.

'You'll be in full training soon enough,' Larsby said. 'Don't worry, this is all just to find out what we need to design a training programme specially for you that will bring you to your optimum performance peak. By the way, sign this.' It was another consent form.

'What is it for?'

'It's just a general consent for us to introduce performance-enhancing agents into your food.'

'Wait, please. Do you mean you want me to take drugs? Mr Larsby, Islam prohibits the abuse of drugs.'

Larsby pursed his lips.

'Well, they're not exactly drugs, in fact, they're not drugs at all, they're naturally occurring chemicals, well, synthetic copies of them, found in the body, that stimulate muscle development, neural responses, and overall growth. Really, you shouldn't call them drugs at all.'

Hammadi signed the form. He could not tell when they started to put the performance enhancers in his meals. At the end of the two weeks of testing, Larsby sent Hammadi for five days of sun, sand, surf, sleep and sex at a Company beach resort down the coast. When he returned having enjoyed all of these bar one, Larsby summoned him to his office.

'Got something for you.' A panel slid open in the wall. Hanging there, in this year's latest pastels and black, with all the logos in all the right places, was a Toussaint Mantene bodysuit. Hammadi tried it on in a small dressing room hidden behind another wooden panel in Larsby's office. As he sealed it shut, he felt it move and settle around his contours, felt the temperature-control mechanism adjust to his optimum heat-transfer pattern, felt the inbuilt film circuitry mesh with his parallel interfacers. Energy poured through him, burned up his spine, along his nerves and sinews. He had never experienced such a total, dynamic communion with his body before. He wanted to run and run and never stop. He looked at himself in the mirror, remembered the pride with which his father had presented him with the cheap Filipino copy.

The training began. Hammadi had thought he would be running every day with the other Company-sponsored athletes. Again he was wrong. Most of the competitive races were run in computer simulation. The few others he did meet in out-of-training hours were mostly boys like himself, lifted from lives of disadvantage and insignificance by the hand of Toussaint Mantene. Different skin, different hair, different eyes, same lives. They had too much in common to be able to communicate. Hammadi trained alone, under the silver dome with its tiers upon tiers of flipped-up seats and the lights that were supposed to simulate sunlight but never quite did.

Larsby monitored the training sessions from a glass box that descended from the roof. It had not taken Hammadi long to realise that, despite the whispered comments on the speaker they had implanted in his mastoid bone, Larsby was his coach only in so far as he was the man who had speculated in buying up the contract of a promising street-runner and invested his time and effort in bringing him to the point where he might some day win him and the Company a lot of money. He had heard from the other Toussaint Mantene athletes of the fortunes in shares and influence points that changed hands at the intercorporate athletics meets.

His real coach was the computer. It regulated his calorific, mineral, nutrient, trace and vitamin intake, it programmed his hours of sleep, it monitored his body functions and vital signs from the moment he pulled his bodysuit on in the morning to when he left it lying in a pile outside the personal hygiene cubicle at night, it produced optimum performance parameters for every action he made while running and programmed them into his muscles through the bodysuit interfacers, it compared his movements and responses with a holographic ideal synthesised from the performances of past champions, it checked Hammadi's real-time performance against his optimised model a thousand times a second and tightened up a neural firing curve here, flattened out a troublesome brainwave pattern there, adjusted the levels of alpha dopamines and K-endorphin groupings so that he was neither too happy nor too sad, too much in pain or not feeling the burn enough.

He saw the other athletes flying off to competition every other week and asked Larsby when he could run for the Company.

'You've got a way to go yet, son,' Larsby said in his always reasonable, always right voice. 'Lot to learn, boy. Lot of mistakes to put right. But you'll get there, don't you worry about that.'

'When?'

'When I say so.'

Months passed, the passage of the anonymous seasons apparent only in secondary, human responses: the changing fashions of the girls who rollerskated along the palm-lined boulevards; the jet-surfers and powerskiers putting on colourful wet-suits, the fat peely women who sunbathed naked on their balconies resetting their apartment lighting to UVB and making appointments to have their melanomas frozen off. Hammadi sent letters and flat-light holograms of himself to his family. In the letters he received in reply his father would say how proud he was that the son of such a humble man could hope to rise so high. His mother would be constantly amazed at how tall he was growing, how broad, how strong, why, she hardly knew him for the same Hammadi. She would always remind him that God honoured those who honoured Him. Hammadi looked at himself in the mirror in his personal hygiene cubicle, the long, deep look he had until now avoided. He saw what the radical replacement surgery, the growth factors, the daily physiotherapy, the muscular-development hormones, the high-energy diet, the muscle-pattern optimisation treatment had done to him. He hardly recognised himself for the same Hammadi.

Now when he trained he was driven by a deep and dark energy. It seemed like determination. It was anger, anger that his father had always, only, loved him for what he could become, not what he was. Larsby noticed the new, driving energy. 'So, what's the secret then, boy?' he asked. 'The computer models never predicted you'd hit this kind of form at this stage in training.'

'I looked at myself in the mirror and saw that I was not what I thought I was.'

'You keep taking that look,' said Larsby. 'And keep liking what you're seeing. I think maybe we might try you at the next race meet.'

Hammadi was flown in another windowless plane to another arcology by another oceanside and another track under its silver dome with tiers upon tiers of seats and lighting that was meant to simulate daylight but never quite did.

'You're entered in the two hundred,' Larsby told him. They were walking the track, letting the real-time analysers in Hammadi's shoes produce a model of the running surface. 'Given the range of entrants, the computer assigned the highest probability of an optimum performance in that event. Friday. Twelve thirty.'

Hammadi stopped walking.

'Could you not have entered me in an event that is not going to be run on a Friday?'

'You have some problem with Friday?'

Hammadi had known Larsby long enough to read a full spectrum of expressions into his practised blandness.

'It's the Holy Day. I can't run on the Holy Day, it would be dishonouring to God.'

Larsby looked at Hammadi as he might some dead thing washed up on the beach from deep in the ocean.

'Okay, so, I respect your religion, I respect every man who believes in something, but, Hammadi, you say God's made you fast, that's the secret of your success, I can accept that, you have a remarkable talent, but answer this, which would honour God more, to use the gift he has given you to show a world which, frankly, does not believe, the strength of your belief, or let that light be hidden, so that no one will see what God can accomplish through you?'

'I don't know. I'll have to think about this. Give me time, will you?'

'Son, you take all the time you need.'

Hammadi went to his apartment. He sat on the balcony overlooking the palms and the ocean. He thought about what his mother said about God honouring those who honoured Him, and her accusations that his father had confused the will of Allah with his own will. He prayed. He waited on God but no finger of fire wrote blazing letters across the yellow tropical stormclouds that clung to the horizon.

He went back to Larsby and said, 'I'll run. If I am honouring God, he will bless me. If I am dishonouring God, I will not succeed.'

Friday. Race day. Hammadi's bloodstream had been boosted with synthetic haemoglobin assistors and doped with adenosine triphosphates. By race time his nervous system was boiling with artificially induced fury. He ran onto the track and as the trackside tech team ran final checks on his biological, physiological and informational systems the cameras looked on, hovering like blue flies on their silent ducted fans. Then the adenosine triphosphate kicked in fully and all he cared about, all he lived for, was to annihilate every other runner on that track. In the blocks, the pulser ticked in the corner of his field of vision, recording World, PanOlympic, Corporation and Personal records. The starter was a ringing blip in his ears and a flash of red across his vision. Cortical electrical activity peaked momentarily to multi-volt levels and sent him burning away from the blocks in a split-second of controlled epileptic spasm. The PCP pump in the base of his skull trickled 3-4-morphoatropine and tyrocine salicylate into his brainstem; he felt he was growing in size until he filled the entire stadium. He could complete the two hundred metres in a single stride. Larsby's voice in his ear spoke through a wash of mantras designed to erase everything unneedful from his attention except winning. He was running like a god, with the great easy strides Allah takes across Creation, galaxies in a single step. Yet, somehow, there were others in front of him. Under his bodysuit his muscles moved into new configurations as the interfacers fed new response patterns to the changing tactical situation.

It was begun and ended in less than ten seconds.

He had come third.

Larsby was ecstatic. 'Third! Third! In your first competition! Boy, you beat runners been competing for three, four, five years, runners who've won PanOlympic medals. I don't know what it was you did, boy, but you ran yourself right off our projections.'

Hammadi was disconsolate. Third. He felt he had failed father, God, Company. He had never felt the down after a PCP high before. He picked his way through the other crashed, shivering athletes for a place to hide and cry.

In his apartment was a letter forwarded from his father. There was a photograph of what looked like several hundred people crammed into the front room of his old home, all cheering and waving. His mother was nowhere to be seen, presumably making mint tea for the men. He might have honoured everything else, but he had failed his mother.

He is beyond it now. Behind him lies the laughter of the condominiums and the dark, desperate pulsebeat of the tourist hotels. The city is a cluster of lights, soft as powder, at the end of the beach, like the jewelled hilt of a sword. He runs on into the night, under the moon and the orbiting factories, past the dark olive groves and fig orchards and the houses of the humble, the olive farmers, the sardine fishermen, people whose lives have been largely passed over by the twenty-first century, except for the satellite dishes on their roofs and the squatter camps of refugees from the war in the south in the shade of their grandfathers' olives. No lights here, these are a people who rise and set with the sun, but from the cardboard and plastic shanties Hammadi can hear the solar-charged televisions the government hands out. He wonders, do they recognise this running figure in its sleek primaries and corporate logos as the same man they cheered on to victory and national glory on those twenty-centimetre screens that are the only sources of light in the fetid, filthy shanties? The same sweet, glossy smell that haunts the condominiums carries to him from the shoreline squats. The condo people buy their highs with smartcards, the shanty people get them free, courtesy of the government as an exercise in social engineering, but they all end the same. Long-term SYNTHC users display symptoms similar to Alzheimer's. The government's generosity to its dispossessed gently shepherds the refugee problem to its own self-imposed final solution.

But Hammadi is the sufi, the dervish of Allah, translated into a purer, higher form of worship which gathers body mind emotion and spirit together in one living declaration of the power of God. This was the part of him the Company could never subcontract, the state of exaltation they could never simulate, for all their chemicals and computers and conditioning, the part where divinity and humanity touched, the unknown fire that drove Hammadi Al Bourhan off their graphs and models and extrapolations.

Every other week he was flown to a competition against another company. Hammadi made steady progress up the ratings from also-ran and third to third and second to second and first. Larsby's wins on the credit and influence stakes grew smaller and smaller as the odds against Hammadi Al Bourhan grew shorter and shorter, but Larsby's eyes were set on a greater horizon. In ten months it would be the PanOlympiad and the chance of glory against the gathered corporations. Hammadi saw that horizon also, but his immediate concern was with a man called Bradley Nullabiri. He had met him first in a training simulation, the man who was to become his closest and deadliest rival. Bradley Nullabiri, Bayer-Mainhof GmBH, born 21 December 2002 Alice Springs Australia one of the final generation of pure-bred Aboriginals: he studied that black man, ran and ran and ran that simulated two hundred metres against him until there was nothing about him as an athlete or a human that he felt he did not know. Then he flew on a suborbital Sänger with Larsby and his twenty-person tech team to run against him in the flesh.

He lost. They met again, in the return meet, when it was Bradley Nullabiri's turn to fly in with his coach and tech team. Hammadi lost. There was one more thing about Bradley Nullabiri that the files didn't cover: Bradley Nullabiri was also a man who had been touched by the hand of God, his gods, the stalking ones, the ancient ones, who had drawn his two-hundred-thousand-year heritage behind them out of the Dreamtime. In every respect, they were the same. Except one, and that was the one that made Bradley Nullabiri unbeatable.

Bradley Nullabiri knew he was unbeatable.

'Question of attitude,' Larsby said. 'Nothing magical about it. You just got to believe you're more unbeatable than he is.'

Hammadi spent the three weeks until their next meeting in the company of the psychologists who never got round to explaining what their tests were for or how he had scored in them. Team Al Bourhan was loaded into an aerospacer and disgorged after the forty-minute flight to do battle with Bradley Nullabiri. Media interest was by now so hyped they were charging two hundred thousand a minute for advertising. The race went to a freeze-frame finish. Hammadi lost by three hundredths of a second.

'Forget Bradley Nullabiri,' Larsby told a depressed Hammadi on the flight home. 'You got to concentrate on the PanOlympics. Every waking and sleeping, you're thinking of nothing but PanOlympic gold. PanOlympic gold. PanOlympic gold.'

'Bradley Nullabiri will be there.'

'So will Hammadi Al Bourhan. PanOlympics are different.'

His father, in his regular letters, gave the same advice: Allah would never permit the Godless to triumph over His Chosen, it was ordained that he would win gold at the PanOlympics and bring everlasting glory to Islam, his country, and the name of Al Bourhan.

Incidentally, thanks to the money the Company put into a trust fund from his account, they had recently moved into a newer and bigger house, thank you, son.

Hammadi no longer replied to his father's letters.

Twenty minutes into the flight, just before the aerospacer went into freefall at the apex of its orbit, Hammadi realised that either he hadn't been told, or hadn't asked, where they were going. The new diamond-fibre doped ceramoplastic ankle joints which enabled him to withstand even more acceleration away from the blocks ached dully in freefall. The anti-rejection drugs were ab-reacting with the freegee tranqs. He felt vast and vertiginous.

India. The room was the same, the television he could not turn off was the same, the balconies with the nude sunbathing women were the same (except that here they were fat and brown rather than fat and pink), the palm-fringed ocean with its cargo of jet-surfers and powerskiers and body-sailers was the same. But somewhere some geographical sense long abused by the mandatory uniformity of the world insisted this was *India*.

And this was the PanOlympiad. The youth of all nations gathered together in the Great Fellowship of Sport under the Eternal Flame and the Six Rings (one for each continent and one extra for the new orbital settlements). With the inevitable exceptions: some of the companies locked in takeover and merger battles were not sending teams, and TSA Lagrange were boycotting the games as protest against the PanOlympic Council ruling that their technique of temporarily suspending their athletes' personalities through massive doses of PGCPE and ergominesterase and giving control of their bodies to the coaching computers was contrary to the PanOlympic tradition of sportsmanship.

Hammadi could not pronounce her name in her native language, but she told him it meant 'Swallow'. He translated that into his native language and she said she liked the sound of it very much. She had been assigned to him by the organising committee as his liaison and guide through the planetary party that was the PanOlympiad. He was mistrustful at first that she was a spy for a rival corporation; performance data was a highly negotiable commodity. He had no illusions that his training schedule had not been prepared with the help of black data. Larsby assured him of his hostess's impeccability.

'It's the PanOlympics, boy,' as he said twelve times a day every day. 'Only comes round every four years, enjoy it, make the most of it.' It was unnecessary for him to add that this might be Hammadi's only chance to enjoy it: Hammadi understood how short an athlete's professional life could be. In three years he expected to retire, with at least one world record, to a condominium on the coast and a life donating sperm to Toussaint Mantene's genetic engineering programme at a million a year. So when he came out from the closed training sessions he was glad to let Swallow whirl him through the colour and movement and gaudiness and loudness of the Pan-Olympic city. She was the perfect hostess: informative, spontaneous, with the intelligence to be a foil to Hammadi's curiosity, witty, pretty (he could not deny that), fun to be with. She never made him feel like a street-racing boy from the global boondocks. The anticipation of her company after training put an extra sparkle in his performance; with his probability models improving every day, Larsby was happy to accede when Hammadi asked if Swallow might be permitted into the sessions. She sat with Larsby in his glass booth and watched Hammadi pit himself against holographic enemies.

'You are so beautiful when you run,' she told him. 'So alive, so you. You are like a big, graceful cat. Like a hunting cheetah.'

Hammadi bowed his head and blushed as he had learned when he was a boy and his father praised him above his brothers. Within was a different heat altogether.

She slipped her tongue into his mouth for the first time in Vidjaywada Shambalaya's, immersed in ethnobeat and video-shriek of interior bio-scapes macro-projected from nano-cameras circling the bloodstreams of the club's resident *drastique* dancers. Further radical replacement surgery had left Hammadi fifty centimetres taller and forty wider than Swallow; pulling her to him to taste her again, he understood how easily he could have snapped her like the bird from which she had taken her name. The *smell* of her enveloped him, erased the din of the club.

'You've never done anything like this before, have you?' she asked.

He shook his head, shyly.

'This is your first time.'

He nodded his head, shyly.

'Mine too.'

Larsby had a singular honour to bestow upon Hammadi. He was to carry the Company Banner in the Grand Parade of All Athletes. Swallow thought he looked most impressive in his specially designed team uniform in the Toussaint Mantene colours. Parading into the stadium at the head of Team Toussaint Mantene under the gaze of two hundred thousand spectators and fifty global Sat-tel networks, he looked long at the place where she had told him she would be sitting.

Later, she said she was so proud of him.

He said it had been nothing. Duty to the Company.

She said she thought he was beautiful.

He said no, she was beautiful, beautiful Swallow.

She said she had never felt about any other man the way she felt about him.

He said he had never known a woman who could make him feel the way he did right now.

She said did he want to make love to her?

And his will said no but his body said yes, yes.

Of course he came too early, before she even turned on. He was embarrassed but she told him it was all right, everything was all right, it was just inexperience, this was new territory for them both, they would explore together, as a team. They made love again and this time it was a slow attenuated coming together that had him roaring like a lion and whimpering like a dog and her growling guttural obscenities in the back of her throat. Afterwards he told her he loved her, he loved her, he loved her, but she had fallen asleep like a small and graceful savannah cat. He woke her with his penis to make love again. Outside in the sub-morning, blimps painted the clouds Day-glo with holographic sponsorship messages and the never-ending world party coiled and uncoiled. The lights of the low orbitals, the new estate, rose to the ascendant and set.

He was too excited to sleep afterwards, though the two hundred metres heats were only two days away. He sat in a soliform chair and thought about Swallow and thought about God. Sexual impurity had been the most heinous of his mother's library of sins. Yet what he had experienced had been so good and so holy that it could only have been a gift from God. Only when he had run himself into a state of sublime awareness had he ever experienced anything as divinely thrilling. He felt no guilt: two adult, responsible humans had been attracted to each other, as Allah had created them; had come together, as Allah had created them; had made love, as Allah had created them. He had enjoyed the creation of God. He had committed no sin. He had not dishonoured God.

He crossed to the bed to look at her in the nakedness of sleep. He stroked her back, her thighs, her breasts, ran his fingers through her hair. His fingers stopped on the ridge of bone just behind her left ear.

Embossed in the flesh were three letters.

TM®.

He knew those letters. He carried them himself, in the places where Toussaint Mantene had replaced his own bone and sinew with their diamond-fibre doped ceramoplastics.

He booked a ticket on a Sänger on the apartment unit. Team Toussaint Mantene Security came bursting in through the door they had told Hammadi only he could open to see just what the hell their prospective PanOlympic star thought he was doing, but he had already slipped away from them through the corridors and arcades and never-ending planetary party. In the acceleration seat he thought about the prostitutes in the almost-grand hotel. The smile subtler, the costume less provocative, the enhanced pheromones less insistent, the approach less blatant. That was all.

He had told her that he loved her.

Despite the gee-shock tranqs, he still threw up. The hostess swiftly vacuumed up the floating globules of vomit before gravity returned.

He sat on the balcony and looked at the sea and waited for Larsby. He was not long coming. It gave Hammadi a dry satisfaction to see the bland carelessness discarded like the mask it was. He let the small man scream himself hoarse, then asked, 'Who was she?'

'Someone, anyone, no one, does it matter?'

'It matters.'

Larsby had been defeated the moment he had walked through the door.

'Just a girl. From our Industrial Espionage Division. A Strength Through Joy girl. You would have recognised one of our own, so we had to do a little camouflaging surgery to, ah, fit her to the role.'

'Don't blame her. It was you got careless.'

Larsby grinned helplessly.

'Tell me why,' Hammadi said.

'Because you still didn't believe in yourself. Because there was still an area in your life where you believed you were a failure.'

'With women.'

'It's all there in your file. PsychCorps saw it the first day you walked in here. You have a massive self-confidence problem with women, you can't believe you can be successful sexually. While that self-doubt remained, you could never have beaten Bradley Nullabiri. So we set you up with a woman who would be irresistibly attracted to you, go to bed with you, tell you she loved you, so you would feel great enough about yourself . . .'

'I know!' Hammadi shouted. Then, more gently, 'I know . . .' He looked at Larsby. 'Did she ever, do you know if, whether, she . . . felt anything?'

'Would it make a difference?'

'Not really.'

'We needed you to beat Bradley Nullabiri.'

'Winning is everything.'

'Yes,' said Larsby.

'You aren't even sorry,' Hammadi said. 'Well, it will just have to go down in history as one of the great unanswered questions in sport.' He handed Larsby an envelope.

'You don't want to do this, boy.'

'Oh, yes, I do.'

On the television you couldn't turn off, Bradley Nullabiri was running in the finals of the two hundred metres. He won. Hammadi did not feel a thing.

With regret the Company accepted Hammadi's resignation and took away his apartment with its view of the palms and the ocean and the naked sunbathing women. It suspended use of his *plastique* card and payment to his account and his parents' trust fund. It stripped him of the pastel and black bodysuit in which he was to have beaten Bradley Nullabiri. It put him into surgery and took back the PCP pump in his brainstem. It removed the sensory amplifiers and implanted neurochips and the biotech interfacers. It took out the diffusers and the synaptic controllers and the bio-assay monitors and the mastoid speaker and the subvocal mike and the parallel ports and the serial muscular triggers and the subdermal blood scrubbers and left him with himself. It took all this away because it was and always had been and always would be Company property, on loan to him under the terms of the sponsorship contract. That was what the man in the Nehru suit told him. The only thing the Company left him were the radical replacement ceramoplastic joints and shock absorbers. To have taken them away would have killed him. He stood two metres thirty in his skin and the weight of his new mortality bore down in him. He felt like an angel cast out of heaven.

The deductions the Company made from his account for the reclaimative surgery left him just enough for a Sänger flight home. The seat-back flatscreen showed him the closing parade of All Athletes in the Great Fellowship of Sport in the silver stadium in Madras. Hammadi felt like he had died.

His father would not speak to him. Disowned him, disinherited him, ignored him, treated him as worse than dead. His brothers wanted to sympathise but were kept from doing so by fear of their father's wrath. His mother kept Al Bourhan from throwing Hammadi out of the house. She listened, long long hours in her mosque-kitchen as her son tried to explain why he had done what he had done. In the next room the television blared. His father's silence blared louder.

'I honoured them, but they would not honour me,' he said. 'They pretended they cared about me, that they respected me as a man, as a Muslim, but all they respected was winning, all they wanted was a piece of meat that could run around a track faster than the other pieces of meat. And to please them, I compromised myself, little by little. I became what they wanted me to be, not what God wanted me to be.'

'You did not compromise,' his mother said. 'Not when it really mattered. In the end, you honoured God.'

'And has God honoured me?'

Jobs were easy for anyone who had done time with the Companies, even a failed star. Hammadi settled quickly into his post at the tourist-bus company arranging transfers between airport and hotels for the people from Dahomey and Luzon and Costa Rica. His work-mates soon learned not to question this over-tall, gangling freak about his racing days.

On his way home along the boulevards and palm-lined avenues he would be passed by street-racing boys, out practising. He could not look at them. His eyes were like lead. When he came home in these moods his mother would say, 'God made you fast, God still makes you fast. He still delights to see you run. He is not interested in whether you win or not, just that you run for His pleasure.'

It took many months for the truth of what she was saying to penetrate his sense of loss. But it was the truth, that in winning he lost, that in losing, he won. God had made him not to win, or to lose, but to run. Now when he saw the street-runners, he would watch them, carefully noting, analysing, mentally commenting, cor-recting, coaching. One night he found his old, old bodysuit draped on the bed. Mothers' intuition. He stroked the silky stretch fabric, rubbed it against his cheek. He smiled at how ludicrously outmoded it was. In the privacy of his room, he stripped, slipped it on.

It was nothing like a real bodysuit, of course, and it clung oddly around his massively re-engineered frame, but it felt right. That night he found his way through the wire mesh onto the private part of the beach and began to run, slowly at first, but with gathering strength and speed, along the white crescent of sand, for the glory and delight of Allah.

It is nearly over now; the white crescent of sand is dwindling away between sea and stone to a horn, a sliver, to nothing. He has left the people far behind, their cities, their hotels and beach clubs and condominiums, their farms and squattertowns and satellite dishes and sardine boats. He is among the eternal things; sea, sand, stone, sky, stars; unchanging things. Godlike things. At the end, where the beach peters out into jumbled rocks, he will stop, and then turn and jog slowly back beneath the moon and orbiting factories to the hole in the wire where he has left his tracksuit. But only at the end. Not before. He will run the race, he will go the distance. He glances at the fluorescent timer patch on the sleeve of his bodysuit. Not bad. Not what he would have hoped for, once. But not bad.

He is close now. The sand is running out beneath his feet, into the sea. He is tired, but it is a good tiredness. He is panting, but he still smiles. He is here. The end. The race is over. He stops, rests hands on thighs, bends over, breath steaming in the cool air. He looks around him, at the white crescent of sand, at the white crescent moon, at the sea, at the lights of the tourist hotels and the condominiums, almost all gone out now, at the eternal glow of the city.

And he leaps into the air. Arms spread, fists raised to heaven. A leap of triumph, a leap of joy. The leap of a man who knows that God has taken pleasure in seeing him run, for Him, just for Him, under the stars and the moon, along the deserted beach. The leap of a man who has won.

TOWARD KILIMANJARO

To every book its inscription. I have written my name in black ink inside the cloth cover but the syllables are harsh and clashing in this land of whispered sibilants and strong consonants. How much better the name Langrishe gave me: *Moon*, generous, looping consonants, vowels like two eyes, two souls looking out of the page. One half of T.P.'s final gift to me, this journal, clothbound and intimate in Liberty print; I treasure it, hug it to me, companion and confessor. T.P.'s other gift I treated less kindly: black dragonfly wings shredded by the impact, struts snapped like the bones of birds. Already the forest is at work on it, converting the organic plastics into dripping stalactites of black slime.

It is over an hour since I lost the beat of the helicopters in the under-song of the Chaga; my crash-landing must have looked sufficiently convincing for them to abandon the hunt. Forgive me, T.P., but you would understand: skimming across the tree-tops towards the looming edge of the Chaga with two Kenyan Army/Air Force Nighthawks behind me, expecting at any second to be smashed into nothingness by a thermal-imaging StarStreak missile; one's options are somewhat limited. Sorry about the microlyte, T.P. But I will be good to the diary, I promise.

I look again at those four letters: Moon. How much of life is a search for our true names, the jumble of ideograms that spells us as we truly are? Some, like T. P. Costello, attain true personhood in being reduced to their initials. Some intimate, cosy souls never become more than their Christian names, to others that name is a useless appendix, their true identity lies in their surnames, like you, Langrishe. And some only find personhood in the names they attract to themselves. *Moon*. They cannot see themselves, it takes another to tell them what they are. Moon. Langrishe. T.P. Our players. No, I have omitted one vital addition to the *dramatis personae*: the mountain.

'Wide as all the world; great, high, and unbelievably white in the sun': Hemingway described it. To the Masai it is *Ngajé Ngai*, the House of God; but most simple and striking is its Swahili name: *Kilima Njaro*, the White Mountain.

You never forget your first view of the mountain, as you never forget your first, nervous, thrilling view of a lover's body. When I flew in to the Ol Tukai that first time, the clouds were hanging low across the mountain but still its presence could be sensed, like God at Sinai. Interviewing Langrishe in his office my attention was increasingly distracted as beyond the window the final rags of cloud dissolved and dispersed and that astonishing white tableland caught and kindled in the African twilight. Spellbound: I watched the shadows move up across the uncanny geometries of the alien forest until the final red glow was extinguished from the snows. You never forget; like that first, electrifying exploration of love, you keep it secret and warm in your heart.

Again, my name, inscribed in black ink inside the front cover of the clothbound journal. I have given much thought to what kind of journal I should keep. A neo-Victorian almanac of wonders and horrors, each neat copper-plate entry headed, Day the –th, Year of Grace 20– ? Tempting. But my choice of travelling companions dictates otherwise. T. S. Eliot. Joseph Conrad. Thomas Merton. Not so much an expedition to the interior as a pilgrimage through the darklands of the soul. Langrishe as Holy Grail? The comparison would please him, arrogant bastard.

Early in the afternoon I came upon the remains of the old Ol Tukai Research Facility. Subtle transubstantiation: I had been picking a path between the vegetation-shrouded bones for some minutes before the nagging tingle of familiarity became recognition. The voracious forest life had long since converted the organic materials to its own matrix of tubes and fans and flows of blue lichen. All changed, changed utterly. It is less than a year since the line of advance engulfed the centre; now only the concrete and steel skeleton enforces some form of human geometrical discipline to the biological anarchy. I paused awhile in the memory of Langrishe's office. Kilimanjaro was lost behind wave upon wave of forest, the mood strange, and I uncertain of my own feelings. From out of the wilderness came a twittering, chiming music, like a child's experiments with a synthesiser, uncanny and alien. I never saw what it was sang that song.

I will not spend the night there. Memories too big.

Wide-eyed and clueless in the pick-up bay at Nairobi airport: I'd been in Kenya a whole half-hour and was still reeling from the *African-ness* of it all. Stepping off the plane into the sour grey pre-dawn drizzle, I'd almost kissed the tarmac; it was surely destined for canonisation, the place where the astonishingly talented girl writer from Dublin town who wrote *the* book on *the* phenomenon of *the* century first intersected with the surface of Africa. Now, two bags on the concrete, waiting and waiting while all around me taxis hire cars limousines shuttle buses were speeding my fellow passengers off to Sheratons Hiltons Intercontinentals Ramadas PanAfrics, the *African-ness* of it all was beginning to pale a little. Another flight came in, another disgorgement of travellers into the hinterland. I watched my own flight take off, onward bound, into a huge sunrise. The sun was well up and about its business by the time a dirty white Peugeot pick-up with what looked like a small greenhouse bolted to the back swung into the parking bay. The window rolled down, a face like an angst-ridden owl looked me up and down from behind immense spectacles and finally bellowed in dearest dirtiest Dublin, 'Bags in the back. You in the front. I'll get a ticket if I hang around here much longer; what'll I get?'

'A ticket?'

'That's correct.'

T. P. Costello: East African correspondent of the *Irish Times*; liaison, contact, mentor, in the end, best friend; the only man in Kenya who was fool enough (or impecunious enough) to be prepared to share an office with me. And the worst driver I have ever known. Some people are born to bad driving. Some aspire to it; to T.P. it was a major social accomplishment. As we took a roundabout at a speed that left rubber on the blacktop, he asked me, 'What kind of underwear have you got on?'

Wondering just what kind of a pervert I had saddled myself with, I told him.

'Throw them out,' he said. 'Nothing but cotton. Nylon traps moisture. You can get fungus. What can you get?'

'Fungus?'

'That's correct.'

Howling down the wide boulevards of downtown Nairobi I noticed we were passing by shining skyscrapers with names like Sheraton Hilton Intercontinental Ramada PanAfric.

'Just where are we going?' (An explosion of hooting as the Peugeot pick-up pulled out to overtake a lumbering green and yellow municipal bus straight into the path of an oncoming Nissan van: I'd never actually seen an expression quite like the driver's before.)

'The Kenyan Island Mission Guesthouse. It's comfortable, it's clean, it's central without you getting a noseful of diesel fumes every time you open your window, it's quiet – most of the guests are missionaries on R 'n' R – Mrs Kivebulaya, the proprietrix, thinks Irish girls are polite, quiet, charming and well behaved – please don't disillusion her – and, above all, it's cheap. Given, the meat can be a bit chewy, but you can afford it.'

We swung up a steeply curving drive and lurched to a halt in front of a relaxed red tile-roofed building, a genial mongrel of colonial and clinker-block ethnic. T. P. Costello busied himself in the back of the Peugeot and appeared with my cases and three chickens strung together at the feet, swinging.

'My compliments to Mrs Kivebulaya,' he said handing cases and chickens to a geriatric porter dressed in a jacket of almost inspirational vileness. T.P. screamed the engine, preparing for another ballistic leap into the traffic. '224b, Tom M'boya Street!' he shouted, and hurled himself into the streets.

I had never eaten chicken gizzard before – apparently it is something of a local delicacy. I enjoyed it much more than I should have.

Impressions from my notebooks: pen-sketches in that early light when we see clearest.

Woodsmoke, shit and diesel, street perfume; sweated from the red earth like a pheromone.

Wonderful incongruity: Colonel Saunders's patrician features intimidating the intersection of University Way and Koinange Street. Do all the black faces make him feel back on the ol' plantation again? Must order chicken gizzard with fries and buttermilk roll.

A man dressed Arab-style pushing what seems to be a small dog kennel on wheels along Kenyatta Avenue. The creeping horror when I glimpsed inside, the glitter of human eyes: a woman, wrapped in Muslim black, save for her hands, and eyes . . .

The Hilton is extravagantly proud of its English fish and chips served in a copy of the London *Times*. T.P. tells me of a certain journalist who goes there every day to order the delicacy, throw away the fish and chips and read the newspaper.

The city of the dance: the people move like liquid in the streets, as if to the mental beat of drums and wires.

The casual bribery of the police: T.P.'s KitKat tin in the glove compartment of the Peugeot where he keeps the bribes for motoring offences. The next best thing to a totally honest police force is a totally corrupt one. Dame Market Forces . . .

For a city under siege, Nairobi is remarkably cavalier about the fact. Since the package came down in the Nyandarua National Park last year, opening a second front, I reckon Nairobi has about a thousand days left before the advancing walls of vegetation close. But life goes on with a blithe disinterestedness that amazes this European girl, who would be running round like Chicken-Licken announcing the imminent fall of the sky. Disinterest, or African fatalism? Too much like a metaphor of death for this white girl, this *m'zungu*.

To every city its municipal obsessions: Dublin's is finding somewhere to park the car, Nairobi's is coin-in-the-slot photo booths.

T.P.'s office was three rooms above the Rift Valley Peugeot Service Depot on Tom M'boya Street where he was apparently offering asylum to an entire family of Asian refugees: mother on the telephone, daughter one on the typewriter, daughter two in reception, father book-keeper, number one son file clerk, number two son runner, honoured grandmother *chai*-maker. What amazed me was that they were so infernally busy all the time. I suspect that they were terrified of T.P. turfing the lot of them out onto Tom M'boya Street; certainly he ran his office with the self-assured smugness of a minor, benevolent dictator.

For my thousand shillings per month I had use of what T.P. called a 'Captain Kirk Chair', a desk, a telephone, a photocopier, a time-share of an asthmatic word-processor, the occasional privileged glimpse into the specially darkened room where the fax machine sat like a presiding deity, unlimited *chai* and biscuits and the pleasure of T.P. Costello's wit, wisdom, and virtually continuous bitching about his immediate superior, one so-called Jacobellini.

And while I sat drinking *chai*, engaging in dubious battle with the word-processor and spending entire afternoons waiting for the operator to connect me with some minor cog in the great quizzical machine of scientists and researchers, humanity's first encounter with an alien life form was advancing towards me one hundred steady metres per day.

Sometimes I felt it would be easiest just to sit and wait for it to come creeping along Tom M'boya Street, up the stairs and into the office.

Even the professional imagination falters before the face of the Chaga. Description fails, only analogy can convey some impression of this landscape through which I am travelling. The experience that comes closest is the time with Langrishe on the coast, when I was working on the book; our explorations of the reef in snorkel, mask and flippers. Crucified on the surface tension, peering down like vacationing Olympians into the underworld. God, how I burned! That night in the *banda*; the wind in the palms and the rattle of the thatch; Langrishe's hands slicing lemons, rubbing the juice into my skin . . . The gentle, painful, almost hallucinatory love-making, me riding him – was that the boom and crash of the surf on the reef, or the roar of my own blood and bone, or the song of Langrishe, inside me?

Shape yourself into some long-legged chitinous arthropod picking across a coral reef and you will have the feel of it. There is a submarine quality to the light that reaches you through the canopy of balloons, bladders, fans, umbrellas; submarine, and ecclesiastical, a cyclorama of colours like the light in a drowned cathedral. Analogy again.

I am beginning to wonder if my supplies will be sufficient, I had provisioned for twenty days, it may take that long just to reach the lower slopes of the mountain. The riotous Chaga-life confounds my sense of time and distance, I cannot judge how far, how fast I have come. I was so certain, then, now my stupidity at thinking that I can find one man, who may not, if I am honest with myself, which I rarely am, even be alive, in five thousand square kilometres of, literally, another world, astounds me. The sense of isolation is colossal.

Thank God for faithful fellow travellers! Conrad, brother explorer into the heart of darkness; Eliot, cartographer of the desert in the heart of man; Merton, pilgrim into the cloud of unknowing on the dawnward edge of faith. They know what it is to venture into an unknown region, into the utter subjective darkness of the interior wilderness.

Some spore is attacking my copy of *Seeds of Contemplation*, the vinyl cover is breaking out in tiny red warts. Amazing, the tenacity of these almost invisible flecks of life; despite my rigorous efforts to rid myself of all plastic and petrochemical based materials, they still managed to bring the little acrylic aglets at the end of my spare pair of laces out in sulphur yellow blossoms. Ironic that, after three years of the most intense scientific scrutiny anywhere on the planet, all the researchers can conclude is that the pseudo-vegetation (their word, not mine, please) of the Chaga is a carbon-based form of life grouped around long chains of what seem to be polymers as opposed to the amino-acid/protein axis of terrestrial life. The phrase 'Plastic Forest' entered the world vocabulary despite the protests of the researchers that really it wasn't plastic at all, rather a kind of long-chain self-replicating carbohydrate pseudo-polymer. Doesn't have quite the same snap, though.

Popular imagination perfumes the place like a decommissioned oil refinery. The reality is quite different: essential oils and musks, spices and incenses that seem maddeningly familiar though the memory can never quite place them exactly ... Sex. The Chaga smells like sex.

The industrial/chemical analogy may be very near the truth. The

Chaga is only partly photosynthetic (and that part which it seems to operate by a system quite different from, and more efficient than, the green green grass of home); some exploit temperature differentials, others make use of catalytic chemical reactions, some employ wind power, others remarkably efficient heat pumps, others still generate electricity directly from what can only be described as solar panels. Some, like the corals they closely resemble, feed off aerial bacteria, some literally eat rock. All are linked together in vastly complex hierarchies of symbiosis. Benumbed biologists I interviewed for the book maintained that it might take decades to unravel just one symbiotic system. The most recent theories, which will form an appendix to the finished book, extend the factory analogy to the microscopic; at the cellular level, the organisms resemble machines more than biological entities.

Henry Ford, cream yourself: will the Industrial Forest usurp the Plastic Forest in the media-fed mind of the Man on the Clapham Omnibus? If T.P.'s sources are anything to go by (and have they ever been anything other than reliable?) the executive singles of the Hiltons Sheratons Intercontinentals Ramadas and PanAfrics are hot-bunking Silicon Valley cyberneticists, brisk Teutonic micro-engineers, tofu-and-bran custom logic designers and giggling Sony-Nihon chip customisers; all engaged in internecine warfare to be the first to bring home the glittering prize to their particular genus of *Homo polycorporatus*. Sorry, boys, but the Good News from the Chaga is co-operation beats competition hands down, and is advancing towards your expense-account suites at one hundred metres per day.

I saw a vervet monkey today; nervous eyes in the shimmering canopy. A webbed sail of ribs, like some remnant of the time of the dinosaurs, grew from its back. I did not take it for a good omen.

I shall spend the night in the ruins of an old game lodge I came across unexpectedly; a memory of the days of zebra-striped Volks-wagen minibuses bristling broadsides of Nikons. One thing the Chaga has done is restore peace and dignity to the land. These foothills of Kilimanjaro feel old in a way the land in Europe never can; it deserves the respect due age. I slung up my hammock on the veranda of the old game lodge. I had meant to write, cook, wash, do something; but a melancholy lassitude came over me. A calling of spirit to spirit almost, as I lost myself in the shafts of green light. The fragile moment of self-unknowing when the consciousness is totally subsumed into the other, when the slightest tremor of self-awareness taps the still waters and the reflection shivers into ripples. Time out of mind. I heard him. I heard him, his voice, out there, a voice in solo flight above the chords of the forest song. I hear you, Langrishe. I am coming.

Towards nightfall the small glade in which the abandoned lodge stood came alive and ringing with songs. Twittering, rippling, passing into and out of phase with each other. As the first of them came out of the gathering dark, I rose to my feet; just the few at first, then the main body, a procession of creatures like faintly luminous jelly-fish rolling and undulating through the air. They separated around the lodge like a river around a rock; they were still coming to break around me as I retired to my hammock, out of darkness, onward into the darkness again.

I'll tell you the exact place and time I fell in love with Peter Langrishe: 17 March, 10.20 p.m., beside the drinks trolley in the garden of the Irish Ambassador's Residence. I could even tell you what we were drinking – me: John Jameson's, neat, just a clink of ice; he: a Glenlivet that had somehow found a niche on His Excellency's strictly patriotic booze wagon.

The annual ambassadorial St Patrick's Day party is the highlight of the expatriate community year. Southerner or Northerner, everyone is an Irishman on St Patrick's Night. Voluntary workers, development engineers, teaching sisters, rural midwives, Bible translators will move heaven and earth to be there for His Excellency's bash. Head of any guest list was T. P. Costello: it was widely known and never officially denied that if His Excellency really wanted to know what was happening in the greater world he would do much better visiting 224b Tom M'boya Street than grinding himself exceeding fine in the tedious mills of diplomatic intelligence.

An expatriate and colleague of T.P., my gilt-edged invitation was assured; knowing my tendency to drink myself horizontal – something I did not much want to do in the presence of teaching sisters rural midwives Bible translators ambassadors, etc. – I had thought of declining until T.P. whispered that it might well be in my best professional interests to attend. I bought a dress for the occasion, the best my means and Nairobi's supply could achieve.

Two weeks of daily exposure to T.P.'s driving still hadn't immunised me to taking roundabouts at forty: dodging red Kenatco taxis, he explained to me that he had come into certain information to the effect that certain highly placed individuals connected with a certain international research community could be in attendance at a certain ambassadorial bash *ce soir*.

'I didn't know there were any Irish on the project.'

'Oh, there aren't,' said T.P., terrorising a flock of pedestrians with his horn. 'But it's good social and better political grace to be seen to be hospitable to the scientific community. Honorary Irishmen for one night.'

Ghosts and illuminations: the assemblage of rented tuxes and almost-posh frocks was lit by outdoor candles on poles and lubricated by the ever-solicitous presence of the servants, all white smiles and freshly ironed cuffs. From the cover of a glass of J.J., T.P. steered me through the clashing rocks to the more noteworthy landmarks. An ectomorphic Norman Bates in animated conversation with a nun. 'Nikolas van Rensberg, Project Supervisor of the Ol Tukai Facility: Grand Pooh-Bah, between thee and me, he's a bit of a wanker.' Laurel and Hardy arguing by candlelight, a raven-haired woman in a dress that earned her my undying enmity trying, and failing, to keep the peace. 'Conrad Laurens from Ol Tukai, the Bouncing Belgian, and Hakko Lemmenjavi, the Frigging Finn, from Nyandarua. Lord High Executioner and Lord High Everything Else. No love lost between the two facilities. The fine, and exceedingly foolish, young creature between them is Annabelle Pasquali, Senior Botanical Supervisor from Ol Tukai. I once had a short, sweet and altogether wonderful affair with her.'

I wanted to know more about the short, sweet and altogether wonderful affair, but T.P. had moved on to a small and typically astringent American woman in Nina Ricci frock and red Reeboks ('Honestly, these Colonials; bad taste is a national virtue'), holding court with a diplomatically bored ambassador surreptitiously searching his pockets for cigarettes. 'Dorothy Bazyn. Project Security. The military exclusion zones around the Chagas were her idea. I once tried, God knows why, to chat her up at a cocktail party in the Hilton and was asked how I'd like a cocktail stick rammed up my dick.' A solitary man by the drinks trolley with a pigtail and a face like a Yeats poem. 'Ah. Now. This one might be worth your while. In fact, of all the luminaries here foregathered, I would definitely say he would pay the best dividend. Peter Langrishe, Head of Xenobiotics, whatever that is, and a fellow Celt, though of the genus *Pictii* rather than the genus *Hibernii*. If you want a dash of Vindaloo in your book, he's the boy to talk to. More wild and woolly theories about the Chaga than you can shake a stick at. Aliens are his pet obsession.'

'Introduce me this instant, Costello.'

T.P.'s smile froze on his face.

'Oh, shit. Jacobellini has just waltzed in with two lumps of silicon implant on either arm. I thought he was well out of it down in Dar. Any excuse for a piss-up. I suppose I'd better go and pay me *devoirs*. Behave yourself. What'll you do?'

'Behave myself.'

'That's correct.'

Disgusting how like *South Pacific* it was, some enchanted evening, you may see a stranger, all that . . . just at that moment our eyes did meet, and hold. I attempted to match my orbit with his, weaving and apologising through the teaching sisters rural midwives Bible translators.

Overheards: 'I tried to get him to talk about the blood, but he wouldn't!' (Then, more vehemently) 'He wouldn't!'

'Are you sure you remembered the chain saw?'

'I mean, can you imagine, going out with the same girl for ten days?'

'And then he told me about the psychopath . . .'

'Yes, but exactly *what* kind of a prick was Proust?'

'You know, some mornings I get up and I just feel so . . . Antipodean, you know?'

We arrived in each other's gravitational field, mutually circling verbal satellites.

'Nice dress.'

I wriggled, consciously counting every centimetre of bare flesh.

'Nice . . . ah, pigtail.'

He told me his name, I told him mine; little hostages, exchanged.

'It isn't you at all,' he said.

'What, my name? An unfortunate inevitability of being born in a Catholic country.'

'No, you deserve better. You should be something more . . . elemental. A come-by-night. A *Moon*.'

Sometimes you can feel your pupils dilate. Sometimes you possess the awareness of the exact state of every muscle in your body. Sometimes the fingers of unseen guests caress your spine.

'Moon. I like it. Moon I shall be, for the evening at least. And do you have an elemental name for yourself?'

I never got to hear.

There was a sudden collective gasp and sigh from the gathered celebrants. A long slow streak of violet light drew a strict terminator across the sky above Nairobi before vanishing beyond the western horizon. Twenty-five personal pagers exploded in frenzied beeping; needlessly, the representatives of the Facility were already stampeding the cloakroom and calling taxis on their cellphones to take them to Wilson airfield.

Not even an apology.

I had to drive T.P. home. He interrupted a major monologue about the dangers of dehydration and the virtues of ascorbic acid in ameliorating the effects of extreme inebriation to throw up his entire night's consumption of John Jameson down the front of my party dress.

His arrival in the office on Tom M'boya Street at twenty to one was wary in the extreme. It took the offer of a late Indian lunch at the Norfolk Hotel to placate me. Over *rogan josh* he told me that the satellite tracking station at Longonot had picked up the biological package coming in from orbit over the Solomon Islands. It had impacted somewhere in West Cameroon and was currently under investigation by an advance team of international researchers.

He tried to make me pay half the bill.

*

The primal heart of the New Africa is shaped like a twin deck CD twenty watt per channel boombox. It beats in 4/4 time from Sony woofers and JVC bass drivers to the pulse of hy-life guitars pickin' three-chord tricks. I have seen Rendille herdsmen, perched in the one-legged attitude of biblical repose, wearing Walkman head-phones, I have seen Nandi Hills coffee growers in the fields with ghetto-blasters strapped across their backs. The first thing you hear when you arrive in Kenya is the Immigration Officer's radio; from that moment on the general dance never ceases. The gaudy, hazy chaos of the country bus station. The voices and colours and perfume of the fruit market. The Asian store where seriously fat women fuss over *kangas*. Sam's Super Shine Stall on Kenyatta Avenue. Along Koinange Street, from every street vendor selling maize and kebabs grilled over Volkswagen hubcaps full of charcoal.

So familiar that I almost didn't realise the utter incongruity of what I was hearing. Sunny-Odé and his African Beats; thirty kilo-metres into the Chaga, on the lower slopes of Kilimanjaro.

The WaChagga may be the last proud people in the New Africa. The invasion of alien flora and fauna had dispossessed them of their ancestral lands on the slopes of the mountain, it had even taken their name; all it had left them was their stubbornness. Not the most obviously useful asset against the advancing wave of life, but where fire, chainsaw, Agent Orange, Agent Green and finally recombinant DNA had failed to stem the green tide, sheer stubbornness, and infi-nite adaptability, had won a small but not insignificant victory. In the general panic to evacuate when it became obvious that Moshi, Himo and a clutter of smaller settlements along the Tanzanian side of the mountain were going to be engulfed, a few recalcitrant WaChagga had slipped under the wire around the resettlement camps and vanished from the twentieth century.

I know how Dr Livingstone must have felt.

The men of the settlement turned out to meet me, from honoured grandfathers to a five-year-old swinging the boombox I had heard over the general voice of the forest.

(They insisted I call it that: the forest; they were the Chagga and they resented it having buccaneered their name.)

Not so much Dr Livingstone, I presume, as Dorothy in Munchkinland. There was even a Yellow Brick Road to follow, hexagonal tiles of hard yellow plastic that concluded in a comically accurate spiral at the centre of the village.

We call tree-dwellers arboreals, but what do we call flower-dwellers? *Floreals?* Sounds too much like a dead bullfighter, but the word fits; the WaChagga lived, literally, in flowers. An impeccably mannered young graduate from the University of Dar es Salaam was assigned as my guide to the wonders of the community his people had created in the forest. Seen by daylight the flower-houses were wide parasols of zip-locked iridescent petals atop a central trunk; in their shade naked children scampered and monolithic women sat, moving only their eyes to look at the *m'zungu* woman. Passing them again by twilight I saw the petals folding down into night-proof bubbles of light and warmth. I was taken to join a circle of women sitting weaving what looked like nylon thread on belt looms while watching a ten-year-old American super-soap (courtesy Voice or Kenya Broadcasting) on a portable Sony colour set (somewhat scabbed and ulcerous, but nonetheless functional) plugged into the trunk of the tree.

'The petals generate electricity from sunlight,' explained my guide. Freshly graduated and already disillusioned with the academic life, he had brought himself and his European Studies degree home to the shadow of the White Mountain, and then the biological package came down. 'The trunk stores power during the day for us at night.' Balloon-sized globes clustered near the top of the trunk were bioluminescent: 'They somehow know to come on when it gets dark. Look!' He turned a spigot-like extrusion from the trunk; water splashed. 'We have hot as well; solar heating. Come!' The friendly imperiousness of the Africans. He guided me around the municipal plumbing system: the huge transparent gourds that were the main cisterns, the obscenely peristaltic organic pumps that maintained pressure, the stacked fans of solar absorbers that heated the water, the distribution system of plastic tubes and pipes to every house. The inspection detoured via the municipal biogas plant to conclude among the orchards that had sprung up around the settlement and which now provided their entire diet.

I was the only woman guest at the dinner in my honour that night;

seated around the central spiral with the menfolk, while the women served up the fruits of the Chaga. As an honorary man, I had debated whether I should follow local fashion and undress for dinner. Casting modesty to the devil, I turned up in old cycling shorts and silver.

As we ate, Chief Webuye spoke to me through his interpreter. 'We did not come to it. It came to us. It was not easy in those early days, before the orchards grew, we could not eat the food, many of us grew sick and died, but the land was ours and the land still knew us, and came to our need. From the bodies of the dead grew the trees that keep us, from their water came our water, from their bones came our bread, from their skins the houses that shelter us. The forest, having taken from us, is bound to give back the homes it took.'

Traveller's wisdom from Chief Webuye: where you see the colour orange, you will always find water. Anything red will always be edible. Always shit before you sleep, and bury it, you will have food in the morning. A drop of blood on the ground and you will have fruit.

Behind me, the jack o' lantern glow of flower-houses closed up for the night, and the comforting jangle of guitars. Africans will always have their music. Not for the WaChagga the adolescent obsession with identity that mars modern African thought, they had found their identity in the heart of the alienness. Eating with them, communing with them, I felt I was no longer a stranger in the forest.

Asleep that night in a pile of spun floss, I thought I heard my name called, very softly, very gently . . . *Moon*. One, two, three times.

'Langrishe?' I unzipped the folded solar petals. My astral name-sake was high and full and casting a silver unreality over the sleeping village. 'Langrishe . . .'

– *Moon* –

The Chaga was impenetrable as death. Haunted, frustrated, I retired to the house. My sleep was ridden by incubus dreams. When next I woke it was to the house petals unfurling to the sun.

Even before I heard the keening, wailing song of the women, I could feel the air stiff with fear and secrecy. They had gathered in a petal-house across the spiral, the women, slumped like black lava, rocking and nodding and moaning their song. One at a time they would rise and go forward to comfort the desolate young woman at the centre of the ring. Totally absorbed with their mourning, they were oblivious to my approach; it was Tibuweye, the guide, who stopped me.

'Please. It is not for you. Constance, the young woman, she gave birth last night, but the child was stillborn. Please understand.'

'I understand. I am sorry. Please tell her that I am sorry.'

I glanced at the circle of women, at the mother racked with the silent tears of complete grief, and, as the women swayed and rocked in their keening, at the baby at her feet. One of the women saw my staring and whipped a sheet over the body.

The child had no arms, no legs; in their place coiling green tendrils sprouted.

Before I left, they gave me two gifts. I am not certain which I treasure the more, the little glass jars that light up when I shake them, or the path that follows the rumour of a man, a mad half-legend half glimpsed by the foresters in the recesses of the forest, upward. All this morning I have climbed through the gardens of the WaChagga, the slopes ringing with the proud, animal cries of the men harvesting. I pause to eat some fruit from a tree; red fruit, it tastes of musk and sex, it tastes of the Chaga.

Did the apple in Eden feel responsible?

It must be one of those laws of universal perversity, the kind of thing you see in sticker form in the rear windows of Fords, that when the thing you want most in the world happens, you don't believe it. When the phone rang and there among the hissing and scratching was Dr Peter Langrishe of the Ol Tukai Xenobiotics Department extending a personal invitation to me to fly down to Amboseli and spend a week at the centre all I was capable of were a few mumbled acquiescences and a numb replacing of the receiver. T.P. said I looked like a victim of a good confidence trick. Four hours later I was standing on the apron at Wilson airfield, bags packed ('nothing plastic, my dear, and that includes Walkman, film and toothbrush') and fighting to maintain connection with my hat in the propwash from the Ol Tukai Twin Otter.

My first sight of the Chaga: glimpsed out of the cabin window as the aircraft banked into its final approach to the Amboseli airstrip. Half hallucinatory, half revelatory; a disc of rainbow-coloured light which broke apart into flows and eddies, a pointillist sea of colour, like a test for some new colour-blindness. Then the plane banked again and we were down, scoring an arrow of dust across the dry lake-bed.

He was waiting for me. God, but he looked good. I scarcely noticed the Kenyan soldiers treble-checking my security clearance on their portable datalink. Ol Tukai was ten miles away on dirt roads the texture of corrugated iron: Volkswagens, apparently; the peculiar beat of the engines is transmitted through the suspension to the ground. Ten miles was the closest safe distance aircraft could come to the perimeter of the Chaga; early overflights with camera-toting tourists had come to grief when the pilots found the fuel in the tanks turning to sludge and every scrap of plastic bursting into bloom. Langrishe fed me such little morsels of data and I sat, grinning like a teenager, hanging on for grim death as the Daihatsu 4x4 took the ruts. Ol Tukai seemed to be in the process of dismantling itself into tea-chests and packing crates; both civilians and military were all check-lists and baling wire.

'Getting ready for the move.' Langrishe nodded beyond the buildings. 'Three kilometres is close enough.'

My first four hours in Ol Tukai I had my security clearance checked eight times. 'They're ashamed of it,' Langrishe said. 'Same goes for the Tanzanians. A kind of national disgrace. Right in the middle of their great and glorious task of nation building, this happens, like a cancer in the body politic they'd rather have kept secret from the rest of the world in case it affected their international credit-worthiness. Like trying to get life-insurance if you're HIV positive. Want to come for a look at it before dinner, after you've finished interviewing, or whatever it is you do?' Note for the book: no one in Ol Tukai ever called the Chaga by name, what was out there was a lurking, polymorphous 'it'.

I had never considered that it might be possible to see the Chaga advance. One hundred metres per day, just over four metres per hour, sixty-six centimetres per minute. One and two-third centimetres per second. On the botanical scale, that's virtually relativistic.

The line of advance was more subtle than I had envisaged, not so much a line of demarcation as an ever-advancing gradation, from thorn scrub and grasses through increasing echelons of polygonal fungus and pseudo-lichen to low bladder plants and gourd-like growths to tube bushes and small windmill trees and plants that sprayed water and lashed whip-like flails and spewed clouds of floating bubbles to the towering columns and fans and webs of the false-corals and sponges at which point the indigenous was totally absorbed into the full climax Chaga. From his backpack Langrishe took a squeaky plastic elephant.

'Carla Bly's kid's,' he explained. 'I did ask first.' He placed the toy in the path of the advance. Following his example, I hunkered on my heels to watch. The smiling green elephant broke out in a psoriasis of yellow spots which multiplied with appalling speed to cover the entire surface. Within fifteen seconds the toy was a mass of sea-anemone-like extrusions. I watched the green elephant collapse and dissolve into a pool of oily sludge which, even as it seeped into the ground, was generating furiously reproducing clusters of sulphur yellow crystals.

'We assume they're alien biological packages because, given a plethora of impossible hypotheses, that seems the least improbable: that the earth is on the receiving end of an alien colonisation programme. Truth is, we have no more evidence for this theory to be credible than the incredible ones: the packages appear out of nowhere on the deep-space trackers, make a couple of fast orbits and then execute an aero-braked descent. We've been scanning the sun's Local Group of stars with our deep-space tracking facilities for the past five years without the slightest hint as to their point of origin. But they still keep coming; that one last month in Cameroon; the one six months back that splashed down in mid-Atlantic: submarine surveys say something's happening along the mid-Atlantic ridge, but they don't know exactly what. This was the first, that we know of, the second one came down in the Bismarck Archipelago, the third hit in the old Aberdare National Park up to the north, another took out a dam in the Amazon basin, another in the Ecuadoran Andes, three others in mid-ocean; but they all came down within three hundred kilometres of the Equator. Fancy a walk?'

He indicated the advancing Chaga. I shuddered. Where the green elephant had sat smiling, a bubble of ochre polymer was expanding.

'Dinner, then.'

Dinner was a fifty-pence romantic-novel fantasia: a table out under the enormous African night; moon, wine, candles; picking at our food and feeding each other choice morsels of biography for dessert, the wheres, whens, whos of our lives. I loved every minute of it, I've never said a harder goodnight in my life.

And with the morning, we flew.

At the sight of the flimsy film wings, the eminently snappable struts and one's utter exposure to sky and gravity this Moon very nearly chickened. Langrishe reassured me the microlytes were equipped with smart systems that made it impossible to crash or stall them, they virtually flew themselves and if I really wanted to experience the Chaga this was the only way I could get close and because this Moon was going to impress or die that morning I said what the hell yes, why not, and while he was filing a flight plan with security I put on my helmet and waggled my feet in the steering stirrups and the solar wing fed power to the engine and the next thing I knew we had shaken ourselves free from the wrinkled skin of Africa; airborne, *flying* at once terrifying and liberating, I wanted to laugh and scream as we banked (flash of iridescence as our wings caught the sun) and wheeled; before us: the White Mountain, casting off its concealment of cloud, the eternal snows high and pure and holy; below us, birds and things that were not quite birds fled from the shadow our wings cast over the jumbled canopy of the Chaga; Langrishe waved, pointed; a flotilla of silver balloons bowled through the air just above the treetops, at his signal we banked our dragonfly craft to pursue – each blimp carried a passenger like a large silver octopus – banked again, Chaga, sky, mountain, all whirled into crazy juxtaposition, and I was lost. Transported. I do not know how long I flew, where I flew, how I flew, I seemed at times a fusion of woman and wing; Icarus ascending on beautiful, foolish arms; the forest, the mountain, the high, white tableland diffracting refracting dazzling hypnotising under the sun – mystical? transcendent? I cannot say what I experienced except to echo Thomas Merton's description of God as the pure emptiness of light where the self dissolves into the cloud of unknowing of which one cannot, of necessity, speak.

On our return to earth we did not speak, we could not speak; the sexual, spiritual tension between us was too strong for words. In his office we tore like vultures at each other, stripped each other, ecstatically, soul-naked for the long, deep, plunge into each other; kisses desperate and naïve as ancient clay cuneiforms. Under the shadow of the White Mountain, desperate, desperate love . . . God, Langrishe, I want you!

It has been several hours since the last skeleton of a baby. Like the others, it was wedged in a cleft of a fan-coral, like the others it was terribly deformed. The pain was so old and eroded that I could pick through the bones with the same detachment that I would examine a dead bird. The tiny, eyeless skull, warped into a sweeping crest of bone; the jaws fused shut in one seamless ridge of enamel; the fingers, long and delicate as those of a bat – the slightest touch snapped them – terminated in rounded open sockets. Like the others I had encountered on the WaChagga pathways, it had been deliberately abandoned. Ritual infanticide. Paradise exposed; the price of compromise of Chagga with Chaga?

Cooler now, higher. I have had to supplement my ethnic fashions with my dearly loved leather jacket. I must look like a fetish-figure from a sword 'n' sorcery fantasy. The unremitting claustrophobia of the forest robs me of a sense of location: I find myself searching for some breach in the walls so that I can re-establish my relationship with the surface of Africa. Certainly, I must be close to the heartlands; the density and diversity of the ecosystem is staggering. Writing this, I am overshadowed by stands of what I can only describe as giant toadstools crossed with oil refineries: all caps and pipes and tubes; elsewhere on today's climb I have encountered groves of coiled cornucopias, vagina-mouths wide enough to swallow me whole (the ultimate penetration?); miniature mountain ranges of what look like bright orange wormcasts three times my height and waving feathery extrusions. Small estates of squat cylindrical pillars, an abandoned adobe, seeping a semeny froth from their open tops. Organisms as transparent and fantastic as marine radiolarin, magnified a thousand times . . . What that cow Dorothy Bazyn would have given for me to have brought a camcorder with me! If she was ever to know . . .

Corresponding with the accelerating diversity of the flora, I am encountering new and quite alien forms of fauna. Creatures like aerial manta rays cluster around a tangle of vivid lilac intestines; the first sight of them winging through the forest towards me sent me diving to cover, two million years of instinct, but as they passed over I saw they had no mouths. How do they feed? Too many mysteries, I haven't the time; as I have said, this is not an expedition, this is a pilgrimage. Heart of Darkness, eh, Conrad? You don't know the half of it. Mistah Kurtz, he dead.

(You damn well better not be, Langrishe. You hear me?

No, I do not think you can be dead. I would know, I would feel it in my heart, as if a part of it had stopped beating, as if a part of me had withered and died. Love it, loathe it, Langrishe, we are bound together: God, Eros, Kismet: we are one. You are out there. I will find you. Moon promises.)

One thing I have noticed: nature here has learned a trick Mother Earth never mastered in two billion years of evolution: it has invented the wheel. Yesterday I encountered impossibly cute little creatures like a cross between a lizard and a Dinky toy, revving and rodding around my feet along the twining plastic footpaths on tiny wheels. Today, the Chaga had a further delight. At first I thought they were over-large dragonflies; ignoring my attempts to shoo them away, they danced closer and I saw that they were, in effect, tiny helicopters; all eyes and whirring vanes. They even possessed tiny tail rotors to prevent spinning. The delightful little creatures accompanied me for the rest of that day's journey. Life in the Chaga takes to the air with enthusiasm and ingenuity. From simple gliders (some the size of T.P.'s lamented microlyte) through a bewildering array of gas bags, blimps and balloons to the helicopters and the mantas, whose means of propulsion seems to be jet-power.

There are others in this new land, like the WaChagga, they have *adapted*. As I progress towards the cloud layer their presence becomes more and more evident: rafts of birds struggling to take wing weighed down by sponge-like encrustations about their heads and legs, others ridden piggyback by objects like diseased organs.

The vervet monkey I saw, with the parasitic dorsal ridge, is no freak here. Some monkeys possess octopus tentacles in addition to their own arms and legs, some sport antlers of green coral studded with hundreds of tiny blue abalone eyes. Some are carpeted in a green mould that I assume must enable them to photosynthesise like plants, for their mouths have fused shut under whorls and ridges of raw bone. Some of the young I have seen clinging to their mothers' backs bear the same deformities I saw in the abandoned children of the WaChagga. Yet none seems in distress from the mutilations, and all are obviously thriving. Is this their absorption into the symbiotic life of the Chaga? Is the law of the jungle being rewritten?

More than monkeys and birds have come to terms with the aliens. A sudden crashing approaching through the understorey, a stand of tall, brittle umbrella trees trampled down, an elephant entered the clearing. It raised its trunk to test taste touch the air, around its neck was a red, veiny mass of flesh reaching down along the tusks to elongate into two prehensile tentacles, each terminating in something shockingly like a human hand. I remained hidden in the cover of a grove of translucent cistern-plants. Scenting the presence of its ancestral enemy, the elephant turned and withdrew into the bush. Another pact with the Chaga.

When I heard the movement in the hooting, trilling dark that night, I feared it was another visit of the long-legged tripod creature that had reconnoitred my camp two nights before; stroking my few intimate possessions with long feathery cilia. I have a deep and entirely proper dread of all things clicking and chitinous. I held my breath.

'Greetings to you in the name of the Lord Jesus . . .'

I almost screamed.

'Peace, sister, I am only a humble servant of my Lord. Pastor Hezekiah, minister to the lost and light to the found. Tell me, sister, do you love the Lord?'

He moved into the range of my biolights.

Hezekiah: bifurcated man; your right side is flesh and blood, your left a garden of tiny white flowers, trumpet-mouths opening and closing flicking forked tongues to taste the air. Hezekiah: your left eye observes the world from a half dome of blossoms and roots, your left arm is a swollen club of green flesh fused shut upon a decomposing black Bible. Too strange to terrify me, Hezekiah. To me you were almost . . . beautiful.

He was dressed in a memory of old Anglican vestments. His speech was deeply beautiful, enriched by decades of exposure to the towering cadences of the Authorised Version. I did not feel any threat or darkness about him, rather, a sad holiness that made me move my little jars of biolight into a circle as an invitation to enter.

He had evolved a complex and curiously satisfying theology around the Chaga in which God had cast him in the role of a latter-day John the Baptist; the voice crying in the wilderness, prepare ye the Way of the Lord! With reverential fervour he expounded his credo that, in the shape of the Chaga, the millennium was at hand, the Kingdom of Heaven come down to Earth: 'Is it not written, sister, that a star shall fall from heaven, and its name shall be Wormwood, and that one third of all the growing things and creeping things upon the earth shall be destroyed? Does it not say that the New Jerusalem itself shall come down out of the heavens?' His brother preachers had been blinded to this truth by Satan and had denounced it as ungodly; to him alone had been granted the vision, and in obedience he had come out from the midst of the scoffers and unbelievers, left his small parish near Kapsabet, and walked the five hundred kilometres to the mountain of God. In the towns he passed through he had preached his new revelation and called the orphans of Babylon to the slopes of Mount Zion and the advent of the Second Adam and Eve. 'Eden!' he declared, including the singing forest with a wave of his Bible-hand. 'The new Eden; the Earth redeemed and cast in the perfect image of God. What we had seen previously as in a glass darkly, we shall now see clearly and without distortion.' His pilgrimage followed a divinely ordered spiral around the mountain, each level corresponding to a new degree of spiritual grace and enlightenment: as he reached the summit and the pinnacle of transfiguration his own personal transfiguration would be completed, changed from glory into glory, into the likeness of Christ his master. It was a mark of God's grace that he was half transfigured already. He touched his mantle of flowers, eyes shining with ecstasy.

I envied him his fine madness. I asked him were the WaChagga disciples of his. 'Degenerates,' he denounced them. 'They would not receive the Lord, so I have shaken their dust off my feet. God has spit them out of His mouth, they shall not see the glory.' I asked him had he seen a white man, a *m'zungu*, in the forest. 'Yes, many months ago, a *m'zungu* from the Research Facility.' When I asked where the *m'zungu* had been headed, he pointed up into the mists. He prayed a blessing over our sleep and in the morning he was gone, moving from glory to glory. But I could not rid myself of the sensation that he shadowed all that day's march: a half-glimpsed suggestion of a figure that could as easily have been a delusion of the prismatic perspectives of the forest. I stopped, called his name, waited for him, several times during today's climb, but the Chaga kept silence.

Hezekiah?

T.P. knew it. Mrs Kivebulaya knew it. Phyllis at the Irish Embassy who let me have her day-old copies of the *Cork Examiner* knew it. The entire office from venerable tea-lady to junior runner knew it.

Moon was in love.

The Celts invented the concept of romantic love.

He actually left messages for me pinned to the Thorn Tree in the café of the New Stanley Hotel, a thing no one has in any seriousness done since the shadow of Hemingway stalked the bars and country clubs; dates and arrangements for champagne breakfasts overlooking the Rift Valley, the night train to Lake Victoria (a teak and brass time machine focused fifty years in the past), hiking expeditions in the N'gong Hills, camera safaris to Lake Turkana, microlyting over the Masai Mara. Impossibly romantic. Horrendously expensive. Moon loved every second of it. T.P. found it simultaneously hilarious and pitiable.

Suddenly the three hundred pages of notes, the hundred and twenty-two hours of taped interviews, the twelve box files full of associated documents that I had been avoiding like a persistent creditor seemed to spontaneously combust under my fingers. T.P. watched in dumb amazement from his Captain Kirk chair as the spirit of the Chaga reached out and possessed me. Finally, to save me from myself, and his afternoons of contemplative crossword-solving and street-watching, he ordered me out of his office and sent me to pursue my demonic muse in the sultry climate of the coast. He obtained an indefinite lease on a beach-edge *banda* half an hour's drive north from Mombasa and sent me off on the overnight train with a ream of A4 and a Remington portable that barely qualified for the description.

Silence and solitude unbroken. I drove that Remington portable into the ground; well after dark, homeward-wending shell-sellers were surprised to see me working chthonically on the veranda by the light of oil lamps. At two o'clock I would tumble through the mosquito nets into bed and sleep until dawn when I would rise and run, or swim, before breakfast in the hotel up the beach. Then I would plunge into the book and not surface until dinner time. By Friday I would be exhausted but glowing and waiting eagerly for the headlights of the Ol Tukai 4x4 to come weaving through the palm trees, the herald of two days of swimming, sunbathing, sleeping with Langrishe.

We all carry around a box of snapshots of our loves. Riffle, shuffle, deal them again.

Two figures running down the surf-line, running for the joy of using their bodies to push at the limits of their selves; the dawn coming up behind black thunderheads out of India and the world waiting in indigo, waiting to be reborn. They make love in the shower, licking the salt sweat from each other's skin.

An ebony bed, brought down by *dhow* from Mogadishu for the Sultan of Mombasa's pleasure. After centuries the wood had not lost its perfume.

Sudden, savage rain beating on the palm thatch.

The moon, huge on the seaward edge of the world. The call of the moonpath: to the sea! to the sea! the man and the woman burst from the water like creatures newly created, like drops of fire from the fingers of God, before they sink again into the amniotic embrace and each other.

Still life, she absorbed in her book with the moths butting softly against the globe of the oil lamp; he is in his wicker chair, watching. Just watching . . .

Then all things were a prelude to sex. Respighi's symphonic poems among the trees at batflight. Wading thigh deep through the blood warm ocean. Hands lovingly oiling me against the sun . . .

After, in that black Arab bed, he would explore his land of heart's desire, the high, white tableland beyond the clouds.

'Who are they? A day doesn't dawn that I don't ask myself that question a dozen times; who are they? The satellite cameras have looked through the clouds to show us the things that are up there; amazing things; forms and systems more complex than any we've yet discovered, entire tracts of forest that seem more like animate cities; why? For whom? When? Are they already abroad in their living cities, have we seen them and not recognised them? Have we indeed seen the faces of the masters of the Chaga in those satellite photographs and not recognised them?

'Or then again, it may be the time is not yet right for them: all is prepared, the stage set, but the principal performers have yet to make their entrances – how could they have put an entire world into something not much larger than this room? Will they make themselves known to us; one day will our survey expeditions go to the edge of the Chaga and find them waiting; will they come soon, will they wait until their grip on our world is more secure; are they delaying so that they may deal with us as equals, or is that moment centuries distant, when the whole earth is changed into their likeness? Who are they? Most of all, that question; every day, every minute, that question casts its shadow over everything else; who are they?'

I would turn away from him, staring at the tracks the beetles left on the wall.

With the morning he would be gone. I was not woman enough to hold him, the mountain had a more primal claim on him. I knew in the end he would have to decide. I knew how he would choose, I knew he would leave me, at the last, for that other love. I almost told him to go, rather than bear the pain of having him leave me. To love someone so much you will give him away rather than lose him, does this make sense? Yet every time that 4x4 cane swinging through the palms, I would throw myself on him and drag him down, into that Arab bed.

I could smell it in the wind, the day the houseboy from the tourist hotel half a mile up the beach came panting to my veranda to tell me there was a telephone call for me, most urgent. I followed in a daze of numb serenity. When Dorothy Bazyn regretted to inform me that Peter Langrishe had failed to return to the Oloitiptip Research Facility after a microlyte survey of the North Western Sector of the Chaga, I experienced a colossal sense of guilty relief, of a kind I have not felt since my mother finally surrendered to the cancer that had taken six years to kill her. I almost laughed, but a preventing hand around my heart restrained me, like a mailed glove. That same glazed calm accompanied me home on the train until I saw T.P. waiting for me amid the porters and taxi drivers at Nairobi Station and all restraint fled. I was shattered like a soapstone pot, the interior emptiness it had shaped was lost in the greater emptiness without. I cried for an hour all over his pure silk suit.

I sank into a deep, dark depression. Weeks, months, disappeared behind me. The book sat three-quarters complete on my desk at 224b Tom M'boya Street. T.P. was always there, to listen when I wanted to talk, merely to be when I could not talk. He preserved me from some of the more disgusting excesses of self-pity: stopping me drinking myself stupid, flushing the cocaine I had bought from an American consular official down the *choo*; I think he would have slept with me if that would have helped the healing.

Strange, that I never once considered that he might be dead. I knew him, the bastard.

Over tea at a questionable Chinese restaurant tucked behind the Kenyatta Conference Centre, I asked T.P. why it hurt so much, still. He said it was because I was in love with Langrishe, still. We toyed with the mottoes from our fortune cookies, pretending all manner of things.

'T.P.'

He lit one end of his motto in the candle flame.

'You're right. I still love the bastard, so bad I know I will never, never be free from him. God, I love him; I am going mad without him; what's the line from that old song?'

'"I can't live, with or without you?"'

'T.P., I have to find him.'

'You know for certain that he is alive?'

'The heart knows, T.P. The heart knows all manner of things. He has gone in search of his aliens, in their living cities up among the snows. T.P., will you help me find him?'

I think that was the only time I ever succeeded in surprising him. The very next day: 'I have a little something for you. Out back, if you would care to take a look?'

I don't know how he had managed to put the thing up in the postage-stamp backyard; certainly his office staff looked very pleased with themselves. The microlyte was black and green, like a proud and beautiful dragonfly. I could not speak, merely run my hands over the wings, the struts, the power unit; appreciating it by touch.

'T.P., it must have cost a fortune.'

'It did. Presuming that, as a typical romantic, you haven't the least idea about how to bring your plan to fruition, I took the liberty of engaging in a little logistical thought: great amusement, by the by. You can dismiss immediately any thought you might have entertained of obtaining a security clearance from Oloitiptip – Dorothy Bazyn does not want a second Missing in Action on her quarterly report – and I presume you have enough wit not even to think of trying to make it past the perimeter patrols on foot; the odds of you ending up in a bodybag, that is, after the soldiers gang-rape you, is in the region of 98 per cent. However, if you were to find a secluded spot, say, fifty kilometres from Kilimanjaro, and fly in just above ground level underneath the radar net, the odds are a little more favourable. At least, if they open up with twenty-millimetre cannon you won't feel anything. So, I made a few, ah, purchases?' I almost kissed him.

We worked fast, furious, we did not stop to consider what we were doing; the face of our madness might have turned us to stone. Deep dark truth in the mirror. 'The Last Safari,' T.P. christened it, but I told him that had been a film with Stewart Granger. 'That was *King Solomon's Mines*,' he said. 'With Deborah Kerr.'

We drove down to a place on the road south, just outside of Ilbisil township; a bend, a baobab and much, much sky. T.P. unpacked the microlyte – he had borrowed the Irish Ambassador's Range-Rover for the occasion ('He owes me, the Garibaldi affair') and assembled the aircraft under the watchful gaze of a dirty, gawky Masai kid, materialised out of five hundred square kilometres of nowhere, as they tend to. All three of us were most impressed when the propeller actually turned.

'Well, aren't you going to give Deborah Kerr a kiss for luck?'

Hands in pockets, T.P. contemplated the landscape. 'Among the Dinka tribesmen of Sudan,' he said, 'the baobab is known as the Tree Where Man Was Born. In Kenya there is a common belief that the baobab disobeyed God by growing where it wanted to, in punishment for which God uprooted it, turned it upside down and thrust it back into the earth again. I think there may be a moral in that somewhere, Moon. What is there?'

'A moral, T.P.'

'That's correct.'

I kissed him anyway.

Five minutes later, I was airborne.

In the cloud forest we face the final confrontation, the ultimate consummation. An appropriate enough theatre, this high shoulderland of Kilimanjaro; in this season the clouds hang unbroken for weeks on end. A landscape of moral ambiguity, all shades of grey . . . is this the Cloud of Unknowing? The Daliesque geometries of the Chaga, the ripples and veils of fog; suitably Macbethian for a Scot like Langrishe.

I came upon the clearing at the end of a heavy day's climb; the air was thin, every footstep was a shard of migraine exploding through my brain; when I found myself on the edge of the small, rocky defile that cut a jagged gash through the ubiquitous Chaga, I knew instinctively this was to be the place. As I made camp the fog capriciously swirled and dissolved; I found myself looking through a tree-lined window over the cloud-speckled plain of Amboseli. To be able to *see*! The many-coloured land sweeping away beneath me to merge almost imperceptibly with the tawny earth shades of Kenya. Those winks of light, that scattering of antiseptic white like spilled salt, the new facility at Oloitiptip (those Masai names, names the earth speaks to itself), those plumes of dust, vehicles, perhaps aircraft taking off from the dry lake-bed; those specks of black moving through the middle air: Army/Airforce helicopters.

It is not good for the soul to look down from the mountain too long: I lingered until nightfall and the more I looked the more I felt myself despising the monotonous, starved landscape beyond the mountain; the more I rejoiced in the colour and diversity of the Chaga. I did belong here.

He came that night. I was expecting him.

'Moon.'

No doubt, no uncertainty this time. I was already reaching to shake my biolights into luminescence.

'No. No light.'

'Why?'

'No light. Or I'll go . . .'

'No! Don't go. Langrishe, where are you? Don't hide from me . . .'

'Moon . . . oh, Moon. Don't make this difficult for me. I want to come to you; more than anything, Moon. Just to see you, here . . . why did you have to come, why could we not have left it where it lay and let it wither?'

'Langrishe, I couldn't leave you. I couldn't let it wither and die; it isn't like that, you know. It won't die, it can't die. Langrishe, listen to me . . .'

A silence. Alone, in the dark, with the whole forest listening, I sat and hugged my knees to my chest. After a time, he spoke again.

'Those living cities among the snowline that we have seen in the satellite photographs – I've been there, up among the snows, Moon, I've explored those cities; the word "city" barely describes what is up there, I've seen things that beggar the human imagination, things far beyond my comprehension; but one thing I understand, there is no race of aliens waiting buried in the soil to step forth and inhabit them. In a sense, we were right when we hypothesised that we might not be able to recognise the aliens; we do not recognise them because, Moon, we are the aliens . . .'

I waited the rest of the night for him to return; shaking, and shaken, in my protective circle of biolights. The clouds were low and cold and drizzling the next day. Miserable hours; wrapped up in my sleeping bag in my hammock I picked and pecked at Thomas

Merton but my mind was too full of birds and doubts to mirror the Benedictine's tranquillity of solitude. Too long since I last read him; the vinyl cover of the book was a nauseating mash of pulpy crystals and froth. I ripped it off, threw it away, read the master in the nakedness of his own pages.

He came at nightfall, in the dripping freezing twilight.

'Evolution, Moon, catastrophic shifts to new levels of complexity, do you understand? You must understand, it's vitally important that you understand. Evolution does not plod through history one steady gene at a time; evolution dances, evolution leaps, from level to level; on the biological clock the second hand does not move continuously, it clicks from one instant to the next. Changes occur simultaneously throughout an entire population; within one generation a population may shift to a higher level. Do you understand? Moon, you must understand!'

'Langrishe!' Empty, dripping darkness. I dreamed about his eyes all that night, terrible, terrible eyes without a face.

Washing in the lukewarm waters of a cistern next morning, I heard my name in the mists.

'Go away, Moon. Before you there were never any choices to make, never another consideration; and when I left to come here, it was that way again. I knew what I wanted, what I was searching for, and now you have turned everything inside out again. I want to be with you, I want to run away from you, I love you, I am terrified of you.'

I turned around slowly, scanning the grey silhouettes of under-growth.

'Langrishe . . . where are you?'

'Here, Moon.' Shadow among the shadows, a man-shaped patch of mist. 'No. No nearer. Please. Listen. I can't stay long. This is important. Fire will not burn it, poisons will not kill it, it thrives on our wastes and pollutions and can provide technological man with his every need: is the Chaga the next evolutionary step forward? Technological man fouls his nest with glee; will the nest reject him, or will the nest adapt itself so that he can live there without destroying it and himself?

'The protein life has had its day, now the new life has come and is sweeping it away. The wave, Moon, the wave.'

As he spoke I had closed the distance between us, one cat-cautious step at a time. I was within a handful of metres of him when he awoke from his self-absorption and noticed my proximity. He gave a cry as we saw each other, face to face. Then in a flicker of movement he was gone.

My heart pounded. Black phosphenes exploded noiselessly in my retinas, my blood roared. Langrishe was still human.

That night, in my hammock, a touch on my cheek, a kiss. Mumbling like a great contented cat, I turned over and looked into his face and the soft sensual mass of his body pressed upon mine. Mouths parted, lips met, I unzipped the sleeping bag to welcome him within, lifted my hands to touch him. 'No,' he said. 'Please. Don't touch. Promise me that, Moon.'

'But why?'

'Because of you. Because I don't understand what it is about you that drives me mad. I'm mad even to think of doing this . . . mad, mad. What is it about you, woman?' I laid a finger to his lips, one second later our mouths met and before I was even aware he had slipped inside me. I gasped in surprise, his tongue was at my nipples, his breath hot on my skin. He smelled of Chaga, musks, essential oils, the intimate perfumes of the orifices. His hands held mine above my head, sexual surrender as we plunged and pulsed in the absolute darkness of the senses. As his thrusts grew more frantic, his pace more urgent, his fingers released mine and my hands automatically fell to stroking his body, over the thighs, nails lightly raking the buttocks, tracing little spider-feet along the flanks, onto the gentle syncline of his back.

At my scream the song of the Chaga fell silent for a minute.

My fingers were entwined in a holdfast of veins and tubes rooted in the base of his spine; a throbbing umbilical that bound him to God knows what out there in the darkness. He leaped away from me, naked, shivering, dripping; I vomited endlessly, emptily.

'Oh God oh God oh God oh God . . .'

'I told you I told you I told you not to touch . . .'

'You bastard you bastard, what have you done, oh my God . . .'

'Why did you have to come here, why did you not go when I asked you, why did you have to reawaken all the things I had forgotten, why did you have to make me human again?'

'Human?' I screamed. 'Human? My God, Langrishe, what are you?'

'You want to see?' he screamed back. 'You want to know? Look. Look well.' He pointed a quivering finger at me. A ponderous crashing from the night-forest, something huge, that knows it can take for ever to get where it wants. 'Look!' screamed Langrishe again and suddenly the ravine was bright with biolights. 'I can do anything with it I like. Who do you think fed you, watered you, watched you, guided you?' Into the amphitheatre of light came a great mound of flesh, taller than a man, wider; ribbed with veins and arteries and patches of scabrous yellow mould. Clusters of organs swayed as it advanced on two massively muscled legs. Lacy antennae feathered from barnacle-like warts along its back; it turned towards me, raised itself up on its clawed feet and extended an array of mandibles and claspers. Its belly was an open vagina, connected to Langrishe by the umbilical cord.

I knew I had gone mad.

The umbilical retracted, drawing Langrishe into the raw red maw. It closed around him, advanced another step towards me. Langrishe's face regarded me from a cowl of red flesh.

'I tried to tell you, Moon, but you refused to understand. Evolution. The future, Moon. The future man. *Homo symbioticus*. The orthobody. A completely self-contained environmental unit. Imagine an end to sickness and disease, bodies that will heal our every illness, that will repair and regenerate our bodies; why, I am effectively immortal. Imagine no pain, no war, imagine the ability of one human to cause another human pain abolished; we can have that, the orthobodies have a system of neurological checks that make it impossible to translate a violent thought into violent action. Imagine, no more want, no more hunger, for the orthobody lives on sunlight, air and water like the plants, and every man will be able to draw what more he wants from the endless resources of the forest. Imagine, a world without ignorance; my brain is linked with the orthobody's brain that can process information with the speed of a computer; what is more, it can link into another orthobrain, so that the total of all human knowledge is accessible by every man, woman, and child; knowledge is no more the privilege of an educated class, the heritage of humanity is the right of all humanity. Imagine, the richness of experience and emotion of a Shakespeare or a Michelangelo the birthright of everyone; imagine eyes that can see into the infra-red and the ultraviolet, new spectrums of hearing, the ability to taste, smell, touch things you never conceived of before, in addition to new senses, new awareness that I cannot even begin to describe to you, Moon!'

'Horrible!' I cried. 'Horrible!'

'No, glorious! The next evolutionary leap. If man could not live harmoniously with his planet, his planet must adapt to live harmoniously with man. Moon, I understand your fear; it looks dreadful, it seems monstrous; believe me, it is more wonderful than you can ever imagine. I feel like . . . a god, Moon. A god.'

Eyes I dare not meet in dreams.

'God, Langrishe . . .'

'So, what will Moon do, then? Will she go back? Will she go down from the mountain-top – to *that*? You can go back, after what you've seen, after the wonder and glory you've touched here? Or will she stay, with me? You loved me enough to come here to find me, do you love me enough to stay? Am I any more monstrous than I would be if I lay paralysed in an iron lung, if I had leprosy? You would love me then, can you not love me now?'

No, not a god, Langrishe, a devil, and a subtle one at that, a driver of devil's bargains. My mind was a firestorm of doubts and confusions; through the conflagration, the numb roaring, I reached out to touch him, lay a hand on the red ridged flesh beside his face. 'Oh, Langrishe . . .'

'You said we were one. You said we were inadequate parts of a unity, incomplete without the other. I'm not saying that you have to become like me; you don't have to pass into an orthobody, you can just stay with me, as you are, and we can know each other as we did, before . . .'

'Langrishe . . .'

'Moon, I love you.'

But I had already fled into the night.

*

The sifting of the ashes: all the emotional underpinnings upon which the life of Moon had been built have collapsed into embers. If only he had not said that. If only he had not said that he loved me, it might have been bearable then – why did you always have to make me the guilty one? Was it always like this, mere explorations of new ways of causing pain to each other? Was all we needed from each other a mirror in which to examine ourselves?

He will come again for me, soon, calling, through the mist and the forest that lies across the shoulders of Kilimanjaro. And I do not know what I will do then. That is why I am completing this journal: the fury of the condemned man's diary. The longest journey is the journey inwards, it is also the journey from which return is least possible. Of all travellers, it is most true for the pilgrim that you can't go home again.

The pilgrim that comes down from the mountain will not be Moon: Moon died, up there under the breath of the snows; what returns to earth will be as changed within as Langrishe is without. And if I stay . . . I cannot become like that. I cannot accept that this is the future for humanity; an eternity of graceless hedonism browsing in the great world-forest, each man an island entirely sufficient unto himself? No, I reject it; do you hear me, Langrishe, I reject it! You have it right, Eliot, humankind cannot bear very much reality.

The last temptation, the greatest treason, to do the wrong deed for the right reason. I must finish now; I can hear him calling, he is coming for me. I have not much time to complete this record and still I am undecided. Maybe this will not be my last entry after all. T.P., if this journal should ever find its way back to you, by my hand, by the hand of another, even if you may not understand yourself, try to make the world understand. It is possible to love the heart of darkness while being repelled by it.

He is here now, I must put down my pen for today. Dust in the air suspended, marks the place where the story ended.

ACKNOWLEDGEMENTS

'Gardenias' first appeared in *Zenith: The Best in New British Science Fiction* edited by David Garnett, Sphere Books 1989; 'Rainmaker Cometh' first appeared in *Other Edens III* edited by Robert Holdstock and Christopher Evans, Unwin Hyman 1989; 'Listen' first appeared in *Interzone*, 1989; 'Speaking in Tongues' first appeared in *Digital Dreams* edited by David V. Barrett, New English Library 1990; 'Fragments of an Analysis of a Case of Hysteria' first appeared in *Tales of the Wandering Jew* edited by Brian Stableford, Dedalus Publishing 1991; 'Approaching Perpendicular' first appeared in *Other Edens II* edited by Robert Holdstock and Christopher Evans, Unwin Hyman 1988; 'Floating Dogs' first appeared in *New Worlds 1* edited by David Garnett, Gollancz 1991; 'Atomic Avenue' first appeared in *Atomic Avenue* edited by M. Nagula, W. Heyne Verlag 1990; 'Fronds' first appeared in *Amazing*, TSR Ltd 1989; 'Winning' first appeared in *Zenith 2* edited by David Garnett, Sphere Books 1989; 'Toward Kilimanjaro' first appeared in *Isaac Asimov's Science Fiction Magazine*, Davis Publishing 1990.

CRITICAL WAVE

THE EUROPEAN SCIENCE FICTION & FANTASY REVIEW

"CRITICAL WAVE is the most consistently interesting
and intelligent review on the sf scene."
- Michael Moorcock.

"One of the best of the business journals...
I never miss a copy..." - Bruce Sterling.

"Intelligent and informative, one of my key sources of
news, reviews and comments." - Stephen Baxter.

"I don't feel informed until I've read it."
- Ramsey Campbell.

"Don't waver - get WAVE!" - Brian W Aldiss.

CRITICAL WAVE is published six times per year and has
established a reputation for hard-hitting news coverage, perceptive
essays on the state of the genre and incisive reviews of the latest
books, comics and movies. Regular features include publishing
news, portfolios by Europe's leading sf and fantasy artists, extensive
club, comic mart and convention listings, interviews with prominent
authors and editors, fiction market reports, fanzine and magazine
reviews and convention reports.

Previous contributors have included: MICHAEL MOORCOCK, IAIN
BANKS, CLIVE BARKER, LISA TUTTLE, BOB SHAW, COLIN
GREENLAND, DAVID LANGFORD, ROBERT HOLDSTOCK, GARRY
KILWORTH, SHAUN HUTSON, DAVID WINGROVE, TERRY
PRATCHETT, RAMSEY CAMPBELL, LARRY NIVEN, BRIAN W
ALDISS, ANNE GAY, STEPHEN BAXTER, RAYMOND FEIST, CHRIS
CLAREMONT and STORM CONSTANTINE.

A six issue subscription costs only eight pounds and fifty pence or a
sample copy one pound and ninety-five pence; these rates only apply
to the UK, overseas readers should contact the address below for
further details. Cheques or postal orders should be made payable to
"Critical Wave Publications" and sent to: M Tudor, 845 Alum Rock
Road, Birmingham, B8 2AG. Please allow 30 days for delivery.

Recent titles available in
VGSF and VG Horror paperbacks

Prices correct at time of going to press (July 1993)

Hearts, Hands and Voices

IAN McDONALD

A lyrical science fiction novel with haunting echoes of contemporary Ireland and Ulster from the 1992 Philip K. Dick Award-winning author.

'He is one of the finest writers of his generation, who chooses to write science fiction, because that is how he can best illuminate our world' – *New Statesman*

'At once disturbing and beautiful: superbly realised' – *The Times*

£4.99   ISBN 0 575 05373 9

Aztec Century

CHRISTOPHER EVANS

In her dreams, Princess Catherine could still see London burning, and the luminous golden warships of her enemies, the Aztecs, as they added yet another conquest to their mighty Empire. Sweeping from occupied Britain to the horrors of the Russian front and the savage splendour of Mexico, *Aztec Century* is a magnificent novel of war, politics, intrigue and romance, set in a world that is both familiar – and terrifyingly alien.

'Intelligent, finely written, and towards the end, absolutely nail-biting' – Iain M. Banks

'A sacrificial *feast* of a story – highly original sf from the first page onwards, an intriguing and compelling thriller to the end' – Robert Holdstock

'Christopher Evans is particularly brilliant at mixing a cocktail of the everyday and the wonderful to make a magical alternative history' – Garry Kilworth

£8.99   ISBN 0 575 05540 5

The Martian Inca

IAN WATSON

Julio and his friends had salvaged a space capsule that had crashed on a remote Bolivian mountainside. They had inhaled the strange red dust that the pod contained, and fallen into comas. Only Julio and his beloved Angelina survived. But now these two view their world in a new light, believing that they have been reborn as terrible, powerful Godlike creatures – the Inca and his Queen.

Meanwhile in Space, a manned mission to Mars is also about to discover the devastating effects of the deadly soil.

What is the mysterious constituent that makes this dust so literally mind-blowing? And can it really increase Man's evolutionary potential?

'This book contains a new, near-poetic dimension. The most formidable fiction [Ian Watson] has yet written, and also one of the most compulsive' – *The Times*

£3.99   ISBN 0 575 05558 8

And Disregards the Rest

PAUL VOERMANS

A critically acclaimed debut novel from a young
Australian writer:

'Vigorous and confident, and richly authentic...
powerfully strange and apocalyptic and elegant
...the debut of a powerful and distinctive new
voice' – Paul J. McAuley, *Interzone*

'An interesting and ambitious first novel...so
different from everything else around these days
that it deserves attention' – *Time Out*

'Enjoyable, sometimes poignant, and far better
written than most standard SF' – *Locus*

£4.99   ISBN 0 575 05282 1

Wulfsyarn

PHILLIP MANN

On its maiden voyage, the *Nightingale*, the most advanced craft in the entire fleet of Mercy ships belonging to the Gentle Order of St Francis, vanished into deep space with its life bays packed with refugees.

Almost a year to the day later, heralded by a distress signal, the *Nightingale* reappeared, damaged in ways that meant its very survival in space was a miracle. Only one survivor walked from that partly mineral, partly sentient craft – its Captain, Jon Wilberfoss.

This is his story, as told by Wulf, the autoscribe.

'A *tour de force* . . . and . . . revelation . . . that haunts the mind long after the book is finished' – *The Times*

£3.99   ISBN 0 575 05162 0